PRINCES AND PEASANTS

THE TSAR'S DRAGONS: BOOK TWO

CATRIN COLLIER

D1824675

For Alan and Hazel Bryant –

wonderful and special friends who are always there for us
whenever we most need someone

When one has nothing left ... but memories, one guards
and dusts them with especial care.
Saki (H. H. Munro)
The Wolves of Cernogratz

Prologue

Owen Parry's ironworkers' cottage, Broadway, Treforest, Pontypridd 1956

Every morning I wake surprised to find myself still on this earth. Is it because I have not yet completed the tasks appointed to me by fate? So many files to read – so many papers, letters and photographs to archive – so many years to record. And not just years – an entire history, not just of a people, but a town – or is it two towns?

First there was the one named for John Hughes, the man the Russians christened 'The Iron Tsar', for bringing industry and railways to the country, catapulting it into the modern age. He imagined the town before a single brick had been laid, nurturing it through the dangerous early years into a wealthy, full, and hedonistic mature life. Then in 1924, in the aftermath of the bloodiest war in history and the revolution it spawned in Russia, John Hughes's town on the steppe, which had evolved into a city, was renamed for a new Tsar. Stalino.

Some say it was named for the steel it produced, not the leader of the state. But either way it will never be Stalino, not to me. It will always bear the name Mr Hughes endowed it with, Hughesovka. My Hughesovka.

I rest my notebook on the frame my great-grandson made so I can work without leaving my bed, and read the pages I've already written.

As I sift through dry, brittle letters, diaries, age tarnished albums and photographs – Glyn Edwards's photographs – so lovingly composed and captured for posterity – scents rise from the papers and the long dead flowers pressed between their pages.

The perfume of old summers fills the air, drifting through the mists that shroud the years, evoking memories of my Russia more vivid and redolent than those conjured by mere words alone.

I pick out Glyn Edwards's letters. Some were written before Mr Hughes imported the Welsh metalworkers and colliers, long before the gamblers and adventurers flocked to colonise the Iron Master's new town. Men and women who saw the possibility of making their own fortunes in the enterprise of Mr Hughes's New Russia Company. They came, first in their hundreds, then their thousands.

Salesmen, shopkeepers, hoteliers, priests, whores and whoremongers, murderers, thieves, the moral and the downright criminal of every nationality, all crowded into a few square miles. Forced to live next to, if not to respect, their neighbours. Every one of them drawn by one man's vision of a brave new industrial town that promised freedom, equality, wealth, and a better life for all who had the strength to work and the courage to join him, no matter what their class, creed, or lineage.

John Hughes had the vision but he couldn't have realised it alone. I look at these papers and see the men and women around him. Men like Glyn Edwards, six and a half feet tall in his stockinged feet, heavily built, as handsome and swarthy as a gypsy. Russian aristocrat Alexei Beletsky with blond hair and mischievous blue eyes that belied his angelic features. Nathan Kharber and his sister Ruth, both slight and dark, with Jewish features and eyes that could pierce the soul. Dr Peter Edwards, who journeyed to Russia only to find death waiting on the steppe. Count Nicholas Beletsky, cold and arrogant, self-serving aristocrat to the core. My brother, Richard Parry, just out of boyhood, with the dark curly hair and blue eyes of the Irish – and myself, Anna Parry, the youngest, smallest, and least significant emigrant, taken to Russia as a charity case because I was the subject of salacious gossip in Merthyr Tydfil.

The women who became closer to me than sisters: Sarah Edwards, healer, mentor, friend; the Cossack Praskovia who could have modelled for Titian with her voluptuous figure, red hair, and emerald eyes; and Sonya Tsvetovna, who saved us all in the end with her self-sacrificing unconditional love.

Every one of us overshadowed by John Hughes, who strode over the steppe and through life with the air of a medieval king: born to govern, command, and, above all, to build...

Now, when the only new experience that awaits me is death, I can truthfully say that I've had a good life. A long one, richer in every way than the one of poverty and bondage to iron and coal that I was born into. I've seen and done things and travelled to places beyond most people's imagination. I've lived like royalty in a St Petersburg Palace and cowered, a hunted animal, in a burrow in the ground, without a kopek or crust to my name. I've broken more commandments than I care to dwell on, including Thou shalt not kill. But I feel no remorse for that sin – if sin it was. Some men are evil and deserve death; if writing that makes me a poor Christian then so be it.

Perhaps that is why I've lived so long. Ninety-nine years on this earth and still God doesn't want me in his heaven. Possibly He's asked Satan to prepare a place for me but the Devil is also reluctant to extend an invitation.

I sense my thoughts meandering into philosophy: the hobby of the ancients, the bane of the young. I'm not so decrepit that I can't recall my irritation when I was on the receiving end of lectures from my elders. I believed I knew everything then, just as my grandchildren and great-grandchildren do now. They sit next to my bed with grave unlined faces, solemn-eyed in the face of my old age and impending death, so sure of their knowledge and themselves.

They try to fool me, and themselves, that I have a future. That my life isn't coming to an end. It is, but it's not over ... not yet, not while I can still hold a pen and dream of the past. My last and most precious possession.

I've often wondered if memories and emotions, like disease, can be transmitted from one person to another. If so, that would explain why I've always felt so acutely the pleasures and pain of those I've loved.

I can pick out his voice above the others in the garden. The language is different, but not the voice. It is his great-grandfather's.

I turn back to my book

September 1871: the month Sarah Edwards and my brother Richard married in a simple ceremony in the Anglican Church in Taganrog, two days before they came face to face on the Taganrog quayside with Edward Edwards, Betty Edwards, Alice Wilkins, and my brothers Morgan and Owen Parry.

September 1871: the continuation of the early wild years when no lone unarmed woman – or man – was safe on the streets of Hughesovka; when a visiting Moscow journalist wrote, 'Hughesovka – all the dregs of mining industry life gather here. Everything dark, evil and criminal – thieves, hooligans, all such, are drawn here. You cannot go out at night without risking violent death.'

Chapter One

Reception, Hotel Bristol, Taganrog September 1871

'The entire third floor?'

The receptionist looked over his spectacles at the German standing in front of the desk.

The blond man was slim and imposing, with an undeniably aristocratic air. His black travelling suit, hat, and cape were expensive and immaculate. He could have just stepped out of a St Petersburg tailor's, not off a boat in Taganrog Harbour

'Prince Roman Nadolny took a liking to the suite on the third floor that overlooked the gardens the last time he was here, he recommended it to me.'

'The suite is free, but the other rooms...'

'I am Hans Becker, the prince's confidential private secretary. The other rooms will be needed by my associate, and Grand Duke Konstantin's private secretary and our valets, for however long it will take our escort to assemble to take us from here to Hughesovka.'

'But there are guests in the rooms.'

'Move them.'

The warning the manager had given him when the receptionist had been given his post echoed through his mind: 'Aristocratic servants are always more imperious than aristocrats.' He steeled himself for argument. 'But they have paid in advance...'

Hans Becker waved the receptionist's 'but' aside. 'No matter. I will recompense them for any inconvenience. You have Cossack officers and troops staying here?'

'Yes, sir. They are waiting for an important shipment to be delivered into the harbour for Mr Hughes's new town.'

'A message for their commanding officer. To be delivered as a matter of urgency.' Hans Becker handed the receptionist an envelope. 'Grand Duke Konstantin's secretary and our valets will be disembarking from Prince Roman's yacht shortly, as well as the prince's associate. Please have rooms ready for the five of us for one, possibly two or more nights. We will be leaving for Hughesovka with the Cossacks. Have the prince's carriages arrived from the Crimea?'

'I think so,' the receptionist stammered.

'Think so?' Hans repeated. 'Either they have or they haven't. Which is it?'

'I believe the senior groom took delivery –'

'Order one of the carriages to the quayside immediately to pick up the passengers from the prince's yacht.'

Overwhelmed by the mention of both the prince and Grand Duke Konstantin, it was as much as the receptionist could do to murmur, 'Yes, your Excellency.'

'I am Herr Becker, not "your Excellency". We will require a meal. Place menus in all five rooms. The Grand Duke's staff, like the prince's and his associates', never eat in public dining rooms.'

'Yes, your ... Herr Becker.'

'I'll need a bellboy to carry my luggage to my suite.'

'Yes, Herr Becker.'

'And a key.'

'Certainly, Herr Becker.' Still flustered, the clerk finally began the process of registration.

Richard and Sarah Parry's suite, second floor, Hotel Bristol September 1871

'Do you want to eat here tonight, or go down to the dining room?' Richard Parry moved away from Sarah, settled back on the pillows and lifted her head on to his shoulder.

She glanced at the clock on the bedside table. 'Isn't three o'clock in the afternoon a little early to be thinking about dinner?'

'We didn't have a very substantial lunch.'

'Only because you suggested we forego dessert and opt for soup and salad, which were already prepared,' she reminded. 'Entirely your fault for looking so appetising, and thank you for that very lovely dessert. Pity we have to actually eat, which necessitates leaving this bed. Although we could telephone down for room service...'

'It's not only food we need, but exercise.'

'If that's an invitation ...?'

'There's more than one kind of exercise, and that tickles,' she laughed as he ran his fingers lightly down the full length of her body.

'This is the only kind of exercise I want to indulge in.' He slid his head beneath the bedclothes and kissed her breasts. 'How people find the time to sightsee when they're on honeymoon is beyond my reasoning.' His voice was muffled by the blankets.

'I can't hear you.'

He emerged from the tangle of linen. 'You don't really want to travel back to Hughesovka when the boat comes in from England, do you? We could stay another week.'

'And travel through the countryside without a military escort as well as risk snow delaying us? If this cold wind keeps up, winter could hit the steppe early.'

'Everyone in Taganrog agrees the weather is unseasonable and bound to change for the better. Look out of the window. The sky's blue...'

'And the air freezing.' She snuggled closer to him under the covers, wrapping her arm around his bare chest before moving her hand lower.

'Do you know what you're doing to me, wife?'

'Yes.'

'So I'm not the only one who wants second helpings of this particular dessert?' He bent his head to hers, and kissed her lips. 'Talking of dessert, if we're going to dine in the suite tonight we should put our order in early.'

'We'll compromise.'

'By starving?'

'By asking that a ten o'clock supper of dolmas be prepared and served to us here. Shortly, in an hour or so – or whenever you decide to let me go – we'll visit the fish restaurant on the wharf and go on to the pancake café afterwards. I fancy a plate of oysters followed by double helping of cherry blinis with whipped cream.'

She cupped his face in her hands. 'If it's not one appetite it's another.'

'I love you, Mrs Parry.'

'That name is going to take some getting used to.'

'You've already had two whole days.'

'It will take longer than that for me to stop thinking about you as a beautiful boy.'

'Husband, not boy, Mrs Parry.' He moved towards her.

Within minutes the only sounds in the room were the ticking of the clock accompanied by their short quick gasps of breath.

The Wharf, Taganrog September 1871

'Have you given a thought as to where we're going to live when we return to Hughesovka?' Sarah asked Richard as they strolled towards the café from the fish restaurant.

'I envy Alexei being able to move into his own place with Ruth, but we have no choice but to return to Mr Edwards's house. I realise it might not be easy for you to carry on living with your first husband's brother, but I thought we could use your bedroom and turn my room into a sitting room to give us and Mr Edwards and Praskovia some privacy. Anna will still have to live there, and as she's my sister I feel responsible for her, so we should invite her to sit with us in the evenings when she's not working.'

'We're both responsible for her,' Sarah emphasised, 'and when we buy a house, Anna will move in with us.'

'I'm afraid our own house will be a dream for a few years yet. I've managed to save some money but nowhere near enough for a house,' said Richard.

'When Mr Hughes starts building houses for his workers, I think we should consider taking out one of the preferential mortgages he's offering, but we'll need more than I've banked with the company before we've enough for a deposit.'

'I have enough money to hire builders now. All we need is the land. I recall Glyn saying something to Peter and me about Mr Hughes earmarking plots for house-building and leasing them at a low rent to company employees. We should choose one as soon as we get back.'

Richard stared at her. 'You have money?'

'I have money,' she revealed cautiously, concerned by his tone.

'I know you've worked as a nurse for some time but it's not that well-paid. I didn't think you'd managed to save enough to buy a house, not after paying for your board and lodge.'

'I have some savings, but Peter earned far more than me, hardly surprising as doctors are well-paid compared to nurses. He invested in Glyn's collieries, which is why they're called the Edwards Brothers Collieries –'

'You own shares in Mr Edwards's collieries?' Richard was shocked.

'The same number as Glyn. He and Peter split ownership. Why are you so surprised? It's usual for a man to leave his worldly goods to his wife when he dies. Peter also took out insurance when we married. He left me with a sizeable annuity as well as a lump sum.'

'I had no idea. People will think that I married you for your money.'

'They'll think nothing of the sort. We're having a child, or have you forgotten?'

'I can't believe this is the first time you mentioned this annuity...'

'Would it have made any difference if you'd known I had money?' she broke in.

'It might have.'

'When?' She raised her eyebrows. 'That first night we made love.'

'I would never have dared.'

'If I remember rightly, I dared more than you, but it's not worth arguing who seduced who now we're married. Peter used to say, "The only time to talk about money is when you haven't any." It's hardly a secret, Richard. It's usual for men to take out insurance so their wives will be provided for if anything happens to them.'

'I've never given a thought as to what will happen to you and our baby if I die. You didn't say a word ...'

'Because you didn't ask,' she interrupted. 'I assumed you knew.'

'I haven't taken out any insurance.'

'We were only married two days ago. There's plenty of time.' Sarah regretted the words as soon as they were out of her mouth. She and Peter had believed they had all the time in the world before he'd died of cholera shortly after they reached Hughesovka.

'I could be killed working in one of the pits. I don't have enough to money to buy a house ...'

'But I do, and you have prospects.' Sarah hooked her arm even more tightly into Richard's.

'You can't live off prospects. I'm an idiot.'

'You're far from being an idiot. But you are an impulsive romantic fool who chased after me when I left you, and for that I'll be for ever grateful.'

Preoccupied by guilt, he didn't hear what she'd said. 'What kind of a husband doesn't think of the future of his family?'

'You're regretting you married me?' She wondered if he'd suddenly been overwhelmed by the responsibility he'd taken on. Marriage and fatherhood at any age was daunting. Richard was barely twenty and she could imagine that he felt crushed, especially given their eleven-year age difference.

'No, never!'

'Richard...'

'Please don't mention the age difference between us again,' he begged. 'Years mean nothing.'

'When the man is older than the woman, perhaps.'

'I like having an older, more experienced wife, and I can't wait to be a father, but I can't possibly live off the money Dr Edwards left you.'

'It's not my money, Richard, it's our money, and we need a house large enough for all of us, the baby, Anna...'

A shout echoed from the other end of the quayside. 'Sarah!'

They turned around to see a group of people dressed in travelling clothes climbing out of one of the small boats used to ferry passengers from the larger vessels into the shallow waters of the harbour. As the group drew closer Sarah recognised Peter's oldest brother, Edward, who'd refused John Hughes's invitation to join him in his venture.

Shortly after they'd arrived in Russia, Glyn had heard that Edward's wife Judith had died. Edward had obviously changed his mind about Hughesovka because he was walking towards them, together with Glyn's wife, Betty, who'd also insisted on staying in Merthyr, two young women, one of whom was carrying a baby, and two boys.

'Sarah, how wonderful to see you. You're looking well.' Edward hugged her and kissed her cheek. He turned from her to her companion.

'Richard?' he murmured uncertainly.

'Mr Edwards.' Richard shook his hand firmly.

'I hardly recognised you. You're a foot taller and twice the weight you were when you left Merthyr.'

'All the good Russian food and vodka.' Richard glanced at Sarah. The news of their relationship had come as a shock to Glyn and they'd been living under his roof. He didn't need to see the trepidation in Sarah's eyes to tell him she feared it would upset and antagonise Edward and Betty.

'Richard!' The two boys flung themselves at him and Richard recognised his younger brothers Owen and Morgan.

'If I've grown a foot, you two have grown three!' Richard joked. Owen was ten and Morgan twelve, but both appeared far older and more confident than when he'd last seen them.

'Your fur coats and hats look expensive. Were they? Are they as warm and heavy as they appear?' Betty fingered the arm of Sarah's coat enviously.

'They're sable like Mr Hughes's.' Richard had purchased his in St Petersburg after receiving a bonus from Mr Hughes for rescuing miners trapped after a fall in one of the pits, but he had no intention of telling Betty how much he'd paid for it.

'I can't believe we've walked into you just after landing. Talk about luck. Is it always this cold?' Edward pulled up the collar of his woollen overcoat.

Sarah laughed. 'It gets much colder than this, Edward. But it is unseasonably wintry for the time of year. Where are you staying?'

'Nowhere as yet.' Edward turned and waved to two porters who were pushing barrows laden with luggage. 'That's our hand luggage. I left instructions that our trunks be offloaded, along with the equipment Mr Hughes ordered to be shipped, in the hope they'd be delivered directly to Hughesovka.'

'They will be,' Richard assured him. 'The local people can't do enough to help Mr Hughes.'

'We're on our way to the British Embassy. The captain of the ship suggested we go there for advice on hotels,' Betty explained.

'No need, our hotel is just behind us and it's excellent,' Sarah advised.

'You think they'll have rooms for us?' Edward asked.

'They should do. The Cossack escort Mr Hughes sent to pick up his delivery are staying there as well. They've been waiting for the ship to come in so we'll probably move out first thing in the morning.' Richard smiled at his brothers. 'Come on, let's get you two sorted. You must be tired as well as cold.'

'Exhausted,' Betty answered. 'Travelling with a baby is no picnic, I can tell you. You remember Alice Wilkins who was Perkins, don't you, Richard.' She pushed one of the girls forward.

Richard had been besotted with Alice Perkins before he'd left Merthyr but it had ended abruptly. Her overseer father, angered by his daughter's relationship with a lowly colliery worker, had paid two thugs, Ianto and Mervyn Paskey, to beat Richard senseless. He'd heard afterwards that Alice had been married off to a much older man. She'd put on weight and aged considerably since he'd last seen her and he doubted he would have recognised her if Betty hadn't told him who she was. He wondered what she was doing in Russia. He offered her his hand.

'I heard you'd married, Alice.'

'I'm a widow.' To his embarrassment she stood on tiptoe, wrapped her arms around his neck, and kissed him full on the mouth.

He stepped back swiftly. 'Let's get all of you indoors and into the warm.'

Amused by Richard's reaction to Alice's kiss, Sarah turned to the young girl carrying a toddler. 'That's a beautiful little girl.'

'Harriet Maud is Glyn's daughter, born eight months after he left Merthyr. Martha is her nursemaid,' Betty revealed.

Martha tentatively returned Sarah's smile and gave her a small curtsey.

'Congratulations, and apologies for not writing to you, Betty, Glyn hadn't told me he was a father.' Sarah took Richard's arm when he offered it. Her smile broadened when she sensed he was using her as protection from Alice.

'That's because I didn't tell him she'd been born.'

'It's too cold to talk here, Mrs Edwards.' Richard shouted in Russian to the porters with the handcarts. 'Follow me.' He quickened his pace and led the way to the hotel, which was only a few minutes' walk away. Edward strode alongside him.

'You said that you and Sarah have rooms here?' Edward checked.

'We do.'

'You're in Taganrog on Mr Hughes's business?'

'Sarah will check the medical supplies. I'll look over the metallurgical equipment before it's packed for the journey to ensure nothing's been forgotten,' Richard hedged, consoling himself with the thought that he hadn't actually lied. He and Sarah would check the supplies against the loading invoices when the Cossacks packed them for transport to Hughesovka. He didn't want to explain to Edward why they were in Taganrog – at least not yet, and certainly not in the street outside the hotel. He stood back when the doorman opened the foyer doors.

—

'As it's only for one night the boys and I can move into your room, Richard, and Betty and the girls with Sarah,' Edward suggested.

'I'm sure they'll have enough rooms available for everyone.' Sarah went to reception while Morgan and Owen ran to the window that overlooked the stable yard that opened on to the back street. Half a dozen Cossack troopers were rubbing down their horses and cleaning tack. Two stable boys were polishing a magnificent black coach, with a raised metal coat of arms fixed to the doors.

'Important nobs must be staying here, Richard,' Morgan shouted.

'Keep your voice down, Morgan,' Richard ordered when several people in the foyer turned to glare at his brothers as they raised their voices.

'Look, Richard,' Morgan shouted as two soldiers rode into the yard side by side standing on their horses' backs.

'I've never seen anything like that,' Edward commented as one executed a perfect somersault and landed upright back on his mount.

'Cossack cavalry love showing off. That's nothing. Wait until you see them riding on their heads in the saddle,' Richard smiled.

'Royalty's arrived?' Sarah indicated the coach as she asked one of the bellboys.

'Their staff and servants, Mrs Parry.'

Sarah glanced warily at Betty lest she'd overheard the 'Mrs Parry', but Glyn's wife was too busy studying the gilded walls and furniture, tiled floors, and profusion of mirrors that lined the staircase, to pay attention to what was being said.

'This is the kind of place where they charge you to take a breath of air.' Betty sniffed disparagingly. 'There has to be somewhere cheaper we can stay?'

'There are plenty of cheaper places, Mrs Edwards, but I doubt you'd want to stay in any of them.' Richard struggled to conceal his irritation.

'If it's only for one night, Edward's right, we'll shift and make the best of it. Better that than waste money. Ask them to put beds up in your rooms for us, Sarah,' Betty set her bag on a chair.

Sarah was already speaking to the concierge manning the desk. Richard joined them. After a few minutes of earnest conversation in Russian, Sarah returned to Edward and Betty.

'They have two suites free. One has a double bed that will accommodate you and Alice, Betty, and a side room large enough to take a full-size cot for your nursemaid, and a smaller one for Harriet Maud. They also have a separate suite with a double bed for you, Edward, and a side room with two singles for the boys.'

'How much are these suites?' Betty demanded as Edward went to the door to pay the porters who'd brought their hand luggage.

'Ten roubles a night for each suite. I negotiated breakfast for all of you in the price, four adults and three children.'

'Ten roubles? That's daylight robbery!' Betty exclaimed, before adding somewhat incongruously, 'What's a rouble worth in pounds, shillings, and pence?'

'At the moment it's roughly eight roubles to an English pound,' Richard answered.

'Over a pound – for a single night! Both of you must be earning too much money if you can afford to waste it. Unless of course it's Mr Hughes's money you're splashing about?'

'The price includes breakfast for all of you,' Richard reiterated.

'I'm not paying for breakfast for Harriet Maud. The child barely eats anything.' Betty crossed her arms across her chest. 'My money's staying locked in my purse and we'll camp in your room.'

'No you won't –' Sarah began.

'I always said you were selfish, Sarah Edwards –'

'It's Parry, Mrs Edwards, Sarah Parry.' Richard steeled himself for disapproval. 'You must excuse us for not wanting to share our room but we're on our honeymoon.'

For the first time in her life, Betty Edwards was lost for words.

Chapter Two

Hotel Bristol September 1871

When Sarah heard a knock at the door of her suite she
hoped it would be the waiter. Richard had invited Edward,
Betty, and the entire party to tea in their rooms, but as he'd
taken his brothers into the yard to introduce them to
Captain Misha Razin and his Cossack command, he'd left
her to greet them.

'Edward,' she looked over her brother-in-law's
shoulder and was relieved to see he was alone. 'Thank you
so much for coming.'

'I'll be your only guest until the boys come up from the
yard.' He walked into the sitting room, 'I didn't know
people like us could live like this.'

'It's a luxurious suite,' Sarah agreed, 'but the Russians
who can afford to stay in hotels demand more opulent
surroundings than we do in Britain.'

'And Richard wanted to make his honeymoon special.'
'That too. I'm sorry –'
The waiter interrupted them. Sarah asked him to wheel the
trolley that held the samovar, pancakes, and
sandwiches next to the table before tipping him. 'Thank
you, Albert, we'll serve ourselves.'

'What were you apologising to me for, Sarah?' Edward
asked after Albert left.

'Any hurt I've caused you by marrying Richard within
a year of Peter's death.'

'If I've learned anything from losing Judith it's that it's
less painful to live in the present than dwell in the past.'

'I was so sorry to hear Judith succumbed to diphtheria.'

'She died horribly. Unable to swallow, then at the end unable to draw breath. The entire congregation of the chapel prayed for her, to no avail ...' He took a moment to compose himself. 'I appreciated your letter, Sarah. It arrived on a day when I desperately needed the comfort it gave me.'

She took his hand. 'Until you experience it, it's impossible to imagine what it's like to lose the person you love the most and are closest to. Or what it's like having to live on in this world without them.'

'Even more so when you doubt the existence of the next.'

Sarah was shocked. Edward's faith had been the cornerstone of his existence. He read the expression on her face.

'I don't want to talk about it, Sarah.'

'I understand. Please, sit down, Edward.'

Edward took the chair she indicated. 'We appear to have forged a bond, you and I, albeit one of grief and sorrow.'

'I'll never forget Peter and the daughter we would have loved so much, who died before she could live. Having no family of my own, I was grateful for the kindness you and Glyn showed me when you welcomed me into your family. Nothing has changed in that respect. I will always think of you and Glyn as my brothers, Edward.' She saw anguish in Edward's eyes and changed the subject. 'You couldn't persuade Betty or the girls to join us for tea?'

Edward shook his head. 'Alice is in hysterics after Richard's revelation that he married you, and as Betty pays Martha's wages the girl doesn't dare ignore her mistress's slightest whim. Betty has ordered her to look after Harriet Maud in their hotel room and that's exactly what she will be doing.'

'I can't understand Alice's reaction. Richard told me they never saw or contacted one another after Alice's father had him beaten, and even before then they'd only managed to snatch a few hours together.'

'From what Richard told me at the time I assumed it was no more than a childish infatuation on both sides, which was why I was concerned when Alice insisted on accompanying Betty and me here. Betty was all for it, because she wanted a woman's company on the journey. When I tried to talk Alice out of making the trip until she'd written to Richard and he'd sent her a reply, she refused because she said she wanted to "surprise him".'

'She certainly did that.' Sarah filled the tea glasses. 'To change the subject, is it worth me trying to talk to Betty to explain why I married Richard?'

'I wouldn't if I were you. Give her time, Sarah.'

'She has every right to be angry with me.'

'No she doesn't. Things are obviously different here to the way they are in Merthyr.'

'Not that different.'

'Please, Sarah, don't feel guilty. No woman could have loved Peter more than you did when he was alive. You don't have to justify your actions to me, Betty, or anyone else. I admit I was shocked by the news, but only because I think of Richard as a boy.'

'As did Sarah until I persuaded her to take another look at me.' Richard walked in, removed his hat and coat, and pulled a chair up to the table.

'Your brothers?' Sarah asked.

'Are having the time of their lives with the Cossacks. When I left, Morgan was on the back of Misha's horse and Owen was grooming one of the smaller mounts. Misha promised to take care of them and the clerk at the desk said he'll send a bellboy up with them so they won't get lost when they come in from the yard. So, Mr Edwards, if you want to berate Sarah and me and tell us what you really think of us marrying, now is the time to do it.'

'I'd like to offer you both my congratulations.'

'I didn't know what to expect from you, Mr Edwards, but it certainly wasn't that,' Richard watched Sarah fill a third glass with tea.

'Tea is served in a glass here?' Edwards commented.

'Always, but you'll soon get used to Russian ways.'

Edward almost gave a smile as he took his glass from Sarah and lifted it in a toast. 'To the new Mr and Mrs Parry.

Sarah and I have just agreed that life is for living, Richard. Now, tell me about Hughesovka. How are Glyn, your sister Anna, and Mr Hughes? Do you think he can find work for me?'

'An experienced manager like you, Mr Edwards? Mr Hughes will grab you quicker than a collier snatches a tankard of beer after a shift underground. That's if you decide to work for him and not the Edwards Brothers Collieries.'

'Glyn wrote and told me that the collieries are already a reality.'

'They are, sir, and once we secure the shafts they'll start producing as much quality anthracite as any Welsh colliery of similar size.'

'That's good to hear, but I wouldn't expect any different from a pit Glyn had a hand in sinking or running.' Edward took a sandwich from the plate Sarah offered him.

'Did Glyn write and tell you about the gold medals the Tsar presented to him, Richard, and Alf, for saving miners after a pit shaft collapsed?' Sarah asked.

'If he did, I didn't get the letter.' Edward slapped Richard on the back. 'Well done, and congratulations.'

'You trained me, sir.'

'In his last letter, Glyn said he was considering making an offer for the house he was renting. I take it he has little intention of ever returning to Wales.'

'He agreed the purchase with the owner when we were in St Petersburg, sir. Wait until you see the place. It's beautiful and so big it's almost a mansion.' Richard placed three sugar cubes in the saucer of his tea glass.

'You both live with him?'

'We do, as does Anna. As Richard said, it's a large house, which you'll soon see for yourself. There's a desperate shortage of accommodation in the town.'

'So I've heard.'

'People have been writing home?' Richard helped himself to a sandwich.

'There've been a few complaints about the primitive conditions in Hughesovka,' Edward concurred.

'Hardly surprising given the highly civilised and luxurious conditions the workers left behind in Merthyr,' Sarah joked.

'So you're saying things aren't as bad as some people are painting them?' Edward suggested.

'That depends on who's saying what,' Sarah qualified.

'Jimmy Peddle's wife seems to spend a great deal of her time writing to everyone she knows in Merthyr, and from what I've heard her letters are less than flattering about Hughesovka.'

'Jimmy Peddle broke his leg in several places,' Sarah revealed.

'A pit accident?' Edward asked.

'A drunken brawl. Since then he's found it difficult to work, but as I said, accommodation is a serious problem,' Sarah conceded. 'Many of the Russian labourers and their families are living in holes they've dug in the ground and thatched with turf. It's the lack of housing that led Glyn to rent out rooms. I'm sure he would much rather have his house to himself. As well as us and Anna, a Russian boy named Alexei Beletsky lives with Glyn, he works for Glyn and Mr Hughes, and then there's Glyn's servants...'

'Glyn has servants?' Edward was astounded.

'A cook, two maids, a boy who does odd jobs and helps Glyn's groom with the horses, a gardener, a laundry maid, and a housekeeper. They have separate quarters at the back of the house.'

'You're saying that my brother lives like the Crawshays!'

'Not quite so luxuriously.' Sarah was defensive. 'He works hard and long hours for everything he has.'

'You're forgetting Alexei won't be living with Glyn after today,' Richard reminded Sarah. 'He's getting married and his grandmother, who owns property and an estate just outside the town, has given him a cottage next door to Mr Edwards's house. In fact it was Alexei's grandmother, Catherine Ignatova, who sold Glyn his house.'

'Will there be room for me at Glyn's?' Edward asked.

'Alexei's room will be free and, if it's needed, one of ours for Owen and Morgan,' Sarah picked up her tea and sat back in her chair.

'And Alice and Betty, and Harriet Maud and her nursemaid?' Edward asked.

Sarah remained tactfully silent in the hope that Richard would answer Edward.

'Alice isn't carrying on to Hughesovka, is she, sir?' Richard questioned.

'I don't know what else she can do, other than travel back to Wales alone.'

'The consulate would offer her accommodation until she can secure a berth on a homeward-bound ship,' Richard suggested hopefully. He didn't wish Alice ill, but he did wish her as far from him as physically possible.

'I doubt Alice would leave Betty. From the way she coped, or to be more accurate, didn't cope, with the journey here I don't think she's capable of travelling any distance by herself, but that applies to Betty as well.' Edward set his glass on the table. 'Glyn did get Betty's letter to say she was joining him in Russia?'

'Not that Mr Edwards told me,' Richard replied.

'He never mentioned the birth of a daughter either, and that isn't like Glyn. I'm sure if he'd known of Harriet Maud's existence he would have told everyone in Hughesovka about her.' Sarah placed a pancake on a plate and handed it to Edward.

'If he knew she existed he would have,' Edward concurred. 'I've had more than one argument about this with Betty. She said she didn't want to tell Glyn they had a child until Harriet Maud was old enough to travel because Glyn would try to persuade her to join him here, and after what happened to Peter...'

'Cholera and typhoid are as rife in Merthyr as they are in Russia,' Sarah broke in defensively.

'You don't have to explain that to me, Sarah. Betty also said her father took such delight in Harriet Maud's company that she didn't want to take the child away from him, which was why she waited until he'd died to join Glyn. My brother will welcome Betty and Harriet Maud into his house in Hughesovka.' He looked at Sarah and his suspicions hardened. 'Won't he?'

Richard and Sarah exchanged glances.

'Glyn's found himself another woman?'

Sarah decided there was no point in trying to conceal what would become obvious once Edward moved into Glyn's house. 'Her name's Praskovia, she's his housekeeper and she's pregnant with his child.'

'Do you think Glyn will ask her to move out when Betty arrives?'

'I think that's a question only Glyn can answer,' Sarah said.

'One of us should say something to Betty.'

'One of us should, Edward,' Sarah nodded. 'But I'm not volunteering.'

'Nor me,' Richard rejoined.

'Is there any way of getting in touch with Glyn before we arrive?'

'If we sent him a letter it would be given to us to deliver. All I can suggest is we entrust a note to one of the Cossacks with a fast horse when we get within a day or two's ride of Hughesovka. With luck he'll get the news of Betty's imminent arrival to Glyn a few hours before we reach the town.'

'I'll write as soon as I've finished this pancake. Have the Paskeys reached Hughesovka yet?'

'The Paskeys!' Richard paled.

'I wrote to tell Glyn they'd signed up to work for the New Russia Company.'

'If they'd reached Hughesovka before I left, I would have heard,' Richard said.

'When did you leave?'

'Just over two weeks ago.'

'I left before Richard,' Sarah volunteered.

'You didn't travel together?' Edward was surprised.

'I was in St Petersburg when Sarah left. She thought –'

'I thought the age gap between Richard and myself was too large for us to marry,' Sarah explained. 'Richard didn't, and as I'm having his child he persuaded me to change my mind.'

'Then it's double congratulations.' If Edward was surprised he concealed it well.

'Thank you, Edward.'

'I hope you'll allow me to become an honorary uncle when he or she arrives.'

'Not so honorary, Edward. How about a real one?'

'Are you sure the Paskeys are going to Hughesovka?' Richard broke in. He couldn't forget or forgive them. It had taken him months to recover from the beating they'd given him before he left Merthyr but he'd eventually come to terms with his injuries, unlike those they'd inflicted on his sister Anna.

'It was all over the ironworks the day after they left,' Edward divulged. 'Deputy Perkins couldn't resist boasting that he'd given the Paskeys references in false names to hoodwink the man who was recruiting workers for John Hughes. Perkins said it was payback for Glyn persuading the police to bring the charges against the Paskeys that had collapsed in court.'

'Charges that should have stuck,' Richard muttered darkly. 'If Anna sees the Paskeys ...' Richard recalled the Cossack soldier his sister had shot dead when she'd caught him trying to rape Ruth. Anna had never divulged exactly what the Paskeys had done to her, but that hadn't stopped him from imagining what she'd suffered.

'You said Anna's living in Glyn's house?' Edward checked.

'And working in the hospital as a nurse,' Sarah confirmed.

'I know my brother,' Edward declared, 'he won't let anything happen to Anna.'

'He won't if he's on the lookout for the Paskeys, but if he hasn't received your letter he won't know they're on their way to Hughesovka,' Richard observed darkly.

Chapter Three

Glyn Edwards's office, New Russia Company, Hughesovka September 1871

Glyn looked up from his desk when Alf Mahoney, who helped to manage the pits Glyn had leased from the Cossacks and renamed the Edwards Brothers Collieries, walked into his office with Ezra Manning. Both men were covered in dust from the building sites that littered the street outside of the enormous wooden warehouse that served as Headquarters of the New Russia Company.

'Ezra, I last saw you in my father-in-law's pub in Merthyr. Welcome to Hughesovka – although as you see the town has yet to be built, hence the racket.' Glyn indicated the window as he left his chair and shook Ezra's hand. The non-stop hammering of carpenters, shouts of workmen, and braying of pack animals and horses wafted in, a loud and occasionally deafening mêlée.

'I admit the town, if it can be called that, isn't what I expected, sir.'

'Give us time, Ezra.'

'I will, sir, and thank you for the welcome, although you might want to send me packing when you hear what I have to say.'

'Doubt it, good men are treasured like gold here and from what I recall my brother Edward saying about you, you're the best. Please, sit down, can I get you anything, tea – blinis?'

'Blinis?' Ezra repeated.

'Pancakes, and very good,' Alf explained.

'Ask Vasily to bring a plate of them and tea for three please, Alf.'

Alf did as Glyn asked before returning and taking the chair next to Ezra.

'You've brought more workers from Merthyr?' Glyn asked.

'Almost a hundred, sir.'

'Colliers and ironworkers?'

'About forty ironworkers and fifty or so colliers. Most good men.'

'Most?' Glyn looked uneasily from Ezra to Alf.

'I heard the Paskeys were on their way here?'

'How did you hear that, sir?' Ezra asked.

'My brother wrote to me.'

'Ianto and Mervyn were on the boat when it left Southampton, sir,' Ezra began hesitantly, unsure how Glyn was going to take the news. 'But when we left I didn't realise who they were. I signed them up as experienced ironworkers in Merthyr. They used the name of Jones, Ianto and Mervyn Jones. I thought they looked familiar but they'd wound scarves around their mouths to hide most of their faces. They said they were getting over diphtheria. It had broken out again in China...' Ezra referred to the roughest area of Merthyr.

'Let me guess: they had good references from Deputy Perkins?'

'They did, sir. And with Mr Hughes wanting to recruit so many experienced men, that's what threw me. I was prepared to take on almost anyone who could show a good reference. I admit I was swayed by Deputy Perkins's letter of recommendation and didn't look beyond it, or too closely at either of the men. I could kick myself for not recognising them, but when I signed them up, both Paskeys had pulled their caps down low over their faces as well as pulled up their mufflers. I should have demanded they uncover...'

'You weren't to know they'd try to join us in Russia,' Glyn interrupted. 'Frankly, until I received my brother's letter it never occurred to me that they would attempt the journey here. Not with Alf, me, and Richard Parry here, ready and waiting to give them what they deserve.'

'No one would give them a job in Merthyr, sir. Not after what was said about them in court.'

'The case against them was thrown out?' Glyn checked.

'Only because the judge said he needed more evidence, sir. Everyone in town knew the Paskeys were as guilty as sin. That poor girl...'

'If I catch sight of them...'

'The Paskeys are here, in Hughesovka?' Glyn cut Alf short. 'That's just it, sir. No one has seen them since we berthed in Taganrog,' Ezra explained. 'They picked a fight with a couple of the crew on board the boat after we left English waters. Some of the boys say it was over a card game, others say the Paskeys stole the crew's money and drink...'

'Alf and I have a wedding to go to this afternoon, Ezra.' Glyn nodded to the painfully thin young man who brought in a tray and handed round glasses of tea and plates of pancakes. 'Thank you, Vasily.'

'Yes, sir. Well, to cut a long story short there was a fight and the Paskeys came off worse. They were both knifed...'

'Badly hurt?' Glyn asked hopefully.

'Bad enough for the captain to take them to a seaman's ward in a charity hospital in Taganrog.'

'How were they injured?' Glyn wondered if their wounds would make them easily identifiable if they did turn up in the town.

'Ianto was stabbed in the neck and chest and Mervyn the hand and arm. They both lost a lot of blood. The crew were Spanish, sir, a race rumoured to be vicious with a knife and...'

'You're sure about the injuries?'

'I saw them myself, sir,' Ezra asserted. 'But when I went to fetch the Paskeys from the hospital in Taganrog ready for the trek here, one of the English-speaking nurses told me they'd left the hospital with a Russian.'

'Did she say who the Russian was?' Glyn asked.

'She said she'd never seen him before and he didn't give his name.'

'So the Paskeys were in Taganrog and could be on their way here?' Glyn mused thoughtfully.

'They'd have more sense,' Alf asserted.

'I'm not so sure. Alert every foreman, Alf,' Glyn ordered. 'Tell them to inform me the moment any man or men answering their description turns up looking for work at an Edwards Brothers or New Russia Company site.'

'I'll do that, sir, but their description will fit half the Welshmen here. Middling height, stocky build, dark hair, brown eyes.'

'Mervyn will have a scar on his right hand. His middle finger and palm,' Ezra volunteered. 'The cut was deep. And Ianto has a scar on the left side of his neck and another on his chin from an old fight back in Merthyr.'

'That may help.' Alf made a note in his pocket book before finishing his tea. 'Not that those two are likely to be looking for honest work even if they do reach Hughesovka. The only "work" the Paskeys ever did in Merthyr was crippling people, usually at Deputy Perkins's command.'

'They were good at that, sir.' Ezra confirmed.

Glyn left his chair and looked out of the window at the dusty unmade road that stretched down towards the hospital. 'I'll warn Anna Parry, but the last thing I want is for her to see the Paskeys swaggering around the town.'

'None of us want that, sir.' Ezra set his tea glass back on the tray next to Alf's on Glyn's desk.

'I can't understand why they weren't put away for life after what they did to Miss Parry,' Alf said with feeling. 'Not when the women in the court were there when it happened and willing to testify.'

'They were in the court off John Street, Alf, but they didn't actually see the Paskeys rape Anna. They saw them leaving one of the houses covered in Anna's blood after they'd finished with her.

'Just talking about it makes me angry. She was twelve years old at the time ...' Glyn clenched his fists in an effort to control his temper.

'Between us we'll keep the Paskeys away from Miss Parry, sir. That's if they do turn up. Given what people think of them I don't think they'd dare show their faces in this town.'

'I wish I could be as sure as you, Ezra. I really do.' Glyn returned to his desk. 'Have you found a bed in one of the dormitories, Ezra?'

'Better than that, sir, a bed in Jimmy Peddle's house.'

'I heard he and his wife are taking in lodgers.'

'They are at the moment, sir, although his wife's not happy. She was only telling me before I came here that if she has her way they'll be going back in the spring.'

'Jimmy Peddle's leg hasn't healed properly after that fall he had outside the beer shop a couple of months back,' Alf elaborated.

'I heard it was a fight, not a fall,' Glyn interposed. 'Word of warning, Ezra, be careful where you step here, especially at night.'

'I'll remember that piece of advice, sir.'

'Here's another,' Alf added, 'watch the company you keep.' 'People here can't be any worse than the ones in Merthyr.'

Ezra looked from Glyn to Alf. 'Can they?'

Dr Nathan Kharber's house, hospital grounds,
Hughesovka September 1871

'I will not, I cannot, allow you to take your sister from this house into a Christian church. It is an affront to God and the name of Kharber.' Asher Kharber stepped in front of his nephew Nathan and raised his fist. Given the disparity in their ages and heights, Asher looked ridiculous but none of the people who'd gathered in Nathan's sitting room were laughing.

'I am my sister's guardian, Uncle,' Nathan asserted. He spoke quietly, softly, but there was no mistaking his determination.

'Your parents are spinning in their grave.'

'The decision has been made, Uncle Asher. Ruth has converted to Christianity and within the hour she will marry Alexei Beletsky.'

'I forbid it.' The old man stamped his foot on the wooden floor sending shock waves that rattled the furniture and the dishes in the cupboards.

'This is my house, Uncle Asher,' Nathan reminded. 'It is not for you to forbid anything within my walls.'

Rabbi Goldberg rose from his chair. 'This is my last word on the subject, Nathan. If you allow your sister to marry out of her faith, she will be dead not only to your family and those present, but to our entire community.'

'Then let me be dead, Rabbi Goldberg.' Ruth Kharber appeared in the doorway in her white lace bridal gown and veil. Her two Christian bridesmaids, Alexei's cousin Sonya Tsetovna, and her friend Anna Parry, stood beside her like bodyguards. Ruth's dark eyes glittered and her mouth was set in a resolute line although the bouquet of white lilies and roses she was holding trembled in her hands.

Nathan moved closer to the rabbi and lowered his voice. 'We made a bargain, Rabbi, you and I,' he reminded. 'I have kept my side, you must keep to yours.'

'Ruth, please,' her Aunt Leah reached out to her. 'You are like a daughter to Uncle Asher and me. Please. I beg you on my knees,' the old woman lowered herself stiffly to the floor, 'don't turn your back on your faith and us. Not after what we've been to one another.'

Ruth didn't trust herself to speak for a few moments. When she did, her voice was clotted with unshed tears. 'It is you who is turning your back on me, Aunt Leah. I am the same person standing before God I've always been.'

'The Christian God is not our God, Ruth,' Rabbi Goldberg thundered.

'That is not what Father Grigor said.'

'Father Grigor wants what every Christian priest wants. More souls to count in his church and pay him his stipend so he can live without having to do any real work. That is why every Christian priest spends most of their time looking for converts. All they really want is to fatten their purses. Whereas we Jews are born into our faith, we have been chosen by God to keep his word, his worship, and our bloodlines pure.'

'All religions teach that God is kind, gentle and all-seeing. He understands people, their frailties and the love they bear one another.' Ruth continued to look at the rabbi. The rabbi refused to meet her steady gaze. 'The Godly know

what has to be done.' It was a command to all the Jews assembled in the room. Everyone present except the bride, bridesmaids, Nathan, and his wife Vasya tore the cloth of their jackets and blouses on the right side of their bodies to signify they were mourning the death of a relative or close friend. The cloth ripped easily in every case, suggesting the gashes had been made in advance and concealed.

Rabbi Goldberg wasn't the only person who'd made preparations. Nathan took three black ribbons and pins from the pocket of his best black suit. He handed one to Ruth, another to his wife, Vasya, and kept the third. 'As Christians you don't need these,' he explained to Anna and Sonya. 'You'll excuse us, Rabbi, if we don't tear our clothes, but these are our best outfits and we're on our way to a wedding.' He pinned the black ribbon over the left side of his body above his heart, to signify that he regarded Asher and Leah, as his closest – newly deceased – relatives. Ruth followed suit. Nathan walked past Ruth, Anna, and Sonya and opened the front door. 'As we are now dead to one another, Rabbi Goldberg, Uncle Asher, Aunt Leah, guests, if you do not wish to attend Ruth's wedding to Alexei Beletsky in the church on Catherine Ignatova's estate, please leave.'

'Remember, Ruth, you brought this upon yourself.' Rabbi Goldberg looked to his niece. 'Vasya?'

She moved close to Nathan. 'I am Nathan's wife, Uncle.'

'Your uncle is your rabbi, Vasya,' her father reminded her. 'He has spoken.'

'A wife's first duty is to her husband before her rabbi.' She pinned the ribbon over the heart of her best dark grey silk dress and lowered her head modestly.

Rabbi Goldberg, Asher and Leah Kharber, and the remainder of the guests walked out of Nathan's living room and his house.

Catherine Ignatova's senior coachmen, Igor and Ivan, were waiting outside in front of the gate with the bridal carriages she'd sent to convoy her grandson's bride and her party to the church. Glyn Edwards had ordered the company workmen to lay a tarpaulin between the hospital gate and the carriage stop for the bride so she wouldn't soil her gown and shoes. Both coachmen tipped their hats to the departing Jews as they walked over it. All the men who'd been labouring nearby removed their hats and bowed. If the rabbi or any of his party saw them make the gesture, they made no reciprocal acknowledgement.

Nathan offered Ruth his arm.

Ruth covered her face with her veil, lifted her head and slipped her hand into the crook of Nathan's elbow. He walked her out to the accompaniment of cheers from the workmen and helped her into the first carriage.

Sonya and Anna offered their arms to Vasya. The three of them linked arms and walked to the second carriage where Ivan assisted them inside.

'Is that a Cossack hymn?' Ruth asked Nathan as they moved off to a musical rendering from the men labouring on the new shops.

'I believe so, Ruth. A serenade to your new life as a Russian Orthodox bride.'

Chapter Four

'Sit down, calm down, take a deep breath,' Glyn ordered Alexei, who was shifting from one foot to the other like a chained bear. 'Very shortly Ruth will take her last steps as a Kharber when she walks down that aisle with Nathan, and her first steps as a Beletsky when she walks back to the door with you.'

'You believe she'll turn up?' Alexei asked. 'Her Aunt Leah insisted on helping her dress. Her Uncle Asher will be in Nathan's house with Rabbi Goldberg and the entire Goldberg tribe. Nathan's wife Vasya is a Goldberg so she'll add her voice to the others when they try to persuade Ruth to change her mind about marrying me. None of them wanted Ruth to convert to the Orthodox Church. They've talked non-stop about ceremonies in the synagogue under a canopy, stamping on glass to break it and converting me to the Jewish faith. I should have converted. Why didn't I convert ...' Alexei's voice rose precariously 'If I'd converted...'

'You would have had to undergo a small but painful operation that would have severely interfered with your enjoyment of your honeymoon,' Glyn interrupted in a whisper. 'You're forgetting that Ruth chose to become a Christian. She also chose your cousin Sonya and Anna Parry to be her bridesmaids knowing that if anyone can keep the arrangements on track it's those two. Ruth will be here because she loves you. Now smile at your grandmother, who's just walked in with Mr Hughes, Mr Dmitri, and Prince Roman Nadolny. I wasn't expecting to see the prince here. When I spoke to him three days ago he told me he was planning to leave Hughesovka.'

'He changed his mind when Mr Hughes asked for his opinion on the way the town is developing. Once he decided to delay his departure my grandmother invited him to attend my wedding.'

'Your grandmother can be very persuasive.' Glyn spoke from personal experience.

Alexei turned around. The immaculately dressed man who accompanied his grandmother, Catherine, John Hughes, and Mr Dmitri into the Ignatova family pew was certainly striking. At nearly six and a half feet, he was almost the same height as Glyn, but of a marginally slighter build. His hair was white- blond, his eyes green, not the more usual dark jade, but a bright, glittering emerald. But the most noticeable thing about him was his face: Oriental, longer and slimmer than a Mongolian's, it was indisputably Chinese.

'I've had a few interesting meetings with him,' Glyn commented. 'He certainly seems to be on Mr Hughes's side when it comes to industrialising Russia.'

Without thinking, Alexei repeated the maxim that had become his mantra since he'd started working closely with John Hughes and Glyn. 'Like the Tsar, the prince sees Russia's need to modernise if our motherland is to take her place amongst the foremost nations of the world.'

'I know he's well-connected and counts not only the Romanovs, but members of the other royal European families amongst his closest friends. I've wondered, but haven't dared ask. Is he Russian or Chinese?' Glyn whispered.

'His mother was Manchurian. And you're right about his friends he's close to the royal family, especially Grand Duke Konstantin and often represents his interests.'

'Is that why he's here?'

'Without a doubt,' Alexei whispered before walking down the aisle to greet his grandmother. He embraced her and shook hands with the prince, John Hughes, and his grandmother's lawyer, Mr Dmitri.

'I'm honoured by your presence, sir,' he said to Nadolny. 'I believe you've met my best man, Mr Glyn Edwards.'

Roman shook Glyn's hand. 'A pleasure to meet you again, sir, on such an auspicious day.'

'Please excuse us, Prince,' Alexei apologised as the choir began to sing.

'Of course, it would be inappropriate to keep your bride waiting while you converse with me.'

Alexei wondered if the prince had made a joke. The prince rarely smiled and Alexei frequently had difficulty determining whether or not he was being serious. He followed Glyn back to their station in front of the altar in the small estate church that had been a betrothal present from Catherine's husband to her on her sixteenth birthday. It had aged well in the decades that had passed since Catherine had walked down the aisle as a bride. The pine walls had matured to deep gold, the stained-glass windows had faded, the bright blues, yellows, and reds turning to less vibrant, muted shades more becoming to a place of prayer and worship.

All the pews were full and people were standing at the back, but Alexei noted the absence of Jews. Every worker and family from his estranged father, Count Beletsky's estate was there, as were all the workers and their families from his grandmother's estate. The Cossacks from the village had filed into the back pews, and Glyn's mistress, Praskovia was sitting with her mother Yelena and feeble-minded younger brother, Pyotr. A contingent of the Cossack troops who'd been sent by the Tsar to keep the peace in John Hughes's new industrial town, had marched in headed by their commander Colonel Zonov and stationed themselves along the side walls. The Welsh were strongly represented and led by Alf Mahoney with his Russian bride of a few weeks, Tonia. To John Hughes delight, Alf and Tonia's had been the first Welsh/Russian marriage in the town.

'So much for a quiet wedding,' Alexei murmured to Glyn when he faced the altar again.

'Given your grandmother's social position you didn't really believe you'd get away with a few witnesses and a quick service, did you?' Glyn asked in amusement.

'I had hoped. What's happening at the door?'

'Your bride's arrival,' boomed an authoritative voice.

Alexei looked up to see the high-hatted, imposing figure of Father Grigor in full regalia looming over him. He turned back to the door and caught a glimpse of Anna and Sonya's cream lace bridesmaids' dresses but they had their backs turned to him.

'You're allowed to watch your bride walk down the aisle, Alexei,' Father Grigor said with mock gravity. 'And when she does, I assure you there won't be a man in this church who won't be envying you.'

The choir broke into the traditional Russian Orthodox wedding hymn, the door opened and Ruth and Nathan Kharber stood framed in the doorway. Glyn felt in his pocket and produced the rings needed for the first part of the ceremony – the betrothal. But Alexei was oblivious. He stared mesmerized as Ruth walked slowly towards him.

He knew his grandmother and Sonya had helped Ruth choose her bridal clothes, but he hadn't expected them to transform her into an angel. Her floor-length dress, train, veil, and cap were simply cut from pure white, handmade lace. The skirt was full and not drawn back into a fashionable bustle. He recognised the white lilies and white roses his grandmother grew in her hot houses in Ruth's headdress and bouquet and saw Sonya's artistic flair in the way they'd been tied with white ribbons. The overall effect was awe-inspiring. The only other time he could recall feeling so affected was when he first saw the icon of the Madonna that graced one of the side altars in the Church of the Annunciation on Vasilevsky in St Petersburg.

Forgetting the directives Father Grigor had given him at the rehearsal, he walked towards Ruth and held out his hand. She took it. He gazed into her eyes and saw his entire future mapped in their dark depths.

'Alexei?' He heard Father Grigor but couldn't tear his gaze away from Ruth. 'Do you want to marry this lovely bride before sunset or not, Alexei?'

Laughter rippled through the congregation.

Alexei grasped Ruth's hand. 'I do, Father Grigor. I most seriously do.'

Catherine Ignatova's house, Hughesovka September 1871

Alexei led his bride into the centre of the ballroom floor. The musicians struck the opening chords of a waltz and the guests applauded.

'You must be very proud.' John Hughes touched his glass to Catherine's as Alexei whirled Ruth around the room.

'I am.' Catherine's smile was strained. 'I only hope Rabbi Goldberg will allow them to live in peace.'

'He will, Catherine.' Nathan appeared at her elbow with Vasya. 'He has to accept that Ruth has made a choice that is recognised by the state and the Russian Orthodox Church. He won't risk irritating either.'

Catherine clasped Nathan and Vasya's hands. 'I can't thank both of you enough for coming to the wedding, for Alexei's sake and mine.'

'And Ruth's,' Nathan smiled. 'She is my sister.'

'Alexei will take good care of her.'

'I know he will, Catherine. Thank you for organizing a wonderful wedding and wedding breakfast. I know that in your world that is the task of the bride's family.'

'Since my daughter and all but one of my granddaughters died in the cholera outbreak, Alexei, his little sister Kira, and my niece Sonya are all I have left, Nathan. It was an honour and a privilege to help plan this wedding for Ruth and Alexei.

'I know you and Vasya will be berated by Rabbi Goldberg and everyone in the shtetl for attending today.'

'Our ears are strong enough to withstand a few harsh words. Thank you so much for your warm welcome, Catherine, but we have to leave. I have already been away from the hospital longer than I intended.' Nathan shook Catherine's hand and Vasya followed suit.

'You'll stay to wave the new Mr and Mrs Beletsky off?' Catherine pleaded. 'They'll be leaving after their bridal dance.'

'We can wait until then,' Nathan capitulated.

'I need to find my coat.' Vasya looked around for a footman. 'Boris will help you,' Catherine pointed her in the direction of her butler. Vasya went to him but when Nathan followed his wife he was waylaid by Sonya.

'It's traditional for the bridesmaid to dance with the bride's father, and as you gave the bride to her new family, that's you.'

'I am a very poor dancer,' Nathan demurred.

'I'll help you improve.'

'You won't allow me to refuse your request?'

'I won't.' She was smiling but there was steel in her voice. Nathan glanced over his shoulder at the dance floor. It was filling up with guests who'd joined Alexei and Sonya. He welcomed the anonymity the crowd offered and held out his hand. Sonya took it and he led her into a gap that opened next to Anna who was dancing with Dmitri.

'You're far from a poor dancer, Dr Kharber,' Sonya complimented.

'I haven't danced since I left Paris and that was a few years ago.'

'Because we have so few dances in the town?'

'Because my religion frowns on men and women dancing together.'

'I've heard dance music being played in the shtetl when I visited the dressmaker, and Ruth is a beautiful dancer. She must have practised.'

'She did with the women, and we men dance together, but dancing with the opposite sex is forbidden.'

'How odd.'

'You, like the friends I made in Paris and Vienna would find many things about my race odd,' he qualified.

'Not once they were explained to me.'

'It's not always easy to explain tradition.' He dropped his bantering tone. 'I'm going to miss you in the hospital, Miss Tsetovna.'

'You weren't so formal in the hospital.'

'We were often alone in the hospital office, now we're in company.'

'And you're married.' She hadn't meant her observation to sound bitter. She loved Nathan with all her heart. She sensed that he loved her, yet nothing remotely personal had ever been spoken between them. But from the moment they'd begun working together in the hospital John Hughes had built, she'd nurtured a secret hope that one day Nathan, like his sister Ruth, would either renounce his faith, or ask her to convert to Judaism so they could marry.

When Nathan had asked to speak to her alone a few weeks ago, she'd half expected a proposal. Instead he'd given her advance notice of his marriage to Vasya Goldberg. Vasya was the Rabbi's niece, a spinster past forty who looked nearer sixty and was ten years older than Nathan. Like everyone else who knew him, Sonya suspected that Nathan's marriage had been Rabbi Goldberg's "price" for allowing the wedding between Alexei and Ruth to go ahead.

'What's it like working for Mr Hughes?'

She looked up at Nathan and realised he'd spoken, but lost in thought she hadn't heard a word he'd said. 'I beg your pardon.'

'It's me who should beg yours,' Nathan apologised. 'You were obviously miles away, I asked about your work with Mr Hughes.'

45

'It's exciting and interesting,' she gushed to conceal her embarrassment, hoping he hadn't guessed that she'd been thinking about him. 'I never believed I'd have the opportunity to put my language skills to use, but Mr Hughes sends letters all over Europe and America, and they all need translating.'

'Exactly how many languages do you speak?'

'Only the principal ones, English, French, German, Russian, Polish, Italian, Spanish, and Latin and Greek of course.'

'Of course,' he echoed. 'You're making fun of me.'

'I didn't mean to.'

The music stopped, she stepped away from him.

'Sonya...'

She looked over his shoulder and saw his wife. 'Vasya's waiting.'

'I wanted to say I'm sorry.'

Sonya didn't need to ask for what. 'Take this.' She opened a small reticule hanging on her wrist and removed a packet of rice.

He looked at it quizzically.

'For you and Vasya to throw at the happy couple.'

'They are happy, aren't they,' he murmured more to himself than her as Alexei escorted Ruth from the hall.

'They are.' Sonya had to force herself to smile. 'If we follow Alexei and Ruth now, we'll get close enough to shower them before anyone else.'

Prince Roman Nadolny watched Sonya lead the guests out of the ballroom and through the doors that opened into the hall. He followed the crowd at a leisurely pace with John Hughes.

'A beautiful bride,' John commented as Alexei wrapped Ruth in a silver fox fur cape that had been a wedding gift from Sonya.

'She is,' Roman agreed,

'Are you looking at the bride or at Catherine's niece, Sonya?' John teased when he saw just who Roman was watching.

'Both,' Roman admitted as the guests followed Alexei and Ruth outside. 'I take it Sonya is Catherine's dipsomaniac lunatic brother's illegitimate daughter. The niece who recently inherited a fortune?'

'Sonya is the only niece of Catherine's I've heard of,' John relied cautiously. 'But if she's inherited a fortune I don't know anything about it.'

'Someone told me the family want to keep it quiet which is understandable. A young pretty girl in possession of two million roubles would attract fortune hunters like wolves to a cemetery.'

'Two million ... Are you sure we're talking about the same girl? Sonya Tsetovna?' John checked.

'How many nieces does Catherine have with that name?'

'As I said, only one I'm aware of,' John confirmed. He glanced at Roman. 'And while we're talking about rumours, I've heard it said that you're the richest man in Russia.'

'I was before I loaned the Tsar money, and invested in your New Russia Company,' Roman said drily.

'So why ask about an heiress?'

Roman turned back to the ballroom and took two glasses of champagne from a waiter. He handed John one. 'Money should marry money. Otherwise half of the marriage will always wonder if roubles were the only incentive for the other half to walk down the aisle. I've been looking for my heiress for some time.'

'You think you've found her?' John enquired.

'You British are always in such a hurry. Time will tell, Mr Hughes.'

'If we're always in a hurry, it's because you Russians are content to live with dreams. Without us Hughesovka wouldn't exist, even on paper.'

'Touché, Mr Hughes. But the world needs dreamers as well as men of action – we're the ones who give practical men their ideas.'

Chapter Five

Alexei stepped down from the carriage, turned and held out his arms to Ruth.

'I can walk,' she protested.

'Absolutely not, Mrs Beletskaya. It's bad luck for the bride to set foot between the carriage and the inside of her new house. Can't you see the devil waiting to watch you trip, and when you do, he'll rain down all his bad luck on both of us.'

'You've just made that up!' Ruth rose from the carriage seat.

'Possibly, possibly not. Bring the lamp over here please, Igor.' He glanced at the uneven ground as Igor lifted the lantern from the hook on the outside of the carriage and held it out in front of them. When he was certain the path was clear Alexei reached up and lifted Ruth into his arms.

'Happy married life, young master, mistress. Good luck.' Igor saluted them as he closed the carriage door.

'Thank you, Igor, enjoy the rest of your evening.'

'The party will be going on a while yet, sir. We'll drink a fair few toasts to you and your beautiful bride and wish you both a long and happy life.'

'Thank you, Igor.' Alexei carried Ruth over the road, which was strewn with building rubble, up the garden path, swung her over the threshold and set her down in the hall.

'Welcome home, master, mistress.'

'Lev, Lada,' Alexei greeted the couple he'd employed to run his household.

His grandmother had warned that he'd never manage with just two servants, but he'd known Lev, who was the nephew of his grandmother's butler Boris, and Lev's wife Lada all his life. Like most Cossacks they were hard workers and he had no intention of employing a large staff like his grandmother, who, given their light duties, had all the time in the world to visit the town markets and spread gossip.

Lev bowed and Lada curtsied. 'Welcome to your home, master, mistress. Everything is as you ordered.'

'Thank you, Lev. See you at breakfast, and not too early.'

'Yes, sir.'

'Goodnight, master, mistress.'

'Goodnight,' Ruth called as she ran up the stairs. She knew the layout as she'd helped Alexei choose the furniture for the house. It had been built around the same time as the house Catherine had sold to Glyn Edwards. Intended to house the estate's huntsman, it had been ideally situated on the barren steppe. But since John Hughes had persuaded Catherine to lease him most of her land, the steppe had been encroached on by Hughesovka. After Catherine sold her brother's house to Glyn, she'd decided it was ridiculous to leave her huntsman living in the centre of the town that had grown up around the cottage, so she moved him to alternative accommodation nearer her mansion.

Alexei had always liked the Cossack-built wooden cottage, and as it was close to the New Russia Company headquarters where he shared an office with Richard, he'd asked his grandmother to give it to him.

There were two bedrooms, a large and a small, on the first floor, and a single fairly large living room on the ground floor. An annexe built behind the cottage housed a bathhouse, kitchen, and two rooms that Alexei had renovated and turned into self- contained servants' quarters.

Alexei saw Lev and Lada out, locked the front and back doors, and walked up the staircase, which like most Cossack houses was intricately carved with designs of animals and plants.

Lada had left the oil lamp burning in the largest bedroom and it cast a golden glow over the polished wood walls and floor. Alexei and Ruth had chosen a plain pine bed and washstand. Chests, cupboards, and shelves had been built into the walls, which they'd decorated with an assortment of family photographs and a selection of Sonya's and Alexei's mother's paintings. The overall effect was that of a rustic, reasonably well-to-do peasant's home.

The allowance Alexei received from his grandmother was generous. He also earned good wages from the New Russia Company, and, given his contacts among the craftsmen in the area, he could have easily afforded to have built a more luxurious and substantial dwelling, but he was determined to live simply, and enjoy Ruth's company – at least until their children came along when he knew that lack of space would dictate a move.

Lev had put the bottle of champagne he'd sent from his grandmother's wine cellar along with a bucket of ice from her ice-house on a table in the bedroom. Next to it were two glasses, and a bowl of strawberries from Catherine's hot-house. Ruth was standing at the window looking down at the street.

'Happy, wife?' Alexei stood behind her and kissed the back of her neck.

'More than I believed possible.'

'I told you we'd be married one day.' He released her, closed the curtains, opened the champagne and poured two glasses. She picked up the cork along with the glass he handed her.

'Why do you want that?'

'Memories.'

'We have our whole lives to make them.'

'We have a saying in the shtetl, "Life is nothing but a dream, but don't wake me up!" This,' she held up the cork, 'is real and will remind me of tonight at a time when I may need to remember.'

'I will fill every day with happiness so you can make new memories. So many memories it will be impossible for you to remember them all. We'll grow old together, you and I.' He took the glass from her, bent his head to hers, and kissed her.

She returned his kiss. 'That bed looks very inviting.'

'I thought brides were supposed to be coy.'

'Not this one. Sometimes I think I've been waiting to be your wife for ever, but I'm glad we waited. This night is going to be very special.'

'More memories?'

'The best.' She turned her back to him again. Heart pounding, he unbuttoned the row of pearls that fastened her gown.

Catherine Ignatova's house, and Madam Koshka's Salon, Hughesovka September 1871

'I will say goodnight, ladies, gentlemen.'

'You're going to bed early, Roman,' Catherine commented.

'Dmitri has persuaded Mr Hughes and I to call on an old friend for a nightcap.'

Catherine nodded. 'I think you are referring to an old friend who also happens to be an old friend of mine. Please give her my special and warmest wishes.'

'I will indeed, madam. Until breakfast.' Roman kissed her hand and left with Dmitri and John. Their valets were waiting with their coats.

It was a short carriage ride into town.

Dmitri disappeared down the corridor that led to the private rooms as soon as they reached Koshka's and John was waylaid in the comfortable salon by a group of building contractors, leaving Roman to bask in the attentions of a pretty young redhead.

Koshka joined them. 'So you stayed on in Hughesovka after all, Prince Roman?'

'Mr Hughes found more work for me to do, which gave me an excuse to stay for Alexei and Ruth's wedding, which was all a wedding should be. Catherine's grandson made a suitably dashing bridegroom and his bride was extremely beautiful. You should have come. I know you had an invitation.'

'I was there. I sat at the back of the church along with the other veiled widows.'

'I didn't see you.'

'My intention was not to attract attention. I have French cognac in my room if you prefer it to the German you're drinking, but if you would like Adele's company...'

'Who could resist your French cognac? My apologies, Adele, but Madam Koshka and I are old friends.'

'Perhaps you'd like to enjoy my company later, sir?'

'Perhaps.' He winked at the girl before following Koshka into her small, exquisitely furnished inner sanctum.

'My boudoir and office.' She showed him in and closed the door, shutting out the noise of the salon.

After the chatter of conversation in the public rooms Roman found the silence soothing. 'I recognise the furnishings from your Tverskaya Ulitsa establishment in Moscow. You and your girls have brought civilization to the steppe, Koshka.'

'We try, but Hughesovka needs to be drastically improved in many ways before it will be a suitable town for a well-bred woman.'

'It's certainly a long way from the capital and your usual haunts. Are you happy here?'

'Reasonably so. There's money to be made in this town, Roman,' Koshka said seriously. 'More than Moscow, more even than St Petersburg. Every one of my girls has at least one regular, most have more, and although our clients may not be as aristocratic as those who frequented my Moscow salon, in general the gentlemen have better manners and are as rich, if not richer. They are also generally gentler and more respectful and appreciative of my own and my girls' persons and feelings.'

Roman sat in one of the plush upholstered gilded chairs and watched Koshka pour two glasses of cognac. 'John Hughes asked me to take a look around the town tomorrow and give my opinion on the way it's developing.'

'Haven't you had enough time to look around it during the past few days?'

'I've attended too many meetings in the New Russia Company's offices, and too many discussions around Catherine's dinner table to make time for an appraisal.'

'So you've met John's employees?'

'Most of the senior ones, and Catherine's family of course as I'm a guest in her house, although my room is in the wing John Hughes rents from her. Her grandson, Alexei, works for John and,' Roman looked Koshka in the eye, 'her niece Sonya is John's interpreter.'

'What of it?' Koshka spoke sharply.

'Have you met the girl? She's extraordinarily beautiful and has been well educated.' He took a cigar from the amber-plated humidor she offered him. 'Thank you.'

'Why would you be interested in Catherine's niece?' Koshka's tone was far from casual.

'Because I've heard rumours she's an heiress. Two million roubles or thereabouts.'

'Who told you that?' Koshka sat tense and bolt upright on her chair.

Roman shrugged. 'You can't stop lawyers' clerks from gossiping, Koshka.'

'They have no right to discuss the affairs of their employers' clients.'

'I haven't called on you to discuss the latest stories that are entertaining the socialites who frequent the Moscow and St Petersburg salons, Koshka. I came to give you advance notice that I intend to make Sonya Tsetovna an offer.'

'Of marriage?'

'Given her mother and aunt I wouldn't dare suggest anything else.' He sipped his brandy. 'This is exceptionally good cognac.'

Koshka wasn't prepared to be waylaid into a conversation on cognac. 'Why do you think I would be interested in your plans?'

'Because they concern Sonya, and you knew her mother.'

'Sonya's mother died shortly after she was born, which is why Catherine took her in and saw to the child's upbringing and education,' she said abruptly.

'I have many fond memories of Sonya's mother's sterling qualities. Her strong character and loyalty to her friends.' He looked her in the eye again.

She looked away first. 'Why Sonya? You're wealthier than the Pope, incredibly good-looking...'

'For someone who's half Chinese.'

'False modesty doesn't become you, Roman. Women are attracted to your exotic looks and you know it,' she countered. 'You're in the prime of life. A snap of the fingers will bring you any woman you want. Two million roubles are not to be sneezed but they are insignificant in comparison to your hundreds of millions. There are richer heiresses in the world. So why chose Sonya Tsetovna?'

'Because she's young, unspoilt, needs someone strong to guide her, and has already had her heart broken.'

'You know a great deal about her.'

'I saw her dance with the Jewish doctor who works in the hospital tonight.'

'Alexei Beletsky and Ruth Kharber are a brave exception in this town. Nathan Kharber didn't possess the courage to marry outside of his race.'

'I met his wife.'

'Vasya is a kind woman.'

'A wife who won't attract envious glances from other men.'

'That is harsh. But to return to Sonya...'

'You have no need to concern yourself, Koshka, I won't hurry her. Just make my proposal and wait until she is ready to accept it or not, as she chooses. After all, she's, what, sixteen, seventeen...'

'Almost eighteen,' Koshka interrupted quickly. Too quickly. 'I had no idea you were on the lookout for a wife, Roman.'

'I've been on the lookout for some years.'

'I would never have guessed from your behaviour.'

'You wouldn't condemn a man for sowing a few wild oats, would you?'

'Not when he sows them along with his roubles in my house.'

'I've always pictured myself as the ideal family man and a faithful husband.' He had the grace to smile. 'Sometime in the future, that is.'

'It's an ideal I've heard about but, given my profession, one I've never become intimately acquainted with.'

'In the meantime, as a bachelor, albeit one contemplating marriage, I'm free to indulge in a little more debauchery.'

'Adele will be waiting and at your disposal. A prince with royal connections is a catch in this house, especially when he's rumoured to be generous.'

'I'll compensate Adele for her time and expertise.'

'I didn't doubt you would. Just a gentle hint that there are other ladies in this house who are also worthy of your attention. Jealousy can undermine the entire atmosphere of a salon when favours are not evenly spread.'

'Always thinking of others,' Roman picked up Koshka's hand and kissed it. 'A pleasure to meet you again, madam.'

'You'll let me know Sonya's reaction to your proposal?' 'Of course. I will return before I leave town.'

'And your real reason for wanting to marry her, Roman?' '

You wouldn't believe me if I told you, Koshka.'

'Try me.'

'Perhaps I will – one day.'

Koshka continued to sit alone in her room after Roman left. After a while she reached for her keys and unlocked a drawer in her desk. She removed the papers it contained and pressed a button at the back. A secret drawer flew open and she removed the album it contained.

The cover was embroidered with a single word. Sonya. She opened it and studied the first portrait. It was of a young woman holding a baby. Had she ever been that young? There was no mistaking the family resemblance. She could be Sonya as she'd seen her earlier that day in her bridesmaid's dress.

And the baby – the baby she'd handed over to the child's father's sister shortly afterwards. She hadn't lied to Roman.

The woman she'd been had died that day and Koshka had been born.

Chapter Six

Nathan Kharber's house September 1871

'Do you have to work tonight?' Vasya asked Nathan as he walked her into the hospital grounds and to the door of the doctor's house that came as part of his salary.

'I'm sorry, Vasya. I have to,' Nathan replied. 'I'll try not to disturb you when I come in.'

'I'll wait up in case you need something.'

'No, Vasya, you're worn out. It's been a very long day. You go to bed. I'll see you in the morning.'

He turned his back on her because he couldn't bear to see the disappointment etched on her face. He was married to a martyr and he was finding it increasingly difficult to live with her self-sacrificing stoicism. He knew what people were saying, not only in the shtetl, but the Cossack village and the town. That marriage to Vasya had been the price Rabbi Goldberg had exacted from him for allowing Ruth to marry Alexei.

It was true.

He thought he'd be able to pay the price willingly, but that had been before he'd had to face Vasya's servility and interminable and effusive gratitude for rescuing her from her spinster state.

Love wasn't a factor in Jewish marriages. Every Jewish child was brought up to believe it followed, not preceded, the religious nuptials. He'd believed it himself before he'd returned from Paris after studying medicine. Until the moment he'd seen Alexei drive Sonya into the shtetl in her aunt's carriage he'd believed "love at first sight" existed only in young girls' imaginations and fairy tales.

Afterwards, he'd almost managed to convince himself that his feelings were no more than admiration for a beautiful girl on the brink of womanhood.

57

Then, when he'd been appointed doctor to the hospital after Peter Edwards's death he'd found himself working alongside Sonya. Impressed by her kindness and consideration for everyone she came into contact with, patient, staff, and visitor alike, he was forced to admit that, inconvenient as it might be, love at first sight was undoubtedly a reality.

Although he'd never found the courage to confide his feelings to her, he soon realised there was no need for words. The looks they exchanged were enough for him to read and understand her thoughts, just as he was absolutely certain she did his.

He glanced across the road towards Glyn Edwards's house. Next to it, set parallel to Glyn's back wall, was the wooden cottage that had belonged to Catherine Ignatova's huntsman before Hughesovka had encroached on her estate. A light burned in the porch and another in an upstairs room: Alexei and Ruth's first night as a married couple in their new home. He hated himself for envying their happiness but when he pictured Sonya in her bridesmaid's gown – so like that of a bride – he couldn't help it.

He walked around to the front of the hospital, pushed open the door and entered his office. A pile of patients' files lay on his desk waiting to be updated. He took his notebook from his desk drawer, sat and opened the first file. After a few minutes he was disturbed by a knock.

'Come in.'

Anna Parry opened the door. 'Good evening, Dr Kharber, Maxim said he'd seen you walk into the building.'

'At this time of night I expect Maxim to be watching the front door, given the influx of dubious newcomers into the town.'

'He is watching the door, but from the street, sir. Two of the Cossack soldiers stationed here are escorting a couple of drunks to the stables. Maxim went with them part of the way.'

'The drunks were here, actually in the hospital?'

'Maxim caught them before they reached the door, sir. They're soldiers out on a night's pass from the barracks. We know because they were waving the passes around. They were probably looking for beds for the night. One of the student nurses, Naomi Rinskaya, saw them through the window of Yulia's ward. They were crawling around the grounds on their hands and knees. She fetched Maxim who called the soldiers. I wouldn't like to be them when they have to face their officers in the morning. Would you like some tea?'

'Yes, please, Anna.' He opened his ink bottle and laid out his pens.

'It was a lovely wedding, wasn't it? Ruth made a beautiful bride.'

'She did,' he concurred.

'Sonya and I agreed, everything was perfect, apart from Sarah and Richard's absence.'

'Any word from them?' Nathan asked.

'None.'

'Let's hope everything works out for them the way they want it to,' he said diplomatically, uncertain how much Anna knew about Sarah's situation. He'd noticed the symptoms of Sarah's pregnancy before she'd left Hughesovka, and been surprised when Praskovia had confided that Richard had pursued Sarah in the hope of marrying her. Given the disparity in Sarah and Richard's ages it had never occurred to him that they were lovers. He'd assumed – wrongly – that Sarah's child had been fathered by her brother-in-law Glyn.

'I hope so too. It would be wonderful to have another wedding in the Ignatova church.'

'You think Richard and Sarah will marry?'

'You don't?' Anna challenged.

'As I just said, I want whatever they want for themselves,' he reiterated.

'You must have an opinion.'

'I try not to voice them lest you Welsh call me a "nosy parker".'

She laughed. 'Well, to repeat my opinion, and Sonya's, Alexei and Ruth had a beautiful wedding and I hope Richard's will be as wonderful.'

'Unless Richard and Sarah choose the same bridesmaids as my sister, their wedding can't possibly be as wonderful. What about your wedding and Sonya's, when the time comes? Will you marry in Mrs Ignatova's estate church?'

'Sonya might,' Anna said seriously, 'but not me. I want a career as a nurse.'

Nathan recalled Anna shooting the soldier who'd tried to rape Ruth, and Anna's insistence afterwards that she wasn't sorry she'd killed the man. Sarah had explained that Anna had been attacked before they'd left Wales, and from the way Sarah spoke, he'd assumed she meant raped. An experience like that would be enough to deter any young girl from all thoughts of men and marriage. He changed the subject.

'You are already a brilliant nurse. The fact that you're here now on night duty after an exhausting day as a bridesmaid is testament to your dedication.'

'Not really,' Anna qualified. 'We've no serious cases on the wards requiring night nursing, so it will be an easy shift.'

'Unless a case is admitted.'

'There's always that possibility.'

'And you also have a cantankerous doctor to cater for who demands tea at regular intervals,' Nathan hinted.

'It's your fault for keeping me gossiping. I'm on my way.'

Anna went into the kitchen, opened the range and removed a small shovelful of hot coals, which she poured into the base of the samovar. After topping the embers with wood and paper until the fire blazed, she filled the kettle and placed it on the coals to boil. She opened the teapot, filled the infuser with tea leaves, and set it aside.

When Ruth, Miriam, and Yulia had first shown her a samovar, she'd thought it a ridiculous, complicated way to brew tea. But she'd since had to admit that tea tasted richer, stronger, and far better brewed that way. She looked into the wards while she waited for the water to heat up. All the patients were asleep, but Yulia and Naomi were sitting at the Nightingale desk in the centre of the men's ward updating medicine charts.

'Tea?' Anna murmured.

'Please,' Yulia replied.

Anna opened the door to the women's ward, where Miriam was checking the patients. She mouthed 'Tea?' and Miriam nodded.

Anna returned to the kitchen. The kettle was boiling. She filled the teapot with water, raked out some of the coals to lower the temperature, set the teapot on top of the kettle to brew and laid out three trays.

'I saw Ruth and Alexei when they came home this evening. They looked so happy.' Yulia joined her and lifted plates down from the shelves.

'They were, and it was good of you and Miriam to start your shifts three hours early this evening so I could go to the wedding breakfast and ball.'

'We were both free to go to the church this afternoon. The service was beautiful. I can't wait for Father Grigor to marry me.'

'You want to marry Father Grigor?' Anna deliberately chose to misunderstand her.

'I wouldn't mind, he's a nice kind man.'

'You're talking about a priest who's at least thirty, if not forty, years older than you.'

'I'm talking about kindness, and I'd settle for that from any man as long as it was accompanied by a little money.'

'Money always helps.'

'Ruth will have no worries married to Alexei. I heard his father cut him off without a kopek but his grandmother is as rich as the Tsar.'

'I doubt she's that rich.' Anna qualified.

'You know what I mean. Ruth will be able to buy as many new gowns as she wants without worrying about the cost. I envy her that, and Alexei adores her so he'll shower her with fine clothes and jewellery.'

'She won't allow him to. She knows the value of a rouble.' 'Don't we all,' Yulia said gloomily.

'Don't you want to be rich, Anna?'

'I am rich by the standards I was brought up in. I have enough food to eat, I can buy all the clothes I need, and I can afford to rent a room in a fine house. What more do I want?'

'Balls, parties, jewellery...'

'You can only wear so much jewellery, and parties and balls would get boring if you went to them more than once in a while. We went out every night when Mr Hughes, Mr Edwards, and Mrs Ignatova took Richard, Alexei, Sonya, and me to St Petersburg. After the third night all I wanted to do was curl up in front of the fire with a book.'

'You're odd.'

'Probably,' Anna agreed as she cut two pieces of the cake Yelena, Glyn's cook, had sent over the day before. She put them on plates and set them on a tray together with two glasses of tea. 'This is for you and Naomi. I'll take Miriam and Dr Kharber theirs. Do you want help with anything on your ward?'

'No thanks, once we've finished the charts I'll be looking for things for Naomi to do. It's good to have a quiet night once in a while, but the busy ones pass more quickly.'

'They do,' Anna agreed.

Yulia returned to her ward. Anna left Miriam's glass and plate of cake on her desk and carried a tray into Nathan's office. He had his head down and was hard at work so she set it next to him quietly.

She stopped as she walked back through the entrance hall and looked across the road.

Lights burned in the porch of Glyn's house and his downstairs bedroom but the rest of the house was in darkness. It was hardly surprising as Alexei had moved out that morning, and Richard and Sarah were away.

She watched the house for a few minutes wishing things didn't have to change. She was going to miss Alexei, his pranks and smiling face. Seeing him next door and around the town wouldn't be the same as living in the same house as him. She wondered if Richard had succeeded in catching up with Sarah before she sailed for Britain. If Richard married Sarah would marriage alter them – and their relationship with her?

Why couldn't everything remain just as it was?

She returned to the kitchen, poured a glass of tea, and cut another slice of cake for Maxim, then took them into the hall. Maxim wasn't in the room off the porch that the hospital porters used for their breaks. She looked out of the window and saw him standing at the gate. She opened the door, walked down the path, and joined him. 'Are the drunks still around?'

'No, the soldiers left them in an empty stall in the stables to sleep off the vodka. I wouldn't like to wake to their headaches tomorrow. The soldiers thought they heard something out back when they returned, so they're patrolling the fence of the hospital grounds. At least that's what they said they were going to do. It could be just an excuse to drink the flasks of vodka the drunks hadn't finished. Can you see anyone up there, next to Mr Hughes's lumber pile?' He took the tea and cake from her.

Anna squinted into the darkness. 'Nothing, but it's black as coal along there. I could take a lantern and go and look?'

'You will not,' Maxim countered. 'I can't go far from the hospital because I'm the only one on duty but when the soldiers return I'll ask them to take a walk in that direction. I'm sure I saw someone flitting about.'

'What did they look like?'

'All I could make out was a black shadow.'

A dog barked further down the street.

'You probably saw an animal,' Anna reassured Maxim.

'If it was a dog, it was walking on its hind legs.'

'Another drunk looking for somewhere to sleep it off?'

'Perhaps. Thanks for the tea, Nurse Parry. Now go back inside and be sure to close all the doors and windows. Lock them all except the front door. I'll watch that.' He accompanied her to the door, closed it, then stood guard in the porch and lifted his rifle from his shoulder.

Glyn Edwards's house, Hughesovka September 1871

'That was a day to remember.' Praskovia draped her shawl over a chair in the enormous bedroom she shared with Glyn that also served as his study and their private sitting room.

'I'm only sorry that given the Russian Orthodox's church's attitude towards divorced men I won't be able to give you a wedding as memorable.'

'You asked Father Grigor if he would marry us?'

'I talked to him about our situation in confidence, but that's all I could do – talk – given that legally I'm still married to Betty.'

'You know that I'm happy just to be with you, Glyn.' She placed a tray of glasses and brandy next to his chair. 'Can I get you something to eat?'

'After all we've consumed in Catherine's house today, no thank you. I'll burst!' He sat down and pulled her on to his lap. 'I have something to tell you.'

'Something serious?'

'I had a letter from my wife. It arrived when I was in St Petersburg.'

'She must have said something to trouble you, if you've waited until now to tell me about it.'

'I put it off as long as possible because I wanted to enjoy our time together without thinking about her. Unfortunately we won't be able to do that much longer.

'She sent it as she was leaving Merthyr. She's on her way here.'

Praskovia could feel her heart beating. It was so loud she was amazed she could hear herself speak. She was suddenly very cold and very frightened. She couldn't imagine a world without Glyn. 'You want me to leave your house so your wife can move in?'

'No, absolutely definitely not. No! And there's something you should know about this house. It's not mine. It's yours. I had Mr Hughes's lawyer transfer the deeds to you after you told me you were having my child. So the house is in your name and you can throw me – and all the others – out any time you choose. I've also had your name added to my bank account so if anything happens to me you'll be able to access my money and you, your family, and our child will be able to continue living here. The lawyer's clerk is bringing the papers here tomorrow morning for you to sign.'

'But your wife?'

'Is well provided for. I bought Betty an annuity years ago –' he saw the look of confusion on her face. 'I paid a large sum of money into an investment scheme which sends money every year to Betty. It's more than enough for her to live very comfortably. I've also redrafted my will, and left her a penny so she and the lawyers will know that I want everything I own to go to you. There is however one other problem. Apparently, Betty gave birth to my child – a daughter – after I left Merthyr.'

'They are both coming here, to Hughesovka, to see you?'

'I told you my marriage to Betty is over, Praskovia. It is. I wrote and asked Betty for a divorce before I received her letter but I have no way of knowing whether she received my request or not because she never answered me. Our letters could have crossed in the post. However, if she did receive my letter, it could be the reason why she's decided to come here. Perhaps she thinks our marriage can still be saved. Which it most certainly can't,' he added.

'But she will want to stay in your house ...'

'I've just told you, it's your house. Not mine.'

'You can't just give me a house, especially not this one. It's large, beautiful, and aristocratic...'

'And yours.' He locked his arms around where her waist would have been if she wasn't pregnant. 'I'll visit the hotel in the morning and reserve a room for Betty and our daughter. When they arrive, I'll tell Betty she can stay only as long it takes me to book return passage for her to Merthyr.'

'What if she refuses to leave you?'

'I've already left her, Praskovia.'

'Glyn, I love you. I can't imagine a life without you, but if she feels the same way – and now there's your child...'

'I told you about Betty from the outset, Praskovia, because I want no secrets between us. I've made my choice and it's you and our child.' He laid his hand on her swollen body. 'This is your house and you can do whatever you wish within its walls, but no matter what happens I'd rather you didn't invite Betty inside, because if you did I've a feeling she'd never leave. That would be embarrassing for you, everyone in this house, and especially me.'

'So, you want me to pretend your wife doesn't exist?' She climbed from his lap went to the bed and turned it down.

'No, I want you to leave Betty to me when she gets here so you can concentrate on running this house and preparations to welcome our child.'

'I'll try, Glyn.' She bit her lip. 'But...'

'But?' he echoed.

'I can't believe you're really mine. That you love me and want to stay with me when you have a wife.'

He went to her, wrapped his arms around her and held her close.

'You're all the wife and woman I want, Praskovia. I told you about Betty's letter because you'd only find out about it when she reached here. Now, I'd like to forget about her – at least for what's left of tonight.'

'There's been no news from Richard and Sarah?'

'None, but I forgot to mention that my brother Edward and Richard's two younger brothers are travelling with my wife. They're probably hoping that we can find room for them here.'

'But of course, they'll stay here. Where else would they go?'

'You can find room for them in your house?' he smiled.

'It's a big house and Alexei's room is free. And maybe Sarah or Richard's if they're married ... Do you think Richard reached Sarah in time to stop her from leaving Russia?'

'I have no idea. What I do know is that it's been a very long day and that bed looks soft, clean, and comfortable.' He sat on the edge, bent down, and unlaced his shoes.

Praskovia lit the lamp at the side of the bed and turned down the one her mother had left burning on the table. She unbuttoned her blouse and skirt and stepped out of them. She sensed Glyn watching her undress.

'I'm fat and ugly.'

'You're becoming more beautiful every day with this little one growing inside you. He took her blouse and skirt from her and draped them over her shawl. 'We couldn't be more married than we are at the moment, Praskovia. I may have a wife but I never knew what love was until you came into my life.'

She reached up, kissed him, and helped him take off his coat.

'We'll talk again tomorrow,' he murmured, 'but not now.'

'You are tired?'

'For you, I'll find a little energy,' he whispered before pulling her down on to the bed beside him.

Chapter Seven

Alexei Beletsky's cottage September 1871

Alexei opened his eyes to darkness. He looked around in confusion. Bright light was flickering behind the curtains and they were on the wrong wall. It took him a few seconds to realise he'd moved out of Glyn's and was in his new house. Then, when he felt the warmth of Ruth's body lying alongside him, he remembered – and reached out and embraced her.

'What was that?' Ruth sat up with a jerk.

'If you heard it too, I couldn't have dreamed it.' He padded naked from the bed, pulled back the curtains and looked out into the street. 'Damn!' He reached for his trousers.

'What's happening?' she left the bed and joined him.

'Fire up the street. Let's hope it doesn't reach here.'

'Our furniture, clothes...'

'Can be replaced. You can't. Dress quickly and run next door with Lev and Lada. Stay there in case it does blow this way. Glyn's house is brick, but if fire takes hold in this house it will go up like a tinderbox.'

'If you're going out to fight the fire I am too.'

'You just took a sacred vow to obey me in church.'

'I lied.'

'Ruth, there's no time to argue...'

'Quite.'

'What are you doing?' He didn't know why he was asking.

She was already pushing her wedding dress and shoes into a bag. 'At least dress before you pack.'

'I can dress later.' She threw a robe over her nightgown before emptying her wardrobe into another bag.

He buttoned his trousers and reached for his socks. 'I saw Roman, Dmitri, Glyn, Nathan, and the soldiers and guards from the hospital fighting the fire. Please,' He grabbed his shirt and dropped a kiss on her lips. 'I need to know you're safe.' He picked up her bags and his boots and ran down the stairs, shouting for Lev. He dropped the bags, thrust his feet into his boots, and his arms into his shirt.

'Lev's already out there, master,' Lada stepped out of the shadows in the hall and opened the front door for him.

'Take Ruth next door to Praskovia. Don't let her pack anything else that will delay you one minute.'

Alexei ran. The lumber John Hughes had stockpiled to build houses and shops, and stored in a yard in front of his warehouses, was ablaze, as were several of the wooden shops and eating and drinking houses on both sides of the street. When he looked further north it appeared as though the entire shtetl was burning.

The slim figures of Jews were silhouetted black against the yellow and orange conflagration, their cartwheel hats enormous on their heads, their dark coats flapping around their knees as they charged backwards and forwards between the buildings, hauling buckets of water and rugs to beat out the flames. The scene reminded him of the woodcut illustrations in the children's books he'd read as a child.

Sparks arced through the air, lightening the sky and threatening the wooden buildings that weren't yet alight, eliciting cries and screams when they landed on the firefighters. Below the shtetl, the entire population of Hughesovka seemed to have poured out of their homes.

Koshka's clients in formal dinner suits were fighting alongside Mujiks in rags who had crawled out of their holes in the ground. Welsh colliers and ironworkers passed buckets to hotel guests in nightshirts and robes who'd lined up to form human chains.

Water was being pumped by Praskovia's slow-witted brother Pyotr from the well in Glyn's yard and passed from hand to hand to Glyn who'd stationed himself perilously close to the fire in the lumber yard. Alexei studied the line and realised that the buckets would move faster if there weren't so many men handling them.

He raced towards the wooden shed where the building materials were kept, shouting to Lev, Vlad, Maxim, and half a dozen others to follow.

'The doors are locked, master,' Lev said when Alexei tried and failed to wrench them open.

'What are you after?'

Alexei turned to see Nathan at his shoulder.

'Tarpaulins. If we smothered the fire on the fringes...'

He didn't have to say any more, Nathan shouted to Maxim to bring an axe.

Vlad was directing the workmen who'd joined them to pull as much of the undamaged timber from the back of the pile as they could safely reach. Maxim returned with an axe. Alexei knocked the padlock from the door and yanked it open.

He stared at a mound of sand heaped inside the door. 'Quick, bring buckets,' Nathan ordered no one in particular. Alexei grabbed a tarpaulin, dragged it out and ran to Glyn.

The centre of the pile of timber was blazing, but they managed to smother one edge with the oilcloth. At the far side of the fire, Vlad and the Cossack soldiers who'd ridden in with Colonel Zonov succeeded in pulling most of the undamaged planking out of reach of the flames.

Nathan heaved up a second tarpaulin. Alexei threw one corner to Glyn. Between the three of them they managed to cover even more of the fire. Maxim handed the first bucket of sand to Alexei who passed it to Glyn.

Alexei stepped back and studied the street. He saw Praskovia and Yelena working alongside Pyotr at the well in Glyn's garden and to his dismay Ruth– still in her nightclothes – working alongside Lada at the well in his garden.

Glyn shouted for another tarpaulin. Alexei ran to fetch it and pulled it behind him.

Nathan was standing motionless next to Glyn, staring at the shtetl. 'Fire is moving in from both sides of the Jewish quarter.'

Glyn and Alexei turned to see Rabbi Goldberg marshalling the Jews. They were attacking the untouched shops in the centre of the shtetl, axing the wooden frames and walls so they would fall in on themselves and starve the fires that burned at both ends of the settlement.

'He's making a firebreak,' Nathan said.

'Let's hope the destruction isn't in vain and it prevents the flames from spreading,' Glyn breathed in a lungful of smoke and began coughing.

'Here comes the relief force,' Alexei shouted when John Hughes arrived in the foremost one of a convoy of Catherine's carriages. All were packed with workers from the Ignatova estate. Sonya leapt out with John. She ran directly to the hospital where Anna, Yulia, Naomi, and Miriam were examining the injured in the grounds.

'Sonya, thank you, we can do with all the help we can get,' Anna shouted to make herself heard above the cries, screamed commands, and crackle of flames. 'Can you sort the wounded? Those with breathing problems over there,' Anna pointed to an area at the side of the building. 'We're dressing minor burns and cuts in the porch. Any serious injuries, send for Dr Kharber.' Sonya nodded and ran to the people who were waiting to be seen.

'Every second man, follow me, the rest of you to Mr Edwards,' John Hughes headed straight for the conflagration that was destroying the Jewish quarter.

'Do you think he'll save the shtetl?' Nathan asked Alexei when they heaved the last tarpaulin out of the warehouse.

Alexei wiped his blackened forehead with the back of his hand. 'Not a chance. I only hope the Jews don't start spreading the rumour that God brought this down on them for allowing Ruth to marry a Christian.'

Glyn Edwards's house September 1871

A thin, grey, smoke-filled dawn broke over Hughesovka at six o'clock to reveal smouldering ruins. The exhausted men, women and children who'd spent the night firefighting were raking over the embers that had cooled enough to fork and scatter. John Hughes stood in Glyn's front garden and studied the North-Eastern sector of his town that had housed the shops. The only buildings that hadn't been destroyed were the two built of brick.

The flames, coupled with Rabbi Goldberg's firebreak that had managed to curtail and concentrate the blaze, had decimated the Jewish quarter, houses as well as shops. The seared posts of the buildings' frameworks stood, blackened skeletons in a sea of smouldering debris. Three of the largest dormitories for the Welsh, French, and Russian colliers, two drinking shops, and two eating-houses that had been erected on the eastern fringes of the shtetl were blackened smears on the scorched earth. The thatched roofs of the Mujik "hole" houses in that section of town had also been devoured by the flames, but philosophical and pragmatic by nature, accustomed to setbacks they invariably attributed to "God's just punishment for sins" the peasants were already weaving replacements.

The brick foundations for permanent buildings that had been recently laid were blackened but appeared structurally undamaged.

To the south of the settlement, the hotel, Madam Koshka's, and Glyn's house, all brick-built, were unscathed, as was Alexei's wooden house and the New Russia Company's wooden warehouses and headquarters in the South West quarter. But most important of all in John's eyes, the furnaces and buildings of the ironworks that waited to be commissioned had escaped the conflagration.

Exhausted and dispirited after the night's work, the senior managers of the New Russia Company gathered around him.

'It could have been worse.' Glyn looked back at his garden. As the sky faded from dark to light grey and light rose from the ground, he saw groups of shadowy, weary figures slumped in every corner of his plot.

Alf nudged Vlad in the ribs. They started laughing.

'What's funny?' Glyn wondered if fatigue had edged them into hysteria.

'Us, all of us,' Alf said when he could finally talk. 'We're blacker than colliers at the end of a shift. You can't tell Cossack soldier from civilian, Jew from Welshman or Russian, and we're all too whacked to fight each other or even trade insults.'

'Perhaps we should cover ourselves in ash every day,' Vlad added in his heavily accented English.

'Might stop people mouthing a few of the stupider comments I heard some of the Russian colliers make about the influx of Welsh colliers and ironworkers yesterday,' Glyn agreed.

John Hughes ran his hands through his hair. 'Everyone is sleeping on their feet. I can't see us doing much work today, so you may as well tell the colliers they've been given a day off, Alf.'

'Yes, sir.'

John parried Alf's questioning glance. 'All the men – and women – who turned out last night will be paid for the shift they put in firefighting.

'Without their efforts even more of the town would have gone up in smoke and the flames might have reached the works.' He glanced at Glyn. 'The ironworkers can have the day off to catch up on sleep, but I'm calling a senior managers' meeting. Headquarters in one hour. That should give us enough time to breakfast and clean ourselves up.

'I'll be there, sir.' Alexei smiled at Ruth who had brought a tray of tea glasses out from Glyn's kitchen.

'Thank you, Mrs Beletskaya', John took a glass. 'Alexei, I'm grateful for what you and your wife did last night. Without your assistance, we wouldn't have saved as much timber as we did, but the company gave you two weeks' leave for your honeymoon. Take it. That's an order.'

'We can honeymoon later, sir,' Alexei demurred.

'I admire your enthusiasm and loyalty, but I can't allow you to make the sacrifice.' John eyed Alexei and Ruth thoughtfully. 'However, if you can spare a couple of hours this morning there is one job you're perfectly suited to. Both of you. Could you go to the shtetl and talk to Rabbi Goldberg, the merchants, and anyone else who lost property last night, sales goods and livestock as well as buildings. I'll send a couple of clerks with you to make notes. Ask everyone affected to list what they need to rebuild their homes and shops. Tell them you have my complete authority and the New Russia Company will underwrite their losses. In the meantime, they can take the notes, which the clerks will write out and you'll countersign, to the company warehouses and draw whatever materials they require to begin rebuilding. If it's not in stock or we run short, inform them I'll have everything that's listed brought into the town as soon as the bullock carts allow.'

'That's very generous of you, sir,' Ruth commented.

'Not that generous, Mrs Beletskaya, most of the losses will be covered by the company's insurers. My main concern is to keep Hughesovka's commerce and building programme on track.'

'We'll do our best to ensure that, sir,' Vlad asserted.

'Tell the clerks to make copies of the notes they hand out and file them in the office, Alexei. Warn everyone that the company will only pay out on notes that either you or Mrs Beletskaya have countersigned.'

'We will, sir.' Alexei winked at Ruth. 'Mrs Beletskaya. Did you hear that?' Alexei took the heavy tray from Ruth and handed it to Pyotr.

'Something else for all of you to think about is the urgent formation of a trained fire brigade,' John lowered his voice, 'that can fight fires and also crime. Several people reported that they saw someone flitting around before the fires took hold last night. The fact that the flames flared simultaneously in so many places suggests the blazes were down to the work of more than one arsonist.'

'If the brigade is to have any credibility we need to recruit men from every race, Cossacks, Jews, Welsh and Mujiks,' Alexei warned. 'Are you sure you don't want me to come to the managers meeting, sir?'

'You're not indispensable yet, boy. Just do as I asked, and while you're talking to Rabbi Goldberg remind him that I sent him the architect's rough sketches for the new synagogue a month ago and I'm still waiting for him to come and discuss them with me.'

'I will, sir.' Alexei saw Anna walking through the gate. He called down to her. 'Was anyone hurt last night?'

Anna joined them. 'Dr Kharber sent me to tell you that there are no serious injuries among the men who fought the fire in this section of the town, Mr Hughes, but he's still waiting to hear from the shtetl.'

'Let's hope the people in the shtetl got off as lightly as us,' John said. 'We couldn't have managed without you and the other nurses, young lady. I saw how hard you all worked last night.'

'All the beds in the hospital are taken and we've treated over fifty people for burns and minor injuries, mainly cuts and bruises, but all the nurses are hoping that there won't be any major catastrophes today.'

'It's not just the nurses who are hoping for a quiet day, young lady.' John eyed his senior staff. 'We can't let this setback affect the timetable for commissioning the furnaces. No matter what, this January we have to go into full production.'

None of the men around John dared point out that the height of winter was almost upon them, bringing with it snow, below freezing temperatures, and, possibly, even worse disasters than fire.

Ruth returned to the kitchen and helped Yelena, Praskovia, and the maids to load another tray that Pyotr carried out to the men in the garden. She looked for Alexei and found him with Vlad and Alf by their well. All three had washed their faces, but the water had only served to plaster the black and grey smuts that covered them in layers over their skin and hair.

'You look as though you've all grown scales like lizards,' she observed.

'If that means we can lie on a rock and sleep for the rest of the day, I'll be happy.' Alf wiped his face with his hands, smearing the grime even more.

Ruth shook her head at Alexei. 'Your wedding trousers are ruined. They're blackened and peppered with burn holes.'

'As I've no intention of getting married again, Mrs Beletskaya, I won't need them.' He slipped his arm around her waist.

'And when we're invited to other weddings?'

'I'll buy wedding guest trousers.'

'You won't be able to wear them with that linen shirt. It's singed beyond repair and your shoes are in ribbons. I'm not much better.' Ruth examined the torn and blackened overall and apron she'd borrowed from Yelena to throw over her nightgown and dressing gown. 'We need to go home and wash and change before we visit the shtetl.'

'No,' Alexei countered. 'The rabbi and the merchants need to see us exactly as we are. That way they'll know we fought the fire as well.'

'I'm not going to the shtetl in my nightclothes,' Ruth protested. 'Rabbi Goldberg would die of shock.'

'Change if you must, but put the overall and apron back on over it, and don't wash the soot from your face and hands.' Alexei felt a tap on his shoulder and turned around.

'Mr Beletsky, sir,' Vasily was standing behind him together with a younger company clerk. Both were carrying notepads stamped with the heading of the Company. 'Mr Hughes said you'd be needing clerks.'

'We will, thank you for coming. We'll be leaving for the shtetl in a few minutes. If there's any tea left go and get yourselves a glass.'

'Yes, sir, thank you, sir.'

Alexei brushed himself down.

'You're making yourself look like a chimney sweep,' Ruth warned.

Alexei glanced over his shoulder. When he was sure only Vlad, Alf, and Ruth were within earshot, he murmured, 'Have any of you picked up any rumours as to who's responsible for the fire?'

'That depends on who you talk to.' Like Alexei, Vlad lowered his voice. 'The Cossacks are blaming the Jews.'

'Unsurprising, but it makes no sense. Why would the Cossacks reason that the Jews set fire to their own shtetl?' Ruth demanded.

77

'The Cossacks are saying that the Jews are angry over Mr Hughes's decision to move their shtetl from its original location.'

'That's ridiculous,' Ruth asserted. 'The Jews have been generously compensated by the New Russia Company for the move.'

'You know that, and I know that, but perhaps the Cossacks don't,' Alexei pointed out logically.

'The few Jews I spoke to in the hospital blame the civilian Cossacks and Mujiks. They say the Russians burned down the Jewish quarter to punish the Jews and Mr Hughes for giving the Jews preferential treatment,' Alf revealed.

'And the Welsh?' Alexei enquired caustically.

'They wanted to burn the town so they could go home.'

'You're joking?' Alexei challenged Alf.

'I wish I was but you haven't heard the craziest rumour.' Alf smiled and his teeth showed white against his grimy face. 'Mr Hughes set the fires so he could claim the insurance money.'

'In other words, no one has any idea who's responsible and gossip is raging wilder than the flames last night, and probably twice as destructively.' Alexei reached for Ruth's hand. 'Let's find out if anyone in the shtetl is talking sense.'

Chapter Eight

Catherine Ignatova's house September 1871

'Did you two catch up on your sleep this morning?' Catherine asked Sonya and Roman as they ate a light lunch in her dining room.

'I managed an hour after Mr Hughes's managers' meeting. I could have slept longer but I knew that if I stayed in bed I'd be awake tonight. Thank you, Boris,' Roman took a bowl of cranberry kisel and honey mousse dessert from Catherine's butler.

'What about you, Sonya?' Catherine asked.

'About the same, but I'm not in the least tired. I didn't do anything physical, like the men. I only helped out with teas and dressings in the hospital.'

'You were still awake,' Roman pointed out.

'After losing an entire night's sleep you should both rest this afternoon,' Catherine advised.

'Before the fire Mr Hughes asked me to look over the town and give him my thoughts on the way the construction work is progressing. Now the fire has given the New Russia Company a more or less clear field to build on in some areas, Mr Hughes asked me to report on the development as soon as possible so he can lay down sound, well thought-out plans for the future rather than allow people to build wherever they like.'

'I don't envy you your task,' Catherine commented. 'The Mujiks have always dug their homes underground with little thought to the convenience of, or proximity to, their neighbours.'

'That's something I'm all too aware of, given my experience with the peasants on my own estates.

'However, as Mr Hughes and everyone who works for the New Russia Company will be busy inspecting the fire damage, I would appreciate Miss Tsetovna's company, knowledge, expertise, and guidance.' He smiled at Sonya, 'that's if you are free, Miss Tsetovna, and have no objection to accompanying and guiding me around Hughesovka?'

'Sonya?' Catherine asked.

'A carriage ride in the fresh air might be just what I need. No exertion and pleasant conversation.'

'I'll ask Boris to order a carriage. Ivan can drive you. Don't forget to take Maria. You'll need a chaperone. I'd go with you myself if I didn't have a prior engagement. I'm expecting my carriage to be brought around at any moment.'

'Maria has taken to her bed with a headache,' Sonya divulged. 'I think it's shock. She was furious when she heard that I was out most of last night. She didn't see my sacrifice of a night's sleep as in the least heroic. I told her I'd driven into town with Igor and Lyudmila and I spent all my time with the nurses in the hospital but she still disapproved. I'm afraid I'm a terrible disappointment to her.'

Catherine smiled. 'That sounded just like one of my daughter's rants when Maria tried to chaperone her. Olga was a disappointment to Maria as well, and unlike you Olga had no headstrong ideas about wanting to work, as opposed to being purely ornamental. I'm afraid that like most convent-educated ladies' maids, Maria has very strict ideas when it comes to a lady's behaviour and what is and isn't permissible. Leave Maria in bed and take Lyudmila. She's always complaining that she never has an opportunity to leave the kitchen.'

'I really am getting too old to have a chaperone, Aunt Catherine,' Sonya protested.

'You'll have one as long as you're under my roof and remain unmarried, Sonya,' Catherine countered.

'Even when I'm sixty?'

'Especially when you're sixty. Everyone knows how wild old ladies can be. Now, if you'll excuse me.'

Catherine rose from the table and Roman and Sonya followed out of deference. Roman folded his napkin and dropped it on to his plate. 'Thank you for an excellent lunch, Catherine.'

'Thank Lyudmila when she joins you. She's my cook. Boris will see to the carriage.'

Catherine glanced at her butler who nodded. 'My pleasure, madam.'

'What time would you like it brought round to the front of the house, Roman?'

'I can be ready in ten minutes, but if Miss Tsetovna would like more time, there is no hurry.'

'Ten minutes will be fine, Prince Roman.' Sonya crossed the hall.

'You'll ask Lyudmila to act as chaperone, Boris?'

'Of course, madam,' Boris loaded the uneaten kisel and mousse on to a tray and carried it out.

Roman stood in the doorway and watched Sonya walk up the stairs. There was a strange expression on his face that Catherine couldn't decipher. He turned suddenly, and saw Catherine watching him. 'I was admiring the fig tree in the hall. I'm surprised to see it flourishing. I would have thought the temperature would drop too low for it to thrive so close to the door in winter.'

'We take care to move all the delicate plants into the hot houses before winter bites. The fig tree will be moved in the next day or two. You'll take care not to tire Sonya?'

'I'll see that she doesn't over-exert herself, Catherine. Until later?'

'Yes, until later,' she repeated.

Catherine watched him run up the stairs. Roman was wealthy as tsars counted wealth. Sonya's two million roubles were not insignificant, but they hardly put her in the same class as the aristocratic St Petersburg and Moscow heiresses from the upper circle of society that Roman moved in.

He couldn't possibly be interested in her niece. Could he?

Madam Koshka's salon September 1871

Adele reached the door of Madam Koshka's private rooms and took a moment to compose herself. In the six years she'd worked in madam's salons, both in Moscow and Hughesovka, she could recall only a few occasions when madam had interviewed girls privately. And then only for one of two reasons: a serious complaint from a client, or confirmation of bad news from one of the routine medical tests madam paid a doctor to carry out on a weekly basis.

Summoning her courage she knocked the door.

Koshka opened it herself. She was alone and dressed in widow's weeds. Her voluminous dress was high-necked with long sleeves, designed to disguise rather than reveal her figure, and her bonnet had a black lace veil that could be unpinned and dropped to conceal her features.

'You wanted to see me, madam?'

'I do, Adele. Thank you for coming so promptly. Excuse me for continuing to dress but I have an appointment and don't wish to be late.' Koshka picked up a pair of black kid gloves and proceeded to pull them on using a silver glove stretcher. 'Please sit down. I'm sorry I can't offer you coffee but as I said, I'm on my way out.'

If Adele hadn't known better she would have said madam was uncharacteristically disconcerted, but as the fire had decimated the town and destroyed the homes of so many people, she presumed madam was concerned about the effect the conflagration would have on business.

'I want to ask you some personal questions. I have good reason to pry, Adele, which I'm not at liberty to explain, because other people are involved. Please don't read anything into my enquiries that isn't intended.'

Adele couldn't stand the suspense of not knowing the reason for the interview a moment longer. 'You are unhappy with my work, madam?'

'I'm delighted to have someone as kind, friendly, and professional as you in my house, Adele. I hope you are as happy here as I am to have you.'

Adele smiled, but didn't lower her guard. 'I am happy to be here, madam,' she replied cautiously.

'I want to ask you about Prince Roman Nadolny. You have entertained him several times?'

Adele was surprised. Madam had very few inflexible rules, but never discussing clients, their foibles, or revealing any indiscreet revelations confided during passionate moments, was one of them. 'As you must know, madam, I have entertained the prince on several occasions both here and in Moscow.'

'Do you like him?'

'As a client? Very much. He is kind, gentle, and always gives me a small present in addition to what he pays the house for my services.'

Koshka finally finished buttoning up her gloves and returned the glove stretcher to a drawer. 'You keep his presents to you, above what he pays the house, confidential between the two of you?'

'I never discuss the presents I receive from any of my clients with the other girls, madam.'

'I'm glad to hear it. Revelations about "presents", especially generous ones, can lead to jealousy and jealousy inevitably leads to discord. As I've said, I have my reasons for asking these questions. Please bear with me because I can offer you no explanation other than to say your answers to my questions are vitally important to me – and will remain strictly private. You say the prince is kind and gentle. Has he made any peculiar or distasteful requests of you?'

'No, madam.'

'Has he ever hurt you, even inadvertently?'

'Never, madam. He has always treated me with the utmost respect, which as you know is not the case with all our clients. He takes the time to converse amusingly, and is as mindful of my pleasure as his own.'

'Then you regard him as a favourite client.'

'The favourite, madam, and not just because of the presents he gives me.'

'Thank you, that's all I wanted to know, Adele. As I explained, I have my own reasons for asking about the prince. Suffice to say he has another life outside of my salon. The questions I asked you are pertinent to that. When we women step out of the public world into the shadowy world of the salon, we can never return to our old lives, whereas men can, and do, move easily between the two.'

'I knew that when I entered your salon for the first time, madam.'

'You have never regretted your choice?'

Adele shrugged her perfectly formed shoulders. 'I made a choice that enables me to live in luxury. It is infinitely preferable to my sister's life. She married a poor but respectable farmer and is pregnant with her fourteenth child.'

'You help her?'

'With money, occasionally,' Adele admitted.

'You don't visit her?'

'As you just said, madam, when it comes to the world of the salon, only men can move freely between it and the world of respectability.'

'You're a good girl, Adele. Thank you. I want you to know how much I value you, not just for your work, but your personality and the respect you show to everyone in this house. Please don't ever refer to this conversation again. I will ask Fritz to put all the money Prince Roman has paid to the house for your services since he reached Hughesovka into your account. You will also receive all the future payments the prince makes for your company.'

'Thank you, madam, that is very generous. You want me to keep entertaining him?'

'Whenever he asks for you. Ensure that he has a very good time, as you always do.'

'Yes, madam.'

'We will never speak of this again.' Koshka opened the door and dropped her veil. Adele curtsied and left the room before her.

Hotel Hughesovka September 1871

Catherine was waiting in the suite she'd hired when her visitor arrived dressed in deepest mourning, her hair and face concealed by a lace veil.

Catherine rose and embraced her. 'As you see, I ordered tea, wine, and cake. What would you like?'

'Tea please and if that's Krendel, the thinnest of thin slices. I haven't tasted it since my last birthday but at my age I only have to look at a piece of cake to put four inches on my hips.'

Catherine laughed, 'You're exaggerating as usual, you have the figure of a young girl.'

'It's good of you to say so, Catherine, even if it's not true.'

'I asked Boris to book this suite as soon as I received your note this morning. It sounded urgent. I made enquiries about your house. I was told that it wasn't affected by the fire, but if it was you could always move in with me...'

'No, it wasn't damaged,' Koshka reassured Catherine. 'But if it had been, my girls and I would have taken refuge elsewhere. If the hotel couldn't accommodate us we would have moved into the stables if no other place was available. We couldn't possibly move in with a respectable widow. Most certainly not one who is hosting Mr Hughes and Prince Roman Nadolny.'

'They are both broad-minded – and busy. Roman is here as a representative of Grand Duke Konstantin who has financial interests in the New Russia Company.'

'So I've heard. I've also heard that the Grand Duke is constantly fending off the petitions of those who are conspiring to thwart John Hughes's industrialization of the Donbas.'

'There appear to be as many short-sighted people in Russia anxious to derail the building of the ironworks as there are to support it,' Catherine observed. 'Although as John is acting in accordance with the Tsar's blessing as well as his commission, I doubt they'll succeed in stopping the march of progress. Not with men like the Grand Duke and Roman watching the backs of the investors in the New Russia Company.'

'Roman's a good man,' Koshka conceded. 'But then if you didn't know that you wouldn't have him in your house. And, of course, you knew his father.'

'As did you, E –'

'Koshka, please, Catherine.'

'We are alone. We never see one another in company so I am unlikely to slip up publicly.'

'But we might not find ourselves alone one day. I suppose Roman is resting after spending most of the night firefighting?' Koshka went to the window and looked down at the street below.

'No, John asked him to look over the town and give his opinion on the way it's developing now he has the opportunity to rebuild in some areas from scratch. Roman invited Sonya to act as his guide. Chaperoned, of course.'

Koshka took the glass of tea Catherine had poured for her and settled in the chair opposite her. 'Roman visited me yesterday evening. In fact he and several of my guests left my house to fight the fire as soon as it broke out.'

'I trust some of the more highly strung wives in Hughesovka didn't notice the direction their husbands came from.' Catherine cut two wafer-thin slices of cake.

'Earlier in the evening Roman confided to me that he intends to ask Sonya to marry him.'

Catherine was speechless for a moment. 'But Sonya's only just eighteen...'

'You and I were both married at sixteen, Catherine,' Koshka reminded.

'Times are different now. And, thanks to your generosity, Sonya is an independent young woman.' Catherine forgot she was serving the cake and sank back in her chair.

'I'm sorry, I didn't mean to shock you.'

'What do you think of Roman's offer?' Catherine asked. 'After all you are Sonya's mother...'

'I gave up all rights to Sonya when I handed her to you when she was three months old.' Koshka lowered her eyes so Catherine wouldn't see the pain that hadn't dissipated or dimmed with the passage of years. 'I asked to see you because I wanted your opinion of the match. You brought Sonya up, you know her better than anyone. Both she and Roman are living under your roof. You've seen them together.'

'I saw Roman looking at Sonya this morning. I did wonder...'

'What?' Koshka pressed when Catherine didn't elaborate.

'What he was thinking.'

'Does he love her?' Koshka asked.

'I don't believe so, but there was an expression in his eyes I couldn't fathom. If he does love Sonya, he hides it well. Did he tell you that he loves her?' Catherine asked.

'He never once mentioned love. If you'd asked me about Roman a few months ago I would have said that like his father, the man is imbued with charm but emotionally stunted and cold. It's not surprising, given his history. His mother died when he was five. His father, never the most demonstrative of men, packed him off to an English boarding school when he was seven and rarely bothered to visit him more than once a year. If it hadn't been for Grand Duke Konstantin taking Roman into his own family after his father died when he was sixteen, the boy would have had only his servants for company. It was Konstantin who guided Roman's education and insisted the boy study at Oxford and Heidelberg universities.

'Roman's manners are impeccable, his education extensive, his culture beyond question. His wealth, pedigree, and Grand Duke Konstantin's patronage have brought him connections and influence in every sphere of life in Europe, Russia, and indeed the world as we recognise it. He's thoughtful and considerate to his friends. Everyone who knows him thinks well of him, but...'

'Say it, Koshka,' Catherine encouraged when she fell silent again. 'When it comes to people there's no one's opinion I value more. This is Sonya's future we're talking about. You were the one who made her an heiress and ensured that no one knew where the money really came from by spreading the rumour that her father had set up a trust for her.'

'I only gave Sonya enough money for her to live on. Financial independence means she doesn't have to marry the first unsuitable man who asks her. And that's all. Two million roubles are not enough to attract the likes of Roman Nadolny. But Roman did say last night that Sonya was extraordinarily beautiful and well-educated – which she is. Has Sonya received many offers?' Koshka asked.

'Admirers, yes. We couldn't move for young men flocking around her when we visited St Petersburg with John Hughes, and that was before you gave her an inheritance. But Sonya didn't reciprocate their attentions. In fact she showed no interest in any of them and soon tired of balls and parties. She couldn't wait to return here.'

'To spend time with a secret suitor in Hughesovka?' Koshka suggested archly.

'None I've noticed. She enjoyed working in the hospital and making friends with the girls there who were training to be nurses, and now she's left the hospital she takes the same pleasure in interpreting for the office of the New Russia Company.'

'Is her talent for languages the only reason she left the hospital to work for John Hughes?' Koshka enquired.

'What other reason could there be?'

Koshka set the two pieces of cake Catherine had cut on to plates and passed one to her. 'I have a fine view of the town from my boudoir window. One of the things I've noticed is the way the Jewish doctor who works in the hospital looks at Sonya.'

'Nathan – but he's recently married.'

'To a woman who looks old enough to be his mother, if not his grandmother.'

'Yes, I've heard Vasya suffers from premature aging, but she's charming, and their marriage was arranged by their families. It's the Jewish way.'

'If what I heard is true, Nathan's and Vasya's marriage was a condition Rabbi Goldbcrg exacted from Nathan, before allowing Ruth Kharber to marry your grandson.'

'I've heard that too but Nathan and Vasya seem happy enough.'

'Vasya perhaps, but I've seen the way Nathan looks at Sonya, and more crucially the way Sonya looks at him. Didn't it occur to you, when Sonya left the hospital soon after Nathan married, that she did so because she felt she could no longer work with him.'

Catherine thought for a moment. 'But if Sonya is in love with Nathan and he with her, their situation is hopeless. He's married –'

'Aside from being married, any Jewish man who allows himself to be used as a bargaining chip by his rabbi will never go against the tenets of his faith. And a man who puts his religion above his wife is not a husband worth having,' Koshka declared forcefully.

Catherine sensed her friend was speaking from experience. 'If what you say is true, Sonya must be desperately unhappy.'

'A broken heart can kill, but we must do all we can to make sure that will not be the case with Sonya. There are many other eligible men in the world. Hopefully Sonya will find another she can learn to love. If she does decide to marry, it has to be to someone of her own choice.'

'And Roman?' Catherine asked.

'I believe him to be an essentially good man who is well placed to give his wife, whoever she is, everything she could possibly want in the material sense. He will shower his family with houses, rich clothes, jewels, and servants. I have no doubt he will look after Sonya, should she decide to marry him. But if she does, it must be her decision and no one else's.'

'And love?' Catherine asked.

'Love is for Roman and Sonya to think about. I know of several successful, and loveless, marriages of convenience.'

'A marriage of convenience is not something I would advise any young woman to embark on, especially Sonya with her loving and tender heart.' Catherine looked Koshka in the eye. 'You do know that Roman has the reputation of being a womaniser?'

'My entire business is built on the desires and penchants of womanisers. I thank God daily for them.'

'And Roman?'

'He patronises my salon. I've heard it rumoured that he has women in every city and town in Russia and every capital city of Europe.'

'He's visited your salon often?'

'Regularly, both here and in Moscow before I moved.'

'Do you think he would be faithful if he married Sonya?'

'Truthfully? Honestly?' Koshka shook her head. 'No. Not on his past performance, but then I know of few husbands who are. Think about it, Catherine. Men who are faithful to their wives rarely find their way to my door.'

'Do you think any man capable of fidelity?'

Koshka smiled when she thought of Glyn and his devotion to Praskovia. 'One or two rare specimens of manhood perhaps, even in Hughesovka, but it doesn't follow that if Roman married Sonya and was subsequently unfaithful, she would be unhappy.'

'I was when I discovered that my Alexei sought solace in other women's arms.'

'Even though he loved only you.'

'Or so he said, and words cost nothing,' Catherine murmured bitterly.

'Most men are capable of separating love from sex. Some crave novelty and variety in the physical act that they believe their wives would find distasteful, so seek fulfilment elsewhere. It does not mean that they love their wives any the less. And some women are only too happy to send their husbands to the salon because they find the physical act disagreeable.'

'And Roman?'

'Is rich, charming, and, like many intelligent men I have met, a closed book when it comes to fathoming his motives and emotions.' Koshka finished her cake and replaced her veil. 'I only came to warn you of his imminent proposal to Sonya, Catherine, not to offer advice I am not qualified to give. I trust you to guide Sonya and help her decide what is best for her. Whether that is marriage to Roman Nadolny or not, it has to be Sonya's decision and no one else's.'

'Not even Roman's?' Catherine asked.

'Especially not Roman's.' Koshka hugged Catherine and left the room.

Chapter Nine

Burned out shtetl, Hughesovka September 1871

Alexei, Ruth, and their attendant clerks found most of the Jewish merchants and Rabbi Goldberg holding an impromptu meeting next to the smouldering remains of the shtetl shops.

The rabbi glared at Alexei and Ruth as they approached. 'If you have come to gloat...'

'We're here because Mr Hughes sent us. He is a little busy today,' Ruth answered.

'As you see,' the rabbi indicated the smoking ruins of the shops, 'we are also a little busy. We've been fighting fires all night.'

'As have we,' Alexei interrupted, indicating his own and Ruth's bedraggled state.

'Now we have established that we are all tired and busy, state your business and leave.'

'Mr Hughes would like you – all of you who have lost property and goods to the fire – to make lists of whatever you need to rebuild your shops and houses. These clerks,' Alexei pointed to Vasily and his assistant, 'will help you to compile them. Ruth or I will look over your lists and sign them once we've agreed on the quantity of materials. Then you can take them to the New Russia Company's warehouse and draw out whatever you require, provided it's in stock.'

'At what cost?'

'Nothing to those who have lost their shops, stock, and houses. Mr Hughes has given his word that the New Russia Company will bear the cost of rebuilding and repairing the damage.

'He intends to claim as much of the cost back as he can on the insurance, but his principal concern is to get the town up and running again so he can concentrate on commissioning the ironworks.'

'You have Mr Hughes's authority to do this?' the Rabbi asked suspiciously.

'We do,' Alexei lifted Ruth's hand in his to show the men that she wielded as much of John Hughes's authority as he did. 'That is why Mr Hughes sent us. Shall we begin, gentlemen?'

'Rabbi!' A group of wailing women ran towards them. Behind them half a dozen men pushed a handcart shrouded in blankets.

'It's Asher and Leah Kharber, Rabbi Goldberg. They allowed their niece to marry out of our faith and God punished them by calling them to him.'

'That's nonsense.' Alexei pulled Ruth close in an effort to protect her from the hostility that was emanating towards them from everyone present. 'That's absolute nonsense,' he reiterated, suddenly nauseous and terrified not for himself, but Ruth.

He looked down at his wife, but ashen faced and trembling she was too distraught to absorb anything beyond the fact that her aunt and uncle were no more.

Hospital, Hughesovka September 1871

'Stop here please, Ivan.' Roman ordered Catherine's driver. 'This is Hughesovka's hospital?' he checked with Sonya.

'We wanted to conceal its whereabouts from hypochondriacs so we decided not to put up a sign.'

'I like your sense of humour. I recall Mr Hughes telling me it has twelve beds.'

'Twenty-four,' she corrected. 'We had a twelve-bed ward when the hospital opened last year. The original ward now caters exclusively for men.

'Two months ago the hospital was extended and we created a second twelve-bed ward for women and children.'

'We,' he smiled, 'you Hughesovkans are so parochial. You see this as your own personal hospital?'

'Everyone in the town is proud of our medical facilities and dedicated doctor and nurses.'

'I know the place will be full after all the injuries that were sustained last night but do you think Dr Kharber might spare the time to give me a quick tour?' Roman opened the door of the carriage. Without waiting for her to answer he stepped down and extended his hand.

'If Dr Kharber is busy I'm sure he'll allow me to show you the facilities.'

'Of course, your aunt mentioned that you'd worked here until recently.'

'Only in the office.' Sonya sensed he knew all along that she'd worked in the hospital. She took his hand and climbed out of the carriage. The hospital door opened and the duty porter, Maxim, greeted them.

'Welcome, Miss Sonya, we miss you.' He recognised her companion and snapped to attention. 'Welcome, Your Excellency, we are honoured, sir.' He thrust the door wide.

Roman looked around the hall. It was spotlessly clean, which he found surprising after the chaos, ash, and smuts of the night. The floorboards were scrubbed, the whitewashed walls pristine. The kitchen door was open and Anna was clearing dishes. She turned when she heard voices and came out to meet them.

Sonya introduced them. 'Prince Roman, this is Anna Parry.'

'The second beautiful bridesmaid. I recognise you from yesterday, Miss Parry.' Roman lifted Anna's hand, which she'd hastily dried in her apron, to his lips and kissed it. Taken aback, wary of the touch of any man, Anna snatched her hand away.

'Forgive my impertinence, Miss Parry, but aren't you a little young to be a nurse,' Roman commented.

94

'Our matron, Mrs Edwards, trained all of us, sir. We may be young but she made certain that we are capable of carrying out every medical procedure expected of nurses.'

'That I can vouch for.' Nathan emerged from his office and offered the prince his hand. 'We met yesterday at the wedding, Prince Roman.'

'It's good to see you again, Dr Kharber.' Roman glanced at Sonya who'd retreated into the kitchen with Anna. 'Mr Hughes asked me to look around the town and give my view on the way it's developing. The one facility everyone can't seem to praise enough is your hospital. It was much needed last night'

'Fortunately, none of the injuries were life-threatening. A few broken bones, cuts, bruises, and burns. But, this hospital is hardly mine, Your Excellency. It was built by and is funded by the New Russia Company although the facilities we offer are open to the entire population of the area, not only company employees.'

'So I understand.'

'Please, come and see the examination rooms and operating theatre.'

Roman accompanied Nathan down the corridor. 'I heard that you were appointed here shortly after Dr Edwards, who travelled here with Mr Hughes, died of cholera...'

Sonya picked up a cloth and began drying the dishes Anna had washed.

'We miss you here, you know,' Anna said.

'So Maxim told me when I arrived.'

'Do you miss us?' Anna glanced at her.

'Of course, but the translation work I do for Mr Hughes is vital for the company, and Sarah did such a good job of setting up the patient filing system here anyone can manage it.'

'Not anyone, Yulia managed to mess it up last week, but Nathan is talking about bringing someone in to run the office as you did.'

'I thought Vasya might take over,' Sonya commented.

'I had the same idea, but when I mentioned it to Yulia and Miriam, they told me Vasya is a Goldberg and the Goldbergs are a traditional Orthodox Jewish family. Apparently, no Orthodox wife would consider working outside of her husband's home and business. Although Nathan works here, the hospital cannot be regarded as his business. Vasya considers her job as solely caring for Nathan and their home.'

'So Nathan is looking outside the shtetl for a new office assistant?'

'Not necessarily. He asked Miriam as well as Yulia to approach their unmarried girlfriends to see if any of them were interested and he also asked me to check if Praskovia knew anyone who could do the job.' Anna washed the last plate and cup. 'Would you and Prince Roman like tea?' She lifted the kettle out of the samovar.

'No, thank you, we've only just had lunch and the prince wants to see as much as possible of the town before the light fades. This is our first stop.'

'There's a lot for the prince to see here. All our wards are full with a mix of burn victims and the injured from last night. We also have a few bullock cart drivers who brought in the new Welsh recruits a couple of days ago.'

'The drivers are suffering from vodka-induced dysentery after sampling the various local brews on the journey from Taganrog?' Sonya guessed.

'That wasn't what Dr Kharber wrote on their medical records but it's closer to the truth,' Anna agreed.

'Apparently the girls on night shift were rushed off their feet cleaning up after them when they were admitted. As for Nathan, he hasn't left here since he came in last night just before the fire broke out. I think he was nodding off over his desk before you arrived. That's him and the prince coming back now.'

Roman stopped outside the kitchen door and shook Nathan's hand. 'Thank you for the tour, Dr Kharber.'

'I'm just about to make tea, would you like a glass?' Anna offered. She was intrigued by the prince, not by his aristocratic status but his blond hair and oriental features. She'd overheard someone at the wedding mention that the prince's mother had been Chinese. In Glyn's library she'd found an album of photographs a European traveller had taken in China. Everything from the gardens and scenery to the buildings and people seemed to be so different and so much more exotic than Russia, she longed to ask the prince about the place.

'Thank you for the invitation, Nurse Parry.' Roman took her hand and kissed it again. 'Some other time perhaps. We have a lot of ground to cover before sunset. Thank you, all of you, for your warm welcome, and especially you for the tour, Dr Kharber.'

Vasya's brother Ruben charged through the door. Still covered in soot and ashes from the fire, he raced to Nathan. 'You have to come to the shtetl, quick.' He gasped for breath. 'It's your sister...'

'My carriage is outside.' Roman offered Sonya his arm. Forgetting all etiquette, Nathan and Ruben ran ahead and climbed into the carriage before him and Sonya.

Hughesovka September 1871

'The shtetl please, Ivan.' Roman ordered.

Sensing the urgency of Roman's summons, Ivan cracked his whip alongside the horses and they galloped past the cold black lines that marked the outer reaches of the flames.

Although Sonya had worked through the night, she'd spent most of it in the hospital. The sight of piles of charcoaled debris where shops, houses, and businesses had stood only the day before brought tears to her eyes. Men, women, and children were out in force, shovelling ash from the ground into bins and salvaging heat-sculptured, twisted pieces of wood and metal.

Half a dozen labourers were hard at work, unloading new timber from the back of the carts that had hauled it from the New Russia Company's yards. Carpenters were sawing the planks into lengths to form the frames of replacement buildings. Ivan drove past them to the outer limits of the shtetl, drawing the horses to a halt in front of a dense crowd that had gathered on the outskirts.

'Stop and stay here please, Ivan,' Roman called out.

The noise was deafening, a mixture of women's sobs, anguished wails, angry shouts, children's cries, and prayers being recited, in a cacophony of Yiddish and Russian.

Nathan opened the door, jumped down, and pushed his way through the throng. Ruben followed.

'Stay here,' Roman ordered Sonya.

'But...'

'No buts, I know the sound of fraying tempers at the point of turning ugly and this is it. Ivan, keep her here and take care of her,' he commanded.

'Yes, sir.'

Sonya noticed Roman check his pockets before he jumped down from the carriage. He fastened the door behind him before disappearing into the crowd that had swallowed Nathan and Ruben.

Burnt out shtetl September 1871

Nathan was tall enough to see Rabbi Goldberg over the heads of the crowd, but the more he fought to reach him the more the people around him closed in and prevented him from moving in any direction. Feeling like a salted cucumber in a pickle jar, he shouted, 'Rabbi Goldberg, where is my sister Ruth?'

'Your aunt and uncle are dead,' Rabbi Goldberg thundered.

Nathan sensed the rabbi had enjoyed giving him the tragic news. 'Dead!' The pain in his voice affected the people around him and they began to inch away giving him room to breathe. 'Are you sure?'

'Yes,' the man who'd pulled the cart assured Nathan. 'There's no mistake. Their house was only partly affected by the fire. The bedroom walls are still standing. Asher and Leah weren't burned but suffocated. You can see them for yourself, Nathan Kharber.'

Nathan was acutely aware of the people surrounding them. 'No one of our faith should look upon a man or woman who cannot look back. I will pray over them, but not here. Not with everyone watching.'

The onlookers finally cleared a path through to a cart. Ruth was slumped, sobbing, over the side, Alexei stood beside her covering her back and shoulders with his arms, shielding her from the people pressing around them.

Rabbi Goldberg materialised beside Nathan. 'Ruth should not be here and neither should you. You told your uncle and aunt that they were dead to you –'

Nathan interrupted him. 'Only after Uncle Asher and Aunt Leah told Ruth that they disowned her and regarded both of us as dead to them.'

'Ruth married outside of her faith. She is no longer one of us.'

The rabbi's observations provoked a tidal wave of agreement that escalated into anger directed against Nathan. A woman spat in Nathan's face. As he lifted his arm to wipe away the spittle a shot was fired.

The crack was followed by absolute silence. Every head turned towards Roman who'd fired in the air from the edge of the crowd.

Raisa Shapiro took advantage of the situation and climbed on to the wheel of the handcart so everyone could see her.

The diminutive widowed sister of Rabbi Goldberg wielded authority over the entire shtetl that was far above her status – an authority every man, woman, and child deferred to, although it was rooted in nothing more than the respect due to a woman of her advanced age and family connections coupled with her overpowering personality.

'Nathan and Ruth are Asher and Leah's orphaned nephew and niece.' Raisa's voice, shrill and piercing, carried to every corner of the crowd. 'They were as a son and daughter to Asher and Leah and closer to them than anyone else here present. Nathan and Ruth are of the same blood. They have more right to be with Asher and Leah than any of you. Where is your compassion? Your religion? Nathan and Ruth are mourning. They need kindness and love, not anger. Rabbi Goldberg,' she addressed her brother, 'Asher and Leah are our dead. They need to be buried swiftly and correctly according to our ceremonies and customs.'

'You are right, Raisa,' Rabbi Goldberg acknowledged, but only after he saw the majority nodding agreement with Raisa's impassioned speech.

'I have heard it said that the Jews are the most righteous and kindest of people. Now I have seen it for myself. Those of us who have no right to be here will leave you to your mourning, but our thoughts will be with you. And should you need our help, we will be honoured to assist in any way we can,' said Roman, though he didn't relinquish the hold on his gun.

'My house was untouched by the fire. Carry Asher and Leah there, and send for the holy ones to wash and dress the bodies.' Raisa embraced Ruth and pulled her gently back from the cart.

'Everything has been destroyed. We have no grave clothes or coffins,' Rabbi Goldberg pointed out.

'The company has coffins stored in their yard. They will let me buy or borrow two if I promise to replace them,' Nathan said.

'I'll go to the yard, Nathan, and fetch them,' Ruben volunteered.

'My house escaped the fire. I have shrouds without pockets, I can make new ones for myself and my husband,' a woman volunteered.

'Come.' Raisa leaned forward and wrapped her arms around Ruth 'Let us bury Asher and Leah Kharber according to the rites of our faith. Nathan, you are chief mourner. Tear your coat. Ruth, tear yours also. The side over your heart. Rabbi, you will be needed to pray over our dead. The rest of you return to clearing the fire damage until the funeral. All of you, except the ones needed to pull the cart.'

Roman waylaid Alexei. 'I will wait for you and Ruth in the carriage.'

'Thank you, but there is no need. Ruth won't leave until they bury her uncle and aunt and I'll stay as close to her as the rabbi will allow me to until the ceremony is over. Please ask my grandmother to send another carriage for us in two hours, but warn her it may have to wait.'

'You don't want to change out of your scorched clothes?' Alexei gave Roman the ghost of a smile.

'Sackcloth and ashes seem appropriate to the situation.' He reached out and squeezed Sonya's hand.

'If you want me to stay...'

'No, Sonya.' Alexei kissed her cheek. 'There's nothing you can do here for me, or for Ruth. We'll see you back at Grandmother's tomorrow or the day after.'

Roman whirled around to see Sonya standing behind him. 'I ordered you to stay in the carriage. Where's Ivan?'

'Here, sir. Miss Tsetovna refused to stay in the carriage.'

'I don't take orders from anyone, Ivan – or,' Sonya stared defiantly at Roman, 'you.'

'So I see. You could have been attacked.'

'Not after you fired the shot and gave Vasya's aunt a chance to talk. Brave woman.'

'Brave woman indeed.' Roman watched Raisa lead the way to a wooden house that had miraculously evaded the ravages of the fire, although the walls were blackened by soot. He watched as Asher and Leah's bodies were lifted from the cart and carried inside. Heads bowed, Ruth, Nathan, Rabbi Goldberg, and Raisa followed.

Raisa was the last to enter. She turned and quietly but firmly closed the door behind her, leaving Alexei standing on the doorstep.

Chapter Ten

Burned out shtetl September 1871

'Do you want to carry on with your tour of the town or
return home?' Sonya asked as Roman turned to her.

He eyed the men who'd returned to the task of clearing
the remains of the fire-damaged buildings. 'I could talk to
the elders about their plans for rebuilding the shtetl. Care
to be my bodyguard?'

'You think I can protect you?'

'If you'll let mc hide behind your skirts.'

'They're only men,' she reminded.

'They look formidable with their black coats and
bushy beards.'

Sonya stood back while Roman approached the elders
and a group of shopkeepers. To her surprise, after Roman
began speaking they actually began listening to him, and
when he started pacing out the ground she realised he was
suggesting they build their shops and homes further apart.

She drew closer so she could hear what he was saying.

'... if you allow for two carriage stops between each
shop, it will be easier to load and unload your goods.'

'And the houses?' one man she recognised as the
blacksmith asked.

'Should have gardens. This area is over a mile from the
main works and factories. I know Mr Hughes has plans to
develop his industrial complex to the south of the town as
far as the river but not the north-east. There is no shortage
of land in this sector. Give your houses large gardens so
you can grow your own fruit and vegetables and make
your streets half as wide again as you've pegged out.
Then, fate forbid, if there's another fire before we have an
opportunity to rebuild in brick, there's less risk of sparks
spreading the flames.' When the men hesitated, Roman
added, 'I know it means undoing some of the work you've
already done...'

'It's not that, Your Excellency. People need room to breathe, but we Jews have never had much of that and find space a difficult concept to understand.'

Sonya looked on in amazement, wondering if she had really seen the men around Roman smile. It was difficult to know. She had never known a Jewish elder to show any emotion – happy or sad.

Roman took a notepad from his pocket, scribbled on it, tore out the page he'd written on and handed it to the elder. 'This is authority from me for you to take more land. When I speak to Mr Hughes this evening I'll ask him to send someone out here to assist you with marking out the plots first thing tomorrow. In the meantime, once you've cleared this area, move the foundations of your shops further apart.'

The elder took the note. 'Thank you.'

'I'll return in the morning. If you think of anything urgent you believe that I can help with, I'm usually in the headquarters of the New Russia Company during office hours. I'm a guest of Mrs Ignatova, so any other time I'll probably be in her house.'

Roman shook hands with the men, walked Sonya back to the carriage, and they moved on. As they travelled through the fire swept areas, he studied the streets and made notes while Lyudmila regaled Ivan with a high-pitched, non-stop stream of local gossip. If the driver understood a word of what the cook was telling him he gave no sign of it beyond an occasional grunt.

The last scattered undamaged buildings of the settlement finally petered out and the steppe stretched beneath the sky, vast, open, and endless around them. Sonya expected Roman to order Ivan to turn the carriage back to Catherine's house. Instead he told him to drive on.

'I need to get a perspective of the town from a distance,' he explained. 'It's difficult to plan a settlement when there's an unlimited amount of land. The temptation is to spread the buildings, but if you do, people – or more precisely workers – will spend half their time unproductively, walking or driving from one area to another. And, as most of the essential community buildings such as the schools, hospital, churches, synagogue, hotel, offices, and shops are either built or destined for a fixed location, they've already dictated where the centre of the town will be. Hughesovka needs to grow around them, not away from them.'

Roman asked Ivan to stop the carriage about two miles from the last buildings. He opened the carriage door and helped Sonya down. They walked within sight but not earshot of Lyudmila and Ivan.

'Is that enough perspective for you?' she asked after fifteen minutes of trying to keep pace with his long-legged stride.

'I'm, sorry. I didn't mean to walk so quickly or so far. You must be exhausted after missing a night's sleep.'

They turned and looked back at the town. The industrial towers loomed above the low-built workers' houses of the settlement. To the south, west, and east they caught glimpses of the rivers between the larger edifices, silver scars in the drab, flat landscape. On the outskirts, a procession of black-garbed figures walked slowly towards the walled Jewish cemetery with its sprinkling of headstones.

'Alexei and Ruth must have borrowed coats,' Sonya murmured, spotting Alexei's tall, blond-haired figure walking several steps behind a group of veiled, black-garbed women, none recognisable as Ruth.

'Listen,' Roman whispered, 'from this distance you can hear the carpenters hammering nails into wood. Even on a day of death, life continues and grows. One day Hughesovka will be a city.'

'You think so?'

'I know so. Given the number of workers needed to run the factories, collieries, and ironworks Mr Hughes is planning, it cannot fail to be just that.'

'Will we live long enough to see it?'

'If we survive another twenty or thirty years, yes.' He slipped his notebook back into his pocket. 'I confess, I had an ulterior motive in asking you to walk with me, and now we can no longer be overheard by the indomitable Lyudmila or silent Ivan –'

'Lyudmila means well,' she broke in.

'I don't doubt it, but I wish her well-meaning wasn't quite so loud or exhausting, for our sake as well as Ivan's.' He offered her his arm. She took it and he closed his hand over her gloved fingers. 'First, I'd like to thank you for agreeing to be my guide. You were truly excellent, I wouldn't have seen as much without your expert direction.'

'Ivan would have done as well.' She wondered what was coming.

'I have a proposition for you. I don't want you to give me an answer right away. It's a question I hope you'll consider carefully. Take all the time you need – a year or more if it results in the answer I hope to receive.'

Suspicions roused, Sonya began formulating gentle replies she hoped would spare the prince's feelings.

'I know a great deal about you, Sonya. You may not be aware you were the talk of St Petersburg when you visited the city with your aunt and Mr Hughes. The stunning beauty from the steppe with the look of an angel. Since then word of your inheritance has leaked out, and now you're not just any beauty, but a beauty who's inherited two million roubles from her father.'

'I'm aware that news of my inheritance has become common knowledge in some circles. Aunt Catherine has already warned me that most of the attention I'll receive from men in future will be for my fortune, not my person. I don't need further counsel from you, Prince Roman.'

'I've no intention of lecturing you, Miss Tsetovna, but given the rumours about my own wealth, I have some experience of your situation.'

'Given the exalted circles you move in, I don't doubt you've met several fortune hunters.'

'I have. After living in Catherine's house and seeing you every day, your company has proved a most refreshing change from the St Petersburg and Moscow socialites who haunt the fashionable salons in the hope of diverting a portion of the assets of the wealthy into their own purses, along with a wedding ring. Angelic looks don't often come with an angelic temper or a generous and kind heart, but in your case your personality is even more attractive than your person. I am asking you to do me the honour of becoming my wife, Miss Tsetovna.'

'Prince –'

'Even if you should refuse me, which I hope you won't, I trust that we can at least become friends enough for you to call me, Roman, Miss Tsetovna.'

She didn't reciprocate by asking him to call her Sonya, not without her aunt's permission. She wasn't even sure how Catherine would react when she told her about Roman's extraordinary and unexpected proposal. 'I have absolutely no intention of marrying, I have my career...'

'I appreciate that you are as indispensable to Mr Hughes as you once were to the hospital. Should you accept my proposal I would not dream of interfering with your plans for making a career outside of whichever of my houses you choose to live in.'

'You wouldn't want your wife to run your home?' she questioned in surprise.

'I have enough trained butlers, housekeepers, footmen, maids, cooks, and valets to organise my domestic life to perfection – in all my houses.'

'Do you have many?' Sonya asked curiously.

'Moscow, St Petersburg, Yalta, Paris, London, Rome. And as business has brought me here, I'm planning to build another in Hughesovka.'

'If you have so many servants why do you want a wife?' Sonya blurted unthinkingly.

'Why does anyone marry?' he shrugged. 'Companionship, and possibly children. I confess I would like to father a child. Do you like children?'

'I enjoy looking after Alexei's surviving sister, Kira. She's just over a year old.'

'I must visit the nursery and make her acquaintance. Would you like your own children?'

'One day, but I intend to love not like them,' she corrected.

'You are right, children should be loved not liked.'

The smile that accompanied his comment caught her off guard. Without intending to, she used his Christian name. 'Roman, I am aware of the great honour you...'

'Please,' he held up his hand, 'spare me the "you have honoured me" refusal speech out of an etiquette book.'

'You've heard it before?'

'No, you're the first woman I've asked to marry me. That surprises you?' he added when she didn't comment.

'It does.' She wished she could think of something more appropriate to say.

The one thing I value above all else, as I hope you'll soon discover, is honesty. I know from the way you looked at Dr Kharber when you danced with him last evening that you love him...' He held up his hand to silence her. 'Please, let me finish. I also know from the way he looked at you that he loves you. However, he is a doctor who practises an honourable profession and is, above all else, an honourable man.'

She couldn't help but notice he'd pronounced honourable as though it was an insult.

'I also saw at the wedding that the good doctor couldn't conceal his lack of love for his wife, yet he treated her with consideration and respect. That alone tells me he will never act on his love for you, nor will he allow you to show your love for him when he knows it would threaten his wife's peace of mind and cast a shadow over his marriage.'

She wanted to tell Roman that he was wrong. That she didn't love Nathan, had never loved him, but when she looked into his piercing green eyes, she knew he would sense that she was lying.

'Unrequited love can damage and blight lives but only if we allow it,' he advised.

'Is that something else you've discovered from personal experience?'

'I doubt there's anyone alive who hasn't loved unwisely,' he replied ambiguously.

'You said that you know a great deal about me. Are you aware my parents weren't married?'

'Yes. Mine were, but only two weeks before I was born. My father didn't want to annoy his parents and he knew they'd be less than pleased with his choice of wife.'

Your mother was Chinese?'

'She was, and I've inherited her features. You've heard she was a princess?'

'No.'

'Good. I've done my best to put an end to the tales told by my father. My mother's parents were farmers. Hardly impoverished but neither were they wealthy. They were of that most boring class when it comes to fairy stories, well-dressed, well-fed, comfortably off Chinese Manchu bourgeois. Do you know much about your parents?'

'Only that my father is Aunt Catherine's brother. I don't remember him. He's ill with tuberculosis and has spent most of his life in a Moscow hospital for contagious diseases. My mother died when I was a baby.'

'So neither of us knows what it is to grow up with a loving mother.'

'I had Aunt Catherine. No mother could have been kinder or more loving.'

'I stand corrected, and I would never try to come between you. I wish I had been fortunate enough to possess such an aunt. All I'm asking of you is that you consider my offer. I don't believe I'm difficult to live with. I'll freely admit to as many of my faults as I'm aware of. I love travelling, I'm impetuous and apt to leave countries and houses at a moment's notice but as I've already said. I employ enough servants to do my packing and clear up after me. I'm fond of wine and vodka, but I know my limits. I gamble, but again I know my limits, and the last time I checked the record I keep of my card losses, I was actually fifteen hundred roubles up on my original outlay of five years ago. I enjoy working so I seek employment although I don't have to. Also,' he lifted her gloved hand to his lips, 'I'd be more than happy for the right woman to mould me into her idea of the perfect man.'

She looked up at him. The one thing he hadn't mentioned was love. But that was hardly surprising when he'd guessed what she'd believed was her deepest and most private secret regarding Nathan.

'You'll consider my proposal?'

'I'll consider it,' she reiterated, 'but please, promise me that you won't tell my aunt or anyone else that you've made it.'

'It will remain our secret until you give me an answer, one way or the other.'

'Thank you.' She felt odd. She'd received her first proposal of marriage. An important milestone in any girl's life. She knew she should feel elated, but all she could think of was Nathan.

If he'd been the one to ask her to become his wife she would have danced all the way back to her aunt's house. But as Roman had just reminded her that could never be. Instead, she allowed Roman to lead her back to the carriage.

Alexei and Ruth's banya September 1871

'I'm beginning to wonder if I'll ever feel clean again,' Alexei scrubbed his forearms as Ruth scrubbed his back.

'I shouldn't even be bathing. No one should while they're in shiva...' She choked back her tears.

Alexei turned and wiped Ruth's eyes with his fingers. 'You couldn't possibly carry on looking like a bear that's rolled in ashes for however long shiva lasts.'

'Shiva's only the first stage of mourning. Nathan and I should sit in Uncle Asher and Aunt Leah's house. It is written that, "Where a person lived there does his spirit continue to dwell." Their presence will still linger there and we should be there to pay homage to them.'

'They won't be in their house, angel, because most of it has burned down.'

'That makes their death worse. All their possessions, the furnishings I grew up with. All the things they valued, Aunt Leah's photographs and embroidered clothes. Uncle Asher's books and wood-carvings...' The tears Ruth had held in check all afternoon finally began to fall.

He wrapped his arms around her. 'Cry it out, angel. Emotion should never be bottled up inside the body.'

'This can't be easy for you either,' she whispered hoarsely. 'It's not long since you lost your mother and sisters.'

'Which is why I know how you feel.' He rubbed her arms with his hands. 'Come closer, you're freezing.'

Her eyes were dark, brimming with anguish and grief. 'Make love to me.'

'What? You don't know what you're saying, you're grief- stricken...'

'Which is why I want you to make love to me. I want to live with every particle of my body and my being. I want to – I need to – know I'm alive.'

Lacking the self-control to deny her, he wrapped his arms around her waist, pulled her close and kissed her. Rising, he lifted her with him and thrust his naked body along the full length of hers. There was nothing gentle about the urgency of his embrace, but his ardour inflamed her after the passion of the evening before. 'Are we clean enough for bed?'

'I can't wait that long,' she murmured.

'Here?' he reached up and pulled the bolt across the door.

'The steam room.'

He swung her from her feet into his arms, opened the door and carried her inside the Banya. He set her on the waist-high shelf and stepped in front of her.

She reached up and tipped water on the hot coals. The room was flooded with thick swirls of steam. Alexei moved even closer, piercing her body with his own.

'Don't leave me. Promise me that you'll never leave me.' She locked her arms around his neck.

'I promise, my angel. I won't leave you.'

She knotted her fingers into his hair. 'Never ... say never...'

'Never. I'll never leave you, my angel. I swear it.'

Chapter Eleven

Inn, four days' journey from Hughesovka October 1871

'No carts for us tonight. We'll have real beds if there are
any spare, but there'll be no mattresses, only hard planking
with coarse woollen bed linen that will itch and scratch.'
Richard brushed a snowflake from his hair. He and
Edward had just spotted the chimneys of one of the many
primitive wayfarer stations that had sprung up between
Taganrog and Hughesovka since John Hughes's bullock
trains had begun hauling supplies from the port to the
town. Richard was driving the cart, with Sarah squashed
between him and Edward who was perched uncomfortably
on the outer edge of the driver's seat.

'The planks can't be any harder than what we're sitting
on,' Edward grumbled. 'I wish I'd had the sense to hire a
comfortable carriage in Taganrog like Hans Becker.'

'Hans Becker didn't hire it, it belongs to his master,
who's a prince,' Richard pointed out. 'And even if you'd
hired a carriage, which would have cost the earth as you
would have had to pay for a double journey because the
driver would have had to return to Taganrog when we
reached Hughesovka, you would still be bumping over the
same rutted steppe. They're not that much more
comfortable, for all the springs built into them.'

'They have to be,' Edward demurred. 'Springs to
cushion the impact on my poor, aged, decrepit, aching
bones, and a roof, doors, windows, and sides to shelter me
from the cold sounds blissful at this moment.'

Richard looked ahead. Twin smoke plumes headed
straight up, scarring the snow-laden, iron grey clouds.
With no breeze to dispel them and the steppe stretching
flat and unrelenting in every direction they were the only
landmark for miles.

'If there are beds, they'll be shared, so keep your clothes on,' Sarah advised Edward. 'The innkeepers never wash bedding and wool is a magnet for fleas and bedbugs. Although the two chimneys suggest there's a bathhouse, which will be absolute luxury after days of unwashed travelling. I can't wait to soak in a bath, even a cold one.'

'All this talk of fleas, bedbugs, and cold baths makes the thought of spending another night in this open cart more attractive by the minute.' Edward reached for his pipe. He filled it with tobacco but made no attempt to light it.

Richard took the reins in his left hand to free his right and slipped his arm around Sarah's waist. 'Hard cart or hard bed with bugs?'

'Hard choice to make,' Sarah quipped, 'but if the biggest bug of all is with me, I'll settle for either.'

'Do you think there's any chance of Betty and Alice listening if I attempt to enlighten them as to the ways of Russian inns?' Sarah asked Edward.

'After the way both of them have determinedly ignored you and Richard since we left the port, I'd say none whatsoever.'

'Alice still following Misha around like an adoring puppy?' Richard asked.

'Surely you're not jealous?' Edward leaned forward so he could see Richard's face.

'Absolutely not.' Richard gave Sarah an unnecessary reassuring hug. 'But he's a Cossack.'

'And?' Edward prompted when Richard didn't elaborate.

'Richard is trying to say Cossacks are lovely people but not quite like us.'

'In a good or a bad way?'

'That depends on whether you're Cossack or Welsh,' Richard answered.

'I couldn't help overhearing Alice telling everyone who cared to listen that she's inherited a considerable sum of money from her husband.' Sarah lowered her voice, although the snorts of the bullocks and the rumble of wheels was so loud there was little chance of their conversation drifting beyond the confines of the cart.

'A thousand pounds,' Edward murmured, 'I've tried to warn her about keeping her business private, but she's so proud of having her own money after first her father then her husband never allowing her to handle a penny, she insists on telling everyone she meets about it.'

'She isn't carrying it with her, is she?' Richard was alarmed by the thought.

'No, I persuaded her to put most of it into the same bank Mr Hughes uses so she can draw on it here. Although it means she has to give notice to the company whenever she needs to access her funds and as there's no bank in Hughesovka ... there isn't, is there?' Edward checked.

'Not yet,' Richard confirmed.

'Good, that means it will take time for her to lay her hands on her money. Do you think men will be attracted to her simply because she has money?' Edward asked.

'Men in Russia are no different to men in Merthyr, Mr Edwards,' Richard declared. 'There are the good, the bad, and the unscrupulous who would marry an ugly old woman to lay their hands on a thousand pounds – and Alice is neither old nor ugly.'

'So you'll warn Alice about predatory men when you tell her and Betty about the bedbugs and fleas they can expect to find in the inn?' Sarah suggested.

'You'll also have to explain how a Banya – a Russian bath house works,' Richard added.

'You're forgetting I've never been in one,' Edward protested.

'When men and women travel together the men always use them first. Richard will explain how they work to you, then you can tell Betty.'

Sarah leaned against Richard and watched the smoke plumes grow gradually larger as they approached the inn.

'Four days and we'll be in Hughesovka,' Richard flicked the reins in a futile attempt to speed up the bullocks. Futile because none of the beasts could move faster than those pulling the cart in front of them, and there were over fifty carts in the train of supplies. 'I'll ask Misha to mount a man on a swift horse and send him on ahead first thing in the morning with a letter for Mr Edwards so he'll have advance warning that Mrs Edwards and his daughter are on their way.'

'You may not need to.' Sarah shaded her eyes with her hand. 'Isn't that Vlad in the doorway of the inn?'

Richard squinted into the sun and made out the figure of the tall, loose-limbed Russian. He was leaning against the doorpost, a bottle of vodka in one hand, his gun cradled in the other.

'Take over for me please.' Richard thrust the reins into Sarah's hand and jumped from the cart.

Edward watched him run. 'That boy can't wait to hear the news from Hughesovka.'

'That boy is my husband, Edward.'

'Sorry.' He gave Sarah a sheepish grin. 'It's hard for me to forget that I was born the same year as his mother. To me he'll always be the next generation.'

'As for Richard wanting to hear the news from Hughesovka, he can't wait and neither can I. It's home now, Edward. In every sense of the word, and from what little I've gleaned from Richard, Anna, and Peter, more home to Richard than Merthyr ever was.'

'Richard's mother could only afford the rent for a hovel, even by Merthyr standards, after his father died. Damn the Crawshays. They should be ashamed for allowing their workers to live in worse conditions than animals.'

'You'll find the same shortage of decent housing in Hughesovka, Edward.

'Some of the labourers can't even afford hovels. They dig holes in the ground, thatch them with turf, and call them home. We've had several epidemics already, not only of the cholera that killed Peter, but typhoid fever, diphtheria, and typhus.'

'Mr Hughes is building more houses, isn't he?'

'As fast as humanly possible given the shortage of labour and materials, but the industrial buildings take precedence.'

'Making money has always comes before people's comfort and probably always will.' Edward looked ahead to where Richard was deep in conversation with Vlad. 'I wish these bullocks would move faster. The inn might be bug-ridden but the chimney smoke suggests it might be warm inside, and unless my nose is playing tricks on me, I believe I can smell hot stew.'

Sarah shivered. 'Winter's coming. You can feel it in the air. Be warned, autumn and spring only last a few hours here. A day at most. The steppe rarely has time to change to autumn shades before it's buried in snowdrifts. It wouldn't surprise me if it starts falling thicker tomorrow or even this evening, and within a day the snow will be six feet deep and rising. At the end of winter the snow will melt just as quickly. The trees will be full of blossoms, and summer will be with us. That's something else you should warn Betty and Alice about. You either need cool summer or extreme winter clothes here. There's no need to buy for an English climate.'

'I'll pass on the message but I've no doubt they'll forget their ridiculous attitude towards you soon and start coming to you for advice.'

Sarah raised her eyebrows. 'After Betty finds out about Glyn and Praskovia and discovers that Richard and I live under Glyn's roof? I don't think so, Edward.'

Wayfarer Inn, steppe outside Hughesovka October 1871

'So, Hughesovka's burned to the ground,' Richard echoed

looking to Vlad to elaborate.

'Last month. Not all of it has gone, the works and the furnaces are fine, but most of the shtetl went, along with a fair number of the wooden shops and houses, but Mr Glyn's and Mr Alexei's houses weren't touched. And the hotel, Madam Koshka's, and the headquarters of the company are all intact.'

'We have to be grateful for that much,' Richard said.

Sarah joined them. 'Please, tell me about Alexei's wedding to Ruth? Did it go well?'

'It seemed to go all right.'

'All right! That's a typical man's answer, Vlad. Was it perfect and romantic? Was the bride's dress very beautiful ... and the bridesmaids' gowns, did they match the bride's? Were the choir and music inspiring and moving? Could you hear the responses in the ceremony? Were the bride and bridegroom nervous?'

'You need a woman to answer those questions,' Vlad answered evasively.

'So it seems.' Sarah took the glass of kvas, a low alcohol bread beer, that Richard handed her, 'thank you.'

'Sorry I can't be of more help, Mrs Edwards ...' Vlad hesitated in embarrassment, 'sorry, Mrs Parry.'

'We've known one another long enough for you to call me Sarah, Vlad.'

'That wouldn't be proper, Mrs Parry. So, what do you say to my proposal?' Vlad prompted, more at ease making practical plans than discussing weddings. 'Because of the information we were given in Hughesovka that this convoy was closer to home than it is, the troika, horses, and me have been taking our ease here for two days while waiting for the supplies Mr Hughes needs urgently for the metallurgy laboratory. I could pack the chemicals into the back of the carriage, you and Mr Parry into the front, and we could move out within the hour and be in Hughesovka two full days before this bullock train reaches there.'

Richard glanced at Sarah. She didn't need to nod agreement.

'Did I hear you say that you're driving straight on to Hughesovka now?' Hans Becker asked Vlad in perfect Russian.

'You did, sir,' Vlad confirmed.

'Could we please travel with you? All we'll have to do is put a fresh team of horses into the carriage harness.'

'You'd be most welcome, Your Excellency.' Vlad had noticed the coat of arms on the carriage and been impressed without realising who it belonged to.

Hans saw Vlad studying the carriage door. 'I'm not Prince Roman Nadolny.'

'I know the prince by sight, sir, and I can confirm that you're not him.'

Sarah stifled her laughter.

'I'm Hans Becker and I work for the prince, which is why I'm travelling in his carriage. When do we leave?' he asked Vlad.

'How long will it take you to unload your luggage from the bullock carts?' Vlad asked Richard.

'As long as it will take Mr Becker's coachman and footman to harness a fresh team.' Richard turned to Sarah. 'Find Edward and tell him we're going on ahead. I'll see to the luggage.'

New Russia Company Headquarters October 1871

'You're absolutely sure about this,' Roman repeated in astonishment.

John Hughes smiled. 'We'll carry out a full test firing of the furnace next month, but all the indications are that if there are no further hitches, by January next year we'll be in full production.'

'You've performed a miracle, John. If you're sure about this I must write to Grand Duke Konstantin at once.'

'I'm sure,' John reiterated drily.

'I'm glad you told me this now. One of my people is leaving for St Petersburg tomorrow to pick up a few things for me. He can take my letters with him.'

'Pick up a few things? You sound as though you've asked him to go down the street because you left your handkerchief behind,' John commented in amusement.

'I don't always carry everything I need; if I did, I'd travel with a veritable caravan of goods. It's much easier to employ extra footmen who can fetch anything I'm missing. I recommend German staff, they're so efficient, they organise me without me even noticing.' He raised his glass of tea. 'Here's to the success of the New Russia Company.'

Glyn knocked John's office door and opened it. 'Sorry to disturb you, but Mr and Mrs Parry have just arrived and they asked if they could see you.'

John smiled. 'Show them in here please, Glyn.'

'Mr and Mrs Parry ...' Alexei repeated the words as he followed Glyn to the door. 'Richard must have caught up with Sarah. I knew he would. Now I can forgive him for missing my wedding.' Alexei stood back as Richard and Sarah walked in.

Glyn swept Sarah off her feet and Alexei hugged Richard. The first time Alexei had embraced him, Richard had been disconcerted. Now, without realising how it had happened, he took the Russian's exuberant demonstrations of affection for granted.

'You're back in time to join us in test firing the furnace,' John announced while Alexei asked Vasily to bring refreshments for Richard and Sarah.

'You haven't met Grand Duke Konstantin's representative, Prince Roman Nadolny,' John effected the introduction. 'Prince Roman, may I introduce my very good friends, and bridal couple, Richard and Sarah Parry.'

Sarah pulled off her glove so everyone could see the ring Richard had bought her in St Petersburg on his last visit in the hope that she'd accept his proposal.

'Please, call me Roman. It's my privilege to meet both of you after hearing so much about you.'

'Has Vlad brought the chemicals we're waiting for?' John asked.

'Yes, he's delivering them to the laboratory now. Your secretary and lawyer also travelled with us, Prince Roman, and an associate of Grand Duke Konstantin,' Richard revealed. 'We left them at an inn this morning so they could repair a broken wheel on their carriage, but they won't be more than an hour or two behind us.'

'The bullock train will be here in two days and it's bringing more people from Wales. Richard's brothers are travelling with them.' Sarah turned to Glyn. She knew there was absolutely no point in trying to hide Betty or his child's presence when everyone in the train knew exactly who they were and why they'd come to Hughesovka. 'Your brother Edward, along with your wife and daughter, will soon be here, Glyn.'

Catherine Ignatova's house October 1871

Hans Becker was accustomed to his master's capricious nature but after the surprise of finding him making plans to stay on in Hughesovka, he considered the prince's latest scheme astounding.

'You want to build a house here? On the barren steppe, sir?'

'It's hardly barren now, Hans, and it will be less so in a few months when Mr Hughes has progressed even further with his building programme.' Roman dipped his cut-throat razor into the bowl of warm water on his washstand. 'Manfred has details of the parcel of land I've bought down by the river. It's larger than I need for the house, gardens, and carriage house, but half of it can be fenced off for horses and stables. It's always as well to keep them close to hand, especially in a town. Send for the architect who designed the Yalta house, I'll talk to him about plans and specifics when he arrives, and if he's still using that Prussian master builder ... what was his name?'

'Albert Salewski, sir.'

'That's the man. Tell the architect I want Salewski to build it and remind Manfred I want a wine cabinet put into the cabin in the boat he's refurbishing.'

'Yes, sir.' Hans was used to his master's grasshopper way of thinking, but this was the first he'd heard about a boat. 'Boat, sir?'

'I bought one to use as a retreat. Catherine Ignatova is a wonderful hostess, and the people here are splendid, but you know me. I need to get away from people, even splendid ones, from time to time.'

'Yes, sir.'

'Wine cabinet to be filled – Manfred will know with what. That's all for now, Hans. I heard that my lawyer travelled with you?'

'Yes, sir.'

'Tell him to come to my office in the New Russia Company at ten o'clock.'

'This morning, sir?'

Roman smiled at Hans's reflection in his shaving mirror. 'You think tomorrow morning would be better, Hans?'

'No, sir.'

'Ask him to come this morning, Hans.'

'Yes, sir. Sir ...' Hans hesitated.

'I can't answer a question if you don't ask it, Hans.'

'Yes, sir. How long do you intend to remain here, sir?'

'You don't like Hughesovka, Hans?'

'You can hardly call the place civilized, can you, sir?'

'Give it time, Hans.' Roman finished shaving, took the towel that had been soaking in boiling water, and wiped his face with it. 'Give it time,' he repeated, 'and while you do, take a look around. This place has many undiscovered charms. If you take the trouble to look.'

'Yes, sir.'

'No need to sound so sceptical, Hans. I'll see you with my lawyer in my office?'

'Ten o'clock, sir.

Chapter Twelve

Glyn Edwards's house October 1871

'Are you sure these will be suitable for your brothers, Richard?' Praskovia had insisted on showing Richard the rooms she'd prepared before his brothers arrived, and as the bullock train had been sighted a verst outside the town, they were expecting them to walk in at any moment. 'If I'd had more notice that they were coming here I'd have had time to prepare something better, or at least repaint the walls. These were always intended to be servants' quarters. I told Glyn we should accommodate your family in the main part of the house...'

'My brothers have never even aspired to servants' quarters, Praskovia,' Richard interrupted. 'In fact these are the first rooms they will have had to call their own. And they're more than fine.' He walked into one of the two identically furnished cubicles and pressed down on the bed with his hand. The mattress was firm, the bedcovers bleached cotton, the chests plain wood. There was a hook on the back of the door to hang clothes, and a travelling washstand. 'Neither Owen nor Morgan could want for more,' he assured her.

'Although they have to share a corridor with the maids, groom, gardener, and my mother? They could of course have Pyotr's room at the front of the house but as one of his duties is answering the bell at night they might not get much sleep.'

'I think they'd prefer it here. They're at a safe distance from me and both Mr Edwardses in case they get up to any mischief they don't want us to see.'

'I'm glad you think they're suitable. Glyn and I discussed the arrangements. It makes sense for Glyn's brother to have Alexei's old room, and as Sarah suggested, you can turn either your room or Sarah's into a sitting room, although you're most welcome to share the one downstairs.'

'We know that, Praskovia.'

'Pyotr will help you to move the furniture around.'

'I wouldn't dare touch anything in the rooms until Sarah's decided what she wants where.'

'Very sensible,' Praskovia agreed. 'The woman in the family is always the homemaker not the man.'

'I seem to have suddenly acquired a large family. Two brothers in addition to a sister and wife. That's quite a crowd. It won't hurt us to have rooms we can spread out in, and next year there'll be two babies in the house.'

Praskovia didn't smile at his reminder. 'You know Glyn's wife?'

'I've met her,' Richard replied warily.

'You travelled from Taganrog with her.'

'She wouldn't talk to me or Sarah.'

'Why?' Praskovia was genuinely perplexed.

'Because Sarah was married to Peter. Some people in Wales believe widows should mourn their dead husbands for the rest of their lives and never remarry. To make things worse, in her eyes I'm still a boy and far too young to have married Sarah, given the age difference between us.'

'You only have to look at you to see you're a man.'

'Thank you, Praskovia.' He suddenly realised how tactless he'd been. The age gap between him and Sarah was practically the same as the age difference between Praskovia and Glyn, only in reverse. 'But that isn't all. An old girlfriend of mine has travelled with Glyn's wife. She was hoping to marry me, and was furious when she discovered I'd married Sarah.'

Praskovia frowned, her thoughts clearly with Glyn. 'I wish Glyn had allowed me to go to the hotel with him to talk to his wife. If she could see us together...'

'She'd what, Praskovia?' he asked gently. 'Realise how much you love one another. That really wouldn't make the situation between her and Glyn any easier, now would it?'

'No, of course not. It's just that...'

'What?'

'I can't stop thinking about Glyn and what he's going to say to his wife and baby daughter.' Tears gathered on her eyelashes. 'I wish I could spare both of them pain.'

'You have spared Mr Edwards the pain of loneliness, Praskovia. I hope Sarah and I will always be as happy together as you and he are.'

Beletsky Mansion, Hughesovka October 1871

'Ilya, the bottles are empty. Bring more whisky cognac, and vodka,' Levsky ordered.

Levsky's manservant left the room and returned a few moments later with a tray laden with full bottles of spirits, fresh glasses, and slices of lemon.

Nicholas Beletsky glanced at the dozen men sitting around his dining table. Levsky was sitting opposite him, depending on the point of view, either at the head or the foot of the long table. Either way Levsky had assumed the mantle of master of the house, and with it the right to direct the servants, although technically the Beletsky mansion was still registered in his name. However, he could hardly object when they were being served by Levsky's retainers and Levsky was paying all the domestic expenses of the Beletsky mansion.

He'd used the house, and indeed most of his other assets, including his Moscow and St Petersburg properties, as collateral against his IOU gambling notes, most of which were now in the possession of Levsky.

Bankruptcy hovered over him like a black cloud above a furnace. Much as he tried to blame his losses on bad luck and his state of mind after losing his wife and all but one of his daughters, he couldn't even convince himself. He knew, as did everyone around him, that his dire financial situation was the consequence of staking and losing more than he could afford at the card table.

'Gentlemen,' Levsky glanced around the table, and signalled to Ilya to refill everyone's glass. 'It's time to commit our concerns to paper and send them to our friends at court. Ilya, when you've finished serving you may close the door behind you.'

Ilya replaced the bottles on the tray and left it in the centre of the table. As soon as he closed the door, Nicholas thumped his fist on the table to gain everyone's attention.

'We have to derail this insane preoccupation of the Tsar to industrialise Russia. It's destabilising Russian society. It's only ten years since he abolished serfdom and we all know where that led.'

Content to allow Nicholas to do the talking, Levsky merely nodded agreement.

'The country is awash with landless peasants. A rootless, thieving, Godless, feral proletariat who care nothing for the land they once worked, or the well-being of those who own that land. Hell-bent on going wherever the wind blows them, including this damned sink of iniquity– this so called "industrial town" of John Hughes. They have no allegiance to anyone or anything other than their own carnal lusts. No thought or respect for their former masters, the church, or even God.'

The men around the table indicated tacit, silent agreement as they drained their glasses and passed the bottles of spirits to one another.

'The peasants are naturally idle. Recent history has shown us they'd rather revolt and fight their God-ordained masters than work.

'As vicious and devoid of morals as a pack of wolves, they terrorise and steal from decent people in the countryside, break into the houses of the bourgeois in the towns, and ambush and strip aristocrats of their valuables whenever we venture out without protection.'

'Hear, hear,' Levsky chanted.

'It has become increasingly obvious that our Tsar Alexander II values his drive to "modernise" and "industrialise" Mother Russia above the wellbeing and safety of his subjects. In short, gentlemen, by unleashing the peasants on us he is actively inciting political unrest.'

Levsky reached down beside his chair and lifted a briefcase on to the table. He opened it and removed a file. He extracted the papers it contained and distributed them. 'We must act immediately, gentlemen. It may already be too late. We can begin by reading and signing these declarations, which I've arranged to be passed on to the Tsar by a "sympathetic friend" in his inner circle.'

Silence reigned while everyone studied the declaration that demanded the reinstatement of regulations restricting the peasants to living on their masters' estates, effectually restoring serfdom, expelling all foreign industrialists from Russia, and confining the building of industrial complexes to the Far East of the country.

The sound of ink bottles being opened and the scratching of pens marked an end to the silence.

'Hasn't the fire halted John Hughes's building programme?' Taras Komansky, an even wealthier landowner than Levsky, asked.

As most of Komansky's holdings were in the East, Levsky suspected that he was hoping to replicate Hughesovka with its lucrative leases on his own property.

'Apparently not,' he snapped. 'The area most affected was the shtetl and the Jews are already putting up wooden shacks to replace the ones that were destroyed. I've also heard that Hughes sent letters to Germany this morning asking his agents to recruit more artisans. His intention is to rebuild in brick.'

Nicholas collected the papers the men had read and signed. He shuffled them into a pile and handed them to Levsky.

'I will get these,' Levsky returned them to his briefcase, 'to the right person.'

'If you need any help in putting pressure on people who are in a position to influence the Tsar, I'm your man,' Komansky boasted.

'The problem is not with the Tsar's advisors, but the man himself.' Levsky filled his glass with cognac. The spirits had flowed freely around the table but it was the first drink he'd allowed to pass his lips. 'I've heard he's even considering some kind of parliament with elected representatives similar to Great Britain, which indicates that the introduction of British industrialists into Russia is already having a detrimental effect on the Tsar's thinking, as well as the pockets of the landowners.'

'So many serfs have left my land there are not enough to cultivate it. Those who still live on my estate will be hard pressed to produce enough food to feed themselves, let alone my servants and the free peasants who have elected to stay,' declared a Moscow landowner.

'By allowing the serfs to move away from the estates that produced the food for Mother Russia, the Tsar has ruined the land,' Nicholas commented. 'As for industry, if the Tsar, as you suggest, Levsky, reintroduces serfdom and returns the Russian workers to their rightful place, I see no problem with continuing to import the goods that we cannot produce ourselves. If the rest of Europe chooses to industrialise and blacken their landscape with filth, dust, coalmines, and factories that is their choice. We will keep Russia a green and pleasant haven.'

'To summarise, gentlemen, we're all agreed that this ridiculous venture of Hughes' has to be stopped here in the Donbas,' Levsky declared. 'I will leave for St Petersburg tomorrow and lobby those with influence to our cause.

'I trust you will do the same in your own parts of the country when you return. Meanwhile I have arranged for the grooms to saddle horses, and the huntsmen to prepare guns and ammunition. If any of you, gentlemen, would care to join me in a hunting expedition on the steppe this afternoon, please meet me in the hall one hour after lunch.'

The men finished their drinks and dispersed. When only Nicholas remained, Levsky opened a narrow door concealed in the wood panelling that led to the servants' quarters. They walked down a stone-built passage until they reached a corridor lined with doors.

Levsky opened the first door and entered a freezing cell. Four men sat at a table. Levsky addressed Ilya. 'You spoke to our man?'

'I did, sir.'

'He read all the reports from bystanders in the town that reached the New Russia Company Office?'

'He did, sir. Your men were seen at the locations of the outbreak of the fires but no one could identify them or give a description other than "shadowy figures".'

'Figures, not figure?' Levsky checked.

'That's what he told me, sir.'

'It's also what I heard in the beer shop, sir,' Gleb attested. 'You two, you wore hoods and covered your faces?' Levsky demanded in English.

'With scarves, sir, we did,' Ianto Paskey spoke for his brother Mervyn as well as himself.

'Keep working on your Russian. When I send you into the ironworks to sabotage production I want you – both of you,' Levsky glared at Mervyn as well as Ianto, 'speaking the language like natives.'

'It's hard, sir,' Mervyn whined.

'No one said it would be easy. How are they progressing, Gleb?'

'Not well, sir,' Gleb replied with more honesty than tact. 'But they could always say they're from one of the Baltic States.'

'When there are as many Lithuanians, Estonians, Prussians, and Latvians in Hughesovka as there are Russians, Cossacks, and Welsh? I don't think so. Keep working, all of you. Not you, Ilya. I need you to supervise lunch and the hunting trip for my guests.'

'Sir.'

Ilya left. Nicholas and Levsky followed him out of the servants' quarters and back into the dining room. The maids were setting the table so by tacit consent they retired to the drawing room.

'You'll remain here and keep an eye on the situation in the town while I'm in St Petersburg?'

Nicholas knew Levsky had given him an order. 'If you want me to.'

'I do. That's settled then.' Levsky sat in the most comfortable chair in the room – the one he knew had been Nicholas's. 'Given luck, and with God on our side, John Hughes will soon smelt his first, and last, iron in his town.'

Chapter Thirteen

Hotel Hughesovka October 1871

Glyn stubbed out his Turkish cigarette, rose from the chair he'd pulled up to one of the windows, and paced uneasily to the second window, although it offered no better view. He looked down on the crowd of workmen and builders milling below his first-floor hotel suite, hoping to see Alf Mahoney or his brother Edward, but he couldn't spot either of them, although the first of the bullock carts had driven into the compound over half an hour before.

He'd hated pulling rank, but he'd had to remind Alf twice that he was the man's boss before Alf had agreed to meet Edward, Betty, and the rest of their party and escort them to the hotel. Alf hadn't been his first choice, but Richard and Sarah had both refused point blank to meet Edward and Betty, reminding him that neither Betty nor Alice Perkins had spoken a word to them on the journey after discovering they were married.

He'd reserved the largest suite the hotel had to offer for Betty as soon as he'd read her letter informing him she was on her way to Hughesovka. Aware that the hotel was almost always full, he'd estimated her arrival date and as a result had already paid a full week for the rooms to remain empty. As well as the sitting room, the suite had two double bedrooms, and he'd asked that a child's cot be put in one. He'd negotiated the option of renewing the reservation for a further month but he hoped it wouldn't be needed that long. A squad of Cossack soldiers was leaving for Taganrog in nine days to pick up supplies for their barracks. He'd requested and received permission for Betty to be allowed to accompany them and had put even more pressure on Alf to act as Betty's escort, if necessary back to Wales.

Alf had been as reluctant to agree as he'd been reluctant to ask. With the works on schedule to smelt the first full production of pig iron in January, Alf, like all the company employees, wanted to witness the historic moment.

The snow that had been falling lightly since morning thickened as Glyn continued his study of the street. Eventually he saw Edward walking beside a man pushing a handcart loaded with luggage. It was hard, slow work over the heavily- rutted dirt street.

Three women walked behind Edward, all swathed in thick woollen coats and shawls. The youngest carried a toddler. He could see his mother's dark-eyed beauty mirrored in the child's face. An overwhelming wave of love engulfed him. An emotion he was totally unprepared for. This child was his daughter. She had every right to expect him to love and guide her through life, to be with her every day...

He turned his back to the window, took another cigarette from his packet and tried to compose himself. He was dreading the encounter with Betty. The more he considered the situation, the less certain he was of her reaction to the news that he'd already left her for his pregnant mistress. He realised he couldn't predict her response simply because he didn't know her well enough. She was his wife yet he didn't know the first thing about her.

When he heard the thumps and scrapes of trunks being hauled up the stairs, he opened the door. Four hotel porters climbed breathlessly on to the landing and dropped two enormous, snow-frosted trunks.

'Where do you want them, sir?' they asked.

'One in each bedroom, thank you,' Glyn replied in Russian.

Betty appeared behind them. She stared at him for a moment then nodded her head. 'Glyn.'

'Betty.'

'I trust you don't expect me to learn that heathen language.' He didn't reply. Standing in the doorway facing her he felt unaccountably foolish. 'Did you have a good journey?' he asked for the sake of saying something – anything.

'That's a ridiculous question considering you must have travelled the same way we did, on rough seas and over even rougher ground in the freezing cold, and now snow, in carts pulled by cows.'

'Bullocks,' he corrected without thinking. When she glared at him he remembered she couldn't stand to be corrected – about anything.

She looked around the corridor. 'Is this the best hotel Hughesovka has to offer?'

'It's the only hotel Hughesovka has to offer.'

'Alf said you wanted to talk to me before the others came up. They're ordering food downstairs.'

'I recognised Alice Perkins, but not the young girl.'

'Martha, she's our daughter Harriet Maud's nursemaid.'

The porters left the trunks in the rooms. Glyn tipped them and murmured, 'Thank you.'

Betty sailed past him into the suite.

'Shall I order something for you, tea or food?' he offered.

'Tea and sandwiches. Plain ones, cheese or ham, no foreign muck in the filling.'

Glyn called to the porters who were halfway down the stairs, gave them Betty's order, and returned to the suite. He closed the door behind him.

'Why am I in a hotel room and not your house?' Betty demanded.

'I wrote to you. You obviously didn't get my letter.'

Alf came up the stairs knocked and dropped two bags just inside the room. 'Excuse me, sir, Mrs Edwards,' he backed out swiftly, closing the door behind him.

133

'Why am I not in your house?' Betty reiterated. 'Don't try telling me that you haven't one. I've been writing to you at a private address, not a hotel.'

'This is comfortable, isn't it?'

'I suppose it will have to do. Who's paying the bill?' Betty looked into the bedrooms, dropped her handbag onto one of the beds, pulled off her gloves and threw them on top of the bag.

'I'm paying, at the moment.' Glyn moved the chair he'd placed next to the window back into the group around the stove.

Betty finally sat down. 'You saw your daughter?'

'Through the window. She's beautiful.'

'She's a lot of work.'

'You look well, Betty.'

'Less of the soft soap. I know you, Glyn Edwards. You've a woman here, haven't you?'

'I wrote to you...'

'You sent me more than one letter over the last two years.'

'The one I'm thinking of asked you to divorce me.'

'I received that letter.'

'You came all the way here knowing I loved someone else?'

'I came to reclaim my rights. My solicitor said I can do that. There's a law. I can go to court and demand,' she hesitated for a moment searching for the exact wording, 'restitution of conjugal rights. That's what I want. A judge can order you back to the marital home.'

'What marital home, Betty?'

'Your home.'

'I don't have one, and even I did there's nothing left between us.'

'There's our daughter,' she bit back.

'Praskovia is pregnant.'

'Praskovia.' She repeated the name and flung it back at him. 'What kind of a pagan name is that?'

'A Russian name. I've never asked but the Russians probably consider our names heathen.' He struggled to keep his temper.

'It's a whore's name,' she spat out.

Glyn suddenly realised it wasn't that he'd stopped loving his wife. He'd never loved her. He'd married her as a young, naïve boy solely to discover the mysteries of sex. The revelation didn't make him happy; if anything it made him despise himself even more. He had to concede that he'd used Betty, but he wasn't prepared to spend the rest of his life paying for his mistake. 'Why are you so determined to see only the ugly side of life, never the beauty, Betty?' he challenged.

'I see what you put in front of me, Glyn Edwards. The Lord only knows that is truly ugly, because you lead an ugly sinful life. And you've chosen an even uglier place to live it.'

'If you won't divorce me, I'll divorce you.'

'As I just told you, I saw a solicitor in Merthyr before I left. A good one, who knew how to charge, but he was worth every penny because he told me exactly how to deal with you. And just so you know, you can't divorce me. You have no grounds.'

'Try desertion. I invited you to come here with me. I bought you a ticket, but you insisted on staying in Merthyr.'

'I'm here now, aren't I? So how can that be desertion? We married before God and our families in chapel, Glyn. And I'll see that we stay married for Harriet Maud's sake.'

'Then it will be a marriage in name only, Betty, because I'm not leaving Praskovia or our coming child.'

'She's a nothing – a nobody. I checked up on that too. Whores have no rights. Your house is mine. I'll move in...'

'I told you I don't have a home or a house, Betty.' He paced to the window, perched on the window ledge and faced her. 'The house I live in belongs to Praskovia.'

'You gave your house to your whore!' Betty shrieked.

'I gave it to the woman I love. The house is hers, Betty. As am I.'

'And me and your daughter? You'd see us beggars out on the street...'

'You're in a hotel room that I'm paying for. I've given you a generous annuity. It's more than enough to keep you and our daughter in the same style as any manager's family in Merthyr. You can live well on the money I've given you without having to run the pub your father probably left you.'

'I sold the pub to come here.'

'That was your choice, Betty, not mine. Go back to Merthyr.' He was tired. Tired of being in the same room as her, tired of arguing with her, tired of confrontation. 'There's nothing for you here.'

'My husband is here.'

'I'm not your husband, Betty. If I ever was I'm certainly not any longer. I'll pay for these rooms until the Cossack soldiers return to Taganrog in nine days' time and not a minute longer. I've already asked Alf to escort you to the port and back to Wales if that's what you want.'

'You can't just wash your hands of us,' she screamed as hysteria took hold. 'I'm staying here.'

He crossed his arms over his chest. 'Why, Betty?'

'Because I have nowhere else to go.' She began to cry. Dry, theatrical sobs designed to evoke pity, but Glyn felt only disgust.

'Your life, your friends are all in Merthyr.'

'Not any more. And don't think my staying here means I'll allow you to see Harriet Maud. I won't, not until you start living with us again.'

'Again? Betty, think– how many days have we lived together since we married?' He kept his voice soft, low, in contrast to hers.

'That wasn't my choice.'

'This town is no place for a woman or a child.'

'Your whore lives here. Sarah Edwards lives here – although she's nothing but a whore as well, marrying a boy young enough to be her son before Peter was even cold in his grave...'

'You have no right to say that. You have absolutely no idea what Sarah's been through or suffered.'

'Suffered! Don't talk to me of suffering. None of you have the faintest idea what suffering is. Living here off the fat of the land in sheer idleness. You haven't had to lift a finger since you left Merthyr,' Betty sneered. 'I overheard Sarah and Richard talking to Edward on the journey here. You have servants. People to do your bidding. You all live in the lap of luxury...'

'Luxury!' Glyn repeated. 'You have no idea how rough this town is, or the sort of men who come here looking for work. They own nothing and have nothing to lose. They live in holes they dig in the ground and they'd slit their own mother's throat for a bottle of vodka.'

'Then Hughesovka is no different from Merthyr.'

'It's different because it's growing. There's an acute shortage of accommodation. This hotel room is expensive. Neither I nor you will be able to afford to rent it for long, Betty, then where will you live? Be reasonable, what would you do here if you did stay?'

'I'll think of something.'

The hint of triumph in the expression on her face alerted him. 'Don't you dare go near Praskovia...'

'Or you'll what, Glyn?' she challenged. 'I have the right to talk to my husband or anyone else I chose to in this town. Try and stop me and I'll go to the police.'

'That just shows how little you know about Hughesovka, Betty. There are no police. There's a Cossack regiment of soldiers, who use their swords and guns in preference to conversation, and a fire brigade. When it comes to disputes between husbands and wives, there's no one to listen. Especially to a complaint made in English.' Glyn picked up his hat from the table.

'I'll go to Mr Hughes...'

'With the workload he has, you wouldn't even get an appointment. Besides, he would never interfere in a dispute between a husband and his wife.' He opened the door. A waiter was standing outside with a samovar trolley set with cups and sandwiches. He waved him in and ran down the stairs.

Alf, Edward, Alice, Martha, and the child were sitting in a corner of the dining room. He beckoned to Edward, who tossed his napkin on to his plate and joined him.

'How did it go?' Edward didn't know why he was asking when the expression on Glyn's face told him all he needed to know.

'Betty's refusing to leave Hughesovka.'

'Why? There's nothing for her here.'

'I've tried all the arguments, Edward. Praskovia's prepared a room for you. You could come with me now.' He looked around. 'Where are Richard's brothers?'

'With Richard. He met us and took them to your house. What about Betty?' Edward looked through the door at the rough-looking men who'd crowded around the bar. 'Will she be safe here?'

'Safer than anywhere else in Hughesovka. The hotel employs its own bruisers to clear out the troublemakers.'

'If you're sure the women will be safe...'

'I'm sure provided they don't go outside. You'd better warn them the streets are dangerous. You can see my garden from here.' Glyn pointed to the gate. 'Praskovia's made a meal. You're welcome to join us whenever you choose.' He strode off.

Chapter Fourteen

Glyn Edwards's house October 1871

'Damned woman wouldn't listen to a word I said. She's determined to stay here. I don't want you talking to Betty if you see her in the street, Praskovia, and I need to know immediately if she dares to knock on this door. No matter where I am, you send for me right away. Understood?' Glyn ordered.

It was the first time she'd heard him speak so vehemently. 'If you don't want me to talk to her, Glyn, I won't. But what about your daughter?' she ventured. 'She's little more than a baby. This argument between you and your wife is none of her doing.'

'I know.' Defeated he sank down on the sofa. 'But Betty made it plain that she doesn't want me to see or speak to Harriet. I might not know my wife very well, Praskovia, but I do know what she's capable of.' He looked up. He'd never needed the love mirrored in Praskovia's eyes more. 'If I let her, Betty will use Harriet Maud to blackmail me, and I refuse to allow her to control and manipulate me, or threaten our happiness.'

'You really think she'll stay in Hughesovka although you told her you intend to ignore her.'

'I think she's petty minded enough to stay and try to damage us in some way, although I made it clear that all I want from her is a divorce.' He reached out for Praskovia's hand. 'I told my brother you'd prepared a room for him here. I know the house is full at the moment...'

'I like it that way.' She sat on his lap and stroked his cheek. 'You can't be serious.'

'My mother is too busy cooking for everyone to find the time to quarrel or find fault with me.

'The maids and Pyotr have plenty of work to do and when they're working they have no time to think of things to complain about. And with Anna on evening and night shifts and Sarah back at the hospital in the day, and you and Richard, and soon your brother and Richard's brothers, in and out of the house at all hours, there'll always be someone here for me to talk to.'

'You won't need too many people to talk to when the baby arrives in the spring.'

'It's good to have people we care about, and who care about us, living in the house.'

'It is.' Glyn would never have admitted it to Praskovia lest he alarm her, but he was thinking more of the advantage of having Edward's and Richard's muscle in the house than company for Praskovia when he wasn't home. He wouldn't put it past Betty to hire thugs to attack Praskovia if she thought it would succeed in persuading him to return to her. He made a mental note to tell Pyotr not to allow his sister to go anywhere alone.

Catherine Ignatova's house October 1871

The senior footman, Marat, was waiting anxiously in the hall when Catherine and her butler, Boris, returned from helping Father Grigor and his cook, Brin, serve bread and soup to the poor in the makeshift kitchen Brin had set up in the headquarters of the Fire Brigade.

Boris helped Catherine remove her cloak, shook the snow from it, and handed it to Marat. 'Is there a problem?' he asked when he saw the expression on Marat's face.

'Count Beletsky is here.'

'Didn't you inform him that madam wasn't at home,' Boris reprimanded.

'Yes, sir, but the count refused to leave. He said he had urgent family business and would wait for madam.'

Catherine checked all the doors in the hall were closed before speaking. 'Where have you put the count, Marat?'

'In the anteroom off the back porch, madam. He wanted to sit in the library or the drawing room but I told him they were locked and I didn't have the keys.'

'Excellent choice of room, Marat,' Catherine complimented. The anteroom off the back porch was where tradesmen waited to be paid. 'Bring me tea in the library, please, then you may show him in. Boris, please accompany me.'

'Yes, madam.'

Catherine went into the library and sat in her accustomed chair, which had been moved comfortably close to the hearth in preparation for winter. She couldn't imagine why her son-in- law had chosen to pay her a visit. She had sent him an invitation to Alexei's wedding, although Nicholas had disowned and disinherited his eldest son when Alexei had refused to give up his position with the New Russian Company. Loathing industry, Nicholas could neither understand nor countenance Alexei's determination to support the Tsar's drive to modernise Russia. When her daughter Olga and all her granddaughters except Kira, the youngest, had died in a cholera outbreak, Nicholas had remained in the town only as long as it had taken to bury them.

Since then he'd based himself in his St Petersburg residence, but Catherine had instructed her lawyer Dmitri to monitor Nicholas's affairs and she was aware that her son-in-law's penchant for high living and gambling had brought him to the brink of financial ruin. He'd not only been forced to put the Beletsky House in Hughesovka on the market, but also his houses in Moscow and St Petersburg, as well as his country dachas outside the cities.

She'd made an offer on the Beletsky house in Hughesovka for Alexei, but the house had been suddenly withdrawn from the market. As she'd heard that Nicholas had returned there, she presumed it was because his lawyer had found buyers for one or more of his other houses.

Marat brought in the tea trolley complete with samovar and glasses. 'You can take away the cake and sandwiches please, Marat, tell Lyudmila I'll eat them after the count has taken his leave,' she ordered. 'Then you can show Count Beletsky in. Boris, you will stay at a discreet distance, but within sight and earshot.'

The butler retired to the opposite side of the hearth.

Marat returned a few moments later. He opened the door, and announced, 'Count Beletsky, madam.'

'Thank you, Marat.'

Nicholas entered.

'Excuse me for not rising, Nicholas. I am tired after helping Father Grigor dispense charity to the poor.'

'I trust you aren't carrying any contagious diseases as a result of your philanthropic whims, Catherine.'

'I hope so too, for both our sakes. You are aware that Alexei married Ruth last month?'

'What Alexei does or doesn't do is of no interest to me, Catherine. When he chose a path that directly contravened all my wishes, I lost all interest in the boy. Nothing has occurred for me to change my view. I did however hear that he'd married a Jewess. Frankly, Catherine, I'm surprised you allowed it.'

'If you've come to berate me for allowing Alexei's marriage...'

'I have not come here to see you, Catherine.'

'Then you wish to see Kira. She will soon celebrate her second birthday. She is a delightful child...'

'Babies have never interested me,' he cut in ruthlessly.

'Even your own. All those babies you forced my daughter to bear for you.'

'Not that again, Catherine. Why do you refuse to understand that it is a wife's duty to bear as many children for her husband as God chooses to send.'

'Thirteen live births, two stillbirths, and two miscarriages in eighteen years are more than any woman can bear. Little wonder Olga had no strength left to fight the cholera that took her.'

'I am not here to listen to your unfounded complaints about my behaviour towards Olga, Catherine. I wish to see Sonya.'

'What possible business could you have with Sonya?' Catherine demanded.

'Private business that is no concern of yours.'

'As I am Sonya's legal guardian, Sonya's business is my business. Boris, tell Marat to go to Mr Dmitri's room and study. If my lawyer is in the house ask him to be kind enough to join us here.'

'Yes, madam.'

'There is no need for you to send for Dmitri ...' Nicholas stopped talking when the noise of the front door closing echoed into the room. The sound of conversation drifted in from the hall. The door opened and Roman, Sonya, and Maria walked in.

'Roman, Sonya, I trust you had a good day at the office of the New Russia Company?'

'Yes, thank you, Aunt Catherine,' Sonya replied.

Catherine continued before Roman had the opportunity to answer her. 'Sonya, Roman, as you see we have a visitor.' Catherine indicated Nicholas who was standing to the right of the door, as she hadn't invited him to sit down.

Sonya had always been wary of the count, although she couldn't have provided a reason for her distrust. She curtsied. 'Count Beletsky.'

'Prince Roman Nadolny, this is my son-in-law.'

'Count Beletsky and I have met at the card tables in St Petersburg.' Roman didn't extend his hand. Neither did Nicholas.

'As I just informed your aunt, I would like a private interview with you, Sonya, to discuss family business. Perhaps we can retire to the drawing room.'

'I can't imagine any business you could have with me, Count Beletsky, that cannot be discussed in front of Aunt Catherine.'

Nicholas looked from Sonya to Catherine, to Roman, and finally, Boris. There was a knock at the door. Catherine called out, 'Enter.'

Mr Dmitri walked in and Maria took the opportunity to move unobtrusively behind Boris.

'Marat said you wanted to see me, Mrs Ignatova.'

'Thank you for coming so quickly, Dmitri. As you see, my son-in-law is paying a visit. Apparently, he has urgent private business to discuss with my niece. We are waiting for him to explain the nature of his "business".'

'Very well, Catherine, as you insist on conducting private matters in public. I am here to invite Sonya to become the next Countess Beletsky.'

Sonya sank down on the nearest chair. The room spun headily around here. 'You're asking me ...' Unable to get the words out she simply stared at Nicholas.

'I am doing you the honour of asking you to become my wife,' Nicholas elaborated. 'I realise my proposal must be overwhelming as well as surprising, but to reassure you, I am fully aware of the disparity between our respective ranks. However, I am prepared to overlook your illegitimacy and antecedents, the fact that your father was a drunkard and your mother a whore –'

'Enough, Nicholas!' Catherine snapped sharply. 'Leave my house now. Boris, call two footmen to escort the count to the door.'

'Not until I receive my answer. Your niece will never receive a better offer.' Nicholas stepped in front of Sonya. 'I am waiting for your reply.'

Sonya found her voice. 'You were married to my cousin, a cousin I regarded as an older sister. I thought of you as a relative.'

'Precisely. I watched you grow up. You are almost family, but not family enough to prevent us from marrying. You are familiar with my house...'

'The house that belonged to my husband's family and was part of Olga's dowry,' Catherine interceded.

Nicholas ignored Catherine and continued as though she hadn't spoken. 'You know how I like my domestic life organised. This is a perfect match for both of us.'

'Apart from the twenty-five-year age gap between you,' Catherine snapped.

'That would be to Sonya's advantage. Every young girl needs an experienced older man to protect and guide her.'

'And this sudden and unexpected proposal has nothing whatsoever to do with the fortune Sonya has inherited?' Catherine didn't attempt to conceal her contempt.

'A man of my status can hardly marry a penniless nobody.'

Sonya looked from Nicholas to Catherine. She knew they were speaking but she failed to absorb or comprehend a single word they were saying. She watched Nicholas's colour rise, saw Catherine grow pale.

Nicholas drew close to her. He set his hand on her shoulders. She felt the warmth of his fingers burn through the woollen cloth of her jacket. She reached up and removed it.

She looked at Roman and saw that he was watching her. 'Prince Roman?'

'Miss Tsetovna?'

'Thank you for your proposal of marriage, and thank you for giving me the time to consider your offer. You honour me. I would like to accept and I would like our marriage to take place as soon as possible.'

Silence, heavy and oppressive, fell over the room.

Nicholas was the first to break it. 'Now I understand. You have the same taste for low life as your father, Nadolny. He consorted with whores so you want to marry the daughter of a whore.'

Boris opened the door to the footmen. Both were larger and heavier than Nicholas.

'Do not allow Count Beletsky into this house again, Boris.' Catherine rose from her chair and went to the window. She watched the footmen bundle Nicholas out of the front door and into his carriage. She didn't avert her eyes until she saw it drive through her gates.

'Aunt Catherine?'

She turned to see Sonya standing pale and trembling next to Roman.

'Those things the count said about my father and mother. That my father was a drunkard and my mother a whore –'

'Gossip and lies, Sonya,' Catherine cut in. 'Pay no attention. My brother drank because of his illness and your mother was labelled a whore by some in society simply because she left a husband who beat her for a man who loved her. Any woman with sense would have done the same.' She gripped both of Sonya's hands in her own and looked into her eyes. 'That is the absolute truth. You believe me?'

'Yes, Aunt Catherine.'

'I'll see you at dinner. Roman, engaged or not, you cannot remain in the same room as Sonya unless she is chaperoned. If Maria leaves, call one of the maids to sit with you.'

'I will, Catherine.'

'We will speak further at dinner. For the moment, I need to sit alone and think.'

'Please, Catherine, don't waste any of your thoughts on Nicholas Beletsky,' Roman advised. 'The man simply isn't worth it.'

'He isn't, Roman,' Catherine went to the door, 'but that won't prevent me from dreaming up tortures I'd like to subject him to.'

Chapter Fifteen

Glyn Edwards's house December 1871

'There is just so much to be done in the Two Firs Colliery, I simply don't know where to start, Glyn.' Edward took the brandy Glyn had poured for him. 'We need to strengthen the shoring on all the shafts before we can think of installing the steam engines, and that's going to take weeks if not months in this cold weather. I'm not even sure if it's worth it with all the other work we have going on in our other pits at the moment...'

'Forget the pits for tonight, Edward, it's Christmas, and for once we don't have to get up before dawn,' Glyn poured out three brandies and handed his brother one. 'What you need is a men's night out. You're welcome to join us, Richard,' he offered when Richard set aside his dessert bowl and reached for his coffee cup.

'Thank you for the invitation, but no, Mr Edwards, and if you don't mind I'll leave the brandy until after I've finished this coffee. Alexei and I spent the whole day crawling around the Four Bears pit. It was uncomfortably close down there and I haven't stopped shivering since I hit the surface. Not even the steam in the Banya could warm me up. All I want to do now is sit in the upstairs living room with my wife, in front of, if not on top of, the stove.'

'Are you and Alexei buying the Four Bears?' Glyn asked.

'We're thinking of it but we won't make a final decision until we've spoken to the geologist in the New Year. There's certainly some good seams of coal down there but not all appear to be easily accessible, and just like the Two Firs, the Four Bears needs a lot of work to make it viable.' Richard yawned.

He'd arrived home late after a long day, lingered in the bath house in an effort to get warm, and hadn't started his meal until after everyone else had finished.

'How are your brothers getting on in the metallurgy laboratory?' Glyn picked up his glass.

'Reasonably well, I think. They don't say much but I talked to their tutor and he seems to be fairly pleased with them.'

'They'll receive excellent training there. The Frenchman Mr Hughes has put in charge of the place knows what he's doing. If Owen and Morgan stay the course that Mr Hughes has arranged, they'll both walk into well-paid jobs at the end of it. Metallurgists can expect better working conditions than colliers, not least a lifetime of mostly working indoors in clean conditions above ground.'

'So I constantly remind them. Have a good evening, sirs.' Richard said when Glyn and Edward finished their drinks and left their chairs.

'Sure you won't change your mind?' Glyn checked.

Richard shook his head. 'I'm enjoying getting to know my brothers again, and Anna has a rare night off. So I have a lot waiting for me upstairs.'

'You weren't joking about your ready-made family,' Glyn smiled.

Pyotr brought Glyn and Edward's coats and hats to the door of the dining room without prompting.

'I finally managed to find the time to look in on Mr and Mrs Parry's sitting room earlier, Pyotr. Mrs Parry and Praskovia did a good job of arranging the furniture. It looks comfortable, and from what I heard they couldn't have managed without your muscle. You not only moved the sofas and tables into the room, you polished up the scarred floorboards so well you'd never think they'd been damaged. Thank you,' Glyn said when Praskovia's brother handed him his furs.

'I'm strong, Mr Glyn.' Pyotr unashamedly basked in the praise.

'You are, and Praskovia, and I, and everyone in this house couldn't manage without you.'

Edward started shivering even before Pyotr closed the door on them. He turned up the collar on his woollen overcoat. 'What is wrong with Pyotr?' he asked Glyn.

'Sarah and Peter thought he might have been brain-damaged at birth. He's a willing worker and invaluable around the house. He does all the heavy lifting and cleaning.'

'He's certainly willing. He cleans my boots every night although I've never asked him to.'

'Praskovia may have prompted him. She insists her brother's happiest when he's busy.' Glyn turned out of his gate and led the way.

Edward flexed his hands inside his gloves in an effort to keep his circulation going. 'I never thought the day would come when I'd envy a man his coat, especially a fur, but I could rip that one from your back, Glyn.'

'I'll write to the furrier in St Petersburg again and tell him to hurry up with that coat and hat I ordered for you. I hoped it would be here in time for Christmas, but he warned me that he had a run on orders. You're going to need it soon as the cold weather's almost here...'

'It gets colder?' Edward interrupted. 'How can it when the snow drifts beside the roads tower above us?'

'January and February will be worse than this.'

'You trying to persuade me to run back to Wales?'

'On the contrary.'

'I think the coldest bit of me is my head.'

'That's because you're bald under your trilby. If you had hair you wouldn't lose so much heat.'

'The day will come when you lose your hair too,' Edward warned.

'Not yet,' Glyn crowed.

'I've asked but you've never told me, how much will this coat and hat of mine cost?'

'To you, nothing. They're my Christmas present to you.'

'I'm not short of money,' Edward protested.

'I know you're not, but I can give my big brother a Christmas present if I want to, can't I? Call it a thank you for me dumping the day-to-day management of the Edwards Brothers collieries on to you. You are managing them – apart from the Two Firs, aren't you?'

'And if I said I wasn't?'

'I'd look around for someone to help you, but I know that I wouldn't have much choice or luck. Mr Hughes has conscripted as many workers as he can lay his hands on to help in the ironworks until we go into full production. Even before I went to St Petersburg I more or less handed over the running of the collieries I'd taken leases on to Richard, Alf, and Alexei, but now with Alexei and Richard in the throes of setting up their own collieries I realise you must be even more stretched.'

'I spoke to Alexei yesterday in the office about leasing more of his grandmother's land so we can build rail heads and storage yards at the Edwards Brothers collieries. Hopefully the track John Hughes is proposing to lay will reach that far.'

'What did Alexei say?'

'That his grandmother has no other plans for that land and he'd talk to her about offering us the same terms for a new lease that she extends to Mr Hughes.'

'I don't think Mr Hughes could have made the progress he has, without Catherine Ignatova's help. I'm glad she and Alexei are extending their largesse to the Edwards Brothers collieries. Roughly fifty per cent of the New Russia Company leases have been negotiated with Catherine. The largest slice of the other fifty per cent are with absent landowners, leaving a small percentage with the Cossacks, and as you've discovered, they mined their holdings with horse drawn winches. We – that is the Edwards Brothers collieries –'

'You did say that you've legalised the formation of the company?' Edward interrupted.

'I have and I talked to Sarah earlier this evening about redistributing the shares now you're here. Initially Peter and I planned to split the company. He'd take forty per cent, as would I, and we intended to give the remaining twenty per cent of the shares to some of our senior workers.'

'Anyone in particular?'

'We discussed giving five per cent to Alf and ten to Richard and keeping the other five in reserve for future employees we felt deserved a stake.'

'Alf I can understand, but Richard? I can't help thinking he's still a boy.'

'No longer, Edward. When we had a seam collapse in a pit we bought from the Cossacks, Richard went down, studied the situation, formulated a plan, implemented it, and hauled men out with no thought to his own safety. His cool head saved dozens of lives that day. He knows all there is to know about both deep seam and open cast mining, which is why Alexei offered him a partnership in Beletsky Collieries. Richard and Alexei are the perfect team. Alexei has the land, Richard the knowledge, and with Catherine investing in their company it's bound to be successful.'

'As successful as Edwards Brothers will be?'

'Not that successful,' Glyn joked. 'But we were talking about Richard. You trained him, Edward, you know what he's capable of.'

'I always knew he had promise. Given the right education he could have made a great engineer.'

'He is a great engineer,' Glyn stated emphatically.

'So who owns Edwards Brothers Collieries now?'

'At the moment, Sarah and I do, but when I received your letter telling me that you were on your way here, I raised the possibly of quartering the company shares with Sarah.

'As she and Peter put all their savings into the venture I suggested she take one quarter, me another, and you the third on condition you work off the amount it would have cost you to buy the shares. When we discussed it again before dinner, she was in full agreement.'

'I know what Peter invested and I can afford to pay the same upfront from my savings.'

'That's good to know. We could do with another two steam engines for the pits.'

'That's three-quarters of the shares accounted for. What about the last quarter?' Edward questioned.

'Give ten per cent to Richard and five to Alf, as I suggested earlier, and leave the final ten per cent in our hands for the present, but eventually distribute it among the senior managers. We'll need at least one for each colliery. Pay them well, give them bonuses, and they'll do all they can for the company.'

'And the Russian, Alexei?'

'As he and Richard are setting up their own coal mining venture I can't see him working for us in the future. We did discuss the possibility of merging the colliery companies a few months back but it's early days and we have to look to the quality and availability of trained men. I believe it won't be long before we're fighting over them.'

'Will Mr Hughes need coal from both companies?' Edward asked cautiously.

'And more. Smelting iron eats as much coal as sheep do grass. As I said, amalgamating the companies is something we can think about in the future, but for the moment I'd rather keep Alexei and Richard's enterprises separate from ours.'

'Is that a pub?' Edward watched the door open on a large wooden warehouse that sported a single window in the front.

Half a dozen men, brawling, shouting, and swearing in a mix of incomprehensible languages sprinkled with a few curses in English and Welsh that Edward did understand, spilled out. A man stepped behind them wielding a broom. From the way he was gesturing, Edward had the impression that he'd literally swept them out of the building.

'It's a beer shop, and too rough for most of the Welsh workers. There's another further down the street on the opposite side that's slightly more refined which caters for the Welsh.'

'I never thought I'd see the day when the Welsh patronised a refined cstablishment.'

'Well, "slightly less rough" is a better description than refined. We, however, are going in here.'

'The hotel?' Edward's spirits rose. The bar was warm and he'd enjoyed quite a few drinks there in the company of Ezra, Alf, Richard, and Alexei. Glyn had determinedly refused to enter the place until Betty moved out of the suite, which he was still paying for despite his threat to stop after nine days. The letters he sent Betty on a weekly basis, asking her to find somewhere else to live, or at least somewhere cheaper, hadn't elicited any response – or if they had, none Glyn had cared to share with Edward.

'No.' Glyn walked past the hotel turned left, opened a gate and headed down the garden path of a fine, brick built house set back from the road.

'Another hotel?'

'The Russians and French would call it a salon, the British a brothel. The people in Merthyr a knocking shop.'

'The last place I want to visit is a knocking shop.'

'Don't look as though you've never heard of one,' Glyn scoffed. 'This salon is run particularly well by a friend of mine. Madam Koshka.'

'Peculiar name,' Edward observed.

'Koshka is Russian for cat. You'll like her and her girls.'

'I'd say the last place you need to visit, with a wife in town and a mistress in your house, is a knocking shop. As for me, I've never been in one yet and have no intention of entering such an establishment.'

'Try broadening your experience of life.'

'Into vice?'

'Leave your chapel ethics and upbringing behind you for the rest of the evening.' Glyn walked into the porch and lifted the iron door-knocker which was cast in the shape of a cat's head. 'I told you, this is a salon. Koshka has elegant, comfortable rooms where men of means and intellect can sit and discuss business or the politics of the day, whichever they chose, while sampling drinks from her well-stocked bar. She also has an excellent cook and serves delicious canapés. It's the only civilised place in town outside of home and the somewhat noisy hotel which my wife has taken root in.'

The door opened and Koshka's German manservant, Fritz, bowed. 'Welcome, Mr Edwards. A very good evening to you'

'And to you, Fritz. This is my brother, Mr Edward Edwards.'

'Welcome to you too, Mr Edwards. We heard you were in town and have been looking forward to making your acquaintance. You'll find madam in the main salon.'

Glyn entered and handed his coat to an attractive young girl who hung it on a rail. He winked at her and noted Edward's disapproving frown. 'No one's asking you to sample the wares, Edward. Give the girl your hat and coat and come and meet some people.' He listened for a moment. 'That is Mr Hughes's laugh?'

'It is, sir,' Fritz confirmed. 'He came in an hour ago with Mr Dmitri and Prince Roman Nadolny.'

'Respectable enough for you, Edward?' Glyn queried.

Edward handed over his hat and coat and followed Glyn up the stairs.

Chapter Sixteen

Beletsky Mansion December 1871

The meal was the same as the one that had been served to the servants the day before and the day before that. A bleak, unappetising mess of cabbage soup and black bread followed by barely cooked, bluish-white sausage skins stuffed with lumps of fat, swimming in a bath of grease. The dish reminded Ianto Paskey of dead fish floating in a polluted river.

He wondered if the servants were ever fed anything else in the Beletsky mansion. The supper was all the more unpalatable for being eaten in the same kitchen that the "master's" dinner had been prepared. The atmosphere was redolent with the appetising aromas of roasting beef, onions, apple pies, gravy, and spices. All of which tantalized taste buds doomed to disappointment. As experience had taught him that the soup was marginally less foul than the sausage, Ianto reluctantly dipped his spoon into his bowl. It tasted worse than he remembered.

'Pass me the salt,' he growled at his brother.

Mervyn picked up the dish and slid along the bench until he was close enough to whisper in Ianto's ear. 'You heard? Mr Levsky, the count, and most of the guests are going to visit Koshka's brothel tonight.'

'So what?' Ianto questioned. 'From what I've heard it's a stuck-up knocking shop that wouldn't allow the likes of us through the door. Even if we had money enough to pay the asking price.'

'Why should we pay, when we can get what it's offering for free? There are plenty of women in Hughesovka. Just like Merthyr, they'll be walking around begging for what we can give them.'

'For what you can give them, you mean,' Ianto snarled. 'You might have forgotten what those bitches did to me after we had our fun with Anna Parry, but I can't. And they would have done the same to you if the coppers hadn't turned up when they did.'

Mervyn shuddered when he remembered the women closing in on him wielding the bloodied tools they'd used on Ianto. A minute more and he'd have been mutilated just like his brother. 'I haven't forgotten, but I saw you take that red-headed whore into the livery stable the night we were released from gaol back in Merthyr. From the noise I heard you both make you seemed to have enjoyed her well enough.'

'I would have enjoyed her a lot more if those bloody bitches hadn't gelded me.'

'Anna Parry's in Hughesovka, isn't she?' Mervyn dug Ianto in the ribs.

'Last I heard. So what?' Ianto kept his voice low. Too many of the other servants understood English for his liking.

'So we'll find her,' Mervyn grinned. 'Just like we did in Merthyr. And when we do you can take your revenge just how you want.'

'Have some sense. From what I've heard the place has a lot of houses. It's big and getting bigger every day,' Ianto snapped. 'We'll never find her even if we look for her. And I don't want to.'

'Hughesovka can't be as big as Merthyr – not yet. And we know Anna Parry's there.'

'All we know is that she went there with the Edwardses and that bastard brother of hers.' Ianto didn't want to think about, much less talk about, Anna Parry and the problems she'd caused him and Mervyn that had resulted in him being castrated and both of them being held in a cell until the judge had dismissed the case against them.

'There are bound to be some people around. We'll ask them where the Parrys are living. It can't be a common name in Russia. All we have to say is "Parry".'

Ianto thought about what his brother had said. 'If that didn't work we could try "Edwards", chances are they might be sharing rooms.'

'Anna Parry and her bastard brother are two people I really would like to pay back. If we can find them. Gleb says this knocking shop is right in the middle of Hughesovka.'

'In which case the Parrys shouldn't be too far away.' Ianto elbowed the man sitting next to him. 'Hughesovka?' He pointed to himself and Mervyn. 'Tonight?'

'It's no good shouting in the man's ear, Ianto – it is Ianto, isn't it?'

'What's it to you?' Ianto narrowed his eyes and glared at Gleb.

'He doesn't speak English, but I do. If you want to go into Hughesovka tonight both of you can ride as pillion footmen on the back of Mr Levsky's coach. My master always travels with two pillions, he thinks it makes him appear important, but he never looks at their faces. He won't be able to see yours if you pull your hats down. But I warn you, we could be kept waiting around in the cold for hours. My master likes to take his time when he visits the ladies.'

'How much will the footmen pay us to take their place?' Ianto asked.

Gleb spoke rapidly in Russian to the table in general. Everyone burst out laughing. He held out his hand to Ianto. 'You pay us twenty kopeks each.'

'To work as pillions? While the men whose places we take sit around on their backsides doing nothing?' Ianto glared at Gleb.

Mervyn put his hand into Ianto's pocket, filched out some coins, sorted through them, and handed Gleb forty kopeks.

'That's my money!' Ianto thumped Mervyn's shoulder. He'd "won" it from the footmen by cheating at cards.

'Just think of paying that bitch back – after she entertains us again.'

'And her brother?'

'If we find him, he's all yours.' Mervyn grinned, displaying twin lines of broken, blackened teeth.

Madam Koshka's salon December 1871

John Hughes shook Edward's hand. 'It's good to have you in Hughesovka, Edward. I've heard a lot about you, not only from your brother but the men here who used to work for you in Merthyr. I'm only sorry we haven't met sooner, but now that the test firing has been successful I'm hoping to have enough time to spend the odd few hours outside of the company offices.'

'I've noticed that every man in this town seems to have been working at twice normal speed, sir,' Edward commented.

'Necessary if we're to get this industrial complex churning out the rails and munitions the Tsar so desperately needs next year. I was ready to give you a manager's post in one of my pits, but your brother snatched you first. Can't say I blame him after hearing about the progress you've made with the Edwards Brothers collieries.'

'Progress?' Edward repeated. 'We've made some but it's slow going, sir.'

'Maybe slow going in Merthyr terms but not Hughesovka's. The snow is making it difficult for everyone.'

'Not underground, sir, the snow doesn't reach as far as what passes for a Russian shaft.'

'Good point, but from what I've heard and seen, all the underground workings need re-shoring and rebuilding,' John concurred.

'There are times when I think it would be easier to sink new pits from scratch.'

'You may well find yourself doing just that soon, Edward. Now the test firing's gone well we'll be in full production in a couple of weeks, and once we start smelting in earnest the New Russia Company will need a great deal more coal than we have stored at present or can produce in the company's pits. Your contribution will prove invaluable, not to mention cut our import bill.'

'Glyn said you'll be able to use all the good quality anthracite your pits and ours can dig out of the ground.'

'And more. I've built up a stockpile and hidden it well, but it won't last more than a month or two once we go into full operation. You'll soon see for yourself how much coal we'll be needing.'

'Considering the difficulties you've met in this inhospitable country you've achieved miracles, sir,' Edward complimented.

'Miracles wrought by hard workers like your brother, Edward. I'll see you tomorrow evening at Mrs Ignatova's?'

'I've received an invitation, so barring accidents you will, sir.'

'Thank you for joining us, Edward. I know the journey here isn't a pleasant one, but I hope you'll think it was worthwhile once you've settled in. Please excuse Mr Dmitri and I, we have to rise early to finalise contracts with a landowner.'

'Count Beletsky,' Glyn guessed.

'He's withdrawn his unsubstantiated claim to the parcel of land Mrs Ignatova leased to us before her daughter's death. The count argued that the ground between his estate and Mrs Ignatova's was part of Olga's dowry and passed to him as Olga left no will. Fortunately Mrs Ignatova had a detailed account of what was included in her daughter's dowry and what wasn't. She's proved beyond all legal doubt that the land is hers and Mr Dmitri has drawn up papers to that effect. The count has agreed to sign them in the morning.'

'I'm glad you set him straight, sir.' Glyn despised the count for abandoning his family and retreating to the hotel in Hughesovka when cholera struck the Beletsky mansion. His brother Peter had died of the disease while trying to help the count's wife and daughters. The count had never thanked Sarah for nursing Olga, or acknowledged the debt he owed Peter for tirelessly working to save the Beletsky family even when he was dying.

'The count's claim was preposterous,' Dmitri declared, 'but from what I've heard he's using every delaying tactic to stave off his creditors. Including filing bogus claims to property that was never his.'

'I thought he'd left the area,' Glyn eyed John Hughes in the hope of gleaning more information.

'He returned to the Beletsky Mansion just before the fire,' John divulged.

'Any connection between the two events?' Glyn wondered.

'None anyone can prove. The count travelled with Mr Levsky, who's stayed on as Beletsky's guest,' John revealed.

'Levsky the industrialist?' Glyn checked.

'They and their associates are walking through the door right now,' John nodded surreptitiously to the entrance where eight men were being greeted by one of Koshka's "hostesses".

'It's rumoured Levsky's bought up all of Beletsky's debts,' Dmitri elaborated, 'but I can cast no further light on their relationship, business or otherwise.'

Glyn knew that John Hughes was as wary of Levsky as he was. Roman had warned that Levsky could be spying on the New Russia Company, as he owned small factories and coalmines on his estates that were in even worse condition than the ones the New Russia Company had taken over in the Donbas. Levsky had also solicited government ministers for munitions and rail contracts before the Tsar had approached John Hughes.

When Tsar Alexander II had awarded the contracts to the New Russia Company, Levsky had lobbied and bribed everyone he knew with any influence at court in an attempt to countermand the Tsar's decision. But Levsky's reputation for paying his workers below subsistence wages and setting such impossibly high targets – some men had literally driven themselves to sickness, even death, while attempting to meet his demands – had only served to sway the Tsar's decision in John Hughes's favour.

'They aren't wasting any time,' Dmitri observed as Levsky, Komansky and Beletsky headed for the door that led to the corridor housing the private rooms. He saw Fritz watching them, and as soon as they left, the manservant knocked the door to Koshka's office.

'We'll talk tomorrow, Glyn, nine o'clock in the office. I've called a meeting of senior management and the management of all our coal suppliers. Please remind Richard and Alexei to attend. Enjoy the rest of your evening, gentlemen, it was good to meet you, Edward.' John signalled to one of the footmen to summon his carriage.

'It was good to meet you too, sir,' Edward stood back to allow Dmitri to pass.

Glyn accompanied Mr Hughes and Dmitri to the door while Edward remained at their table. Koshka's salon was more luxurious and exotic than anything he'd seen in Wales. Even the "best" bar of the Black Lion in St Mary Street in Cardiff would have looked primitive in comparison to Madam Koshka's. It resembled the photographic illustrations he'd seen of the interiors of aristocratic mansions and palaces.

The men sitting at the tables around him were better dressed than any of his superiors had been in Wales, even in the Coal Exchange in Cardiff. The score or so "girls" in the room were eye-catching.

He guessed their ages at between fifteen and thirty. Every one of them strikingly attractive and beautifully dressed in gleaming, shimmering gowns that showed more of their charms than he'd seen music hall actresses display on stage. The atmosphere was intoxicating, a heady mix of musk-laden scents, the babble of alien tongues, and a positive feast of female flesh to titivate the senses.

Glyn returned to the table. Koshka, accompanied by Fritz, joined them 'So this is your brother, Glyn. I'm very pleased to meet you, Mr Edwards.'

Edward rose and shook Koshka's hand. She wasn't young but she was elegant, richly and, compared to her girls, conservatively dressed in grey silk that shimmered in the lamplight. Her bodice was low-cut and displayed her full, rounded breasts to advantage. Her blonde hair was beautifully dressed, her perfume sensual. He found himself moving closer to her just so he could savour it.

'Have you everything you need, Mr Edwards?' Her voice was melodious, seductive.

Glyn answered for him. 'Your girls are looking after us extremely well, Koshka, as they always do. As you see, my brother is overwhelmed. He didn't expect to find such sophistication in Hughesovka.'

'We are doing our best to bring civilisation to the steppe.' She beckoned to a grey-eyed blonde, older than most of her "girls". 'This is my very good friend Xenia, Mr Edwards.'

'Pleased to meet you,' Edward extended his hand.

Xenia took it. Close up, Edward realised she could have been any age between a careworn thirty and a well-preserved forty-five. She took Edward's hand and kissed his cheek without relinquishing her hold on it.

'You must tell me what you think of our Hughesovka, Mr Edwards.'

Koshka signalled to a girl who was acting as hostess. 'Two glasses of champagne for Xenia and Mr Edwards.'

'Yes, madam.'

The champagne appeared on Edward's table. Xenia sat and patted the chair next to her.

'You must tell me about your journey here, Mr Edwards.'

'It was very boring.' He remained standing as Koshka did. 'Are you Russian?'

'I am from Vienna and the longest journey I've ever made was from my home city to Moscow, and from there to here. I am fascinated by the world and would like to see more of it.'

'You should visit Wales. It's a beautiful country. A hilly country, not a bit like here, this place is as flat as a Welsh cake ...' Edward began talking and once he did he couldn't stop.

Xenia sat forward, apparently enthralled by his every word.

Koshka drew Glyn back from Edward's table. When Edward saw Glyn retreat he finally sat next to Xenia.

'Your brother will be safe with Xenia, she is very kind and attentive,' Koshka assured Glyn.

'So I see.' Glyn looked sideways at her. 'You are a born engineer, madam. The social kind that can match people to perfection.'

'Your brother appears lonely. He left his family behind in England?'

'In Wales,' Glyn corrected her. 'No, he left no one behind. His wife died a few months ago.'

'Children?' Koshka enquired.

'None.'

Koshka nodded sagely. 'I was right, Xenia is definitely the woman for him.'

'Unlike me he's very religious – and moral. But I have no doubt he will appreciate her conversation.'

Koshka smiled enigmatically.

Edward left his chair and tapped Glyn on the shoulder.

'Xenia has a private room with a fire which is warmer than here. You know how cold I've been since I arrived. She's invited me to have a drink with her.'

163

Glyn struggled to keep his equanimity. 'Be careful when you walk home.'

'Fritz will send one of my porters with your brother to ensure that he arrives safely at your door, Glyn,' Koshka interceded.

'No matter what the time, just ring the bell and Pyotr will let you in,' Glyn advised.

Edward nodded before following Xenia out of the door and into the corridor that led to the girls' private rooms.

Koshka's smile broadened. 'As I said, Xenia is the woman for your brother. Would you like me to find someone for you, Glyn?'

'Not with Praskovia waiting for me in a warm bed at home.'

'She must be some woman, your housekeeper, for you to neglect my girls.'

'She is.'

'And your wife?'

'You've heard she's arrived?'

'It's the talk of Hughesovka. The Mrs Edwards whom Mr Edwards has paid to stay in the hotel so she doesn't disturb his happy domestic life with his housekeeper, and has only visited once, and that was on the day of her arrival.'

'I'm hoping my wife will leave Hughesovka soon.'

'And if she doesn't?'

'I'll try to persuade Mr Hughes to move the town,' he joked.

He kissed her cheek. 'That's for looking after my brother.'

'Don't expect to see him before morning, Glyn. Xenia can be very beguiling.'

Chapter Seventeen

Hospital, Hughesovka December 1871

Nathan sat back in his chair and read the clock on his office wall. He had no excuse to linger. He suspected that everyone who worked in the hospital with him had noticed that he was staying later and later in the evening in preference to rushing home when he'd finished work for the day. Hardly the behaviour of a man who'd only been married a few months, and all the more noticeable when he saw Richard charge home for his evening meal, or Alexei ride up to his small wooden house shouting for Lev to take his horse before he even reached the gate.

It wasn't that his home was uncomfortable. Jewish girls were taught the art of homemaking and cooking from birth. Thrift was instilled in each and every one of them and they all knew how to stretch a kopek to do the work of a rouble. Not that he was short of money or kept Vasya on a tight budget. Given his well-paid position as the New Russia Company doctor, he gave his wife a weekly allowance most Jewish wives in Hughesovka could only aspire to in their imaginations. He didn't doubt that Vasya saved half, if not more of it. Their home was cosy but hardly extravagant. Vasya had furnished it with hand-me-downs from her family, solid pieces she'd covered with embroidered cloths to conceal the worst scars of age and use. She spent her days cleaning, washing, and preparing meals that were appetising, well- planned and presented – and eaten in silence.

That silence was the problem. It was as though she was afraid of him. Without raising the subject he knew she was aware that he'd been coerced into marrying her.

She'd seen him and Sonya together when Sonya had still worked in the hospital, and although he'd done his best to conceal his feelings he wondered if Vasya had guessed his secret. And worse – if Vasya knew that every minute he spent with her he pictured what his life would have been if he'd been allowed to follow his heart and make Sonya his bride.

He left his chair and exchanged his doctor's coat for the plain black coat he'd hung on the back of the door. Vasya had warned him that morning that the entire Goldberg family, including her uncle the rabbi, were coming to dinner. He hoped it would turn out to be a social occasion. The Goldbergs had only dined with him and Vasya once since their marriage. After the meal the rabbi had taken him outside – ostensibly to advise him on the area he'd dug over in the hope of turning it into a vegetable plot – only to berate him for his lack of religion and absence from a Goldberg family meal on the Sabbath.

He'd explained that a doctor's life could not be timetabled, even to meet religious demands, and that at the time of the meal he'd been busy fighting an epidemic of typhus that had broken out in the "hole houses", but Rabbi Goldberg had refused to listen. To him the Sabbath was the Sabbath, its laws sacrosanct and to be adhered to no matter what the emergency – medical or otherwise. On that occasion he'd managed to bite his tongue, but he was doubtful he'd be capable of remaining silent a second time.

He left his office and, mindful of the patients' files and drugs inside, locked the door. Since the night the fire had decimated the shtetl, the number of porters on duty had been increased to three at night and two in the day. One of them was sitting in the cubicle off the entrance hall that the porters had claimed as their territory. The door was open, his rifle propped in the crook of his elbow.

'Good evening, Doctor.'

'Good evening, Egor. Everything quiet?'

'As the grave. I've just spoken to Kolya and Bogdan. There are no shadows flitting around the town tonight – as yet.'

'It's reassuring to know that you are all here to protect the nurses.' Nathan heard a noise in the kitchen. He glanced in and saw the trainee nurse, Naomi, washing dishes.

'I thought your shift finished half an hour ago, Nurse Rinskaya.'

'It did, Dr Kharber, but we've eaten the cakes Yelena sent over.'

'So you thought you'd wash and return the dish in the hope she'd send over more tomorrow.'

'You know your nurses so well, Dr Kharber.'

'Good evening, Nurse Rinskaya.'

'Good evening, sir.'

Nathan left the kitchen and pushed open the door to the men's ward. Anna was sitting at the Nightingale desk in the centre. The only light emanated from the oil lamp she'd placed close to the midwifery text-book she was studying. He smiled when he looked over her shoulder.

'Studying in the hope of delivering Sarah and Praskovia's babies?'

She turned to him, her blue eyes shining. 'I'd like to help.'

'I'll have a word with both of them and try to arrange their babies' arrival when you're on duty.'

He rarely joked and she returned his smile in the hope of encouraging him. 'Thank you, Dr Kharber. Have a good evening.'

'You too, a quiet one so you can study.' He left her and went into the women's ward. Miriam was also sitting at the desk in the middle of the ward but she was reading a dog-eared fashion magazine that he suspected had been passed around the women of the shtetl at least twice.

He wasn't surprised by the discrepancy in the nurses' reading material. Anna was the youngest nurse in the hospital, but she was also the most dedicated. He'd seen her filching copies of The Lancet that his predecessor had ordered to be sent from London as soon as he'd finished reading them. He knew he was fortunate to have her working alongside him as a nurse, but he also felt that given the right opportunity she'd make an even better doctor.

He waved to Miriam who'd seen him standing at the door then, finally having run out of excuses to linger, he left the building and walked around to his house behind the hospital.

Madam Koshka's salon December 1871

'It's good to see you, my prince.' Adele closed the door of her room behind him.

'As always, good to see you, Adele.' Roman shrugged off his jacket and dropped it on a chair.

'Bed?' She raised her eyebrows.

'Chaise longue. It's not as comfortable, so there's less risk of me falling asleep. I have an early meeting in the morning.' He flicked the button at the back of her dress and watched her dress slide to the floor. 'I love doing that, it's just like pulling the dust drapes from a marble statue.'

'You remove dust drapes from statues?'

'As a child, it was a task the housekeepers in my father's various homes reserved for me whenever we arrived, because I liked doing it so much, but, although your skin is as pale as white marble, you look infinitely more real – and enticing.'

'Thank you, sir,' she gave a mock curtsey. 'Stockings and garters on or off?'

'Off, because you're wearing the pearl-studded ones again and they dig into my thighs.' He stripped off his waistcoat and shirt and unbuttoned his trousers.

She lay on the chaise. He took her hand and pulled her up. 'That's where I intend to be.'

'You expect me to do all the work?'

'Absolutely. I feel lazy.' He finished undressing, lay down, grabbed her hand, and pulled her towards him. She eased herself on to him and massaged his chest.

'I've heard rumours you're engaged.'

'From where?'

'Here. One of the girls overheard Mr Hughes and Mr Edwards talking about it. You're going to marry Catherine Ignatova's niece?'

'I hope to,' he confirmed.

'Congratulations.'

'Thank you.'

'You'll still visit us here from time to time?'

'Given your talent for satisfying my needs, and the salon's status as a bastion of civilization in this wilderness, I intend to.' He caressed her breasts and eased her body closer to his.

She gasped as she stared deep into his eyes.

'Not to mention your theatrical skills.'

'Why, you...'

'Beast?' He laughed before pulling her down onto him again.

When they had finished, Roman kissed Adele's shoulder, then lifted her from him and deposited her behind him on the chaise. He went to the washstand, washed, and picked up his clothes.

'You're not going already?' she complained, turning on to her stomach, watching as he pulled on his underclothes and trousers.

'I have to. I told you I have an early meeting.' He felt in his pocket and set his customary "present" on the dresser.

'But you will come again – and soon.'

'In every sense of the word, my sweet Adele.' He blew her a kiss before opening the door and leaving.

Adele lay, luxuriating in idleness for five minutes, before going to the washstand. She was buttoning her dress when she was disturbed by a knock at her door.

She called out, 'Enter,' hoping Roman had returned. Instead Fritz opened it.

'I saw your last gentleman leave. Another is asking for you.'

'Have I seen him before?'

'Not to my knowledge.' He stepped inside the room and whispered, 'He's just left Felina. Complained she was ... unsatisfactory.'

Adele saw the door move and said loudly, 'Show him in please, Fritz.'

Taras Komansky walked in.

'Sir.' She curtsied.

He laid his cane on the table and unbuttoned his jacket.

Fritz closed the door, but he didn't walk back down the corridor. In the decade he'd worked for Madam Koshka he'd developed a sixth sense when it came to trouble. Right now he could sense it hovering, just waiting to manifest itself behind the door.

Hughesovka Main Street December 1871

'It's bloody cold out here,' Mervyn grumbled as he and Ianto huddled behind Levsky's coach. The drivers who'd conveyed their masters to Koshka's in a stream of carriages had congregated around a brazier at the entrance to Koshka's coach house. They'd formed a circle, effectively consigning the footmen who'd acted as pillions to the open air, from which vantage they could watch the drivers drink vodka and eat the potatoes they'd baked in the fire.

'Is that who I think it is?' Mervyn squinted down the street as a young girl huddled in a long cape and a nurses' hat left a large brick-built house. A thickset man stood in the doorway behind her. She turned and shouted, her voice carrying in the still, snow-laden air.

'There's no need to wait to see me across the road, Pyotr. It's cold, go inside.'

'Not until you walk into the hospital, Miss Anna.'

Ianto turned to Mervyn and nodded. They left the back of the carriage and walked up the street. They saw Anna Parry go inside the hospital. Watched the front door close on the house she'd left.

'What now?' Mervyn asked.

'She left this house. It's getting late. I'm guessing she'll return soon. And when she does we'll pick up where we left off in Merthyr and make the bitch pay for what her neighbours did to me, and for running to the police and telling tales on us.'

'It was the women in the court who sent for the police,' Mervyn reminded his brother.

'Our solicitor said we wouldn't have spent an hour in a cell or gone to court if Anna Parry hadn't pressed charges.'

'You sure she's going to come back?'

'No young girl stays out all night.'

'She was dressed like a nurse.'

'Whatever she was dressed like, she's too young to be a nurse.' Ianto glanced up and down the street to check no one was looking their way before opening the gate. He dived out of sight of the street, behind the front fence. 'Come around to this side, we can't be seen and it's more sheltered here.'

'But they'll spot us from the house,' Mervyn whined.

'No they won't, the curtains are drawn.' Ianto crouched down so he couldn't be seen from the road. He brushed away the snowflakes that were falling thicker than they had done earlier in the day and handed Mervyn a flask of vodka.

'Where did you get this?'

'Gleb's pocket. Payment for the kopeks you handed over.'

'And now?'

'We watch and wait for the bitch.'

'And if we're needed for the carriage?'

'They'll have to find us.' Ianto took the flask from Mervyn and drank deeply.

'We'll freeze to death.'

'No we won't.' Ianto peeked over the fence and saw a young girl in a nurse's cape and hat leave the building opposite. 'Our entertainment for the evening is on its way.'

Nathan Kharber's house December 1871

Nathan entered his dining room to find the Goldbergs sitting around his dining table. Rabbi Goldberg had taken his place as master of the house at the head, with Vasya on his right. On the rabbi's left sat Vasya's father, Levi, who'd asked Nathan for Ruth's hand in marriage for his son Abraham before Nathan had finally conceded to Ruth's pleas and given her his permission to marry Alexei.

Nathan's brother-in-law Ruben, Ruben's wife Rebekah, and Vasya's aunt Raisa, were sitting below them, leaving Nathan the empty chair at the foot of the table.

Resenting the Goldbergs' intrusion into his life at the end of a long day, Nathan moved away from the door. Vasya rose from her chair the moment she saw him, 'Excuse me, Rabbi Goldberg, Father, I'll serve the soup.'

'Good evening, Rabbi, everyone. Excuse me, please, I need to wash.' Nathan went into the washroom which was next to the kitchen. Pretending he hadn't seen Vasya gesture to him, he poured water from the pitcher into the bowl and washed his hands and face.

'We thought you'd be home earlier than this, Nathan.' Rabbi Goldberg took his watch from his waistcoat pocket and opened it as Nathan sat on the only vacant chair.

'I operated on two people today. I like to monitor them until they have recovered from the effects of the chloroform.'

'Is there no one else in the hospital who can do that?' the rabbi asked.

'Nathan is always very busy. There are twenty-four beds in the hospital now, and Mr Hughes is talking of building another ward to make it thirty-six. A children's ward this time,' Vasya added, conscious that she was over-explaining Nathan's unpunctuality.

'Will Mr Hughes hire another doctor to help you when he opens this extra ward, Nathan?' Rabbi Goldberg asked.

'He hasn't mentioned taking on any extra staff to me.' Nathan waited until Vasya had served everyone with the goose soup and matzo balls before picking up his spoon.

'Then you must suggest it. He cannot expect you to continually put the welfare and concerns of his hospital before those of your family,' said Levi.

'Nathan doesn't do that, Papa,' Vasya protested in his defence.

'The hospital belongs to the town, not Mr Hughes, although his New Russia Company pays for it,' Nathan said pointedly. 'This soup is delicious, Vasya,' Raisa complimented.

It was painfully obvious that Vasya's aunt was trying to diffuse the mounting tension in the atmosphere by changing the subject.

'Thank you, Aunt Raisa,' Vasya murmured.

'It tastes different in some way. Spicier. Have you put in extra onions or pepper?'

'No, Aunt Raisa, I followed Grandmother Shapiro's recipe exactly.'

'Face it, Aunt Raisa, Vasya is a better cook than you,' Ruben joked, joining his aunt in attempting to lighten the atmosphere.'

'What else can we expect to eat tonight, Vasya?' Rabbi Goldberg asked.

'I made cholent...'

'It's not a holiday,' Levi protested. 'You should have bought cheaper meat than beef, and where did you buy it?' he asked suspiciously. 'You didn't shop in the shtetl today.'

'Ruslan the butcher brought us two large joints of beef yesterday as a thank you to Nathan for curing his son of whooping cough.'

'You used meat that wasn't kosher!'

'Ruslan takes his cattle to our slaughterhouse, Father. It's all kosher.' Ruben reminded.

Levi sniffed to show what he thought of his daughter taking meat from a shop outside of the shtetl.

'I also made potato knishes.'

'They would have been sufficient without the cholent,' Levi snapped.

'Don't be so hard on your daughter, Levi,' the rabbi chided. 'A bride is entitled to show off her skills to her relatives in her new home.' He sniffed the air. 'Is that apple cake I can smell?'

'Yes, and I also made Medovik honey cake and cream horns.'

'A veritable feast, Vasya, and we thank you. Now to business, as this will affect the entire family.'

'Can't it wait until we have finished eating, please, Rabbi?' Vasya begged.

'No, the sooner we put the proposition to Nathan the sooner we will know how he stands.' Rabbi Goldberg leaned back as Vasya rose from her chair and began collecting the empty soup plates.

While Vasya carried the bowls into the kitchen, the rabbi began. 'No Jewish family is complete without children.'

'Vasya and I have only been married a few months.' Nathan hoped to put an end to the conversation before it began, but neither Levi nor the rabbi was willing.

'Vasya is in delicate health,' Levi hinted.

Nathan stared at him. Raisa and Rebekah exchanged glances, tactfully rose and headed for the kitchen with a barely audible, 'We'll help Vasya.'

'Before you say another word, please remember that I am a doctor.' Nathan warned.

'Exactly. You are earning good money. You have good prospects. God gave you those gifts to share with those less fortunate. Vasya is made to be a mother. You are clever, you would make a good father who will educate and guide his children well.'

'If I had any.' Nathan struggled to reign in his temper.

Ruben saw his brother-in-law's face darken. 'Nathan's right, he and Vasya have only been married a few months...'

'You're forgetting the children,' Levi cut in.

'What children?' Nathan questioned.

'My cousin's children. I received a letter from my son Abraham, who left here to help my cousin Moshe Goldberg in Ekaterinoslav.'

Nathan had a feeling he would soon regret asking the question, but he asked it anyway. 'Why did your cousin Moshe need Abraham's help?'

'His rabbi wrote to me to inform us that Moshe was seriously ill and could no longer work or care for his family.' Levi pulled an envelope from the breast pocket of his coat as proof. 'Moshe, his wife and twin baby daughters,' Levi, Ruben and the rabbi all stared at the ceiling and broke off to chant, "May their memory be a blessing to all who knew them," 'have all died of diphtheria. At the moment Abraham is caring for their three sons and remaining daughter, but he cannot stay in Ekaterinoslav because I need him to help in my business, and when he leaves the children will be taken to the Jewish orphanage.'

'You can't seriously expect us to take in four children just after we've married!' Nathan was furious that Vasya could even allow her father and the rabbi to countenance the idea.

'You are the perfect people to do just that. They are family, but I am too old to look after children, and I no longer have a wife or daughter to run my household, only a daughter-in-law and sister who visit me when they can spare the time.

'My sister Raisa is too old to take them in. Besides, she is poor and has no experience of children. You earn much more – probably ten times more than Abraham and Ruben do, helping me in my butcher's shop. And soon, very soon, Rebekah will present Ruben with a child, so they will be too busy looking after their own children to take in my cousin Moshe's. All our houses are too small to take in four extra children. That leaves you. And look at this table! The boards are groaning with gifts of food, so many gifts, you have more than you and Vasya can eat.'

'I have family of my own,' Nathan reminded tersely.

'Since Asher and Leah have been buried, only your sister Ruth, who as we all know has married out of our faith. And by marrying Alexei Beletsky she will never have to worry about money again. These children have nowhere to go other than the orphanage and no one to care for them...'

'They have you.'

'Nathan.'

'No, you listen to me for once...' Nathan was interrupted by a knock at the door. He rose to answer it but he was still determined to tell Levi what he thought of his proposal. 'I work long hours in the hospital...'

'No one disputes that...'

'I married Vasya,' Nathan cut in ruthlessly. 'I promised before God to care for her and I will. I did not promise to take on a ready-made family. I have no time to look after anyone other than Vasya and my patients. As for Vasya, as you say, she is in delicate health. She is, yet she has a full-time job – caring for me. If it's money you want I may be able to make a contribution to the upkeep of your cousin's children, but I will not take them into my home, nor will I meet them. That is my final word on the subject. Now, if you'll excuse me.'

He left the room and went to the front door. Still in a temper, he wrenched it open. Kolya was in the porch.

'I am sorry to disturb you, sir. Madam Koshka has sent for you. One of her girls has been hurt. She asked if you could come at once.'

'Thank you, Kolya. I'll pick up my bag.'

Vasya appeared in the hall behind him. 'You have to go?' she questioned timorously.

'I do.'

'Nathan, this is a family meal ...' Levi admonished from the doorway of the dining room.

'Someone has been injured. I am needed.'

'Our discussion...'

'Is over, Levi.' Nathan picked up his hat and jammed it on his head. 'Good evening.' He took his bag and left, slamming the front door behind him.

Chapter Eighteen

Madam Koshka's salon December 1871

Several men had gathered outside one of the carriages that lined the drive to Koshka's house. When Nathan drew closer he recognised Fritz and three of the liveried men Koshka employed to keep order in her establishment. They were loading a comatose man into a closed vehicle.

'Is he sick?' Nathan questioned.

'Sleepy,' Fritz answered in a tone that discouraged further questioning. 'He's not the reason we sent for you, Dr Kharber.' Fritz slammed the door of the carriage and shouted up to the driver. 'Take him away and don't bring him back here again, do you understand?'

'I'll give my master your message when he wakes.'

'Do that, because if I see him here again he'll be leaving in a coffin, not a carriage.'

The driver tipped his hat and drove off.

'Thank you very much for coming so promptly, Dr Kharber.' Fritz led Nathan through the kitchen entrance and up the back staircase to the corridor that housed the girls' rooms. He tapped one of the doors. Koshka opened it.

'Dr Kharber, thank you for responding so quickly. Fritz, would you please check that the gentlemen who came in with Adele's last client are not causing us any problems. And when you talk to them please explain exactly why I asked you to enquire after them.'

'Yes, madam.'

'Leave one of our men outside this door, please. Ask him to remain there until someone relieves him.'

'Yes, madam.'

'Dr Kharber,' Koshka ushered him into the room. 'Adele, look, Dr Kharber has come to take care of you'

Nathan wouldn't have recognised Adele if Koshka hadn't mentioned her name. She was lying propped up on pillows in the bed with the sheet pulled to her chin. Her face was swollen out of all recognition, coloured by bruises that were already turning purple, burgundy, and black. Her jaw jutted sideways at a painfully unnatural angle.

He sat on the edge of the bed and examined her.

'Is there permanent damage?' Koshka asked anxiously.

'The skin isn't broken, which is a good sign. The swelling will eventually go down and the bruising, although severe, will fade. It will however take time, a month, maybe more. Adele, your jaw is dislocated, but I am going to try to manipulate it back into place. If you understand what I'm saying, please don't try to talk, but blink once.'

Adele stared at Nathan and blinked. He took the opportunity to lift her eyelids and check her eyes.

'You have burst blood vessels in your eyes. Is your vision blurred? Two blinks if it is. One blink if it isn't.'

Adele blinked once.

'Have you sent for the Fire Brigade, madam?' Nathan opened his doctor's bag.

'No need, we dealt with this matter in-house. Fritz has attended to everything that needed to be done.'

Nathan wrapped his hands gently around Adele's face. 'Please don't fight me. I know you're in pain but try to relax. Do you understand?'

Adele blinked once again.

Nathan moved closer to her on the bed, clamped his hands around her face and made a swift and sudden wrenching move.

Adele cried out. Then stared at him in astonishment.

'Can you open your mouth?'

'Yes,' she whispered. 'But it feels strange.'

'Don't say any more than you absolutely have to. I am going to bandage your jaw into place.' He removed a roll of crepe bandage from his bag and proceeded to wind it around her head. 'Don't loosen this support or try to open your mouth wide for at least six weeks, or your jaw may pop out again. If you must yawn or sneeze, support your jaw and hold it firmly in position.'

She looked up at him and blinked once more.

'You're every doctor's dream, an excellent and compliant patient. Now I'm going to give you an injection to help you sleep, but before I do, do you have any other injuries?'

Adele turned back the sheet and Koshka winced. An angry welt ran from Adele's navel up to and across her left breast.

'I should have told Fritz to horsewhip the brute.'

Nathan examined the welt. 'Like Adele's facial injuries, the skin isn't broken. It will take time but it should heal without a scar.'

He covered Adele again with the sheet and injected her arm. 'She will need looking after and she should only take liquid food for a week and, depending on her rate of recovery, possibly longer.'

Koshka nodded and went to the door. She spoke to the man outside. 'He'll fetch a maid to sit with Adele.' She reached for Adele's hand and squeezed it. 'We'll take good care of you, my dear.'

By the time the maid arrived, Adele's eyes were already closing.

'Stay with her. If there's any change in Adele's condition, please come and find me immediately.'

'Yes, madam.'

Nathan checked Adele's pulse one more time. 'I think she'll sleep now. I'll call in again in the morning.'

'Thank you.' Koshka went to the door. 'Would you care to join me in my room for a brandy, Dr Kharber? I think we both need one after this.'

'Thank you, madam.' Before Nathan reached the door, Kolya appeared and called to him.

'Sorry to disturb you again, Dr Kharber. The Fire Brigade has taken a young woman to the hospital. The nurses say she has been very badly injured.'

'Did they say who she is?'

'Too badly beaten around the face to see, sir. Whoever attacked her, stripped and violated her. She was brought in naked and unconscious.' I'm sorry, Dr Kharber, it seems as though tonight is going to be a busy one for you.'

Hospital, Hughesovka December 1871

Yulia and Miriam were gently sponging the raw and swollen face of the naked girl lying on the bed in the treatment room. She was battered and filthy, covered in blood, dirt, urine, and excrement. There were deep cuts on her body but her head injuries were the worst. Her hair was so soaked in blood it was impossible to hazard a guess as to the colour. Her eyelids were puffed, dark blue and purple pillows over her eyes.

Nathan administered the morphine he'd prepared and stood back, waiting for it to take effect. The girl groaned, but he doubted the sound was the result of pain from the needle. A pin- prick and infusion of cold opiate would be insignificant after the violence she'd been subjected to.

Nathan prepared a second syringe and left it in the tray. He hoped it wouldn't be needed – for the patient's sake. He checked her pulse again and placed his fingers on her neck.

'Be careful when you wash her, Yulia. Sponge only the undamaged skin. Be careful not to dislodge any blood clots. Miriam, go to the porters' cubicle and ask Kolya if Maxim or Bogdan have returned from their search of the area where she was found. Whoever did this to her tore off her clothes. They have to be somewhere and they might tell us who she is. I want to know the minute they find anything significant.'

'Yes, Dr Kharber.'

'Has anyone turned up from the Fire Brigade yet?'

'Vlad, sir, he sent a man to the Cossacks' barracks to ask for help to search for whoever attacked her.'

'Ask Vlad to wait please. I'd like a word with him before he joins the other searchers.'

'Yes, sir.' Miriam bobbed a curtsey and left.

Nathan watched Yulia wring the sponge out in a bowlful of clean water. Her eyes were brimming with tears and he doubted she could see anything. When she spoke her voice was so low he had to strain to hear what she said.

'She's dying, isn't she, sir.'

Nathan realised from the way Yulia spoke she hadn't asked a question. She knew the girl's condition was hopeless.

'Losing patients, is the hardest thing for any doctor or nurse to bear. I'm sorry, Yulia, she's been too badly beaten to survive. She has too many serious injuries and has lost too much blood. All we can do is ease her pain.'

'There is something else,' she contradicted angrily. 'We can wash the filth from her, bandage her wounds, cover her in clean sheets and ... and ...' she fought back tears, 'and...'

'Her pain is fading, Yulia. Look, you can see the morphine beginning to work.'

Miriam returned. 'Vlad is waiting to see you, sir. He's in the kitchen with Kolya. There's fresh tea in the samovar.'

'Thank you, Miriam.' Glad of an excuse to leave the foul-smelling room, Nathan stepped into the corridor and stretched his limbs. He joined Vlad and Kolya in the kitchen. The samovar was steaming but they'd opened their flasks and he detected the heady, astringent scent of raw home-brewed vodka. Not for the first time he wondered if it were possible to get drunk on the stench alone.

'Colonel Zonov has sent twelve Cossacks and an officer from the barracks to help the Fire Brigade search the town for anyone bloodstained who looks suspicious, sir,' Vlad reported.

'At this time of night that's anyone who's leaving a beer shop,' Nathan commented. 'Fights invariably break out at this hour.'

'No harm in them looking. Colonel Zonov also said he'll send half the regiment into town to take over from them at first light.'

'That's sensible, it's black as a rabbi's coat out there and whoever did this has probably gone to ground to clean themselves up. Is there any word on who the girl might be?'

'I asked in the hotel, Madam Koshka's, and Mr Edwards's house, but the girls living in all three are where they should be, apart from Anna.'

Nathan left the kitchen and went into the hall. He opened the door to the ward. Anna was sitting at the Nightingale desk. She looked up at him.

'Do you need me, sir?'

'I might later, Anna, if I do I'll send for you. You can cope here?'

'Of course, sir. I checked the injured girl when she came in. When I realised there was nothing I could do for her I asked Yulia and Miriam to take over so I could watch over the wards. The two patients you operated on today are restless. I gave both of them laudanum.'

'Are they sleeping now?'

'Sleeping but restless, sir.'

'Let me know if their condition deteriorates.'

'Of course, sir.'

Nathan returned to the kitchen in time to hear Vlad say, 'If the girl is from the hole houses she might not even be missed for a few days. From what Bogdan and Maxim said she's unrecognisable and there was nothing on her to indicate who she is.'

'How was she found?' Nathan asked.

'An officer from the Fire Brigade thought he saw someone moving behind Mr Edwards's fence.'

'A shadow?' Nathan guessed.

'Someone in dark clothes, that's all the description he could give. When he went to take a closer look he literally fell over the girl. He picked her up and carried her straight here.'

Maxim ran in, his arms full. 'We just discovered these behind Mr Edwards's fence not far from where the girl was found, sir.' He held out a soiled, torn nurse's dress and apron and pieces of china.

Vlad took the china and dropped the fragments into the sink.

'These could have been thrown away by a servant who broke a dish and didn't want to be blamed for it, but the nurse's dress...'

Nathan stared at the pattern on the china.

'You've seen these before, sir?' Kolya asked.

'When the dish was whole. Naomi Rinskaya was washing a cake plate with that pattern when I looked into the kitchen just before I went home for the evening. She should have left at the end of her shift, but she'd stayed to wash the plate because she wanted to return it to Yelena in Glyn's house.'

'What time was that, sir?' Vlad asked.

'I reached home about seven o'clock. Vlad, take those pieces to Yelena. It could be a common pattern but I've never seen another dish with it. Ask Yelena if Naomi called on her this evening. Kolya, check with all the nurses to see if they know anything about a missing nurse's dress. We can hope, but everything indicates the girl who was attacked is Naomi Rinskaya.' Nathan took the pieces of china and wrapped them in one of the towels used to dry dishes before handing them to Vlad.

'What if Naomi didn't call to see Yelena and the dish is hers, sir?' Vlad ventured.

'Borrow one of Mr Edwards's carriages. Go to the shtetl, find Naomi's family, and bring them here as quickly as possible.'

Nathan thought rapidly. Yulia and Miriam were already upset by the condition of the girl; they'd be even more upset if she turned out be someone they knew. As for Anna – she'd been correct when she'd said there was nothing she could do for the dying girl, but the fact that she'd handed care of the patient over to Yulia and Miriam and remained to oversee the wards suggested she couldn't bear to nurse the victim of such a vicious rape, whoever she was.

'Vlad, while you're in Mr Edwards's house ask Mrs Parry if she'd be kind enough to come here and help. Tell her ... tell her I need her. And hurry, Vlad,' he added. 'If our patient is Naomi, her family don't have much time to say goodbye.'

Madam Koshka's salon December 1871

'There seems to be a great deal of activity outside the door,' Edward commented as he sat with Xenia in her room.

'People coming and going. You get used to it. To return to our conversation about the Russian winter, you'll need fur-lined boots as well as a fur coat and hat, Edward. There are two excellent cobblers in the Jewish shletl,' Xenia recommended.

'I've already ordered them, and paid in advance, but the cobblers warned me it will take them about six weeks to make them given the tide of orders they've received from the latest influx of people into the town.'

'You should have offered them a bribe to move you up the list.'

'I tried to give them double the asking price, they wouldn't take it.'

'That's the Jews for you, they're born with integrity.'

'And talking about money brings me a question I've been meaning to ask you...'

'It's as well to get it out of the way,' she agreed. 'Ten roubles for the first hour of my time, fifteen for two, thirty for an entire night. You pay the house, not me, but as it's your first night in Koshka's salon, shall we say twenty for all night? And, like your brother, Glyn, I'm sure Fritz would be delighted to open an account for you that will also cover the bar and any other expenses you incur, that you can settle at the end of every week.'

'Madam will pay you from my account?'

'Madam meets all her employees living expenses, which are not inconsiderable. Some of our clients leave small presents on their pillows when they leave, some don't. It's by no means obligatory and depends on the goodwill of the client and the size of their purse. There's no need for us to discuss this matter further unless you are unhappy with my services and do not wish to pay for them. Another brandy?' She picked up the bottle.

'I should be getting back to Glyn's house.' Embarrassed by her directness, Edward took his pocket watch from his waistcoat and checked the time. 'It's after midnight.'

'Bedtime, and my bed is very comfortable.' She dropped to her knees in front of his chair and ran her fingers lightly and expertly over the front of his trousers.

Embarrassed, he squirmed as she unbuttoned his flies, slipped her hand inside his trousers and underpants, and teased his burgeoning erection.

'I ... it's been a long time,' he stammered.

'Which is why we'll take things slowly. Here, in the chair, or the bed? It's your choice.' She rose, stretched her arms behind her back, and flicked a button at the nape of her neck. Her gown fell to the floor, the gold fabric forming a puddle at her feet, leaving her naked apart from a pair of flesh-coloured silk stockings fastened by white lace garters.

'That's incredible.'

'The dress is madam's own design. It's quite unique and everyone who works here has at least two of them.'

Edward had a sudden image of his wife Judith. He could even feel her presence, tight-lipped, disapproving. In over fifteen years of marriage he'd never seen her unclothed, and now a woman he'd only just met had disrobed solely for his benefit and was standing before him, proud, entrancing, and unashamed.

'The bed?' Xenia looked back over her shoulder at him as she turned down the covers. Her back was long, slim, her skin as white as the alabaster figures in the hall of the Crawshays' mansion in Merthyr. Her buttocks, full, rounded at the top of her thighs, were alluring globes he longed to caress.

Weakening at her smile he nodded. One night – just one night of female company – what harm could it do? Judith was dead and even before her death she'd been frail – too frail for years to "meet her wifely obligations and fulfil his demands". He'd been without a woman for so long...

He left the chair, his trousers supported by his braces. Xenia helped him remove his jacket and waistcoat, and unbuttoned his shirt. He shed his braces, trousers, and underclothes.

She fingered his erection. 'Perhaps we won't need to take it slowly after all, Edward.' She led him to the bed and lay beside him.

'I ... never knew it could be like this,' he murmured as she stroked his lips, his chest, and his nipples with the tip of her tongue before moving slowly, sensually, down his body.

He ran his arms down her sides, fingered her breasts, felt the full rounded weight of them in the palms of his hands, but he couldn't rid himself of the feeling that she was toying with him, using her knowledge to play him like a musician. Yet her tune was so beguiling – he allowed her to do exactly as she wanted.

Later he lay quietly in her arms, his head cushioned on her breasts, his hand nestling between her thighs.

'Comfortable?' she murmured.

'And tired.' He could feel himself drifting off as he closed his eyes, but the novelty of his situation wouldn't allow for sleep. He was in a brothel. He'd only ever heard about them until today. Glyn and Peter had talked about them often enough when they'd visited the "gentlemen only" bars in the Merthyr pubs. It had been obvious to him that Glyn had frequented many "houses" in the various countries he'd visited while working for Mr Hughes, and Peter's duties as a relief police doctor in London had included carrying out medical examinations on whores.

Whores: even the word sounded foul. It conjured images of the filthy, pox-raddled, brawling drunks who plied their trade on the outskirts of "China", the vice area of Merthyr.

But this house was as far removed from the rough and ready doss houses in China as Xenia was from his image of a "lady of the night". He felt warm, comfortable, cosseted, and domestic – that was it, domestic. He suddenly realised that he felt more at home in Xenia's bed with her lying next to him than he had done in all the years he'd lived with Judith.

Chapter Nineteen

Hospital, Hughesovka December 1871

Sarah moved her chair behind the door of the treatment room so Mr and Mrs Rinski could sit close to the bed. Miriam and Yulia had done their best to mask the marks of violence on Naomi, but her face was unrecognisable as that of the pretty, dark- haired, dark-eyed girl she'd interviewed and taken on as a trainee nurse only a few months before.

Naomi's mother sat, crouched, pale faced, and tense. She was holding one of her daughter's bandaged hands between her own and Sarah could almost feel Mrs Rinskaya's concentration as she willed her child to live with every fibre of her being. Her eyes were focused on Naomi, her lips bloodless. If she was aware of anyone's presence in the room beside her daughter, she gave no sign of it.

Sarah had diagnosed Mrs Rinskaya's silence as shock, but the woman had refused to take anything to alleviate the symptoms. Mr Rinski had fallen to his knees when he'd first seen his daughter, alternately crying and praying to God to preserve her life. He hadn't calmed until Nathan had given him laudanum.

The laudanum had done more than dull Mr Rinski's pain. It had taken away his capacity to feel any emotion. He sat at the foot of the bed, dull-eyed, mouth slack, his hands folded loosely in his lap.

The door opened and Anna entered with two cups of tea. She offered one to Mrs Rinskaya, who shook her head without looking away from Naomi. Anna pressed the other into Naomi's father's hand. Anna handed the cup Mrs Rinskaya had refused to Sarah.

'Dr Kharber asked if he could see you.'

Sarah relinquished her chair to Anna. She left the room and closed the door softly behind her. She felt as though she had been sitting with Naomi and the Rinskis for weeks not hours.

Yulia and Miriam were in the kitchen preparing breakfast trays. She looked in. 'Miriam, can you take over from Anna please.'

'Of course, Mrs Parry.' Miriam was surprised but she left.

'How are you coping on the wards?' Sarah asked.

'We're coping, Mrs Parry,' Yulia answered.

'The patients?' Sarah added.

'Are all sleeping or resting at the moment. Naomi ...' Sarah shook her head. 'Look after Anna when she gets here and don't allow her to return to the treatment room.' Sarah didn't know if Anna had told her fellow nurses she'd been raped before she'd left Merthyr. But they all knew she'd taken a gun from the office drawer and shot and killed a Cossack soldier who was attacking Ruth. She was afraid that Naomi's condition would rekindle horrific memories for Anna. Memories, Sarah suspected, that had never been buried far beneath the surface of Anna's consciousness. To her relief Miriam didn't ask any questions.

When Sarah passed Anna in the corridor she held out her hand.

Anna grasped it. 'The Paskeys did that to Naomi.'

'You can't possibly know that, Anna.'

'I know it,' Anna contradicted stubbornly. 'The marks on her arms, her wounds, they relieved themselves on her, treating her like a lavatory ...'

Sarah held out her arms but Anna didn't embrace her. She stared at her, white faced, defiant. 'It was the Paskeys. I know it was the Paskeys,' she reiterated stubbornly.

'The men are out looking for whoever hurt Naomi.'

'They'll find the Paskeys and when they do, I want to see them.'

Sarah nodded. 'If they find them and that's what you want, Anna, you will see them.'

'You're not just saying that to keep me quiet?'

'If it was the Paskeys who hurt Naomi, and if they're found, you have every right to see them.' Sarah watched Anna walk into the kitchen before knocking the office door.

Nathan was at his desk, staring at the window. He hadn't closed the blinds and although a medical textbook was open in front of him, Sarah knew he hadn't been reading.

'Will it be much longer?'

'I'd say minutes rather than hours,' Sarah diagnosed. 'But you know as well as I do, prophesising death is not an exact science.'

'Should I send for Rabbi Goldberg?'

'In my opinion, yes.' She looked through the window into the darkness. A light burned on Glyn's porch, and further back a lamp flickered on the doorpost of Alexei's house.

'It's strange how so many people die the hour before dawn.' Nathan left his chair.

'The matron in the London hospital where I trained used to say it was because the body's defences were at their lowest ebb at that point.'

'One of the Catholic nuns who nursed in the Vienna hospital I worked in for a few months said it was because God reaped the souls of the dying along with the night's shadows.' He buttoned his coat. 'You go back in. I'll be with you as soon as I've sent a porter to fetch the rabbi.' He sank his head in his hands.

'You should get some sleep.'

He shook his head. 'I keep thinking back to last night when I saw Naomi in the kitchen. She told me she was going to return the dish to Yelena in Glyn's house. I should have insisted that one of the porters went with her.'

'She was about to go home, wasn't she?' Sarah checked.

'She didn't say as much but I assumed so as her shift had finished for the day.'

'The porters don't walk the nurses home at the end of their shifts. If they did, they'd be so busy walking the girls back and forth, they'd never do any work.'

'But Naomi wasn't going home ...'

'No, she crossed the road to Glyn's house to return the dish. The fact that she was found alongside the outside of Glyn's garden fence with the broken dish suggests someone grabbed her and dragged her out of sight of the road. That is hardly your fault, Nathan. No doctor or member of staff could possibly watch all of our nurses day and night.'

'If she cried out ...'

'If she'd cried out someone in Glyn's house would have heard her. There are enough of us living there. You can't possibly blame yourself for this attack on Naomi. Please, Nathan, you have absolutely nothing to feel guilty about.' Sarah looked him in the eye. All her instincts told her to hug him but she held back. Nathan was not a demonstrative man and given the Jewish taboo on men touching women who were unrelated to them, she sensed he would find the gesture disturbing. 'I'll go in and relieve Miriam. Naomi may not have worked here very long, but all the nurses regarded her as a real friend and understandably they're having trouble coping with what some evil brute has done to her.'

Sarah returned to the treatment room. Naomi's breathing was lighter, shallower. She sent Miriam out, moved next to the bed, slipped her hand beneath the bedclothes and monitored Naomi's heartbeat. It was slowing, its beat fading, diminishing in strength and intensity.

Mrs Rinskaya looked at Sarah. Her eyes were bleak, pleading.

Unable to bear the sight of Mrs Rinskaya's grief, Sarah concentrated on the dying girl. She had no idea how long she stood there monitoring Naomi's heartbeat. It could have been minutes, it could have been hours. Every time she heard a step outside the door she expected to see Nathan open it. But the footsteps always moved on.

When Naomi's heart beat for the final time, Sarah pulled the sheet to the girl's chin and withdrew from the bed. 'I am so sorry, Mrs Rinskaya.'

Mrs Rinskaya's only reaction was to tighten her grip on Naomi's hand.

Naomi's father clutched Sarah's arm and stared mutely at her.

'She is with your God, Mr Rinski.'

He began to sob, making harsh violent sounds that seemed to tear from the very depth of his being.

The door opened and Nathan appeared with Rabbi Goldberg. Sarah didn't blame him for waiting to enter the room until the rabbi arrived.

Feeling like an interloper she crept out, leaving the Rinskis with Nathan and the rabbi. She went into the office. A few moments later Anna appeared with two glasses of tea.

'Thank you.' Sarah took the tray and sat in the visitor's chair in front of Nathan's desk.

'I thought Dr Kharber would be here.'

'I have no idea how long he'll be. Why don't you drink the tea? You look as though you could use it.'

'I will, thank you.' Anna perched on the edge of Nathan's desk.

'Are, you, all right?' Sarah asked solicitously.

'Fine,' Anna snapped, tight-lipped.

'You don't have to be brave, and you can talk to me about anything, any time you want.'

'I'm not being brave. I'm angry that men like the Paskeys can do the things that they do to women and no one seems to be able to stop them.'

'They'll be stopped as soon as they're caught.' Sarah refrained from adding, 'if it was the Paskeys'. Unlike Anna, she was far from convinced, despite Edward's assertion that the Paskeys were headed for Hughesovka.

'They weren't stopped after what they did to me. The police took them away but they were set free.'

'We explained why they didn't go to gaol, darling.'

'Because I wasn't there to tell the judge what they did to me, and because they lied,' Anna interrupted. 'If Auntie Maggie and Betty hadn't found me when they did after the Paskeys attacked me I would be dead like Naomi. She is dead, isn't she?' 'Yes.'

Anna bit her lip and shrank back when Sarah tried to hug her.

'If someone had found Naomi sooner...'

'Her head injuries were so severe, darling, she would have died even if she'd been brought here straight after the attack,' Sarah consoled.

'Miriam said Dr Kharber will want to move Naomi's body to the Jewish mortuary as soon as possible.'

'He will, and her family won't want us to lay out Naomi, they have their own special people to do that called the Chevra Kadisha,' Sarah warned, having presided over several Jewish deaths in the hospital. 'The funeral will probably be held today, as the Jews like to bury their dead as quickly as possible.'

'We'll be allowed to attend, won't we?' Anna asked.

'You'll have to ask Dr Kharber that, but not being of Naomi's faith we may not be welcome.'

'What should you ask Dr Kharber?' Nathan questioned as he entered the office.

'Whether or not we can attend Naomi's funeral, sir?'

'I'm afraid that won't be possible, Anna. Rabbi Goldberg will want to limit the mourners to members of our faith.'

'Can we at least send flowers?'

Nathan shook his head. 'Unlike Christians, we Jews keep our funeral services very simple. We bury our dead as quickly as possible and we don't put flowers on our coffins.'

'So, there is no way that we nurses can mourn Naomi?'

'You can say goodbye to her in your prayers, Anna. And perhaps you can light a candle and put it in the hall window tonight when you come on duty. Then whenever you walk past it, you will remember her.'

'I won't need a candle to remember her, sir.'

'No, I don't expect you will.'

'Would you like tea, Dr Kharber?'

'Please, Anna.'

'Shall I take some in to Rabbi Goldberg and Mr and Mrs Rinski?'

'No, Anna, leave them to come to terms with what has happened for the moment. Rabbi Goldberg told me that he has ordered the Jewish mortuary cart to call here at first light.' He turned to Sarah. 'Thank you for coming when I sent for you, and thank you for staying all night, but now, as your doctor as well as your friend, I am ordering you home to get some rest, not only for your own sake, but that of your child.'

Realising there was nothing more she could do for Anna, Naomi, Mr and Mrs Rinski, or anyone in the hospital, Sarah didn't argue. She went to the door.

'Get one of the porters to walk you across the road.'

'Don't be silly, Nathan, I'll be in plain sight.'

'Not in the darkness you won't, and don't tell me that you can look after yourself, not after what happened to Naomi. I'll be watching,' he warned her.

'I'll ask whoever is in the porters' room to accompany me,' she capitulated. 'I'll see you this afternoon after I've slept.'

'Take the day off. Hopefully nothing will happen in the town the next twenty-four hours.'

'If it does the girls can send for me.'

'Thank you again, Sarah.'

'For what?' she asked.

'Being you, and comforting Mr and Mrs Rinski.'

'I did and said nothing.'

'Precisely. The rest of us would have tried. And there are no words of comfort that can be offered. Not in the face of such a loss. It takes someone who's experienced it to know that.'

Chapter Twenty

Hughesovka December 1871

The only illumination emanated from the eerie, blue-white glow of the snow and the yellow oil lamps that burned on the porch of the hospital and in the doorways of the houses.

Nathan stood in front of the hospital and watched the Jewish mortuary cart drive towards the shtetl. Rabbi Goldberg and Mr and Mrs Rinski stumbled hesitantly behind it. Knowing Glyn Edwards would be the first to offer, he'd suggested that Rabbi Goldberg and the Rinskis borrow one of Glyn's carriages and a porter to drive it and them back to the shtetl, but the rabbi had refused. Seeing Mrs Rinskaya falter and Mr Rinski slow his step until they both fell some distance behind the rabbi, he hoped Naomi's parents would reach their home without collapsing.

Seeing a light flicker behind Glyn's house, he walked across the road and down the outside of the fence that enclosed the back of Glyn's garden. Maxim was searching with the aid of a lantern, poking at the snow covered ground with a long stick.

'Have you found anything else?' he asked the porter.

'Nothing, sir,' Maxim answered grimly.

'Naomi had been hit on the head with something hard. A stone? Or a stick. It will be covered in her blood.'

'The snow has obliterated everything, sir. There's nothing, sir. No bloodstains or any more of Naomi's clothes. Bogdan told me her stockings and underclothes are missing. All we found was the broken dish, sir. Vlad, Mr Edwards, and Mr Parry organised a search of the town. They questioned everyone who was out and about last night but no one saw anything – at least nothing they would own up to. I thought I'd take one last look around here before the Cossacks come into town. I saw the Jewish mortuary cart outside the hospital. Is Nurse Rinskaya...'

'She died less than an hour ago, Maxim.'

'I'm sorry to hear that, sir. She was a pleasant girl. She had a kind word for everyone.'

'Yes, she did.' Nathan turned back and retraced his steps. He stopped when he reached the corner of the fence and looked across the road at the hospital.

Dawn was breaking. The snow-blanketed town was bathed in a thin, cold light that lent the deserted buildings and quiet street a grim, sinister air. He shivered. He was cold. He knew he should go home to catch up on his sleep but he was in no hurry to face Vasya or her silent, suffering martyrdom after the scene at dinner. Was it really only last evening?

He didn't even want to return to his office in the hospital. It would only give him the time and opportunity to reflect on his deficiencies as a doctor. Naomi had been so young. She'd had her whole life ahead of her – and for all his training there'd been nothing he could do to save her. Nothing at all.

He looked down the road and saw a company of Cossacks riding in, Captain Misha Razin at their head, and recalled what Maxim had said about the soldiers coming to help search for Naomi's killer.

Too tired to think, walk, or volunteer to help the Cossacks, all he wanted to do was sit somewhere quiet and clear his mind of the unbearable tragedy of the night so he could come to terms with it as much as he ever could.

If only he'd insisted Naomi leave in the company of a porter ... It had been kind of Sarah to say it wasn't his place to suggest that, but he knew he would be haunted by the thought until the day he died.

It was then he remembered one place where he'd be offered tea, a comfortable chair in front of the hearth, and innocuous conversation about nothing in particular. He pushed his hat down further on his head, set his face to the snowflakes blowing in on the east wind and walked down the street towards Koshka's.

'Dr Kharber?'

He turned to see Sonya alight from a carriage. Her chaperone and a footman were with her.

'You're up early, Miss Tsetovna.'

'Mr Edwards sent a message to Mr Hughes at my aunt's last night that one of the nurses from the hospital had been attacked. Prince Roman Nadolny and Mr Hughes went to the company office to co-ordinate the search for the perpetrator. I knew the nurses would be upset and Sarah would be here helping, so I thought I'd come down early to see if I could do anything. Is it true? Was the nurse...'

Nathan didn't wait for her to finish her question. 'Naomi Rinskaya. She died less than an hour ago.'

'I'm so sorry, Dr Kharber, I only met her a few times, but she seemed a sweet girl. How are the rest of the nurses coping?'

'Come and see for yourself. You know the girls, they're always happy to make tea.'

'Sarah?'

'I ordered her home after Naomi died. She sat up with Naomi and Mr and Mrs Rinski all night, which is tiring for anyone but exhausting for someone in her condition. I hope she's taken my advice and gone to bed.'

Sonya looked at Glyn's house. Smoke was drifting upwards from the chimneys, which meant Pyotr had laid and lit the fires, but the drapes hadn't been opened in the family rooms at the front of the house, and she wondered if Glyn and Richard were still out searching the town with the rest of the men, looking for whoever had attacked Naomi.

'Maria, go to the office of the New Russia Company please, and tell Mr Hughes and Prince Roman Nadolny I'll be at the hospital or Mr Edwards's. If no one needs your help in the company offices, you can go home. Tell Boris to send a carriage to the office for me at the end of the day as usual.'

'You don't want me to stay with you, Miss Sonya?'

Sonya heard the disapproval in Maria's voice. 'I'll be quite safe in the hospital, and company office, as I am every day, and I may even be home early if Prince Roman returns this afternoon as I'll travel home with him. Don't worry about my being chaperoned, we'll have the driver.'

'Yes, Miss Sonya.'

Sonya ignored the frost in Maria's voice and walked alongside Nathan to the hospital. Anna had seen them from the window and set a tray of tea on Nathan's desk as they entered. Sonya noticed Anna's damp eyes and pale face and hugged her.

'You don't have to wait on me.'

'The tea's for Dr Kharber, all I did was put an extra glass on the tray for you.'

'Thank you.' Sonya removed her hat and cloak and hung them on the hooks the nurses used behind the kitchen door.

'I hope you're here to sort out the mess Yulia has made of the filing system.'

'As there's nothing else I can do until I'm due to start work in the company office at nine, I'd be happy to help out.'

'Sit down and drink your tea first,' Nathan poured two glasses before sitting behind his desk. 'Has the day shift of nurses come in yet, Anna?'

'Yes, Dr Kharber.'

'Then please go home, and tell Miriam and Yulia to do the same. Ask one of the Cossacks or a porter to escort all of you to your respective doors and tell whoever it is to walk you across the road first. Until the madman who killed Naomi has been caught, no woman will be safe in this town.'

'The porters have work to do. They're busy...'

'And they'll be busier still, escorting all you, nurses, to and from this place. I don't want any of you setting foot in the streets by yourself from now on.' He softened his voice. 'Go, Anna. You've had a dreadful night. You need to rest. All of you. See you tonight.'

'And you, sir?'

'Tell the nurses I'll either be here or in my house if I'm needed for an emergency.'

'Yes, sir.' Anna left, closing the office door behind her.

'Did Yulia really mess up the files that much?' Sonya asked.

'Oh yes,' he concurred, 'but drink this before you look at them.' He handed her a glass. 'If what I've heard is correct, I should congratulate you on your engagement.' When she didn't answer, he said, 'You are engaged to Prince Roman Nadolny?'

'I am.'

'Is your ring as grand as the diamond one Alexei gave my sister?' He didn't know why he was asking. He had no interest in engagement rings, diamond or otherwise, and had bought Vasya only one ring, a plain gold band when they had married.

'I have no ring as yet.'

'There are no fine jewellers who deal in diamonds in Hughesovka,' he observed.

'Precisely.' She didn't tell him that Roman hadn't mentioned a ring and she, in all honesty, hadn't even thought of one.

'I wish you and the prince a long and happy life together.'

'Do you? Do you really?' Sonya fought to control her pent- up frustration with Nathan.

'Miss...'

Sonya finally erupted. 'Don't you dare "Miss Tsetovna" me. Not when you know how I feel about you and what you feel for me.' She saw him flinch as though she'd struck him. She'd intended to hurt him but instead of triumph, she felt numb, empty, and unaccountably nauseous.

'It would never have been possible between you and me, Sonya.'

'Why? Because I'm a Christian?' she demanded. 'Ruth was Jewish, Alexei a Christian, and you not only allowed them to marry but gave them your blessing.'

'It was either that or lose my sister, and I couldn't bear the thought. Besides, the situation was entirely different...'

'Because Ruth is a woman? Or because she was prepared to give up her religion for the man she loved? And you weren't prepared to make that sacrifice for me.'

'I'm not as brave as Ruth, Sonya. My faith is the framework on which I've built my entire life.'

'If you'd asked me I would have converted to your faith, just as Ruth converted to the Russian Orthodox Church for Alexei. No sacrifice would have been too much if it meant that we could have spent our lives together.'

'You would have found the ways of the shtetl strange, and the customs and constrictions we expect our women to live under, even stranger.'

'I could have learned. I would have done anything for you.'

Unable to bear the love and pleading in her eyes he walked to the window, turned his back on her, and stared blankly at the street. 'In the beginning perhaps you could have borne the sacrifice. But in time you would have resented it. Someone brought up as you have been, to value the freedoms of aristocratic life...'

'Aristocratic? Me?' she interrupted angrily. 'Until recently I was a penniless bastard who never knew my father or my mother. Is that it? Is that why you wouldn't marry me?'

'I never considered your parentage.' He turned to face her and she saw he was speaking the truth. 'What I did think of was the different worlds you and I have inhabited and still inhabit. We're mushrooms and toadstools, Sonya. Fine when kept separate; put us in a pan together, and the dish turns to poison.'

'Which one of us is the toadstool?'

'Me,' he answered with a self-deprecating smile. 'The Tsars know just how lethal and dangerous we Jews are, which is why Catherine the Great and her successors have restricted us to living "beyond the pale" in this small corner of all the Russias. So it wouldn't only be the restrictions of my faith that would bind you, but also the laws the Tsars have passed to control every aspect of Jewish life, and limit our influence to our own settlements, thereby sentencing us and our children to eternal poverty.'

Realising the futility of questioning the justice or otherwise of Russian laws governing Jews, a subject she knew very little about, she blurted, 'Roman knows about us and he knows that I love you.'

'You told him you loved me?' He was shocked. 'When we've never spoken about it until now?'

'I didn't tell him anything. He saw us dancing together at Alexei and Ruth's wedding, and guessed.'

'In which case one of us must have been wearing our heart on our face.'

'Possibly both of us.' She couldn't quell the bitterness she felt. 'I hope Vasya didn't notice as well as Roman.'

'She knows.'

It was Sonya's turn to be dumbfounded.

'You told her?'

'I've never said a word about you, but like your fiancé, she knows.'

'She loves you. You do realise that?'

'Almost as much as the prince loves you.'

'Roman doesn't love me.'

'He told you that?'

'He asked me to marry him but it would be a business arrangement. He's rich, I have some money.'

'A man doesn't marry a woman as a business arrangement, Sonya.'

'You did,' she challenged. 'You married Vasya so Ruth could marry Alexei.'

Unable to contradict or face her, he ran his hands through his hair and turned back to the window. He saw one of the Cossacks who was out searching the street look towards the hospital, and closed the blinds.

'You'll have to be more careful when you look at me in future.' She left her tea untouched and rose from the chair.

'How careful will you be, Sonya, when you've promised to marry a man you don't love?'

'As I can't marry you, it doesn't matter who I marry. Least of all to you,' she added cuttingly.

'It will matter when you find yourself living with someone you'll see every single day for the rest of your life.'

'When you married Vasya, you made a decision for both of us, Nathan. What I do or don't do with my life is no concern of yours.'

She moved to the door. He turned and faced her. One step, at the most two, and he would be close enough to touch her. To gather her into his arms. To kiss her...

He didn't move.

She opened the door and head high, eyes focused straight in front of her, walked away.

She was so intent on ignoring Nathan she didn't see Roman passing in one of John Hughes's carriages.

Roman glanced past Sonya to the window of Nathan's office. The blinds were closed, which was why he noticed a chink on the right hand side. A chink just wide enough for someone inside to have moved the slats so they could see out.

'Stop here, Manfred.'

'Here, sir?' Manfred asked in surprise.

'Just for a few minutes. I need to make some notes and I can't while the carriage is moving.'

Roman continued to sit in the carriage pretending to make notes until Nathan left the hospital. Only then did he alight and order Manfred to return the carriage to the stables behind the company offices.

Chapter Twenty-one

Glyn and Praskovia's house December 1871

Exhausted, hungry, and thirsty after a sleepless night, Richard and Glyn stamped the snow from their boots on the doormat before exchanging them for felt slippers. They shrugged off their damp hats, coats, mufflers, and gloves and handed them to Pyotr. Alerted by the sounds of the door opening and of voices, Sarah walked down the stairs to meet them.

Richard kissed her cheek. 'Good morning, sweetheart. The snow is falling thicker by the minute.'

'I saw.'

'You went out?'

'To the hospital to sit with Naomi and the Rinskis.'

'We heard she died. I'm so sorry, Sarah.' Glyn hugged her.

'All three of you look as though you need a good breakfast.' Praskovia said. She and Sarah had cried over Naomi when Sarah had come home a couple of hours ago. Both were struggling to keep their emotions in check lest it affect the others, especially Richard's young brothers.

Praskovia opened the door to the dining room. Morgan and Owen were leaving the table after breakfasting on buckwheat pancakes, eggs, and cured ham.

'Straight to the laboratory, no snowball fights on the way,' Richard warned.

'Richard, please,' Morgan countered with all the wisdom of his twelve years. 'We're too old for snowball fights.'

'Your brother and I aren't,' Glyn teased. 'We tossed snowballs at one another all the way up the street.'

'Excuse us please, Mr Edwards, Sarah, Richard, Praskovia.' Morgan pushed ten-year-old Owen through the door, 'we promised to arrive early so Monsieur Picard could go through the assignments he gave us yesterday.'

'You're excused.' Sarah had trouble keeping a straight face. Glyn noticed the empty chairs.

'Edward not up?'

Praskovia raised her eyebrows. 'Not yet.'

From that Glyn surmised that his brother hadn't returned home.

'Did you find the people who attacked Naomi?' Sarah asked Richard. She'd tried to sleep when she'd returned from the hospital but, expecting Glyn and Richard back at any moment, she hadn't undressed. Neither had she slept. The moment she'd heard the door open, she'd run downstairs.

'We found nothing.' Richard sat at the table. He frowned as he looked around. 'Is Anna back from her night shift?'

'One of the porters brought her home an hour ago. She was too devastated to eat and insisted on going straight to bed. I asked my mother to make Anna's favourite shashlik and rice for dinner, so hopefully she'll eat later.' Praskovia handed round the dishes on the table.

'I spoke to Anna before I left the hospital. She saw Naomi when she was brought in and is absolutely convinced it was the Paskeys who attacked her.'

'What made her think that, Sarah? Thank you,' Glyn smiled at Praskovia when she filled his coffee cup.

'The injuries were similar to the ones the Paskeys inflicted on her,' Sarah said. 'I think seeing Naomi brought the whole horrible experience back to the forefront of her mind.'

'Whoever killed Naomi will be found and brought to justice sooner or later,' Glyn helped himself to eggs and ham.

'Let's hope it's sooner,' Richard said feelingly.

'Naomi's killer will be bloodstained. If they turn up in one of the communal dormitories they'll be seen and someone will report them,' Sarah observed.

'We can but hope, sweetheart,' Richard commented, 'but you know what this town is like late at night.'

'I occasionally hear peculiar noises but I can't honestly say that I know what it's like.'

'Just as well,' Glyn observed.

'There are fights that draw blood in every bar – Russian, Welsh, German, and French,' Richard elaborated.

The front door opened and they heard Edward speaking to Pyotr. He walked in and joined them.

'Early morning walk, Edward?' Glyn asked pointedly.

'Trying to get my bearings, this place isn't quite home yet, but it's cold out there,' Edward complained, 'and it's snowing more heavily than it was earlier. Nothing like we get in Wales. This breakfast looks marvellous,' he said to Praskovia as she pushed the tureens of food closer to his plate.

'Did you see or hear anything unusual?' Glyn asked.

'No, I bumped into Alf and he told me what happened. Awful news. Is there anything I can do to help?'

'Richard and I will be going to the office after we eat, come with us, and you'll find out,' Glyn passed Edward the bread.

'I saw Cossack soldiers out searching with Vlad and Alf.'

'Misha Razin and his platoon came in this morning to relieve the men who'd been out all night,' Richard commented.

'He wasn't doing much searching when I saw him. Yes please, Praskovia,' Edward nodded when she offered him the pancakes. 'He was sitting at one of the window seats in the hotel with Alice Perkins when I passed a few minutes ago.'

Richard and Glyn exchanged glances.

'Could Alice and Betty finally be planning to return to Taganrog with the Cossacks when they next go to get supplies?' Richard asked.

'The Cossacks won't be going anywhere again until the spring.' Praskovia handed Edward a basket of rolls. 'Misha called on our mother yesterday. He told her they're expecting the last platoon that went to Taganrog to return to the barracks next week and no one will be leaving again until the snow melts. He also said that Colonel Zonov's made him winter duty officer.'

'Does that mean that now the snow's here, Betty and Alice will have to remain in the town until spring?' Richard asked.

'Unless they find someone prepared to drive them to Taganrog in a sleigh, and I doubt any competent driver would risk it for fear of hitting a snowstorm. Misha also told Yelena that he was thinking of getting married.'

'Did he give her the name of the lucky girl he's picked out?' Glyn asked.

'No, other than to say she's rich.'

Edward looked uneasily at Richard. 'One of us should call on Betty and Alice and say something.'

'Say what exactly, when neither Alice nor Mrs Edwards is talking to anyone in this house except to nod "hello" to you and my two young brothers, Mr Edwards?' Richard asked. 'And Betty didn't even acknowledge the boys the last time she saw them out with me. Cut us dead when we greeted her in the street. Pass me the butter please, Glyn.'

Hotel Hughesovka December

'Your table is ready, Captain Razin.'

The waiter ushered Misha and Alice from the window table in reception to a secluded booth in the dining room. After pulling out a chair for Alice, he picked up her napkin from her place setting and laid it with a flourish over her lap. 'Your menus, miss, Captain.' He handed Alice her menu first, then Misha.

'Thank you.' Misha smiled at Alice as the waiter left them. 'I'm sorry I haven't been able to come into town to visit you since our arrival here, but my colonel has kept me busy in the barracks.' He shrugged. 'No officer in a Russian regiment, especially the Cossacks, can call his time his own.'

She reached across the table and grasped his hand. 'You're here now, that's what's important. I've missed you.'

'I've missed you too,' he lied. 'And I've been worried about you and Mrs Edwards, alone here in the hotel with Martha and the child. You only have to look at what happened last night...'

'That poor nurse.'

'You know?'

'One of the porters speaks English. He told us that she'd been...' she lowered her eyes. 'Ravished before being murdered.'

'He was right. Last night proves that this is not the town for unaccompanied ladies, especially when the lady is as beautiful as you.'

Alice accepted the compliment with a coy, well-rehearsed smile.

'Does Mrs Edwards intend to return to Wales soon?'

'No, she says she has nothing there to go back to.'

Misha was surprised. 'I heard that her husband does not want to live with her. He won't even allow her into his house.' 'He has signed over the deeds of his house to his mistress.'

'Has he now,' Misha mused, savouring the titbit his mother hadn't passed on to him.

It could be useful to have a sister who owned a house as grand as the one Glyn Edwards had given her. He filed away the knowledge, suspecting that it might come in useful one day.

The waiter interrupted them with coffee pots and their breakfasts of pancakes, butter, and cherry jam.

'So what will Mrs Edwards do here?' Misha probed.

'She doesn't know, other than move out of the hotel as soon as she can. Neither of us can afford to continue living here indefinitely. If we tried we'd have no money left after a year or two.'

'But you'd have lived well,' Misha smiled.

'That would be of little consolation if we were reduced to existing on the street. We both agree that we need to do something to earn a living. Mrs Edwards has been talking about opening some kind of business, something that we can do together. She ran a very successful hotel in Merthyr.' Alice stretched the truth. The Boot Inn could have been described as many things but 'successful hotel' wasn't one of them. 'Drinking den and cheap doss house for bachelor colliers' might have been nearer the mark.

'And you, Alice? Would you like to run a business?'

'I might,' she said airily, 'as long as it was something I was interested in, like ladies' gowns, hats, perfumes, and face creams. I wouldn't like to leave Betty – Mrs Edwards, that is. She really is a very close friend. Probably the closest friend I have.'

'So you will stay in Hughesovka as well?'

'I have no immediate plans to leave.'

'I'm glad because I have something for you.' He took a small box from his pocket and handed it to her. She opened it. Inside was a three-banded ring, one in yellow gold, one in rose gold, and one in white gold.

'It's a Russian wedding ring,' he explained, 'from the very best Moscow jeweller.'

He'd debated whether to tell her that much. He'd bought the ring for Sonya when he'd been stationed in Moscow after he'd been informed by his commanding officer that he was being posted back to his home territory. He'd hoped to rekindle the relationship he and Sonya had shared as children. He'd been devastated when Sonya had refused his proposal.

After her rejection, he'd returned the ring to its box, dropped it into the bottom of his chest and forgotten about it – until the moment Alice Perkins had told him that she had money.

'Misha, are you ...?'

'Asking you to marry me. Yes.' He locked his fingers into hers. She left her chair, flung her arms around his neck, and smothered his face in kisses. Their table was set back in the alcove but not far enough for him to avoid embarrassment. Sensing the other hotel guests watching them, he untangled himself from Alice's embrace.

'The ring is made of gold in three colours because the yellow gold is "for then" – that is, the past when we fell in love – and the white gold is "for now".'

'And the rose gold?' she asked, slipping it on to her finger.

'Is for the future, or as the jeweller would say, "for ever".'

'Thank you, Misha, I will be proud to be your wife. Of course I'll marry you, and then our life will be complete.'

The waiter arrived with more coffee and his congratulations. As Misha watched him fill their cups, he wondered how long he should wait before asking Alice to 'lend' him enough money to buy himself out of the regiment and into the horse-trading business he intended to set up as a civilian.

Beletsky Mansion December 1871

'We didn't realise the Paskeys had taken the place of the pillions on the back of your carriage until we reached Madam Koshka's, sir.' Ilya hadn't lied. He'd seen the Paskeys whispering to Gleb at the supper table, but he'd left almost immediately to take advantage of the servants' mealtime to secrete a few bottles of his master's finer wine in his hidden – very hidden – personal store.

The first thing he'd learned at his master's house parties, was that when the wine started flowing freely his master's check on the number of bottles consumed became less stringent. Also, as the evening progressed his master's guests' taste buds dulled, and it wasn't difficult to pour the contents of cheap bottles into emptied expensive ones. That freed the odd bottle which brought a good price from agents who weren't too particular where their stock came from.

Gleb took over the conversation and began to relate the story he'd concocted with the other drivers and footmen to cover their involvement in Ianto and Mervyn's expedition into Hughesovka.

'As you know, sir when we reached Koshka's salon, it was dark. I joined the other drivers in the carriage house to wait for you, sir. When I looked out of the door, I saw Mr Komansky's two pillions standing at the back of his carriage. When one of them took off his hat I recognised him as Mervyn Paskey. I shouted to him but he and his fellow pillion, that I took to be Ianto Paskey, ran off.'

'You went after them?' Levsky asked.

'A few of us did right away, sir. But as I said, it was dark.'

'It was snowing. There would have been lanterns in the carriage house. You could have followed their footsteps,' Levsky suggested.

'There were a lot of people about, sir, going in and out of the beer shops and drinking dens. All of them making too many tracks in the snow to follow any one set in particular. When we didn't find the Paskeys after an hour or so, we decided to go back to the carriage house in case they'd returned there.'

'More like you wanted to get back to the brazier and carry on drinking vodka,' Nicholas guessed.

'We all needed a warm, sir,' Gleb conceded.

'We were walking back down the street when we heard someone shout from behind a big house,' Ilya volunteered. 'I looked in the direction of the voice and saw the Paskeys running alongside a garden fence towards the road. They were covered in blood.'

'You said it was dark,' Nicholas reminded.

'It was, sir. But as you said we had lanterns.'

'And you could see the blood on them from a distance?'

'Then what happened?' Levsky snapped, annoyed with Nicholas for interrupting Ilya.

'I thought the Paskeys had been in a fight, sir. I knew you didn't want any trouble that would attract attention to you or Count Beletsky, so I asked Gleb to fetch a carriage as quick as he could. One without a coat of arms on the door.'

'Didn't whoever shouted follow the Paskeys?'

'No, sir. Not that we saw. We heard more shouts for help, sir, but from somewhere behind the house. I thought the Paskeys had been fighting with someone.'

'You didn't see the girl.'

'No, sir,' Gleb lied stoutly.

'Ilya?'

'No, sir, we didn't. When I heard the shouts, I told the Paskeys to run down the street until they saw Gleb. But given the problem Mr Komansky encountered at Madam Koshka's, sir, Gleb was delayed. The Paskeys were almost at Koshka's when Gleb left with a carriage.

'He stopped it, and as Mr Komansky was unconscious Gleb, me, and the Paskeys decided to climb in to look after him and protect him in case he should be attacked again, because Mr Komansky was in no state to help himself, sir.'

Levsky allowed the pathetic explanation as to why Ilya, Gleb, and the Paskeys had ridden inside, not outside, the carriage to pass. 'You drove straight here?'

'Yes, sir.'

'And neither you, Ilya, nor you, Gleb, saw the girl?' Levsky demanded.

'No, sir. We didn't even know a girl had been attacked until the other drivers returned.'

'You're sure you didn't join the Paskeys in their idea of fun?' Levsky stared directly into Ilya's eyes.

Ilya returned his master's stare unflinchingly. He'd had a great deal of practice. 'We only knew where the Paskeys were after we heard the shouts, so there was no time to join them, sir.'

'What did you do when you came back here?' Levsky continued his interrogation.

'Locked the Paskeys in their room, and told them to clean themselves up.'

'The livery they were wearing?'

'I told them to wash it, sir.'

'It's bloodstained?'

'Soaked, sir.'

'Burn it. I'll compensate Mr Komansky for the loss.'

'Yes, sir.'

'Did any of the house servants see the Paskeys come in?' Levsky checked.

'No, sir. I brought them in through the back door.'

'Good.' Levsky pointed to the door to the Paskeys' room.

'Open it. I want to talk to them.'

Levsky and Nicholas stood back as Ilya unlocked the door.

A fetid, animal-lair stench redolent with the metallic tang of blood wafted out. Ianto and Mervyn were cowering at the far end of the room. Both were stripped to the skin, the livery they'd worn lying in a bloodstained pool at their feet.

Ianto pointed to a bowl of bloody water balanced on a chair. Rags floated in it like sewage in a stagnant cesspit. 'We need fresh water.'

'After you've cleaned this filthy room, you can scrub yourselves down in the trough in the stable yard.'

'It's snowing out there,' Mervyn whined.

'It would be no loss if you both froze to death.' Levsky turned to Ilya. 'Watch them, as soon as they've finished cleaning this room and themselves, bring them back here and lock them in. And keep them locked in until I tell you otherwise.'

'Sir.'

Levsky turned back to the Paskeys. When he spoke his voice was soft, low. Ominously so. 'What happened in Hughesovka?'

'The girl...'

'Start at the beginning. Why did you go into the town?'

'Me and Mervyn ... well, sir ... we'd been cooped up for weeks in here. When we had supper in the kitchen we heard the other men, the drivers and footmen, talking about going into town. We'd been hearing about Hughesovka all the time since we've been here, but never been there so we asked two of the footmen if we could take their places ...' Ianto's voice trailed under Levsky's cold stare.

'And they agreed?'

'Not exactly, sir,' Ilya broke in. 'Not until Ianto offered them money.'

'You paid them?'

'Yes, sir,' Mervyn chipped in, oblivious to Ianto's warning look. 'We paid them twenty kopeks apiece.'

'Is that right?' Levsky demanded of Ianto.

Deciding there was little point in denying it, Ianto conceded, 'Yes, sir.'

'So you rode pillion into town at the back of Mr Komansky's coach, then what?'

'When we reached town we saw a girl we knew...'

'How did you know a Russian girl?' Levsky narrowed his eyes sceptically.

'She's Welsh – Anna Parry – gave us a lot of trouble back in Merthyr, sir. She went to the police and accused us of attacking her and –'

'Did you attack her?' Levsky demanded of Ianto.

'We had some fun with her, that's all, sir. She enjoyed it as much as we did.'

'You sure about that?' Levsky continued to stare at both men.

'Girls always say no when they mean yes, sir. Everyone knows that.'

'And the girl you attacked in town last night?'

'We didn't mean to hurt her, sir.'

'No?' Levsky looked pointedly at the bloodstained clothes on the floor.

'She didn't seem to remember us, sir,' Mervyn gushed, trying to be helpful again. 'She started lashing out at us. She hurt us...'

'One girl against two of you and she hurt you?' Levsky was incredulous.

'Ianto pulled her back behind the house...'

'That's enough, Mervyn,' Ianto snapped.

Nonplussed, Mervyn continued. 'The girl carried on fighting, sir. She scratched and bit us, Ianto told her to be quiet but she took no notice.'

'You dragged her behind the house?' Levsky held up his hand to silence Ianto when he tried to answer for his brother. 'Is that right, Mervyn? You dragged her behind the house?' he reiterated.

'We didn't drag her, sir,' Mervyn answered. 'Ianto carried her.'

'You followed?'

'We did, sir,' Mervyn admitted.

'We?' Levsky turned to Ilya and Gleb.

'All four of us, sir,' Mervyn beamed.

'Four of you,' Levsky reiterated. 'So who exactly is lying here?'

'The Paskeys stripped her, not Ilya and me,' Gleb intervened in an attempt to fix the blame firmly on the Paskeys. 'She was lying there waiting...'

'Asking to be raped?' Levsky's voice was chill, unemotional.

'Exactly, sir,' Gleb said, misunderstanding him.

'Who beat her?' Levsky cut in.

'She tried to run, she fell and hit her head.'

'You expect me to believe that?' Levsky stared at Ilya.

'It's the truth.'

'I heard the girl was covered in injuries and bruises.'

'She struggled a bit.'

'Four men and one girl – you're real heroes, if it took four of you to subdue one girl,' Nicholas jeered.

Levsky had heard enough. 'Ilya, Gleb, clean this room and the Paskeys. After they come in from the yard lock them in here, and from now until they leave this house they stay here. They don't leave this room under any circumstances. Their food will be brought to them here, either by you or Gleb, understood?'

'Yes, master,' Ilya said contritely.

'The four of you are aware that you murdered that girl?' '

She was alive when we left her,' Ianto protested.

If she's dead she's putting it on, sir,' Mervyn blurted without thinking what he was saying. Ianto kicked him. 'What was that for?' he whined.

'Someone must have killed her after we left if she's really dead,' Ianto protested. 'She did something the same in Merthyr. Had the police and everyone in town believing that she was knocking at death's door...'

'I have no idea what you think you did, or who you thought you "had fun" with, but you didn't attack a Welsh girl. She was a Jewish nurse from the shtetl. If the Fire Brigade find you – any of you –' Levsky stared at all four men, 'they'll string you up on the nearest post for murder. One wrong step from any one of you and I'll send for them myself. Is that understood? Is it?' he repeated when his words were met by silence.

'Yes, sir,' all four men chorused.

'I'll speak to Mr Komansky in the morning. He'll be planning to leave for his estates in the east as soon as possible,' Levsky predicted. 'Hopefully tomorrow. You two,' he glared at Ianto and Mervyn, 'will ride pillion on his carriage when he travels. Mr Komansky has coal mines and a small iron foundry. If he can't find work for you when you reach there, you'll have to shift for yourselves. Either way I don't want to see you back here again after you've left. If I do, I'll take pleasure in shooting you myself.'

'Sir,' Ianto ventured. 'I don't suppose you'd consider sending us back to Taganrog. From there we might find a ship to take us back to Wales...'

'You don't suppose right,' Levsky broke in. 'You have a choice. East with Mr Komansky or the end of a rope strung up by the Fire Brigade.'

'We'll go east, sir.' Ianto attempted to look contrite and humble.

'I wouldn't blame Mr Komansky if he put a bullet in your heads before you arrive.'

'You don't think he'll kill us, do you, sir?' Mervyn was terrified by the thought.

'I'd applaud him if he did.' Levsky strode back down the corridor with Nicholas dogging his steps.

Chapter Twenty-two

Betty Edwards's suite, Hotel Hughesovka December 1871

'Not a bit like a Welsh engagement ring, or even a Welsh wedding ring come to that,' Betty sniffed disparagingly after glancing at the Russian ring on Alice's hand.

Betty was annoyed with Alice and had no intention of keeping her disapproval to herself. Before she'd finished her breakfast, or even dressed her hair for the day, Alice had bounced into their hotel suite bringing Misha Razin in with her without a word of warning. As if that wasn't bad enough, Alice had compounded her transgression by showing off the ring Misha had given her and announcing that she'd accepted Misha's proposal of marriage, without asking for Betty's approval.

'Alice said you wanted to open a business here, Mrs Edwards?' Hoping for an invitation to sit down, Misha hovered next to the breakfast table. He believed that the best way to get the older woman on his side was to make her indebted to him. He was already formulating a plan to help Alice realise her ambition of going into business – with luck in partnership with Betty Edwards. For all of Alice's claims to wealth, he'd heard mention of the pub Betty had inherited and sold, and suspected that she had even more money than Alice.

'What's it to you whether I open a business or not, Captain Razin?' Betty snapped.

'It's none of my concern, Mrs Edwards, unless I can volunteer my services to help you in some way. This town is my home – or rather the Cossack village that was here before Hughesovka is. Now, with so many people moving here, there are plenty of business opportunities. I'm even thinking of going into business myself.'

'You're a soldier.'

'Only at the moment, Mrs Edwards. I'm making plans to leave the regiment. Transport is proving a problem in Hughesovka. I have contacts among the Cossack horse breeders and I'm considering setting up a horse-trading establishment, not only to serve the local population but also the army. Every Cossack regiment needs a regular supply of good-quality bloodstock.'

'Isn't there a stables in the town?' Betty knew full well that there was. She'd even hired a carriage from there so she could look around the area.

'There is, Mrs Edwards. A fine one that rents out carts, carriages, and horses. They also need to buy their horses from somewhere.'

'You've never mentioned leaving the regiment before, Misha.' Alice said reproachfully. She liked the idea of marrying a Cossack captain and had been looking forward to the Russian version of the regimental "ladies' dinners" in the officers' mess, something she'd read about in novels set in English military society in India.

'Of course I'll leave the regiment before we marry, my love,' Misha confirmed. 'Officers' wives lead miserable lives. They are forever packing and unpacking and following their husband's postings to the uncivilised borders of the Russian Empire. I've been in the army almost five years. It's time I settled in one place. I'm especially looking forward to taking orders from no one other than my wife.' He reached for her hand and kissed her fingertips.

Betty snorted.

Misha launched another charm offensive in her direction. 'Alice mentioned that you would like to open a shop that sells ladies' gowns, accessories, face creams, and perfumes, Mrs Edwards.'

Betty glared at Alice. 'You discussed our idea with a stranger.'

'Hardly a stranger, Betty. We're to be married.'

'Just as soon as it can be arranged after I have gained my colonel's authority to resign my commission.' Misha kissed Alice's fingertips again. 'My wife to be speaks of you as her most highly regarded, respected, and trusted friend, Mrs Edwards, and I hope that in time you will also extend that friendship to me.' Misha gave Betty the full benefit of his most dazzling smile. When she didn't reply, he ventured. 'I think a ladies' fashion and beauty shop is something that is desperately needed in this town.'

'Now you're an expert in ladies' fashion?'

'I would never claim to be an expert when it comes to ladies' gowns, especially to you and Alice, Mrs Edwards. Your style and elegance speaks for itself. But before I came here I was stationed at St Petersburg and Moscow. I spent several months in both cities, which was long enough to realise that when it comes to ladies' clothing, the steppe is decades, not months, behind current fashion.'

'You are right. The question is, would there be a market for a sophisticated ladies' dress shop in Hughesovka?'

'I believe there would, Mrs Edwards.'

'Then why haven't I seen one on the few occasions I've left the hotel?'

'Because no one has as yet thought of opening one,' Misha answered. 'There are tailors in the Jewish quarter. One or two even carry a limited stock of fabrics, but mainly men's suiting. Most of the Russian women, Cossacks included, make their clothes at home.'

'Out of what?' Betty demanded, 'is there a warehouse close by I haven't yet found?'

'They use whatever materials the pedlars carry with them. They generally visit once or twice a year.'

'Where do women go to purchase their cold creams, perfumes, gloves, scarves, shoes, jewellery ... undergarments, and all the other things they need?' Betty queried. 'And don't try telling me that pedlars bring all those things too. We had pedlars in Merthyr. They could never supply everything a woman needs.'

'Until Mr Hughes arrived this place was barely a village, Mrs Edwards. If we didn't produce it, or the Jews didn't make it, we had to do without. Now we have managers who are married to fine ladies.' He saw Betty scowl, remembered Glyn and Praskovia and moved the conversation on swiftly, while uttering a silent but heartfelt prayer that she wouldn't discover Praskovia was his sister until his ring had been firmly placed on Alice's finger in front of the priest.

'There are some ladies I wouldn't allow to set foot over the threshold of my shop,' Betty barked.

'Of course. No one could expect a fine lady like yourself to cater for some of the ... less respectable women in the town,' he phrased delicately. 'But you only have to look at the visitors staying in this hotel to see the quality of the people who would patronise your shop. And once the ironworks begins smelting at full capacity, and all the collieries are working under the guidance of managers who will bring their attendant wives and daughters to the town, you will find yourself with an enormous number of customers eager to exchange the money their husbands and fathers are earning for your luxury goods.'

'Where will you get your stock, Betty?' Alice asked.

'If John Hughes can ship in everything he needs for his furnaces, factories, and collieries, I can ship in the stock for my shop. I've the addresses of a few warehouses, including the ones in Pontypridd and Cardiff where I know the managers. I'm sure they'll supply me, even here, if I offer to buy from them at the right price.'

'Once I leave the army I could escort you and Alice to Taganrog, St Petersburg, and Moscow. There are large stores and warehouses in all three cities. I am certain they would be only too pleased to support you in your venture, and,' Misha flashed a smile again, 'I could translate for you.'

'Yes, I can see you'd be useful. But before I do anything else I need to buy premises, a shop with living accommodation above for myself, Harriet, and her nursemaid. And for Alice before she marries you,' she added pointedly.

'I can help you there too.' There are many empty plots of land after the fire.'

'All the builders are busy replacing the burned-out houses and shops. Given the difference between what I can pay and what John Hughes can pay, I have a feeling I'd be far down the list of their priorities when it comes to carrying out the work that I want done.'

'Not at all, Mrs Edwards. I have a simple solution to your problem. Cossack houses are made of wood. Fairly easy to take down, move and erect again on a new site.'

'I'm not too sure of a wooden house after the fire...'

'It would only be temporary until you could replace it with brick, or you could commission a builder to erect brick walls outside of the wooden ones.'

'You know of such a house?'

'I own one, Mrs Edwards,' Misha said confidently, conveniently forgetting that legally it was his mother's and after her death would be as much Praskovia's and Pyotr's as his. Another detail he'd need to sort out was alternative accommodation for the three families who were presently lodging in the house and paying his mother rent.

'You really could arrange a house for us?'

'Give me a month,' he boasted recklessly, 'just leave it with me.'

'Would it be large enough for all of us?' Alice asked.

'It has four rooms on the second floor and a large open area on the ground floor, perfect for a shop.'

'And the cost?' Betty wrinkled her nose.

'Will be dependent on many factors, Mrs Edwards, but I'm sure we could come to an agreement.' Misha picked up the bottle of vodka the maid had brought with Betty's breakfast.

He filled three of the glasses on a side tray, passed one to Alice, and another to Betty. He raised his glass.

'To a successful and wealthy future.'

Alice's eyes glowed with love as she repeated his toast. Betty drank slowly, grimacing, and her look became even more wary when Misha hurled his glass into the hearth.

Blast Furnace, New Russia Company Ironworks, Hughesovka January 1872

'Gentlemen,' John Hughes looked at the men crowded around him in the sub-zero temperature. All were shivering in the biting wind that had hurtled over the snow-steeped steppe before hitting the blast furnace.

'Please, take a glass of champagne from the trays that are passing among you. Hold it close and breathe on it lest it freeze before you drink it.' He stepped up on to a box and watched the clerks move through the crowd so he could check that everyone had a drink.

When he was certain that everyone had been served, he looked pointedly at the molten iron pouring from the blast furnace. 'There you have it, gentleman. The New Russia Company's first scheduled production of pig iron. The forerunner of a veritable river of molten iron that will transform not only this town, but this country. Our British and Russian employees have proved our detractors wrong, and helped produce this iron in record shattering time. Gentlemen?' He lifted his glass high in the air. 'We've done it. The Tsar will have his rails to build a network of iron roads and engines from one end of this vast country to the other. Russia will not only be industrialised as a result of our efforts but revolutionised. Twenty – no, ten – five years from now this great nation will be unrecognisable. Gentlemen, please toast with me, "The New Russia Company, and every one of its workers".'

Glasses clinked as the toast echoed and resounded around the blast furnace.

John raised his glass a second time. 'And here's to the success of whatever else the Tsar and his government contract us to produce. The New Russia Company is here to stay.'

John stepped down from his box and smiled when he saw Glyn, Roman, Alexei, and Richard all fish ice from their glasses.

'I warned you to drink before the contents froze. In the meantime, I suggest we retire to our offices or draw closer to the blast furnaces before we freeze to death.'

Roman led the way back to the waiting carriages. 'Tell me,' he looked from Glyn to John, 'did you really believe a year ago that you would be going into full production of pig iron by January this year?'

John winked at Glyn. 'We never doubted it for one minute, but we have one major advantage over you.'

'What's that?' Roman asked. 'We're Welsh,' John laughed.

Hospital and Madam Koshka's salon February 1872

Nathan left his desk, packed his doctor's coat into his bag, dressed in his black coat and hat, and, after informing the duty porter where he was going, left the hospital for Koshka's. It was part of his duties as company doctor to visit the brothel on a weekly basis to examine the girls but Koshka hadn't needed a directive from John Hughes to persuade her to agree to the monitoring. She'd asked Nathan's predecessor, Peter Edwards, the first time she'd met him to check her girls' health.

He stepped out of the front door and came face to face with Sonya and her chaperone Maria. He tipped his hat to them.

'Good morning, ladies.'

Sonya nodded, too taken aback by seeing him to speak. At that time in the morning she'd either expected him to be at home or safely out of sight in his office.

'We have brought more fruit from Mrs Ignatova's hothouses for the patients, Dr Kharber,' Maria explained.

'It is much appreciated, ladies.' Nathan touched his hat again and quickened his pace as he headed across the street. As usual, he went to the back door of the brothel. Koshka's manservant Fritz opened it at his knock.

'Good to see you, sir. Madam is breakfasting. She asked me to invite you to join her if you arrived early. If you give me a moment to announce you I'm sure she'll be glad to see you.'

'Welcome and good morning, Dr Kharber. Come and sit by the fire while you wait. What can I get you?' Koshka's cook asked.

'Just a loan of some of your heat, please.' Nathan was constantly surprised by the friendly welcome he received at Koshka's, so unlike the suspicious reception he received in most of the Russian and Cossack homes in Hughesovka. He stood in front of the stove and stretched out his hands to the warmth.

'Madam asks that you join her in her boudoir, sir.' Fritz held out his hand for Nathan's bag. 'Would you like me to place that in the examination room for you, sir?'

'Yes please, Fritz.'

'You know the way, sir.'

'I do, Fritz, thank you.'

'Dr Kharber, how lovely to see you.' Koshka rose to meet him as her maid, Minna, laid cutlery and an extra plate at the table in her private quarters.

'How is Adele?' he asked.

'Her bruises have almost faded, just as you said they would – all thanks to your expert care of course. She is so well she has insisted on returning to work, albeit with an extra layer of powder on her face.'

'My apologies for arriving early, madam. I hoped you wouldn't mind. An emergency was admitted in the early hours and I was restless after being up all night.' Nathan took her hand and shook it.

'A serious emergency?'

'A child with diphtheria. From one of the hole houses.'

'Those "houses", for want of a better word, are a disgrace, but what can any of us do when word has got out far and wide that there is paid work to be had in Hughesovka. Starving people will go anywhere that offers the promise of a meal without a thought as to exactly where they will eat the food. Will the child survive?'

'Hopefully, now we have him in the hospital.'

'There is a family?'

'A mother, two sisters, two brothers, and a father who has already found work. As hole houses goes, it isn't too bad. The mother has done her best to make it comfortable and the father has built a makeshift stove out of the bricks Mr Hughes is distributing. The cold weather actually helps. Of course it will be different once the snow melts and water gets into the holes.'

Koshka opened a box on a side table, extracted a leather purse, and pressed it into his hand. 'For the family, or any other family who need a little help, especially the ones with children – but promise me, not a word to them about where it came from.'

'Madam...'

'Koshka, please. It's only money. You can't eat it or wear it so it means nothing in itself, but it is all I have to offer and hopefully mothers and children can exchange it for something they do need. Tea, roll, butter?'

Nathan looked down at the table and realised he was hungry. 'Yes, please.' He sat down and helped himself to a bread roll. It was softer than Vasya's bread, made with more refined flour than the one she used, and the butter was paler, with a rich clean taste.

'My cook's preserves are excellent.' Koshka pushed a jar of cherry jam towards him. 'I ordered Fritz to have the girls ready in half an hour, so please, take your time, enjoy your breakfast. Tell me, am I right in thinking no further progress has been made in finding whoever killed the poor nurse from your hospital?'

'Naomi Rinskaya. You would be, madam,' Nathan confirmed. 'Through no fault of the Fire Brigade or Mr Hughes's men. They made a thorough search at the time and still continue to question people who were out and about in the street that night.'

'I did wonder about the timing, given what happened to Adele.'

'I spoke to Mr Edwards and some of the men from the Fire Brigade, madam. They all agree it would have been impossible for the man who beat Adele to have killed Naomi Rinskaya. Nurse Rinskaya was attacked shortly before Adele, and her attacker would have been covered with her blood. The man who beat Adele had been in your house for about an hour and had no blood on him.'

'So we have two lunatics on the loose in the town. Or we did have until the man who attacked Adele left. I've been assured by the friends who brought him here that he won't be returning to this area.'

'That's comforting to know. Your ladies...' Nathan proceeded delicately. 'They are vulnerable to violent men.'

'Violence from men is one thing I do know about, Dr Kharber. I have taken precautions to help my girls deal with the small percentage of our clients who have – how shall I put this – peculiar tendencies.'

'In other words, they are violent with the girls?'

'They would be if Fritz and the men I employ didn't stop them. The girls have bell-pulls in their rooms that connect directly to a board which is constantly monitored by one of our men. The slightest sign of trouble, the girls ring for help and it arrives within seconds. It's a crude system, and reliant on the girls being able to reach the pull, but it has prevented some attacks in the past. Our main asset is Fritz. He has a sixth sense when it comes to troublesome clients. If he didn't, I have no doubt Adele's injuries would have been far more serious. Was Naomi Rinskaya beaten?'

'Yes, but not with fists. She'd been battered with something large and heavy, a stone or possibly a stick.'

'She hadn't been whipped with a leather thong?'

'There were no whip marks on her, only cuts, scrapes, and bruises. You have someone in mind?'

'Fritz escorted a gentleman out last night. He had a whip he'd tried to use on one of my young ladies. Fritz confiscated it before he could wield it but such a man always has a second instrument. It was a standard horsewhip.'

'I suppose it could have been the same man,' Nathan said slowly. 'If he didn't have a whip, he could have resorted to the first thing that came to hand. You have his name?'

'I do, and I will pass it on in confidence to Mr Hughes.

Given past experience I am certain that he will refer the man to the Fire Brigade so they can monitor the miscreant. It will be up to them to decide whether the man in question is worth questioning or not.'

'He is a man of influence?'

'Not as much as he thinks. But come, Dr Kharber, this is no topic for breakfast. Let's talk of more pleasant things. How is your wife?'

'Well, thank you.'

'I see her out shopping at the food stalls occasionally.'

'You do your own marketing, not your cook?'

'My cook would never trust me to buy our provisions,' Koshka replenished their coffee cups. 'But I often take a turn in my carriage in the afternoon. I also like to sit in front of my window when I read. This town is full of life, something always seems to be going on. Not all of it tragic.'

'Thankfully not.' He reached for a second roll.

'I saw Miss Tsetovna enter the hospital this morning before you arrived,' she tried to sound casual. 'She isn't ill, I hope?'

'Not at all.' He struggled to keep his voice steady. 'She frequently calls in with gifts of fruit from her aunt's hothouses for the patients.

'She may no longer work for us but her thoughts are always with the nurses and patients. She's a close friend of both Mrs Parry and Miss Parry, and like the rest of us, is concerned that Mrs Parry doesn't work too hard at the moment.'

Koshka wasn't about to allow him to move the conversation on to a discussion about Sarah Parry's finer qualities. 'I have heard only good things about Miss Tsetovna.'

'She is a kind, generous, and remarkable young woman.'

'You enjoyed working with her in the hospital.'

'Very much. We all miss her and her efficiency.'

'Then the hospital's loss is Mr Hughes's and the New Russia Company's gain. Forgive me my poor manners, Dr Kharber, but I have a few things to attend to. Fritz will give you your fee when you have finished. 'Please feel free to avail yourself of whatever you wish before you leave. It has been a pleasure to see you as always.'

'Thank you.' Nathan rose to his feet as Koshka left the room. He was flustered, as he invariably was whenever Sonya's name came up in conversation. He only hoped Koshka hadn't seen just how disconcerted he'd been by the mention of her name. He looked at his roll. His appetite was gone. He pocketed the purse Koshka had given him and left his chair.

Koshka was one of the kindest most generous women he'd ever met. Not for the first time he wondered at the mores of society that made outcasts of women who forged successful careers with nothing more at their disposal than their charms.

And at the hypocrisy of men, who were happy to use those women within private walls and yet treated them as pariahs whenever they ventured into the wider world.

Chapter Twenty-three

Madam Koshka's salon February 1872

'Adele, your turn next. Lucky last,' Xenia winked as the door closed on Michelle, one of the few authentic French women who worked in the salon. 'You do realise that if you succeed in inveigling the handsome doctor into bed as a thank you for tending to your bruises, you'll be the first to seduce him in this house.'

'That's the challenge.'

'He's very good-looking, isn't he?' Natalya, a young Cossack Koshka had just taken on, declared. 'I saw him and his wife walking through the town yesterday. She looks like a wrinkled old prune. Do you think he sleeps with her?'

'Presumably, as he married her,' Xenia said. 'But whether he does or doesn't it's none of your business.'

'She looks years and years older than him. I'd entertain him for free if he asked,' Natalya continued. 'He's so good-looking. All I had last night were greybeards who took for ever, and three two-rouble tips. Is it true madam will give you ten roubles for making the doctor happy?'

'Five roubles,' Xenia corrected. 'And aren't you supposed to be checking that the wine glasses are clean for tonight.'

Natalya made a face behind Xenia's back as she flounced off.

'I saw that,' Xenia called after her.

Natalya ran and slammed the door behind her.

'How could you possibly have seen that face she made?' Adele asked Xenia.

'I didn't, but I've seen too many young girls like her come into the salon. Full of themselves, thinking they know it all.'

'I heard your admirer stayed the night again. He's getting to be quite a regular. A friend of Mr Hughes and a Welshman, lucky you. Is he very rich?' Adele probed.

'He's nice, good company, a gentleman, and always leaves me a present. I'm getting quite fond of him, but he's not in the same class as Prince Roman. Not many of us can aspire to aristocratic clients.'

'The prince is a good friend, but I have no idea how much longer he'll keep visiting me. You've heard he's engaged?'

'To the heiress niece of Catherine Ignatova. I overheard Mr Hughes and Mr Dmitri talking about it. But since when has an engagement – or marriage come to that – stopped a man from visiting Koshka's?' Xenia asked.

'It'll stop the prince,' Adele prophesied gloomily. 'He's not like most of our clients. He prizes honesty in all aspects of his life – and he likes his women one at a time.'

'Honesty! One at a time! In that case he must be truly unique. Who was it said that all men, like cats, are grey in the dark? They're cheaters by nature.'

'They're cheaters until they find the right woman,' Adele contradicted. 'Most men only want comfort and a quiet private life, including in the bedroom.'

'In my experience, only after a good few years of excitement.'

'I'm coming,' Adele called in reply to a knock on the door. She pulled the belt of her robe tighter as she left her chair. 'Good luck with the seduction,' Xenia called after her.

The first time Nathan had examined Koshka's "girls" he'd been more embarrassed than his patients. He'd treated prostitutes in hospitals in Paris and Vienna but he'd never felt at ease in their company, particularly when they'd begun discussing their intimate problems openly without a hint of the modesty that was ingrained into Jewish girls from birth. They'd stripped off in front of him without a qualm, deliberately setting out to arouse and excite him, and laughing in his face when they succeeded.

233

Sensing his nervousness, Koshka's girls had treated him more kindly than their counterparts in France and Austria. After a few months of weekly visits, a friendship of sorts had developed between them, but Nathan never felt he was the one in authority when he was with them. Their profession and way of life was so alien to his own, their frank directness so different to Jewish women's reticence, he was never quite sure how to treat them.

'Last one, Dr Kharber.' Adele walked into the room used by Nathan because it had a high raised sofa as well as a double bed. Without waiting for him to ask, she dropped her robe. She lay on the sofa, and watched his face intently as he examined her. He pretended not to notice her staring at him.

'You're fine.' He turned his back to her and washed his hands in the basin on the washstand.

'Thanks to the care you bestowed on my face, madam's precautions, and a plethora of French letters.'

He was unsure how to respond to the flippant remark, so he didn't. 'Any problems with your jaw now?'

'None, thank you.' She opened her mouth wide to prove it.

'You can get dressed.' He picked up Adele's robe from the chair where she'd left it and handed it to her.

She continued to look into his eyes as she rose to her knees. Instead of taking the robe, she stroked the front of his trousers. His cheeks flushed red.

'Madam has instructed me to entertain you.'

'That isn't necessary.'

'We should accommodate your every wish, Dr Kharber – on the house. After all, you look after us so well, the least we can do is look after you.'

'I'm ... married,' he stammered.

'So are most of our clients. You also look very tired. I'm not suggesting you should do anything you don't want to, but this sofa is very comfortable, the bed even more so. If you lay down I'll give you a massage to help you relax.'

234

Nathan had never been so tempted. He glanced at the bed. The sheets gleamed white, freshly laundered and starched. Just like earlier when he'd realised he was hungry, he suddenly felt in desperate need of sleep after working most of the night.

It was as though Adele sensed his exhaustion. 'You have no pressing business to attend to, do you?' She reached up and gently caressed the back of his neck with her fingertips, pushing her naked breasts against him as she did so. 'Just a few minutes – a small gift in return for all you do for us.'

Intoxicated by her perfume and proximity, he turned. Adele then did something she reserved for very few clients. She kissed him, full on the mouth. When she finished kissing him, they were both on the bed, and most of his clothes were on top of her robe on the chair.

Madam Koshka's salon February 1872

'I am so sorry to keep you waiting, Roman, it's my morning for dealing with tradesmen and placing orders for the coming week. Like all business people every one of them was in a hurry and none were prepared to wait.' Koshka joined Roman in her boudoir.

'Fritz has been taking good care of me.' Roman indicated the bottle of cognac and glass at his elbow.

'He said you wanted to see Adele?'

'He told me she's with a client. I was amazed to hear that she's working again. Is she well enough?'

'It was her decision to return to work, not mine.'

'In which case I'm not surprised that she's in demand even before ten o'clock in the morning – or is he a leftover from last night you haven't managed to eject?' he enquired archly.

'I'm sure she'll be delighted to see you as soon as she is free,' Koshka replied diplomatically.

Roman pulled a leather purse from his pocket and set it on the table. 'I only wanted to give her this. I've been meaning to visit her for weeks but we've been busy in the works.'

'I heard – full production of pig iron, no less.'

'Mr Hughes has done exactly what he promised he would, upsetting all his detractors in Moscow and St Petersburg who said he'd set himself an impossible task. But to return to my reason for calling, I thought Adele might need money as she hasn't been able to entertain clients for a while.'

Koshka glanced at the purse that was full and looked heavy. She didn't doubt it contained gold coin. 'Very thoughtful of you. Will you continue to visit Adele after you marry Sonya?'

Roman searched for but didn't find a hint of reproach – or approval – in Koshka's tone. 'If I get married.' He reached for the brandy. 'Forget I said that.'

'Something's happened between you and Sonya?'

'No, I ...' he thought better of elaborating. 'No, really it's not worth discussing.'

'You saw Sonya enter the hospital early this morning and she appeared upset when she left?' Koshka suggested.

'Her chaperone mentioned that they'd called into the hospital before she started work. You saw Sonya too?'

'From my window. You do know that Dr Kharber left the building as Sonya arrived?'

'No, I didn't.'

'It's Dr Kharber's morning for checking my girls, but he arrived just after eight o'clock. I believe he wanted to get away from the hospital after spending all night caring for a young diphtheria patient. It must be emotionally draining trying to save the lives of children, and even more devastating to lose them, especially young ones, as he so often does despite all the care he lavishes on them. However, Nathan told me that last night's patient survived, let's hope that the boy continues to make a full recovery.'

'You're sure Dr Kharber was upset because of the youth of his patient and not because he saw Sonya?' Roman countered.

'He raised his hat to her and Maria. Even allowing for his lack of sleep I hardly think raising his hat would prove to be an upsetting experience.'

'You said he was upset.'

'I didn't. You said Sonya was.'

'I saw Sonya wiping away tears. For her to be visibly distraught...'

'It is cold outside. Enough to make your eyes water.'

'It is,' he agreed.

'But you've drawn a different conclusion?'

'And if I have?'

'If you believe that Nathan Kharber has upset your fiancée, shouldn't you be talking to her, not me, about it?'

'I didn't come here to discuss my fiancée with you, Koshka, but to make sure Adele has everything she needs.'

'You are fond of Adele?'

'You know I am. I assume she is with Nathan Kharber?' '

You know better than to ask that, Roman. The first rule of the house is I never discuss my clients with anyone.'

'Then Nathan is not just your doctor, he's also your client?'

Annoyed with herself for speaking unguardedly, Koshka took a notebook from her pocket and dropped it on to her desk. 'I just told you I don't discuss...'

'Clients?'

'Or my doctor.' She settled on the chair behind her desk and swung it round so she faced him. 'If I were you I would think very hard about marrying a young girl who is infatuated with another man and in all probability nowhere near ready for marriage.'

'Sonya's ready for marriage, she just doesn't know it.'

'If she marries you I hope you're proved right, Roman.' Koshka opened a drawer in her desk and dropped the notebook alongside a pile of others. Roman recognised one of the books in the drawer, a brown embossed leather volume.

'That's an interesting book.'

'What book?'

'That book.'

Koshka tried to close the drawer but Roman was too quick for her. He lifted it out and opened it.

'I thought it appeared familiar, but although I devoured my father's copy cover to cover several times, I failed to make a note of the binding. But then,' he held up the closed book. 'It looks just like any other book, except it's missing a title and author on the spine.'

'I believe the intention of the publisher was to do just that. Produce a book that resembled "any other" so as not to draw attention to anyone reading it in public. I give a copy to all my girls. It should be recommended reading for every woman over the age of eighteen.'

'Really?' He was surprised. 'Even virgins?'

'Especially virgins. Contrary to general belief, inexperienced girls are not little angels who need protecting from the realities of life.' She took a clean glass from the drinks tray and poured herself a small cognac.

She held the bottle up to him. He shook his head. 'Just like boys, girls are immensely curious about sex. Yet well brought-up young ladies are taught it is a subject never to be mentioned in polite company, indeed never to be discussed even in private with one's husband. I give the book to my girls because it's a useful guide if they have cause to question their clients' ideas of the boundaries of acceptable behaviour.'

'Acceptable behaviour?' he questioned incredulously. 'Have you read that book? It sets no boundaries for acceptable sexual behaviour.'

'Yes it does, Roman. The most important boundary of all. That there are no boundaries, provided every party involved freely consents and no one is injured, physically or emotionally.'

He sipped his brandy. 'Sound common sense, but then you are renowned for that – and for your kindness.' He flicked through the book.

'You can keep it if you like.'

'Did Adele suggest I need the titillation?'

She laughed. 'I just told you...'

'Gossip about clients and their penchants is forbidden,' he finished for her. He set the book aside. 'I still have my father's copy in one of my houses, although I could probably reproduce that book, line for line including illustrations, from memory given the number of times I sneaked into my father's library and stole it to read behind the locked door of my bedroom.'

'Did you learn anything from it?'

'Enough about how sex works to please myself, and hopefully my partner du jour.'

'And Sonya?'

'If we marry I'll take care of her needs, and wishes. But when it comes to the emotional side of relationships, I learned everything I know from you during that last visit I made to my father when I was fifteen. Do you remember it?'

'How could I forget. You were such a charming boy.'

'As opposed to man.'

'Now you're a charming man, but like all aristocrats educated in England I can't help feeling there's something disingenuous in your personality. That your charisma is merely a veneer. Crack it and insincerity will ooze out.'

He laughed mirthlessly as if to confirm her suspicions.

'You're right, of course, just as you always are. It's the result of the grounding boys are given in English public school. Etiquette and manners at the expense of feelings. When I arrived in St Petersburg for that holiday I wanted to believe that my father had invited me to visit him so that we could get to know one another. I didn't even realise he was ill that summer until the house master sent for me a month into the new term to tell me that he'd died. Thank you for being so kind to me, and especially for making me understand that my father's coldness towards me was none of my doing.'

'As I've already said, you were a charming boy, but I couldn't help noticing that you were also very lonely.'

'I was religious in those days and used to pray to God every night that my father would marry you.'

'A prince and a notorious courtesan,' she murmured, 'more than prayers would be needed to make that work.'

'Tsars have been known to give dispensations.'

'When aristocrats wanted to marry an innocent girl who was socially beneath them, like Count Sheremetev, perhaps, but a courtesan, particularly one as infamous as me, would have ruined your father's reputation – and yours.'

'The sins of the father are invariably handed down no matter how his children may try to avoid them.'

'Your father had many faults, Roman. Not showing or telling you how much he loved you was probably the worst.'

There was a knock at the door. Koshka called out, 'Come in.'

Fritz opened it a crack and stuck his head into the room. He didn't see Roman who was sitting behind the door. 'Good morning again, madam.'

'Good morning again, Fritz. You wanted something?'

'The doctor has just left, he told me to tell you that all is well. And Adele wanted you to know she was victorious.'

240

'Thank you, Fritz, but next time you have private information to impart please wait until I'm alone.'

Roman leaned forward so Fritz could see him. 'Good morning again, Fritz.'

'Good morning again, Prince Roman. My apologies, sir, madam. I didn't expect to see the prince still here.'

'So I gather, Fritz. Would you please tell the rest of the staff that I do not want to be disturbed?'

'Yes, madam.' Fritz withdrew and closed the door behind him.

'So, Adele was victorious,' Roman repeated. 'I take it that means she enticed Nathan Kharber into her bed?'

'Not all victories are related to clients, Roman.'

'Really?' he enquired sceptically.

'Occasionally the girls use the word when they've attracted a new regular visitor,' she capitulated. 'But you really do appear to be fixated on Nathan Kharber, Roman.'

'Interested, not fixated.' Roman picked up his brandy and finished it. 'That is excellent cognac, you must give me the name of the brand. As Adele has spoken to Fritz I assume she is now free, so I will say my goodbyes.'

'Don't forget the purse.'

'Thank you for reminding me,' He picked it up, pocketed it, rose from his chair and kissed her hand.

'Roman, it's none of my business, but why this headlong rush to marry Sonya? She's young –'

'But as I said, not too young to marry. Business necessitates that I leave Hughesovka shortly for St Petersburg. If I don't marry Sonya I can't take her with me unless we drag along her chaperone, and frankly I find Maria somewhat inhibiting as well as boring. If I left Sonya here in her unmarried state, any lout could come into the town while I'm away, catch her on the rebound from Kharber, and snatch her from under my nose.'

'Lout?' Koshka questioned.

'Have you seen some of the men walking around the town?' he asked.

'I try to avoid the rougher elements.'

'And I'm trying to protect Sonya from them. She's beautiful enough to ornament the court.'

'You want to introduce her to royalty?'

'Royalty are no different from the common herd.'

'Given my acquaintance with aristocrats, I'd say no different at all, especially when it comes to the baser urges,' she agreed.

'That was a poor choice of words. Please, replace royalty with "educated, civilised people, royal and otherwise".'

'So your plans for Sonya are entirely altruistic?'

'Not entirely,' he conceded, 'I'm tired of fending off solicitations from society mothers anxious to marry their daughters off to me simply because I have money.'

'So in return for protecting Sonya from "louts" you want her to protect you from ambitious mothers?'

'I wouldn't argue with that.'

'So you see your forthcoming marriage as one of convenience?'

'Of course.' He went to the door.

'You must love Sonya very much.'

He faced her. 'Who says I love Sonya?'

'You might fool her, and maybe even yourself, but not me, Roman. But don't worry, your secret is safe with me. Just don't wait too long to tell Sonya how you feel.'

'For once your intuition has failed you, Koshka.'

'Perhaps, perhaps not. I notice you still have the book. A present for Sonya perhaps?'

'I thought I'd pass it on to her. You did say it should be recommended reading for every woman over the age of eighteen.'

'I did. Even should your marriage prove to be a happy one, you'll still come and visit us from time to time?'

'Whenever I'm in Hughesovka, and who knows, if my marriage never takes place or if it does and proves unhappy, perhaps you will find me another young lady to take Adele's place now she has a new regular.' Roman blew Koshka a last kiss before walking out of the door.

Chapter Twenty-four

New Russia Company Headquarters February 1872

Tears blinded Sonya's eyes as she sat in her cubicle next to John Hughes's office in the company headquarters. She saw Vasily glance oddly at her when he brought in the morning mail. She began to open it, but she couldn't concentrate on the letters. When she tried to read them, all she could see was Nathan's face, as he'd said, 'Good morning, ladies'.

He hadn't looked her in the eye or paid her any more attention than he had Maria. Yet again, she recalled the words that had burned into her mind and haunted her since the day he'd spoken them. She could even recall the inflection in his voice...

We're mushrooms and toadstools, Sonya. Fine when kept separate, put us in a pan together, and the dish turns to poison.

Poison – was that how he thought of her, poison? Something foul that would contaminate him and the religion he prized above all else. Even love ... If she'd ever needed confirmation that the feelings she'd borne – and still bore – for him would never come to any fruition, she'd received it that morning.

'You feeling all right, Sonya?'

She glanced up. Alexei was standing in front of her desk. 'Fine.'

'You don't look fine.'

'I'm just cold.'

'It's warm enough in here. I'd say almost tropical,' he added after glancing at the fire that blazed in the stove in the corner of her cubicle. 'If you're cold you could be sickening for something. You should go over to the hospital.'

'No, really. I probably just spent too much time walking outside before I came in here. Maria and I took some of Aunt Catherine's fruit to the hospital.'

'I hope you didn't go into the wards. Ruth saw Sarah yesterday and she told her that diphtheria and scarlet fever are rife in the hole houses.'

'I only went as far as the kitchen, Alexei, and you know how strict Sarah is about barrier nursing. Really I'm fine.' She searched for a handkerchief to wipe her eyes. Before she found one he handed her his.

'You look anything but fine to me. Why don't you go home? I could send for my carriage. It's no trouble. Lev would probably welcome the opportunity to escape from Lada for an hour if he could spend most of it sampling Lyudmila's baking in her kitchen.'

'Thank you for the offer but no, Alexei.' She left her desk and reached for her coat and scarf. 'I'm probably in need of some fresh air.'

'You just said you spent too much time walking outside in the cold. You're not thinking straight.'

'Perhaps I'm hungry. It's almost lunch time. I'll call on Sarah and Praskovia and see if there's anything Aunt Catherine or I can do to help the people in the hole houses.'

'I doubt it. Mr Hughes has called a meeting otherwise I'd go with you, but I'll ask one of the clerks to escort you.'

'The Fire Brigade is patrolling the town.'

'They are, but it won't hurt you to have a personal guard. I shouldn't have to remind you that we still haven't caught whoever killed Naomi.'

'It's daylight. Mr Edwards's house is a five-minute walk, Alexei. Besides, you have a meeting and I'd rather be alone.' She pinned her hat to her head without even checking in the mirror to see if it was on straight, before walking out of the building.

Alexei saw Vlad in the corridor, he beckoned him over.

'Mr Alexei, sir.'

'Follow Miss Sonya at a distance. Make sure she doesn't see you and that she gets safely to Mr Edwards's house.'

Sonya resisted the temptation to look towards the hospital windows. Oblivious to Vlad who was following her at a discreet distance, she acknowledged the members of the Fire Brigade who waved to her as she passed. When she reached Glyn's house she opened the garden gate and went to the front door. Pyotr opened it before she reached the step.

'Hello, Miss Sonya, how are you today?'

'I'm fine, thank you, Pyotr. How are you?'

'Very well, thank you for asking, Miss Sonya.'

Hearing voices, Praskovia left the dining room. 'Sonya, what a lovely and welcome surprise. How nice to see, you. Come in and go through to the drawing room. Pyotr, after you've taken Sonya's coat and hat, go into the kitchen and tell them we need tea, sandwiches, and cake.'

'Not for me please, Praskovia,' Sonya demurred.

'In that case, we'll wait until lunch is on the table. Tell them to just make tea, Pyotr.' She followed Sonya and drew two chairs close to the fire that blazed in the hearth. The clock struck the midday chimes as they sat down. 'Knowing Sarah she'll be up soon, although she missed a night's sleep. Dr Kharber sent for her to help him operate on a diphtheria patient. His airways were too swollen for him to breathe.'

'Is he all right?'

'Sarah said he survived the operation and his prognosis is good.'

'I hope you feel as well as you look, Praskovia,' Sonya commented.

Praskovia removed a cushion from the back of her chair in an effort to get comfortable. 'If by that you mean I'm the size of one of the bullocks that pull Mr Hughes's carts, you'd be right.'

'I meant nothing of the sort.'

'Strange isn't it, Sarah's baby will be born only a few weeks after mine,' Praskovia rested her hands on her swollen abdomen, 'yet she's half my size.'

'That's because mothers – and babies – come in all sizes and shapes.' Sarah swept in and kissed Sonya's cheek. 'I heard voices. So I came down to see who was here. I'm glad I did.' She pulled a chair close to Sonya's.

'You should be resting,' Praskovia admonished.

'If I sleep all day I won't sleep tonight.' Sarah looked at the clock on the mantelpiece. 'Besides I should look in on the hospital this afternoon.'

'You're not going to work after being up all night?' Praskovia reproached.

'I'll only be training the new nursing recruits for an hour or two. Hardly onerous, unless something happens and we take in more patients.'

'Given that scarlet fever, diphtheria, and scabies are sweeping through the hole houses I think we've enough happening in this town.' Praskovia picked up the cushion again and moved it behind her head.

'Not easy to get comfortable when you have another one on board, is it?' Sarah eyed Sonya. 'You seem upset. You haven't had an argument with Prince Roman, have you?'

Sonya shook her head as tears streamed from her eyes.

Praskovia pulled a white lawn handkerchief from her pocket and handed it over. 'It's crumpled but clean.'

'Thank you.' Sonya dried her eyes. 'I'm sorry.'

'Don't be,' Sarah spoke with feeling. 'You don't have to talk if you don't want to but if you think it will help, we're here.'

'It's just that ...' Sonya suddenly realised that she couldn't tell Sarah or Praskovia that she was in love with Nathan. If the news reached Ruth or Alexei she'd be mortified. It was bad enough that Roman and Vasya knew she and Nathan loved one another.

She searched her mind desperately trying to think of something – anything – believable that she could tell Sarah and Praskovia, but Sarah interrupted her thoughts.

'It must be daunting being engaged to a prince.'

'It is,' she said without thinking what she was admitting. 'Having second thoughts?' Sarah asked gently.

'I can't seem to think further than the wedding. The prince ... Roman ... he's very kind, but...'

'He's a man?' Praskovia joked.

The doorbell rang and they heard Ruth talking to Pyotr. She joined them. 'Hello, everyone. She kissed Sarah, Praskovia, and Sonya's cheeks. 'Your mother told me to tell you that the maids have laid lunch on the table, Praskovia, and the stew is being kept warm in the chafing dish as you instructed.'

'My mother doesn't like the chafing dish,' Praskovia explained. 'She calls it a new invention, although I've tried to explain to her that the principal is the same as a samovar – apart from what's in it. It's just something for keeping food warm.' She glanced at the clock. 'The men should be in soon, if they're coming.'

'Mr Hughes called a meeting,' Sonya warned.

'In which case, they may not be in until supper time,' Praskovia observed philosophically, 'so we can have a good gossip while you all eat twice as much as normal, so my mother won't be annoyed at the waste of food.'

'I saw Alexei before I left the office. He looked happy, marriage agrees with him,' Sonya forced a smile.

'It agrees with me too,' Ruth pulled up a chair and joined their semicircle around the stove. 'Although I wish he'd let me carry on working in the hospital.'

'Don't let him bully you,' Sonya reached out and grasped Ruth's hand. She was suddenly aware of how very fortunate she was to have good friends she could call on any time she chose.

'Dare I ask how your wedding plans are coming along, Sonya?' Sarah ventured.

'Thanks to Aunt Catherine, they've come along as far as my dress.'

'You've found one, that's marvellous! What is it like?' Praskovia signalled to the maid to place the samovar on a side table.

'Aunt Catherine had hers brought out of storage the day I accepted Roman's proposal. It's beautiful, decades old, but she'd packed it away so carefully it looks as though it's just left the dressmaker's workshop. It's Empire line, white silk overlaid with white lace. The hem, puffed sleeves, and bodice are embroidered with real gold thread and beads, as are the veil and train. Aunt Catherine said she'd always hoped that her daughter would want to wear it on her wedding day, but full skirts were fashionable when Olga married Count Beletsky and he said a figure-hugging gown in the French Empire style would be regarded as indecent, so Olga had one made in a design he approved of.'

'Does it fit you?' Praskovia suppressed a pang of envy. Every time Glyn apologised for not being able to marry her she insisted she didn't mind. But she couldn't lie to herself. She dreamed of wearing a wedding dress, and marrying Glyn in church. Her gown wouldn't have to be as beautiful or costly as Ruth's, or a family heirloom like Sonya's, just a dress she could wear to walk down the aisle to meet Glyn in front of the altar.

'As Aunt Catherine said, it looks as though it was made for me, not her.'

'Will Anna wear the bridesmaid's dress she wore for Ruth and Alexei's wedding?' Praskovia asked.

'She's coming to dinner as soon as she has an evening off to try on the bridesmaid's dress Aunt Catherine's mother had made to match the wedding gown. It's blue lace and silk, cut in the same style as the wedding dress, with the same gold embroidery and just as beautiful.'

'I can't wait to see it,' Sarah enthused.

'You will if it fits Anna.'

'My grandparents told us children many stories of Mrs Ignatova's wedding day but they were mainly descriptions of the pig roasts and pails of vodka set aside for the people who lived and worked on the estate. They never once mentioned Mrs Ignatova's gown or a bridesmaid. Who was she?' Praskovia moved her cushion – again.

Sonya looked sombre as she frequently did whenever she mentioned the parents she had never known. 'My grandparents and Aunt Catherine's parents were great friends, so Aunt Catherine chose my mother to be her bridesmaid. She was fifteen at the time, a year younger than Aunt Catherine and the same age Anna is now. A year later she was married herself.'

'To your father who was Aunt Catherine's brother?' Ruth was interested in Alexei's family's history and eager to learn all Sonya could tell her.

'No.' Sonya shook her head. 'I don't know the name of my mother's first husband or anything about him other than he beat her and she left him. She fell in love with Aunt Catherine's brother – my father – much later.'

Sensitive to the tone in Sonya's voice, for the first time Ruth suspected that Sonya's parents hadn't been married when she'd been born.

'Stay there, Praskovia, I'll serve the tea.' Sarah reached out and wheeled the samovar closer to her chair. 'Do you remember your parents, Sonya?'

'No. I wish I had something, just one memory of them that I could cling to, but my father was diagnosed with consumption before I was born and sent to an isolation hospital where he's remained ever since. He's so contagious he's not even allowed to write letters. My mother died a few months later. All I have are the photographic portraits Aunt Catherine has given me.'

'I don't even have that much to remember my parents by,' Sarah confessed.

'They died when you were a baby?' Sonya took the glass Sarah handed her.

'I've no idea. I was taken to a workhouse as a new born by an Anglican vicar who left his name and address. When I was old enough to be given a day off from the hospital wing where I'd found work, first as a ward maid then a nurse, I went to the address the Workhouse Master gave me. The vicar who'd brought me to the orphanage wing had moved on and the new vicar knew nothing about me. He was kind. He invited me to have tea with him and his wife. He even asked his housekeeper, who'd known the old vicar if she could tell him anything about me, but it was hopeless. The parish was in the East End of London: an area packed from the cellars to the rooftops with immigrants on their way to – or from – somewhere. It was also full of,' Sarah rolled her eyes and lowered her voice, in an attempt to lighten the atmosphere, 'ladies of the night.'

Praskovia and Ruth burst out laughing and even Sonya managed a smile.

'Have you settled on a date for the ceremony yet, Sonya?' Sarah finished serving the tea and returned to her chair.

'Father Grigor is coming to dinner when Anna can make it so we'll decide then. Roman would like us to marry soon so I can travel with him to St Petersburg. He wants to report to Grand Duke Konstantin on the progress Mr Hughes has made and to talk to him on Mr Hughes's behalf about future government contracts.'

'How soon is soon?' Ruth asked her.

'As soon as the snow melts enough to make travelling easier.'

'So in the next month?'

'Yes.' Even as she confirmed it, Sonya didn't quite believe her wedding could happen – ever – let alone within a month.

Whether it was the lack of opportunity to talk to Roman about anything even remotely personal because of the constant presence of her chaperone Maria, or the feelings she had for Nathan, that try as she may she simply couldn't control, she felt as though nothing was real in her life.

It was as though she was trapped in a dream world where nothing mattered because sometime soon she would wake up and her life would begin again, afresh and anew – and Nathan wouldn't be married.

'Then you'll go to St Petersburg,' Ruth sighed. 'This place won't be the same without you. When will you be back?'

'I've no idea. Roman mentioned that he has houses elsewhere but we've never talked about where we'll live.'

'You will settle here permanently, won't you?' Praskovia said hopefully.

'Roman warned me that he likes to travel, but as he has business interests with Mr Hughes I hope we'll be spending a great deal of time here.'

'I hope so too,' Praskovia said feelingly. 'I hate change and it's as if the village I grew up in has galloped into a town and now the town's galloping away from us. New people are moving in all the time, Welsh, Russian, German, every nationality under the sun, changing the atmosphere.'

'That's not a bad thing, is it?' Sarah asked.

'Not for the people coming in, but we Cossacks are beginning to feel overwhelmed. Now that the blast furnace is in full production even more people will settle here in the hope of finding work. I feel as though everyone who lives here is losing control, even Mr Hughes. We have fights in the street, drunks around all the beer and vodka shops, and so much violence and...'

Sarah interrupted Praskovia before she could mention Naomi's murder, a subject that was on everyone's mind, but one she felt that there was little point in discussing as it invariably led to upset and even tears.

'Glyn, Richard, and I talked about the way Hughesovka is growing over breakfast. We agreed change is inevitable and that perhaps our dream of building utopia on the steppe was unrealistic given the nature of the heavy industry Mr Hughes is pioneering, and the type of rough and ready uneducated men willing to do hard physical work in the furnace and mines. But in a few years Hughesovka will settle down, and there'll be more opportunities for educated and skilled workers. Then, I think we can expect things to become calmer and dare I say, more civilized.'

'I hope you're right,' Praskovia set down her tea glass. 'I can't help thinking that our children will grow up in a very different world to the Cossack village that was my childhood home.'

'Looking back it was idyllic. What I remember most are long summer days spent riding, building hides in the woods, and hunting with your father, Praskovia. He taught us all so much and told us so many stories.' Sonya looked up at the clock. 'Time I was getting back to the office.'

'You'll stay to eat something,' Praskovia pressed.

'Brides have to keep up their strength,' Sarah added. 'Otherwise they run the risk of fainting at the altar.'

Sonya capitulated. 'There wasn't that much correspondence that needed translating this morning so I suppose another half hour or so won't make any difference.'

'Let's load up plates in the dining room and bring them back here where it's warm and cosy,' Praskovia went to the door and opened it.

'And talk weddings,' Sarah suggested. She was tempted to add, or about anything except Naomi's tragic death – not to mention the fear she sensed stalking the town like a suffocating cloud of poison gas.

'And what marriage is really like,' Ruth's eyes sparkled.

'Tell me,' Sonya asked.

'I was looking forward to sleeping with Alexei every night and waking up next to him in the morning, but I never thought it would be as wonderful as it is,' Ruth confided. 'When he puts his arms around me in bed it feels as though I've crawled into his cocoon and nothing exists outside of our world.'

Praskovia laughed. 'There is nothing like sleeping with the man in your life – in every sense of "sleep". Making love with Glyn makes me feel alive in a way I never felt before.'

None of them saw Anna on the stairs. She heard what Praskovia said and shuddered. Unable to sleep, she'd intended joining the others, but as she stood at the foot of the stairs and listened to the conversation grow more risqué and intimate, she grew increasingly nauseous. Treading softly and carefully she turned and silently retraced her steps.

Chapter Twenty-five

Hospital, Hughesovka February 1872

Nathan Kharber left Koshka's and returned to his office.
He was exhausted and had almost fallen asleep in Adele's
arms, but he had one task to complete before he went
home to his own bed.

He sat behind his desk, took a clean sheet of notepaper
from the drawer and wrote a short letter.

Dear Miss Tsetovna,
I would like to thank you and your aunt for the fruit you
brought this morning for the patients. It is much
appreciated.
Yours sincerely,
Nathan Kharber (doctor)

There was a hidden message in the polite note. He
hoped for both their sakes Sonya would understand what it
was, because he was spending so much time dwelling on
and regretting what could never be, it was affecting every
aspect of his life.

He placed it in an envelope, sealed it, and wrote
Sonya's name on the outside; locking his office door
behind him he handed his keys and the letter to the duty
porter.

'See this is delivered to Miss Tsetovna in the New
Russia Company Office as soon as possible. It's a thank
you for the fruit she brought this morning.'

'Yes, sir.' Maxim took the keys and letter from him and
shouted to Bogdan who was in the kitchen. 'You're
needed to deliver a letter to the New Russia Company
Headquarters.'

Nathan looked in on the wards. The trainees were practising bed making under Miriam's eagle eye.

'If there are any emergencies I will be at home, Nurse, I'm going to catch up on some sleep.'

'Yes, Dr Kharber.'

'You look as though you could do with some rest too. If it's quiet, lie down in one of the treatment rooms and allow the trainees to run the wards.'

'Yes, sir.'

He knew that unlike Anna, who drove herself harder than any of the other nurses, Miriam would take his advice.

He left the building and pulled up the collar of his coat. It had finally stopped snowing but the sky was heavy with grey clouds, and he could feel the temperature dropping by the minute. He trudged through the snowdrifts around the side of the building and walked up to his front door. The porters had cleared a path and shovelled sand from the company yard on to it to make for easier walking.

Vasya was hovering in the hall and it was obvious that she'd been waiting for him. She opened the door before he even reached the porch.

'You look exhausted, Nathan.'

'It's been a long night and morning, I need to sleep.'

'Would you like me to sleep with you?'

'No,' he snapped quickly. Too quickly, he realised, when he saw Vasya flinch.

'You must be hungry?'

'I breakfasted earlier.' He didn't reveal where. He glanced at the wall clock that had been a wedding present from Vasya's father. 'If no one comes to fetch me sooner please wake me at six o'clock.'

'You're going to the hospital tonight after working for more than twenty-four hours?'

'My patients need me, Vasya.'

'You sure I can't get you something? If you don't want a meal, then cake or a sandwich, and tea...'

'Nothing.' He was angry with himself for being short with his wife, but he knew that if he didn't curb her she would continue until she'd itemised everything in the pantry. 'Nothing at all,' he reiterated in a marginally softer tone.

'My father called again this morning. About his cousin's children,' she began timidly. 'My father and uncle...'

'I have told you a dozen times, my word is final, Vasya, I will not adopt your father's cousins.'

'Then there is no point in discussing the matter, although they will soon be here in Hughesovka?'

He heard her father's demand behind the gentle request. 'None whatsoever,' he replied. 'Please don't bring the matter up again, Vasya.'

She hung her head.

Hating himself for hurting her, furious at her subservience, he was beginning to understand men who beat their meek wives when the women gave no apparent cause for complaint. Wishing that just once Vasya would stand up for herself, he went into the bedroom and closed the door behind him. Tripping over the single bed Vasya had placed at the foot of the marital bed, so she could sleep as an orthodox wife should – at the feet of her husband – he flung off his clothes, crawled between the sheets and tried to sleep.

Sonya, Vasya, and Roman Nadolny's images whirled around in a kaleidoscope, interspersed with those of Rabbi Goldberg, his father-in-law, Levi, and four faceless children, three boys and a girl, all dressed in deep black mourning with tears in their coats above their hearts to signify they were mourning the loss of their parents.

But it was Sonya's face he kept trying to hold to the forefront of his mind. Sonya, pale and reproachful as she'd been when he'd ignored her as she'd approached the hospital that morning, wearing the pain he'd inflicted on her face.

New Russia Company Headquarters February 1872

Vasily waylaid Sonya when she returned to the office.
'These were delivered when you were out, Miss
Tsetovna.' He handed her a package wrapped in brown
paper and a letter. She looked at the address on the
package. It had been written in an educated hand, but she
didn't recognise the penmanship. She turned it over. There
was no return address, only her name on both sides, and
below it marked in large letters PERSONAL AND
PRIVATE.

'Did you see who delivered it?' she asked the clerk.

'Not the package, Miss Tsetovna. It was just left on the
counter in the front office. The letter came from the
hospital.'

'Thank you, Vasily.'

He looked at the parcel she'd made no attempt to open.
'Will there be any return messages?'

'If there are I'll bring them to you, Vasily.'

'Thank you, Miss Tsetovna.'

Sonya waited until the clerk left her office before
opening the letter. She read it and understood Nathan's
reasons for sending such a terse formal acknowledgement.
He was married, she was engaged. They should never have
voiced their feelings for one another. Short and formal
were the only exchanges possible between them if his
marriage was to survive and she was to make any kind of
life for herself.

She had to forget him. To that end, she almost tossed
the letter into the bin, then thought better of the idea. If
ever she needed a reminder that nothing beyond a polite
exchange of platitudes could exist between them, this was
it. She returned the letter to its envelope and filed it away
in the top drawer of her desk.

She opened her package. She shook out the paper
hoping to find a card, or at least a slip of paper with the
name of the sender but there was nothing.

It contained a book beautifully bound in embossed brown leather. She opened it.

There was a handwritten line on the flyleaf.

This book contains information an engaged woman about to be married needs to know, and is sent with the best of intentions.

She flicked through the pages and stared in disbelief at the illustrations. Colour flooded her cheeks, hot, burning. Her aunt had been open and honest with her about sex and what was expected of a woman – complete chastity before marriage and the reverse, but solely with her husband, once the wedding ring was on her finger. As for the mechanics – no child brought up on a country estate, as she'd been, could have failed to have seen horses at stud and other animals mating. When it came to humans, her cousin Olga had been almost continually pregnant from the day she'd married the count.

But these illustrations went beyond the sexual act as she'd imagined it. When she started reading the text she realised it was a guide to gaining as much pleasure as possible from lovemaking.

Until that moment she'd thought of love between a man and woman as pure, beautiful, romantic, and, from something Olga had said, sacrificial and noble on the part of the woman. Whenever she'd thought of it in a personal context she'd imagined lovemaking as an extension of the feelings she had for Nathan, which she'd never associated with the naked writhing of the man and woman depicted in the pictures.

She was still immersed in the book when Roman breezed into her cubicle. She hastily snapped it shut, dropped it into a drawer and closed it.

'Caught you?'

'Pardon.' She knew her cheeks were flaming because she could feel them burning.

'Reading novels in work, tut, tut,' he teased. 'But your secret is safe with me, I won't tell Mr Hughes. Is it interesting?'

'What?' she stared at him blankly.

'The book, of course?'

'I don't know, it's just been delivered.'

'A present?'

'There's no card or return address.'

'I'm not sure I approve of my fiancée receiving presents from strangers. May I see it?'

She changed the subject. 'You have work for me?'

He dropped a basket on to her desk. 'No, I've come to kidnap you and I've brought English afternoon tea.'

'That looks like one of Lyudmila's baskets.'

'It is,' he confessed, 'she promised me that she's put all your favourite foods into it.'

Sonya dropped her pen on its stand and, suspecting that she wouldn't be doing much work for the next half hour, screwed the top back on to her inkwell. 'Such as?'

He lifted the towel from the top of the basket and peered inside. 'Her best white dinner rolls, filled with caviar of mushrooms, liver pate, and caviar of aubergines. He sniffed. 'I also smell salt herring salad and cheesecake with vanilla and fruit sauce. Do you want to eat here or the perfect hideaway I've found?'

'I can't take time out in the middle of the afternoon to picnic with you in the snow. Aside from the fact that we'd freeze to death I have work to do for Mr Hughes.' She picked up a pile of letters from her in-tray to prove her point.

'I asked Mr Hughes to give me his blessing. He knows I have an important question to ask you, and as everyone here is too busy basking in the glory of having the blast furnace in full production to go looking for new projects, those letters can wait until tomorrow.' He lifted her shawl from the hook on the back of the door and draped it around her shoulders. 'I have a carriage waiting.'

'With driver and chaperone?'

'Your aunt's grooms, drivers, and servants were all busy.' His eyes shone as he raised his eyebrows.

'Even Lyudmila?' she persisted.

'Especially Lyudmila.'

'That's odd. I happen to know that my aunt is lunching with Father Grigor in his house today, so Lyudmila only has the servants to cook for, and at this time of year she makes chanakhi or goulash for the staff's lunch which can be easily heated up.'

'I confess, I didn't press Lyudmila after she told me that she'd made plans for her afternoon off.'

'So considerate of you.'

'Wasn't it? And then again I assumed that your chaperone would be with you.' He peered under her desk and opened a cupboard. 'I can't see Maria lurking anywhere. Is she likely to jump out and attack me for attempting to spirit you away without a moral guardian?'

'Maria is at the hospital. They're short-staffed so I asked her to help out in the kitchen.'

'Do you want me to fetch her?'

Sonya tried to push the illustrations in the book from her mind. She'd promised to marry this man on a whim, principally to belittle Nicholas Beletsky and show the count exactly what she thought of his ridiculous proposal. But she couldn't say that she knew the prince, or even liked him, simply because she didn't know him well enough. She found his direct manners and blunt way of speaking, especially in relation to Nathan Kharber, disconcerting.

Nathan Kharber ... she pushed the image of him that had risen unbidden to her mind aside. This was one afternoon she was determined to forget Nathan and concentrate on Roman. If for no other reason than she owed it to her fiancé to get to know him, as she'd accepted his proposal of marriage.

Although they lived under the same roof, Maria had taken care to ensure that they'd never been left alone together – not even for a moment–during the Christmas and New Year celebrations. Given her aunt's penchant for entertaining and welcoming a constant stream of guests, the house had been even fuller than usual during the holidays, and the scope for private conversation severely limited both at the meal table and drawing room.

And now – no matter how hard she tried to forget the book that had just been delivered – the depictions of lovemaking had burned into her consciousness, exciting far more than just her curiosity, holding the promise of a delicious, erotic tang of forbidden sensual pleasure that she had a feeling no well brought-up lady should be aware existed.

'Shall I fetch Maria?' he prompted.

'No, they need her in the hospital.'

'In that case let's be little devils, shall we?' He stretched out his hand. 'Shared secrets already, fiancée. But I won't tell if you don't.'

She hesitated but not for long. 'Pass me my coat, please. It's too cold for just a shawl. You'll find it hanging in the cupboard.'

Chapter Twenty-six

Boat berthed of the bank of the River Donets, Hughesovka February 1872

'As you see, the perfect spot.' Roman jumped down from the carriage and offered Sonya his hand.

'This is where you're building your house?' She looked at the waist-high brick walls.

'Our house,' he corrected. 'It is.'

'It looks as though it's going to be enormous.'

'Forty rooms, but as that includes kitchens, still rooms, storerooms and the usual offices that are the province of the servants, it won't be that enormous. That area fronting the river is going to be part conservatory and part outside terrace. We can entertain out here in summer and when it gets cold we'll retreat to the conservatory. Remind me to show you the plans sometime. My hideaway is down here, next to the river.' He offered her his hand. They passed a large shed where carpenters were working on doors and window frames. Roman shouted to Manfred.

'See the horse is cared for and covered with a blanket, will you please, Manfred, we'll probably be an hour or two.'

'Yes, sir.' Manfred barked an order at one of the workmen who ran back to the carriage.

'All these men work just for you?' Sonya asked.

'These are just a few who are doing the preliminary work on the house, there are many more.' He offered her his arm as well as his hand.

'Thank you.' She was grateful for his support as they negotiated the icy path that had been hacked through the snow down to the bank.

She stood and looked around when they reached a bluff that overlooked the river, which was thickly clotted with ice floes.

'There are no buildings,' she said suspiciously.

'Look again at the end of the jetty below you, but not for a building.'

'A boat?'

'Boris mentioned a fisherman friend of his had made so much money selling his catch since Mr Hughes had moved here with his workers, he could afford to buy a larger boat. I'd been looking for somewhere quiet where I could sit and plan out the finer points of the architecture of our house, away from the distractions of the office and your aunt's house, not that your aunt's house isn't wonderful...'

'But at times it can resemble an Orthodox Church at Christ Arisen Easter service.'

'She's so hospitable people love to flock to her,' he agreed. 'Anyway, to return to the subject, I viewed the fisherman's old boat, and made him an offer. When he accepted it, I had the boat moved to this spot, ordered a jetty built, and asked my valet to refurbish the cabin and make it more comfortable. Careful on that plank, it's sound but narrow. One slip, you'll be on the ice, through it, and frozen to death before I can haul you out.'

He held her hand as she walked on to the deck, then opened the door to the cabin. Heat blasted out to greet her as she entered. It was surprisingly large, the furniture carefully arranged to make the most of the space. The walls were panelled in varnished pine, two cushioned bench seats and a table made of the same wood were screwed to the floor filling one corner, the table was covered by a white damask cloth and a silver vase that had been filled with her aunt's hothouse roses stood in the centre. The wall behind the door held a long, wide-cushioned sofa. A tall, thin cupboard had been pushed alongside it, and a small, and if the temperature was any indicator, surprisingly efficient oil stove stood in the remaining corner.

Roman went to the table, set down the basket and opened it.

'These flowers smell heavenly. Did you pick them yourself or ask your valet to choose them for you?' Sonya sat on the bench, bent a bloom to her nose, and breathed in the scent before taking the plate, napkin, and cutlery he handed her.

'I spent hours choosing them this morning.' He lifted the plates of food from the basket.

'Really?'

'No. I spent most of the morning with Mr Hughes, as you well know. My valet, Manfred picked them – with your aunt's permission, of course.'

'Of course.' She left the bench and opened the cupboard alongside the sofa. 'A wine cellar. On a boat?'

'Hardly a cellar. It's above the water line. And wine is an essential component of any retreat.'

'Yours, perhaps.'

'Not yours?'

'I regard good wine as a luxury, especially in the middle of the afternoon.'

'What makes the middle of the afternoon different to the evening?' he asked.

'Because one glass is enough to send me to sleep.'

'I must remember that, the next time I want to catch you off guard.'

She allowed the comment to pass without remark. 'Do you intend to make a habit of organising picnic baskets?'

'Only on special occasions. It could be a new tradition.' He uncovered the bowls of rolls, caviar, pate, and salad and lifted out a bottle of chilled wine and two glasses that he'd packed at the bottom of the basket. He opened the wine, filled the glasses, and handed her one, before taking a bottle from the cupboard and dropping it into a basket outside the door she presumed had been left there for the purpose. 'In this weather that's the best way to chill it.'

'A two-bottle lunch?'

'One bottle each, it sounds less that way. Have you given any thought as to exactly when you'd like to marry me?'

That book! And the images it contained. Why was she having such trouble forgetting it, and why was she mentally undressing Roman?

'This week, month, year – decade?' he prompted.

'You said there was no hurry.'

'There isn't. But this will make our relationship official. My apologies for not giving it to you on the day you accepted my proposal but it was in a vault along with the rest of my family jewels in St Petersburg. Uncertain of your reaction to my offer I thought I'd tempt fate if I sent for it before you agreed to be my wife.' He slipped his hand into his coat pocket and lifted out a ring box. He opened it before handing it to her.

'That stone. Is it...'

'Real. Yes.'

'Roman, that emerald is enormous.'

'It's not an emerald. It's a green diamond. My father had it set for my mother when they fell in love. He wanted a stone that matched her eyes. As you see, I inherited the colour, so instead of matching your eyes I thought this would remind you of mine. I hoped you'd wear her ring but if you'd prefer a new piece, you can choose one the next time we are in St Petersburg, though I doubt we'll find another stone as flawless.'

'It's beautiful, Roman.'

He took it from the box and slipped it on her finger. 'It's too small.'

'No it isn't.' She pushed it down. 'Just tight, which is good. It means I won't lose it.'

'You want to wear it? I mean all the time.'

'Not when I'm scrubbing floors.'

'When have you ever scrubbed floors?' he enquired in amusement.

'In the hospital when we were fighting typhus.'

'As you no longer work there you won't have to do that again.'

'I suppose I won't.' She suppressed a twinge of regret.

When she'd left the hospital she'd hoped, without cause or reason, that one day she'd return. She couldn't bear the thought of anything happening to Vasya – but she'd dreamed of Nathan returning her love, if not as her husband, then as her lover, although she was pragmatic enough to realise that could only remain a dream. If she had an affair with Nathan and it became public knowledge, she would lose her reputation and he would lose the one thing he held most dear – his religion.

She looked at Roman and forced herself to concentrate on him – and only him.

Roman stared back at her for a moment. There was an odd expression in his eyes. She was still trying to decipher it when he touched his glass to hers.

'To us, and a long and happy marriage whenever it starts.'

They drank and she replaced her glass on the table. 'Is the ring a hint that you'd like us to marry soon?'

'Only if you want to. Now the furnaces are in full production, I'm making plans to travel to St Petersburg to make my report on Hughesovka to Grand Duke Konstantin. I hope to persuade him to accompany me back here so he can see just how much progress John Hughes has made for himself. If you come with me to St Petersburg...'

'As your wife?'

'Or fiancée, whichever you decide, we'll stay awhile and spend Easter in the city. It's beautiful at that time of year. A snow tipped plethora of golden palaces – and talking of palaces, before I drift into poetry, the Tsar will undoubtedly invite us to stay in the Gatchina. He almost never resides anywhere else these days'

'Roman, what Count Beletsky said about my parents...'

'Your aunt told you the truth. When your father was diagnosed, he drank to forget how ill he was and was labelled a drunk. Contagious and condemned to live out his days in a sanatorium, he received more punishment than any sinner who develops a liking for vodka should receive. That's if drink can be regarded as a sin. If it is, ninety-nine out of every hundred Russians are sinners. And probably the remaining one per cent are babies who are too young to drink.'

'You knew my father?'

'Only by reputation. As a child I occasionally heard my father and his acquaintances speak of him. They were friends.'

'I didn't know.'

'The aristocratic world of Moscow and St Petersburg is small. The young men's social circle of card tables, horse racing, and duels even smaller. Your father and mine were young together.'

'And my mother...'

'Any woman who dares leave her husband to live under another man's roof is given a foul name by polite society. Especially by women who suffer in secret and lack the courage to do what your mother did and forge a better life for themselves.'

'You can't shrug off gossip, some of it will stick and reflect badly on you for marrying me.'

'Years-old gossip? Watch me ignore it, Sonya. I want to marry you, not your parents. And I never want to speak of them again.'

'Because they are shameful?'

'Because they are nothing to do with us, or you. Catherine is the one who brought you up. She is in effect your only parent.'

'If we aren't married she won't allow me to travel with you without a chaperone.'

'If you don't want to marry before I leave for the north, Catherine could accompany us.'

'And Alexei's baby sister?'

'In my experience babies are not good travellers.'

'You have experience of babies?' she asked in surprise.

'Some of my servants have fathered children and tried to take them on journeys with me. It's never a pleasant experience. It might be better if Kira remained here with Alexei and Ruth.'

'It might.' She continued to sip her wine.

'If we did marry, I wouldn't make any demands of you.'

'For example?' She was amazed how easy she was finding it to talk to him.

'I'd never try to climb into your bed.'

'You'd wait for me to climb into yours?' She felt audacious for even suggesting such a thing.

'Exactly, on the understanding that the invitation to climb into mine would be open to you anytime you chose to take me up on it, day or night, whether we are married or not.' He winked at her.

'So we'd have separate bedrooms if we married?'

'It wouldn't be my choice.' He picked up the bottle, refilled his glass, and topped up hers. 'You think of our marriage in terms of "if", not "when"?' he asked, suddenly serious.

'You're a prince...'

'I haven't kept my rank a secret. And a prince is insignificant in the hierarchy of Russian aristocrats, as you'll soon find out. One of my ancestors was a minor turncoat Siberian warlord who helped out Ivan the Terrible during his conquest of Siberia. Rumour has it he was hoping to be rewarded with gold, but instead he received the title of prince. Cheaper for Ivan, but not so profitable for my family. Disappointed, my ancestors devoted themselves to making their own money. Most of our wealth is the result of inter-marriage with wealthy heiresses, not always of Russian or even noble blood, and various illegal enterprises.

'So there you have it, my line was a mongrel one even before my father married my Manchu Chinese mother, and as for royal blood – a treacherous Siberian warlord is the highest rank you'll find. But a plethora of roubles can open the doors of the most aristocratic of houses, even those of a Tsar.'

'But you're still a prince and I'm having difficulty imagining myself as a princess.'

'There's no law that says you have to use the title. And the marriage bed of a prince and princess is no different from that of a coalminer and his wife.'

'Aside from the linen.'

He eyed the sofa. 'That looks very comfortable, even without the linen. If you feel so inclined I could live with a little sinning before we climb into the marital bed via the altar.'

She felt her cheeks flame again. 'I'll remember that,' she murmured without giving a thought to what she was saying.

'Please do. I think I can safely promise you a pleasurable experience. However, to return to practicalities,' he picked up his glass and drank, 'my main concern is should you should decide to marry me before we leave for St Petersburg, it wouldn't give you, your aunt, or the priest much time to plan our wedding.'

She found herself wondering what exactly he'd expect of her when they were married – naked – and in the privacy of their bedroom.

'My innocent and blushing bride.'

'I'm not blushing,' she protested.

'You most certainly are.' He smiled. 'Are you blushing at the thought of marriage or what comes afterwards?'

'It's warm in here.'

'Would you like me to turn down the stove?'

'No, it's just the change in temperature from outside. I'll soon grow accustomed to it.'

'If I turn it down and you get cold again I could keep you warm. Manfred's arranged that sofa well. It looks very comfortable, and there's a rug on it that I could wrap you in – or both of us if you get cold and you'd like me to warm you. What do you think? Shall we picnic at the table, or under a rug on the sofa?'

'I think that if we're considering getting married before you travel to St Petersburg we need to start planning a wedding.'

'And inviting guests. Your relatives, and friends, and the few close friends I have here, which in my case would be John Hughes and Glyn Edwards.'

'Aunt Catherine's already asked Father Grigor to dine with us tonight along with Alexei, Ruth, Glyn, Praskovia, Anna, Richard, and Sarah.' She shivered and not from cold.

He offered her his hand. She took it. He pulled her towards him. His arms banded tightly around her until she felt she could no longer breathe. Then he kissed her. She'd expected him to brush his lips lightly over hers. Instead he kissed her deeply, thoroughly, passionately, holding her body so close to his she could feel his muscles, hard, tense pressing into her.

His fingers burned her skin through the layers of clothing she was wearing. His pulse beat, until she was aware of the blood coursing through both their veins. She opened her eyes and saw his, twin green jewels brighter even than the diamond he'd given her, staring down into hers.

'My apologies. I was almost carried away there for an instant.' He released her and she stumbled, falling back on to the bench. 'So,' he continued, 'your aunt has invited Father Grigor to dinner?'

She nodded dumbly, astounded that he could continue the conversation as though nothing had happened between them, when she felt as though her entire universe had been turned upside down.

'How long will you need for the wedding preparations. One week – two?'

'I'll be ready when Father Grigor is.'

'If you need anything, let me know. I can always send a messenger to Taganrog. A pity St Petersburg is so far away. Salad?' He offered her the plate.

She glanced from the salad to Roman. The one and only thing she could be absolutely certain of was that the last thing she wanted to do was eat.

Part of her wanted to slap him. Another part to repeat that kiss. The third part was already imagining her and Roman acting out the illustrations in the book she'd seen. She wondered if he'd sent it in the hope of arousing more than her curiosity?

'You want another kiss?'

'Roman...'

'You're ready to forget Nathan Kharber?'

'I have forgotten him,' she lied.

'You sure?'

When she didn't answer him, he pulled her to her feet and kissed her again. He pulled back her jacket, and unfastened the buttons on her blouse, undressing her with a speed and expertise that surpassed her maid's.

When she was naked apart from her chemise and drawers, he locked the cabin door and drew the blinds over the portholes before divesting himself of his own clothes. He rearranged the rug on the sofa and pulled her down beside him.

Feeling clumsy, foolish, and gauche she wrapped her arms around his neck and buried her head in his shoulder lest he see the expression in her eyes, and guess at her nervousness and inexperience.

He slipped the straps of her chemise over her shoulders. 'Your breasts are magnificent.' He caressed them, fingering her nipples to firm points that pressed against his thumbs. He slipped his hand beneath her chin and lifted her face until he could look into her eyes.

'There's nothing to be afraid of. Do you want me to stop now and dress you?'

She shook her head.

'You do realise that in a few minutes it will be impossible for me to stop?'

'Yes.'

He helped her to her feet and out of her chemise and drawers. His skin was silk against hers. His touch, light and gentle, set flames burning inside her, and when he finally pierced her body with his own she was prepared for the pain, brief though it was, but not the sensations it evoked.

He held back for a moment, resting on his arms, and gazed into her eyes.

'Please,' she begged. 'Don't move away, not yet.'

As he relaxed once more against her she whispered, 'Not ever.'

Chapter Twenty-seven

*Boat berthed on the bank of the Donets, Hughesovka
February 1872*

Roman reached out to the table where he'd piled his
clothes, fumbled through them until he found his
waistcoat, and took his watch from the pocket. He opened
it.

'I thought so from the fading light. It's almost four
o'clock. Even allowing for the explanation I gave John
Hughes about wanting to give you your engagement ring,
we'll be missed soon, not least by the indomitable Maria.'
He pulled her close to him, nestling the length of her
naked body alongside his, and dropped a kiss on her neck
behind her ear. 'Time to dress, princess.'

'Please let that be the first and last time you call me
that.'

'You prefer "your Ladyship"?'

'I prefer Sonya.'

'"Sunshine" suits you better, it goes with the colour of
your hair.' He kissed her again, on the lips this time,
before throwing the rug aside. She clung to him for a
moment. He gently unclasped her arms from his waist and
left the sofa.

'Must you go?' She couldn't stop staring at and
admiring his body, long, lean, and covered with golden
down.

He turned and smiled at her. 'Only until next time.'

'When will that be?'

'When I sneak into your bed tonight.'

'Maria will castrate you.'

'She'll have to catch me first. Leave your balcony door
open.'

'Your bedroom isn't even in the same wing of the
house.'

'Your room is above the library?'

'I ... how do you know?'

'I made it my business to find out. It's a short climb up the columns that frame the windows and on to the balustrade.'

'You'll fall and break your neck.'

He pulled the rug from her grasp so he could admire her. 'I wouldn't dare when I have this waiting for me.' He handed back the rug, turned aside, and slid the panelling on a section of the wall opposite the sofa to reveal a washstand complete with jug of water, soap, and towels.

'A bathroom,' she said in surprise, 'and fitted into such a tiny space.'

'A bathroom of sorts,' he qualified.

'I'm impressed. You really have thought of everything in your hideaway.' She covered herself with the rug again.

'A modest woman.'

'Cold, not modest,' she contradicted. 'After what we've just done, it seems too late for modesty, false or otherwise.'

'I'm glad you think so. I'll make a note to remind my servants to stoke the stoves up well in all my houses. I've always wanted a woman who's not afraid to display her charms.'

She leaned back on the cushions and watched him pour water from the jug into the basin.

He saw her gazing at him in the mirror. 'The first man you've watched wash and dress?'

'The first man as opposed to boy I've seen wash and dress and certainly the first man I've seen naked.'

'Boy?'

'Alexei when we were children. I have memories of swimming naked with him in the river and our nursemaids bathing us in the same tub afterwards. I also recall helping the nursemaids wash Alexei's five brothers along with his sisters when they were small.'

'Catherine told me that Alexei's brothers arc all in a military college.'

'In Allenstein in East Prussia. All five of them. Alexei went there but couldn't wait to leave. As he's so fond of telling everyone, he managed to escape before his eighteenth birthday.'

'Will the boys return here to work for Mr Hughes?'

'Not if Alexei's father has his way.'

'Ah, your would-be suitor, Count Nicholas Beletsky.'

'That's not funny.'

'I don't think you'd have been amused for long if you'd married him,' he agreed. 'Well, I'm the first man you've seen washing and naked, and hopefully I'll be the last. But I promise you, you'll soon get bored with the spectacle.'

He dried himself, tipped the water he'd used into the slop bucket, and dressed. When he finished he turned to the table and repacked the basket. 'We never did get around to the picnic.'

'There's always another day.'

'All the days of all the years of our lives Now I've enticed you into my bed – metaphorically speaking – and my life, I have no intention of letting you go.' He lifted up the basket. 'I'll put this in the carriage and give orders for the horse to be harnessed. Don't leave until I've returned to help you over the jetty.'

'It'll take me ten minutes to dress.' She picked up her chemise from the floor and pulled it over her head.

She was in the "bathroom" when he opened the door seconds later. 'To repeat myself, when do you want to marry me?'

She looked over her shoulder as she filled the basin with clean water. 'As soon as Father Grigor can arrange the ceremony, but he'll want at least three weeks' notice to call the banns.'

'Damn the banns.'

'If the banns aren't called the old wives will assume I'm pregnant.'

'What if you were?'

'We'd be the subjects of salacious gossip.'

'Then damn the old wives as well.'

'If it was up to me I'd marry you tomorrow.'

'That's the answer I've been waiting for.'

'Aunt Catherine will defer to Father Grigor.'

'What does he drink?'

'Berlin schnapps. You're going to try to bribe a priest?'

'Of course.'

Sonya was grateful for the privacy after he left her. She'd expected to feel embarrassed and different somehow after making love for the first time, but all she felt was confused. Roman had made what they'd just done feel so natural – so normal– nothing like the earth-shattering event she had expected losing her virginity to be.

Yet again she thought of Nathan, and when she did she realised he'd been lost to her from the outset and long before that day. She'd "made love" with Roman but didn't love him. Not in the way she loved Nathan. But then what did she know – really know – about either man?

Nathan had made it clear that he valued his race and religion above anything he felt for her. Roman was easy to talk to, easy to get on with, and, if his lovemaking was any indication, kind and considerate – and when she gazed at the ring he'd given her, very generous. And not just with money, which any wealthy man could be, but with his most treasured possessions. But feelings? If he felt anything resembling love for her he'd never voiced his emotions.

By the time he'd returned, she'd finished washing and dressing, had pinned her hair up and was studying her reflection in the mirror above the washstand.

'Looking to see if I left the devil's mark on you?'

'No,' she smiled at his reflection.

'Here, I'll take that,' He took the towel he'd spread beneath them on the sofa, which was stained with her blood, and wrapped it together with the sheet they'd lain on and pushed them into a bin that stood alongside the slop bucket. 'My valet will dispose of them later.'

'Your valet?' She was shocked at the thought of Roman's manservant knowing what had happened between her and Roman in the cabin.

'Manfred is the soul of discretion, and that is not an invitation for you to ask me how often he's needed that discretion in the past.' He offered her his hand. 'Let's see how quickly we can arrange a wedding.'

Hughesovka and the Beletsky Mansion February 1872

The man was tall. It was difficult to make out his build as he was swathed in layers of clothing. He wore a felt hat that covered his head and had draped a long thick knitted shawl over it taking care to cover his nose and mouth. He waited until darkness fell, dense and obscuring, before leaving the dormitory he shared with twelve other workers.

He hovered behind the walls of a half-built warehouse across the street from the stables until the ostler disappeared into one of the beer shops. Only then did he cross the road. Tipping the orphaned boy who lived in the hayloft, he extracted a promise from him to keep the transaction secret, before hiring a sleigh and a stocky, solid Cossack horse. The snow that had been threatening to fall all day began to drift down from the sky as he left the stable and headed out to cover the verst of steppe that separated Hughesovka from the Beletsky Mansion.

The wind picked up before he left the town limits, and the snow fell thickly enough to blind him. Drifts swept over the track covering the road such as it was, until it was impossible to differentiate between the route he'd intended to take and the steppe. The horse slowed and more than once he heard a sharp crack as the animal stepped on ice hidden beneath the snow, momentarily losing its footing. Hoping he hadn't strayed as far as the river he cracked the whip, but still the animal stumbled and struggled and it took him over two hours to reach the gates of the mansion.

He was frozen from the core of his body to the tips of his woollen-gloved fingers and felt-booted toes. He reined in the horse in the stable yard and banged the stable door.

'What do you want?' a grudging voice demanded.

'Shelter for my horse.'

'Go to hell.'

'Your master won't be pleased.'

'My master's in St Petersburg.'

'Count Beletsky isn't.'

The man inched open the door. 'If you want to put the beast in here, get it in.' The groom peered upwards. There was no sky, only a blanket of snow that filled the air. 'If you're staying the night, you can strip the harness from the horse and give her a rub down.'

'I'm not staying.'

'I'll be damned before I rub her down or do any extra work I won't be paid for.' The man upended a vodka bottle into his mouth.'

'If you do, there's ten kopeks in it for you. But only if she's been fed, watered, dried, and made ready to tackle the return journey.'

The man held out his hand. 'Twenty.'

'Do the work and you'll see the colour of my coins.'

'If I do it and you don't pay, I'll lame the horse.'

'Try it and you'll be sorry.'

The groom laughed.

The man pulled out his gun.

The groom reached for a horse blanket.

The wavering, yellow light of the oil lamp that burned above the back door of the kitchen quarters was barely visible through the dense white blizzard. The man trudged across the yard, reached it, lifted his hand, and knocked.

Gleb opened the door and stared down at him.

'Message for the count,' the man muttered.

Gleb moved closer. The man pushed his hat to the top of his head. Gleb recognised him and nodded. He opened the door wider.

278

The man looked in. Seeing the cook and kitchen maid sitting at the table, he pulled his hat back down on his head and covered even more of his face with his shawl.

Gleb ushered the visitor through the kitchen, picked up an oil lamp, and opened a door that led into a long, windowless, stone-flagged corridor. They walked the full length until they reached a door at the end. Gleb knocked. When he received an answer he opened it, told the visitor to wait, and disappeared. He re-emerged a few minutes later, inclined his head, and held the door open.

'Go in.'

The man walked through the door which was panelled on the back. When Gleb closed it behind them, it was indistinguishable from the walls of the room and impossible to see unless you had prior knowledge of its existence.

Nicolas Beletsky was sitting in a chair that had been pulled close to the fire. A bottle of vodka, a glass, an oil lamp, and a book were on a side table next to him. He glanced at the man. 'Uncover your face,' he ordered.

The man did as he was bid.

'You must have news to travel this far from town during a snowstorm.'

'The first of the Edwards Brothers collieries is going into full production next Monday.'

'You're certain of this?'

'I am, sir. They finished shoring up all the shafts they intend working today, and put in the last of the pit props this afternoon. They also carried down extra timber for repairs.'

'Glyn Edwards and John Hughes haven't been recruiting new workers. We would have heard about it if they had.'

'Glyn Edwards put Richard Parry in charge of hiring. He has only taken on Welsh workers he knows or have been vouched for by one of the two Edwards brothers.'

'No Russian or Cossack workers?'

'A few, but only men who have been vouched for by Vlad or your son.'

'The only sons I have are in the military academy in Allenstein,' Nicholas snarled.

'My apologies, sir.'

'Is there any way you can get our men into the colliery?' 'The men who've been asked to work there have been given special identity cards, and I've heard that the only cage operators employed by the collieries will be men who will be able to recognise the workers by sight. If you had enough money it might be possible to bribe –'

'Forget that,' Nicholas interrupted. Levsky had left him barely enough money to pay the domestic expenses of the house and the wages of the informers they'd hired to report on the progress of the New Russia Company. 'Do you have one of these identity cards?'

'No, sir. They've only been given to the men concerned.'

'No spares?'

'No, sir. Richard Parry supervised the distribution himself.

He trusted no one else, not even the men who travelled over here from Wales with him. He warned all the men to take care of their ticket and as far as I know none of them have let one out of their sight, but I did get this for you.' He slipped his hand into his pocket, pulled out two sheets of paper, and handed them to Nicholas.

Nicholas's eyes narrowed as he held the papers to the lamp and scanned the names on them. 'Is there any chance we can waylay one or two of these men and replace them with ours?'

'No, sir, as I told you there'll be men operating the cage who will spot any men we try to put in. And without a bribe...'

'We don't have enough silver to bribe a kitchen maid to give us slops.' Nicholas continued to peruse the list. 'Monday, you're sure?'

'Yes, sir.'

'Anyone see you coming here?'

'No, sir, I waited until dark.'

'You're sure you weren't followed?'

'A blizzard is raging outside, sir. I'm sure. I stopped several times, not always because I wanted to. I couldn't see my hand in front of my face let alone the road.'

Nicholas nodded.

'Dismissed.'

'My payment is due, sir. I wasn't paid last month.'

'Bring me my desk, Gleb.'

The servant picked up Nicholas's travelling desk and set it on the table beside the vodka. Nicholas unlocked it, took a small purse from inside and handed it over.

'This will be your last payment until Mr Levsky returns from St Petersburg.'

The messenger pocketed it. 'Will he be returning soon, sir?'

'I have no idea.'

'Is there anything you want me to do, sir?'

Nicholas turned the question back on him. 'Is there anything that you can do?'

'Not that I can think of given the heightened security around the New Russia Company and Edwards Brothers Collieries, sir.'

'But you can walk in and out of the works?'

'Only when I have messages to deliver from the office and even then, I need a permit signed by the senior member of staff who sent me there.'

'We'll have to rethink our plans. If I need you, I will get in touch. Don't come here again unless like tonight you have urgent information to impart. Stay where you are, and keep your eyes and ears open. Copy any documents you think we may find useful while carrying on your work for the company. You're too useful to us where you are to take any unnecessary risks that may unmask you as sympathetic to our cause.'

'Yes, sir.'

'Show him out, Gleb.'

After they left, closing the panel behind them, Nicholas sat staring into the flames. He wished Levsky was close at hand, but he wasn't. None of them had envisaged the ironworks or the collieries going into production so soon and, what was worse, he was powerless to sabotage either of them without the money to finance an operation. Gleb returned.

'You heard everything, Gleb?'

'I did, sir.'

'Any ideas?'

'The New Russia Company and the collieries are both operating with mainly Welsh labour. The Paskey brothers are Welsh, sir.'

'And at the other side of the country.'

'Yes, sir.'

'If we brought them back here, do you think they'd be taken on if they applied for jobs with the company or the collieries?'

'No, sir, but we might be able to sneak them in,' Gleb suggested.

'If we pay bribes with money we won't have until Mr Levsky returns.'

'Yes, sir.'

'I'll mention your idea to Mr Levsky when he returns. Just out of interest, do you trust the Paskeys?'

'No, sir, which makes both of them expendable.'

'What are you suggesting?' Nicholas asked bluntly.

'That they succumb to an accident after they've succeeded in sabotaging whatever we've asked them to.'

'A crude idea, but possibly one worth considering at a future date. Tell the cook I'll have a beefsteak tomorrow.'

'I'm not sure there are any, sir.'

'There will be in Hughesovka. Drive her in and keep your eyes and ears open.'

'Yes, sir.'

'And while we're confined to the house by the snow, make sure that all the men on the estate know how to shoot. You can practise in the barn.'

'Yes, sir.'

'Let me know when all of them can hit a target every time.'

'Yes, sir.'

'Dismissed, Gleb.'

Chapter Twenty-eight

Catherine Ignatova's house February 1872

'Here comes the bride and bridesmaid, returned from viewing their gowns.' Catherine smiled as Sonya and Anna walked into the drawing room accompanied by Sarah, Praskovia, and Ruth. 'Still happy with the bridesmaid's dress, Anna? No second thoughts about wearing something that's practically an antique?'

'None, Mrs Ignatova. It's truly beautiful, and as you said, it fits me like a glove. I can't wait to wear it.'

'And I can't wait to see you wear it and reprise your role as beautiful bridesmaid, Anna. So, Father Grigor,' Roman took the glass of vodka Boris served him, 'how quickly can you marry me to Sonya – or is it the other way around? Either way, I hope it will be this week. Although, if there are problems I may – at a push – settle for next week, but not a minute longer.'

Catherine looked at Roman in concern. 'Why the rush?'

'First I don't want to give Sonya the time or opportunity to change her mind,' he winked at Sonya, 'and secondly, we still have several long, hard winter weeks ahead of us. I hate waste and would like to make use of the dark evenings to get to know my wife.'

'Are you never serious, Roman?' Catherine reprimanded.

'I am being serious, Catherine. In fact I hoped that I'd be married to Sonya by now. I didn't realise a simple wedding would take so much organising.'

'In which case you should have spoken to me, I'm an expert at organising weddings,' Alexei commented, his tongue firmly in his cheek.

'Is that why you left your own wedding to your grandmother, Sonya, and Ruth to arrange,' mocked Glyn.

'Richard and I were in Taganrog when you met Sonya, Roman,' Sarah reminded him. 'I've been meaning to ask, was it love at first sight between you two?'

'It was certainly something at first sight, Mrs Parry,' Roman replied evasively.

'A thunderbolt?' Richard asked.

'Isn't it always,' Alexei chimed in.

'So speaks one happy bridegroom,' Richard commented.

'Hardly a bridegroom. Ruth and I have been married for months now.' Alexei reached out, grabbed Ruth's hand, and pulled her down on to the sofa beside him.

'I stand corrected, old married man,' Richard sipped his brandy.

'We were married the same time as you,' Alexei reminded.

'Children, no quarrelling,' Catherine said lightly.

'And, all four of you are still smiling after months of marriage,' Roman observed. 'If I get in trouble with Sonya I'll have to come to you for marital advice. So, Father Grigor, can you please put me out of my misery by at least naming the month that we might marry?'

'The first Sunday in April,' the priest suggested. 'That will give me enough time to announce the ceremony in advance in church. And give the old ladies, who keep the estate church cleaner than the hospital wards, enough time to polish all the wood in honour of the occasion.'

Roman looked at Sonya. 'Can you be ready by then?'

'As Aunt Catherine has solved the problems of my dress, there is only the wedding breakfast to be arranged.'

'You can leave that to Lyudmila and me,' Catherine interposed with a frown. As the others began talking about guests and music, she watched Roman. Like Koshka she was beginning to suspect Roman's motives in marrying Sonya.

Roman's wealth was well documented as was his position in society. Rumours of his liaisons with well-connected and even wealthier girls than Sonya were rife.

There was no denying that Sonya was beautiful, but Catherine was realistic enough to accept that Sonya was no more beautiful than many of the St Petersburg heiresses who had a great deal more money plus a far higher social position to recommend them.

Had Roman become suddenly and inexplicably drawn to Sonya for no deeper reason than she was a passing fad or fancy? She hated having to ask the question but couldn't help wondering, would he tire of Sonya just as suddenly as he had courted her?

Glyn and Praskovia's house February 1872

When they returned home after visiting Catherine, Glyn went to his desk in the study area of his and Praskovia's bedroom. After calling goodnight to Sarah, Richard, and Anna as they climbed the stairs to their sitting room, Praskovia checked all the downstairs rooms as she did every evening before going to bed.

She heard her mother's voice raised in anger as she approached the kitchen door. Steeling herself for one of Yelena's volatile outbursts, she opened it to find Yelena and Pyotr sitting hunched over the stove while her brother Misha paced up and down in front of them.

She knew without being told that they had been arguing. 'Problems?' she ventured from the doorway.

Pyotr who never understood the nuances of any discussion and always took everything at face value, blurted, 'Misha wants to sell our house in the village.'

'Is that right, Misha?' Praskovia looked to him for an explanation as she lowered herself onto a kitchen chair.

'It's not as if you haven't another house,' Misha rejoined irritably. 'Your lover has given you this one.'

'Where did you hear that?' Praskovia asked.

'Your lover's legal wife.'

'You've spoken to Betty Edwards about me?' Praskovia struggled to keep her temper.

Misha ignored her comment. 'You didn't think to inform me that you'd come into riches?'

'Owning the house you live in hardly makes you wealthy. And as a family we've never discussed money.'

'Only because as a family we've never had any money – until now.'

'We haven't any money now. When we were growing up, Papa and Mama owned the house we lived in...'

'A house he built.'

'Which was as comfortable as this one.'

'Hardly as grand.'

'As Papa used to say, it's for every person to find their own way in the world, Misha.'

'You certainly found yours,' Misha sneered. 'You landed on your feet by playing the slut and spreading your legs, dear sister. It's a great deal easier than working for a living. I take my hat off to you.' He did just that to emphasise his point, tossing his officer's cap on to the table. 'Mistress of your own big house, which you can keep even if your lover tires of you, and should he die young, you can still keep it, because he has written his legal wife and child out of his will.'

'His legal wife and child, as you put it, have been well provided for by him.'

'You think so...'

'I know so because Glyn told me...'

'So it's Glyn now, not Mr Edwards...'

Sensing Misha was about to say something neither she nor Praskovia wanted to hear, Yelena interrupted the conversation. 'Misha wants me to evict my tenants from our Cossack house, Praskovia. He wants to sell it to Mr Edwards's wife so she can take down the building, move it into town, and rebuild it as a shop, with living quarters for her and her friends in our bedrooms.

'That house is not yours to sell, Misha, it is our mother's,' Praskovia reminded him.

'Our mother has no need of it. All she does is sit here and collect the rent as well as her wages, and stockpile money I could use to buy myself out of the regiment.'

'If you wanted to buy yourself out of the regiment you should have come to me and asked me to lend you the money,' Yelena reproached.

'"Lend"! You expect me to pay you back my father's money. My father built that house.'

'For me.'

'And his children.'

'Exactly, for all his children,' Yelena reminded.

'I am the eldest son. I am entitled to that house and all the rent money that you have collected since you moved out. You have a home here with Praskovia. Glyn Edwards pays you and Pyotr wages,' he stared pointedly at Praskovia's swollen waistline, 'and I don't doubt that you do all right when it comes to luxuries.'

'How dare you...'

'Don't come the high and mighty with me, Praskovia. Or you, Mama, when you rent out our house to strangers while your own son hasn't a roof over his head.'

'The strangers pay rent that our mother sets aside for her old age and Pyotr's. You want to take the house and see our mother and Pyotr destitute?' Praskovia's voice rose precariously.

'Destitute,' Misha repeated the word and spat it back at her. 'They are living in luxury with you and being paid for it. You never told me that you owned this house, let alone invited me to come and live here with you.'

'You are an officer in the Cossack regiment, Misha, you live in barracks –'

'And when I have leave?'

'Glyn – Mr Edwards invited you to come and stay here any time. We set aside a room for you.'

'In the servants' quarters.'

'Only because all the other rooms are permanently occupied. Even if you had taken Glyn up on the invitation you wouldn't be here very often.

'As you've discovered, accommodation is a problem in the town. Do you expect me to reserve one of the main bedrooms and throw Glyn's friends and family out on the streets just so you can sleep here a few days a year?'

'I expect you to give the same consideration to your brother that you do to your lover's friends and family.'

The constant use of "lover" to describe Glyn was infuriating Praskovia but she managed to keep her temper – unlike her mother.

'Every single time you come here, you make trouble, Misha. The house your father built, he built for me. It's mine and no one else's. I am not about to give it away to anyone, including you three children. The rents my tenants pay I give to Mr Edwards to bank for me along with half my wages so I will have money enough to live on in my old age when I can no longer work...'

'When Praskovia throws you out of her house, you mean.'

'I would never throw our mother or Pyotr out of this house,' Praskovia countered angrily.

'So you say now. But what will happen when our mother gets too old to cook or look after herself?'

'You talk about me getting old, Misha. I am not yet fifty and your grandmother was cooking for old Mr Ignatov when she was eighty-five.'

'She dropped dead making soup for him.'

'Better that than trying to stop her ungrateful children from snatching her possessions before she'd even died. I'm a long way off from dying, Misha, and I'm not about to hand over my house to you.'

'You'd rather give it to Praskovia who already has a mansion.'

'I'm not about to give it to any of my children. Especially the one who's come here to cause trouble.'

'I came here to invite you to my wedding, but forget it. I don't want to see any of you ever again.'

Praskovia had heard the threat many times before. 'Misha, you know you don't mean that.'

'Oh yes I do, dear sister, I mean exactly that.' Misha opened the back door and disappeared into the night. Praskovia went after him, but when she heard the sound of hoofbeats she closed the door, turned, and doubled over in pain.

Pyotr leapt up and ran to her. Yelena was slower to her feet.

'The baby?'

Praskovia nodded. 'Pyotr, run upstairs, fetch Mrs Parry.'

'Not when you're hurting, Praskovia...'

'Go, Pyotr, Mrs Parry will make me feel better.'

'I'll see to her, Pyotr.' Yelena wrapped her arm around her daughter. 'Can you walk to your bedroom?'

Praskovia smiled as the pain subsided. 'To my old bedroom next to the silver store. Glyn needs his rest.'

'You don't want me to fetch him?'

Praskovia shook her head. 'Not yet.'

Road from Hughesovka to the barracks February 1872

Misha spurred his horse on as he threw caution to the wind and galloped over the snow-plastered steppe. He heard his horse's hooves crunch on ice, but, angered to the point of blindness, he ignored the warning sound along with the risk of his horse slipping. Indignation and fury boiled within him, even worse than when he'd first returned from Moscow and Sonya had rejected his proposal of marriage.

He knew Praskovia was right. There was a shortage of housing in Hughesovka. When he'd looked for houses in town, people had laughed at him.

He'd arranged leave at the end of the month to marry Alice, but given Mrs Edwards's suspicious attitude towards him, coupled with Alice's revelation that most of her cash had been invested by Edward Edwards in the company bank, he'd decided not to ask her for the money he would need to buy his way out of the regiment until after the ceremony.

By which time, Alice's money would be legally his to do with as he saw fit.

He knew the women's hotel bills hadn't been paid by Glyn Edwards since the end of November, which presumably meant that both of them were dipping into their savings. Given the cost of rooms and food in the hotel, he didn't doubt that their expenses were making serious inroads into both their nest eggs.

He'd asked his colonel for a three-hour pass so he could ride into Hughesovka that night, ostensibly to check on his pregnant sister's health. Given the snow and risk of delay if another blizzard took hold, Colonel Zonov had been reluctant to give his consent. Misha knew he wouldn't get leave again until the weekend he'd booked off for his wedding.

He'd hoped to secure the house and arrange to have it transported into the town before then, so he and Alice could move in there for their honeymoon. He'd even approached a couple of his late father's friends who'd agreed to do the work for him – for a price. Given his mother's point blank refusal to hand over the house to him, that was now out of the question. He had no choice but to ask the colonel if he and Alice could move into rooms in the barracks building that was reserved as married quarters.

All his meticulously laid plans to leave the regiment and set himself up in business were in tatters, at worse abandoned, at best mothballed, at least until the spring when building work would be resumed in Hughesovka. And then ... so much depended on exactly how much money Alice had and how much he could coax out of Betty Edwards to finance his venture.

Worst of all, he had no choice but to remain in the regiment, and live in barracks until after his marriage, because thanks to his mother's obduracy, he had nowhere else to go.

Catherine Ignatova's house February 1872

———

Usually Sonya lingered at bedtime, taking time to talk to her maid while she brushed out her hair, but, unable to stop thinking about Roman and his promise to climb up to her bedroom, she ushered her maid out early. When she closed the door of her bedroom behind her, she did something she'd never done before. She locked it.

She leaned back against it for a moment and looked around. The room had been hers since the day Olga had married Count Beletsky and vacated it. She was so accustomed to seeing it she rarely took time to admire and savour the beautiful furnishings Catherine had so generously provided. It was smaller than the state rooms and guest bedrooms in the mansion, but large enough to contain everything a young girl could possibly want.

The furniture was French Empire, enamelled white, ornamented by gilding. A four-poster bed, hung with blue and white silk curtains that matched the bedcover and pillows, dominated the centre of the wall opposite the windows that overlooked the gardens. French doors opened on to a balcony that ran around the entire first floor storey of the house. A desk and chair stood to the left of the French doors, a matching dressing table and chair to the right. A cheval mirror, two bookshelves, and bedside cabinets completed the furniture. Doors led to a small bathroom fitted with a marble washstand and slipper bath, and another door led into a walk-in clothes and linen cupboard.

Sonya turned up the oil lamps on the bedside cabinets and turned down the wicks on the ones on the desk and dressing table. She checked her reflection in the mirror. A white ghost stared back at her in the subdued glow. She picked up her hairbrush and pulled it through her waist-length hair one last time before plaiting it, as she did every night before bed. She reached for her perfume bottle, upended it on her finger and dabbed her favourite vanilla scent on her wrists and behind her ears.

She went to the French doors and unlocked them. On impulse she opened them and stepped out. A bitterly cold wind blew in carrying ice shards in its blast. She retreated and shut the doors hastily but did not lock them. She ran to the bed, picking up a book of Shakespeare's sonnets from one of the bookshelves on the way.

She untied her robe, tossed it on to the bed and climbed between the sheets. She opened the book and began to read but it was hopeless. She simply couldn't concentrate on anything or anyone except Roman. She wondered, not for the first time that evening, if his comment about climbing up the columns to the balcony outside her room had been a joke.

It wasn't only cold outside it was icy. The snow would be frozen and slippery and it would be even more dangerous than usual to try climbing up to the first floor. She looked at the small ormolu clock that had been her sixteenth birthday present from Alexei. It was ten minutes after eleven o'clock. Long past her usual bedtime. Still holding the book, she snuggled down and listened to the small familiar sounds of the house shutting down for the night.

The footsteps of the maids and footmen, as they climbed the back staircase that was sandwiched between the two wings of the house and led from the cellars up to the attics that housed the servants' quarters; Boris's firm heavy tread as he walked down the corridor outside her door to wind the clocks on the gallery; male laughter echoing up from the library below her room as Mr Hughes, Mr Dmitri, and Roman shared a final nightcap with her aunt.

She tried to focus on her book again, but her eyelids grew heavy. She hadn't meant to sleep but she woke with a start when a cold draught blew across her bed.

She opened her eyes. A shadowy male figure stood outlined in the open doorway, his silhouette thrown into relief against the moon. She sat up quickly.

'Roman...'

'Were you expecting someone else?'

'I wasn't sure if you were joking about climbing up to my room.'

'As you see, I was serious, but I warn you I don't have entirely altruistic intentions for being here.' He closed the door behind him, walked to the bed, and began to undress, tossing his clothes on to one of the chairs.

'Did you really climb up the pillars to the balcony or did you walk along from your room?'

'I climbed rather than risk disturbing the sleepers in the rooms I passed on the gallery. I would have been here earlier but unfortunately Mr Hughes and Dmitri wanted to talk and talk – and even after they went to bed I thought it circumspect to give them, and everyone else in the house, time to fall asleep.'

He dropped the last of his clothes and climbed into bed beside her. 'Now,' he pulled her close, 'I expect you to warm me up.'

'You're asking a great deal,' she murmured as he pulled her gown aside and pressed his frozen limbs against hers.

He lifted his finger to his lips, leaned over her, and turned down first one lamp, then the other. 'Now where did we leave off this afternoon?'

Chapter Twenty-nine

Glyn and Praskovia's house February 1872

Sarah knocked the door that connected the servants' quarters with Glyn's bedroom – a door Glyn and Praskovia had found very useful before Praskovia's pregnancy had forced them to make their affair public.

Glyn was out of his chair in seconds. Sarah smiled when she saw Richard sitting in front of the stove nursing a glass of vodka. He'd obviously left their room to keep Glyn company after Pyotr had called her.

'Praskovia would like to introduce you to someone, Glyn.'

Glyn ran past her down the corridor. Richard held out his arms and Sarah went to him.

'Mother and baby?'

'Both doing well.'

'Boy or girl?'

'Boy, with Praskovia's red hair. I hope I have such an easy time of it.'

Richard laid his hand on her. 'Not long now.'

'Two, maybe three weeks.' She looked at the clock on the dresser. 'In four hours, we'll have to get up.'

'Me, not you.'

'Come and meet Pavlo Peter Edwards,' Glyn called from the doorway.

Richard took Sarah's hand and they walked down a short corridor into a narrow bedroom. Praskovia was propped up on pillows, cradling a baby who was lying quietly staring up at her. Praskovia held the baby out to Glyn who took him gently in his arms.

'We've named him after Praskovia's father and,' Glyn glanced at Sarah, 'my brother. We hoped you wouldn't mind, Sarah.'

Richard and Sarah pretended they hadn't heard Yelena snort in the corner where she was making up a wooden cot with sheets and bedding she'd warmed on the stove. She hadn't had many good things to say about her husband when he was alive, and even fewer since his death in one of the Cossack pits – a death she attributed more to his consumption of vodka than a lack of safe working practices.

'I'm proud that you've given your son your brother's name, Glyn. Thank you.' Sarah knew that her voice sounded strained. She brushed a tear from her eye as she looked from Richard to Glyn.

'If you intended to call your baby Peter...'

'A girl might object to that name,' Sarah smiled. 'Now, you men get out of here while I make Praskovia comfortable and Pavlo's grandmother nurses him to sleep. I'll let you know when you can come back in, Glyn.'

'You mean I have to go?'

'I'll be as quick as I can.'

Praskovia looked at Glyn cradling his son. 'Sit in the corner until my mother has prepared the cot. You'll be out of the way there.'

Glyn sat on the chair in the corner, and Praskovia and Sarah both laughed as he tried to make his massive body shrink.

'You out,' Sarah shooed Richard through the door. 'Keep our bed warm for me.'

'I'll go across the road and tell Anna the good news first.'

'She'll be annoyed that she wasn't here to deliver Pavlo.' Sarah followed Richard to Glyn's bedroom door.

He fell serious. 'Do you think our child will be a girl?'

'I have no idea,' Sarah confessed.

'You told Glyn that we hadn't thought of a name for our son...'

'Or daughter,' Sarah cut in.

'You don't have any family names?' he asked.

'I only wish I had. The only family names I have were Peter's.'

'If he's a boy we could call him Edward, for every Mr Edwards who has done so much for me and my family.'

'That's a wonderful idea, Richard.'

'And David Victor for the two brothers I lost to the cholera.'

'And if it's a girl?' Sarah asked.

'My mother's name was Mary.'

'How about Maryanna, and we'll ask Anna to be godmother if it's a boy or girl.'

He kissed her. She gripped his hand, caressed his fingers, and watched him walk through the door.

Hotel Hughesovka April 1872

The porter opened the door of the hotel and bowed as Misha escorted Alice and Betty Edwards inside.

'Congratulations on your marriage, Captain Razin. The table you ordered in the restaurant is ready for your party, sir.'

'You sent food up for my daughter and her nursemaid?' Betty snapped in English. As she'd warned Glyn, she'd categorically refused to learn the 'heathen language', and although Misha suspected Betty Edwards understood a great deal more than she would admit to, she still refused to say a single word in Russian

Misha repeated her question to the doorman. The man was careful to look Betty in the eye when he replied. 'I saw the waiter go up a few minutes ago, Mrs Edwards.'

'As you ordered, their meals have been taken upstairs,' Misha translated.

They entered the restaurant. The waiters had set a table for three with a white cloth, polished silverware, and candles but no flowers

The only place in Hughesovka flowers could be obtained at that time of year was Catherine Ignatova's hothouse. Given the strained relationship between him and Alexei, and the fact that Alexei was close to Praskovia and Glyn, Misha hadn't even approached Mrs Ignatova. In fact, he'd told no one other than his colonel that he was getting married that day, and he'd only informed Colonel Zonov because he'd needed his permission.

'The table looks lovely.' Alice smiled as the waiter first pulled a chair out for her and then Betty. She'd bought a white silk gown in Cardiff before leaving Wales and packed it in the hope of marrying Richard, but it was summer weight, too thin for the time of year, and she was shivering. Misha saw her tremble and solicitously draped her shawl higher around her shoulders.

'Champagne, Captain Razin, Mrs Razina, Mrs Edwards?' The waiter prised the cork from the bottle.

'Without a proper chapel to marry in, I don't quite feel married,' Alice giggled as the waiter filled three glasses.

'I assure you that we are.' Although Misha wouldn't have admitted it, he didn't feel married either. Of choice, he would have preferred a Russian Orthodox wedding, but Alice had insisted on their civil ceremony being blessed by a chapel minister who hadn't yet raised sufficient funds from his Welsh flock to build a Methodist chapel in Hughesovka. The only good thing about the ceremony was that it had been easy to keep all knowledge of it from his fellow officers. He knew that they would have insisted on giving him a bachelor party in the mess and a guard of honour at the church, along with a few ribald jokes about his marrying for money – jokes he didn't doubt Alice would have picked up on. Unlike Betty Edwards, she was eager to learn Russian and took every opportunity to practise it with the waiters and chambermaids in the hotel.

Misha watched the waiter fill their glasses, then picked his up and touched it to Alice's and Betty's. 'To us and our future.'

Betty echoed the toast.

Misha steeled himself for disapproval and disappointment. 'About the house I said I'd find...'

'We won't be needing it, Misha,' Betty broke in.

'You intend to stay in the hotel?' Misha was alarmed by the thought that Alice would expect him to pay her bill now they were married.

'Alice and I will be moving into Jimmy Peddle's house first thing tomorrow morning. 'I bought it from him as a going concern and signed all the papers yesterday afternoon. It's already mine.'

'You're going to run a boarding house?' Misha was stunned. 'What about the shop you intended to open?'

'That may come later. Everyone says that the snow will melt in a week or two. As soon as it does, Jimmy Peddle and his wife will be off.' Betty studied her knife and polished it in her napkin. 'They can't wait to return to Wales and I don't blame them. Nasty heathen Godless place that this is.'

'Then why stay here?' Misha countered.

'Because I've bought a ready-made business that will bring in enough to keep me and Harriet Maud in comfort and enable me to save for our future. The boarding house is full of paying guests and makes a nice tidy profit every week, unlike my pub in Merthyr that was dependent on the town's workers. Whenever they were laid off by the Crawshays our takings plummeted. Jimmy Peddle and his wife have given up two of their rooms so we can move in right away. Martha and Harriet Maud will share one room, Alice and I the other, and we can run the business together.'

'You're going to be cooking and cleaning up after people ...' Misha began.

Once again Betty cut him short. 'Jimmy Peddle already employs two skivvies and a cook who live in an outbuilding at the back of the house. We'll keep them on to do the heavy work. All Alice and I will have to do is supervise them to make sure that the place is kept clean and run properly.'

The waiter arrived with the fish course of baked carp and they fell silent while plates, sauce, and salt were handed around and their glasses refilled. When they were alone again Misha looked directly at Alice.

'I've arranged for you to move into married officer's quarters in the barracks tomorrow morning.'

'This is the first I've heard about you wanting me to move into the barracks,' Alice complained.

'I didn't mention it until now because I was hoping to find a house that you and Mrs Edwards could buy.'

'You didn't find one?' Betty asked.

'Just as well, isn't it?' Misha challenged. 'If I had, you wouldn't have wanted it, not after buying Peddle's boarding house.'

'If it had been cheap enough, I might have stretched to buying the two,' Betty said airily.

'Houses don't come cheap in Hughesovka, Mrs Edwards.'

'There's cheap and there's cheap. You have no idea how much money I have, Misha Razin.'

'Or don't have, Mrs Edwards. I don't like people who play games and go back on their word. Alice, you will pack today. I'll hire a carriage from the stables so you can travel to the barracks with me first thing in the morning.'

'I wouldn't have minded if you'd warned me that was what you wanted me to do, Misha, but now Betty has bought Jimmy Peddle's boarding house and we're going into business together I can't see how I can move into the barracks. You see the business is mine, too,' Alice said proudly, looking to Misha for approval.

'You've invested money in the boarding house!' Misha was horrified at the thought that Alice had already dipped into her savings without asking his permission.

'It's a good investment,' Alice defended.

'As Alice is going to work with me in running the place, it makes sense for her to have a stake in the business,' said Betty.

'A wife should live with her husband.'

300

'And when you're on duty?' Betty demanded. 'You're the one who's always saying your work doesn't allow you any free time to visit Alice.'

'Which is why my colonel has allocated me married quarters so I can see Alice whenever I'm not on duty.'

'And when you are on duty? What's Alice supposed to do then? Sit and twiddle her thumbs.'

'Keep house, cook, sew, meet the other wives, learn Russian,' Misha suggested.

'Do you intend to stay in the regiment then?' Betty poked at the carp on her plate.

'What I do or don't do is none of your business, Mrs Edwards.'

'It most certainly is my business, Misha Razin, when you're married to my best friend.'

Misha ran his finger around the inside of his collar. He felt suddenly and, given the temperature of the room, quite inexplicably warm.

'You were the one who said you wanted to buy yourself out of the regiment, Misha,' Alice reminded.

'And I will, in my own good time.'

'What are you waiting for, Misha? Alice to give you the money to buy yourself out?' Betty goaded.

Furious because Betty had guessed the truth, Misha glared angrily at both women. 'If I bought myself out tomorrow where would Alice and I live? I'm not giving up my officer's quarters and servants to move into a common boarding house.'

'It's not a common boarding house.' Betty's colour heightened. 'We cater for the best people. Managers...'

'And colliers,' Misha sniped. 'Don't try to deny it, I've seen them walking in and out of the place.'

'It's my house too, Misha,' Alice murmured tremulously.

'How much did you pay Mrs Edwards for your share and what size is your share?'

'It's a good investment ...' she began defensively.

'Have you signed any documents or handed over any money?' he demanded.

'Everything was completed and signed legally yesterday,' Betty informed him. She abandoned her carp, dropped her knife and fork, and crossed her arms over her chest to emphasise her point.

'How much did you pay for your half a share of a bedroom, which appears to be all you've been promised, Alice?'

'I own a quarter of the house ...' Alice began hesitantly, intimidated by Misha's anger.

'How much?' Misha reiterated.

'I gave Betty a draft against my account for five hundred pounds.'

'Five hundred English pounds. For a quarter share in a house that's worth,' Misha did a quick calculation of roubles into pounds, 'no more than four hundred pounds.'

'There's a shortage of houses in Hughesovka,' Betty asserted. 'I paid a lot more than that.'

'I'm well aware there's a shortage of houses, Mrs Edwards, but if you gave my wife a quarter interest for her five hundred pounds, that means you must have paid two thousand pounds for a house that's not worth a penny more than four hundred.'

'I paid more than that,' Betty blustered. 'We'll have expenses...'

'How much did you pay for that house?' Misha repeated. 'That's between Jimmy Peddle and me.'

'And my wife, who so generously and gullibly handed you five hundred pounds for a quarter share. You, Mrs Edwards, have robbed my wife of her money. You'll be hearing from my lawyer.'

'The contracts are signed. As I said, we'll have expenses to meet in running the place. We have to buy food for the boarders, bed and table linen, pay wages to the servants...'

'Expenses!' he raised his voices. 'Five hundred pounds' worth, which I'll wager is more than you paid for the house in total. The contracts may be signed but I doubt that five hundred pounds in exchange for a share of a bedroom would be regarded as fair in any country. We'll see you in court.'

'There is no court here.'

'There is one in Taganrog.' Misha left the table.

'You really think I've been robbed, Misha?' Alice paled.

'Without a doubt. You may think of this woman as a friend, Alice, but she's a thief and I intend to make sure the entire town knows it.'

'You really won't move in with us, Misha?'

'I have no intention of setting up married life with a third person sharing our bedroom.'

'Then buy yourself out of the regiment and set up your own home,' Betty snapped.

'All my money is tied up in investments,' Misha lied. 'I have no intention of taking it out until I have a promise of a larger return in interest.'

Betty turned to Alice. 'I warned you not to marry him. He's nothing more than a Flash Harry. He only married you because he expects you to give him enough money to buy his way out of the regiment. It's as well you invested your money with me. It's safer...'

'Can Alice retrieve her money any time she wants?' When Betty didn't comment, Misha added, 'I thought not. Now you have it you won't be letting it go until the court makes you. As for the regiment, I will resign my commission when my business is viable and not a moment before.'

'But you just asked Alice to move into officers' quarters with you,' Betty reminded

'Temporarily, and only until I can get my business up and running. As soon as I have, I will leave the regiment, but not before I buy a house for Alice, with the money I will reclaim from you with the court's assistance.'

Realising Misha was serious about making an official complaint, Betty attempted to mollify him. 'There is no need for you to buy a house. When Jimmy Peddle and his family move out you and Alice can move into one of the bedrooms, so you can just go ahead and open your business.'

'I'll not live in the same house as you.'

'Misha, it's my house too...'

'It may be partly yours, Alice, but you've paid dearly for the privilege and it's not an investment I would have allowed you to make.'

'Allowed!' Betty repeated. 'With her own money.'

'We're married and that makes it our money. Money Alice has thrown away.'

'It's a husband's duty to keep his wife. I expect you to pay something towards Alice's keep.'

'You have made enough money from my gullible wife, you will not be getting any more from me.'

'The five hundred pounds Alice gave me is just for the business...'

'And I will ensure that Alice uses the remainder of her money to hire a trustworthy Russian lawyer. Good day to you.' Furious that Betty Edwards had outmanoeuvred him, Misha turned to Alice. 'I have booked a room here for us.'

'Waste of good money if you ask me,' Betty said.

'No one was asking you, Mrs Edwards. It's time for us to retire to that room, Alice.'

'But the rest of the meal?' Alice reminded him.

Misha signalled to the waiter. 'I will order them to deliver dinner to us later.'

'Have you started buying horses?' Betty made a final attempt to prove to Alice that Misha had only married her for her money. 'An officer like you must have a tidy nest egg.'

'Now you want to see my bank balance as well as my wife's so you can steal from me too? You won't find me quite so foolish or accommodating, Mrs Edwards.'

'I believe that finances between husband and wife should be open and above board. Alice has told you to the penny how much money she has, it's only fair that you reciprocate.'

'As you said Mrs Edwards, finances are between husband and wife.' He addressed the waiter who'd responded to his summons before turning back to his wife. 'I will see you in our room, Alice.'

'But our wedding breakfast? You can't just leave it.'

'I don't like the company at our table. I've reserved room twenty-one on the second floor.'

Betty watched him walk out of the dining room. 'Your husband has a temper, Alice. Best to curb it from the outset, otherwise your married life is not likely to be a smooth one.'

'I should follow Misha, after all it is our wedding day.'

'Finish your meal,' Betty advised. 'He'll only be after one thing. I can see our next course being wheeled through the door. Whole roast suckling pig with buckwheat. You don't want to miss that.'

'I should ask them to take some up to Misha.'

'It can keep until dinnertime. We have a lot to do before we move out of here tomorrow, it's time we started talking about it and making plans for the business.'

Hotel Hughesovka April 1872

Misha paced impatiently from one end of the hotel room to the other as he waited for Alice. He was furious with her for investing in the boarding house without discussing the transaction with him first. He was aware that Betty Edwards wielded considerable influence over his wife, but he hadn't realised quite how much until that morning.

After Betty's gibes about him only marrying Alice for her money, which had been too close to the truth to sit comfortably with his pride, he suspected that Alice would think twice about handing over the remainder of her money to buy him out of the regiment – and even if she did, there certainly wouldn't be sufficient left over to set himself up as a horse-trader.

He'd married for money, only to be disappointed, and was now saddled with a wife who, although widowed, he doubted would be as competent sexually as the whores who serviced the officers in the barracks, and was likely in the long run to prove far more expensive.

He had to wait a full two hours before Alice entered the bedroom, hours that only served to escalate his temper and vodka consumption.

'Where have you been?' he growled when she finally walked in.

'I finished our wedding breakfast. It would have been a waste not to. It was very good. The roast suckling pig was excellent. I asked them to keep you some in the kitchen and bring it up at dinnertime. Misha,' she reached for his hand. 'This is our wedding day.'

'Precisely, and you didn't think to be entirely honest with me in every way beforehand.'

'I have been honest. You know to a penny how much money I have. I thought my investment in the boarding house would be a pleasant surprise. You can't really believe that Betty set out to steal from us.'

'That is exactly what she's done, and she deliberately set out to do it before we married because she knew I would never let her fleece you. A husband has the legal right to control his wife's money. You never mentioned that you were thinking of giving it to Mrs Edwards to invest in a boarding house of all things. I would never have allowed you to do it.'

'Betty said I will make it back in five years or even less. And should we decide to sell the business I will have my original investment returned to me plus a percentage of whatever profit we make. Given the way the town is growing the house is bound to accrue in value. And I have £500 left. Isn't that enough for you to set up in business?'

'Now that you intend to live in a boarding house and share a bedroom with Mrs Edwards I'm not inclined to put in the work needed to start a business. What's the point in my working for a future for my family if my wife prefers to set up home with another woman. I may as well stay where I am, living comfortably in the barracks.'

'Misha, please, I'll give you a draft for the rest of my money.'

'For what's left after you've given most of it to Mrs Edwards, you mean.'

'Betty explained that she needs the money to run the business.'

'She's played you for a fool and you can't even see it. I've only ever heard her talking about her business, never about your business. You'd better give me your copies of the contract you signed so I can get a lawyer to check them.'

'Betty has them.'

'Then get them from her. Now.'

'Betty's talking about opening another business – a shop this time. She's promised to look after us and I'm sure she will. Once you've bought yourself out of the regiment and set up as a horse trader you can invest the profits with Betty. She's a good businesswoman, Misha.'

'I would as soon think of investing in a cockroach farm.' 'Misha, this is our wedding day!'

'Thank you for reminding me,' he snapped caustically.

'Undress.'

Alice froze.

Her first husband had been old, but not too old to demand what women in Merthyr referred to as 'husband's rights', which in her case had consisted of somewhat embarrassing fumbling beneath the sheets at bedtime.

'Didn't you hear me?'

'Yes, Misha...'

'Undress and kneel on the bed.' He reached for the bottle of vodka he'd asked for when he'd booked the room. He'd almost emptied it while waiting for Alice to join him.

'Misha...'

'You're my wife. Didn't I just hear you promise to obey me?'

Alice turned her back so he wouldn't see the tears – and fear – in her eyes. 'I need help.'

'What's the matter now?'

'I can't unfasten the buttons at the nape of my dress.'

He finished the vodka in his glass, then hooked his fingers into the neck of her dress and pulled. It tore from the neck to the hem. Alice screamed.

'Not so loud,' he hissed. He pushed her face down onto the bed and locked the door.

She looked up at him over her shoulder, terrified of the monster he'd become. He grabbed her legs and pulled her down to the edge of the bed.

'You're hurting me.'

He closed his fingers painfully into the back of her neck, hauled her up, and pushed a pillow beneath her head. He grabbed the waistband of her drawers and tore them from her.

'Don't move.'

He unbuckled his trousers, dropped them to the floor, and raped her.

Chapter Thirty

Catherine Ignatova's house April 1872

Catherine sat quietly in a chair next to the hearth in the library, ostensibly reading while covertly watching and listening as John Hughes, Dmitri, and Roman played cards. When the clock struck ten John laid down his hand and scooped up the coins from the centre of the table.

'Thank you, Roman, I must have won as much as two roubles from you tonight. Another few centuries of nightly poker and I might make a slight dent in your purse! But you can't have it all ways. You know what they say, lucky at cards...'

'Lucky bridegroom is enough for me,' Roman shuffled the cards together. 'Did you lose much, Dmitri?'

'A few kopeks. Not as much as you,' the lawyer commented.

'I'm for bed.' John rose to his feet and stretched. 'Tomorrow I'll see how much of my apprenticeship in Crawshay's works in Merthyr I remember. I'll attempt to puddle a perfect pig of iron for you to take to Grand Duke Konstantin when you honeymoon in St Petersburg, Roman. My gift to him and a foretaste of our production.'

'I'll ask Sonya to wrap it in ribbons,' Roman joked.

'And decorate it with roses, white ones,' John smiled. Catherine set her book aside and left her chair. 'A final nightcap, gentlemen?' She saw John hesitate.

'A small one.'

'You've persuaded me.' Roman went to the tray on a side table and poured four small vodkas. He handed them out.

'To our hostess,' John toasted as Roman and Dmitri joined him in touching their glasses to Catherine's.

'To brides who permit their bridegrooms to plan a working honeymoon,' Catherine countered.

'My fiancée is very understanding,' Roman smiled.

'You're not married yet,' John warned. 'He finished his vodka. 'Goodnight, Catherine, gentlemen.'

'Sleep well,' Catherine called after him and Dmitri who followed John out of the door.

'I think I'll read for a while, if you don't mind.'

'I don't mind, Roman.' Catherine returned to her chair. 'Please, join me, the fire is warm and the flames invite dreams.'

Roman picked up the book he'd chosen.

'What are you reading?' Catherine asked as he took the chair opposite hers.

'Turgenev's Fathers and Sons.'

'Very apt, considering the conflict it depicts between those who support the new industrial Russia and those who adhere to the old Russia of class constraints, serfdom, and peasants tied to the land. Both Alexei and Sonya have recommended the book to me, I've been meaning to read it for some time.'

'Something stopped you? This is a first edition, you own it and it's ten years old.'

'I order all the latest books to be delivered from Moscow on publication but I rarely find the time to read them. Perhaps I will be able to catch up in advanced old age.'

'When everyone within a day's ride stops turning to you in the expectation that you will solve their problems for them?' he teased gently.

'Something like that.' She remembered why she'd lingered after John and Dmitri had left the library. 'I'd like to talk to you.'

'About Sonya?' he guessed.

'To be more precise, her mother. Your insistence on taking Sonya to St Petersburg after your marriage could cause problems for both of you given Sonya's parentage,' Catherine said seriously. 'People have long memories, especially when it comes to scandals.'

'You think people will connect Sonya with her mother, although she uses her father's name?'

'Infamous people excite gossip that can sometimes come too close to the truth. Koshka is infamous,' Catherine reminded him.

'As is Elizabeth Komanskaya for leaving her husband and setting up home with your brother, but I doubt anyone not directly concerned realises the two are one and the same person.'

'You're sure Taras Komansky didn't recognise Koshka when she had him thrown out of her house?' Catherine asked.

'I think Komansky would have been angry enough to say something before Fritz knocked him senseless if he had. Fritz told me he warned Koshka that her husband's brother was in the house. She didn't enter the public rooms until Komansky was in a private room. When Fritz threw Komansky out he took care to keep him away from Koshka.'

'She is fortunate to have such loyal staff.'

'She inspires loyalty,' Roman said thoughtfully. 'When I heard people talking about Sonya in St Petersburg after your last visit, it was as your brother Sergei's daughter and your niece. No one mentioned her mother, not even to repeat the story I presume you and Koshka put about that she'd died shortly after giving birth to a daughter.'

'What did they say about my brother?'

Roman looked Catherine in the eye. 'Things no sister would want to hear.'

'That he was a gambler and a drunk who lost his inheritance and fortune at the card tables and his health in a brothel.' She said what he couldn't bring himself to say.

'Words to that effect,' he hedged tactfully.

'And that he went mad and wandered around the streets of Moscow in his nightshirt brandishing a gun?'

'That too.'

'Nothing was said about her mother?'

'No. In fact I was surprised that Nicholas Beletsky knew as much as he did.'

'Nicholas knew Elizabeth as an old family friend. He was dining here the night I received the message from Elizabeth to say that my brother was sick and destitute in Moscow. My husband had just died; Olga had not long given birth to Alexei but was already expecting another child. To be honest, I was glad of the excuse to travel. As you know, I didn't only find my brother physically sick but mentally. Fortunately, Dmitri had travelled with me and he arranged for my brother to be admitted to a sanatorium.

'Sonya's mother had had every excuse to desert my brother but hadn't. She was no longer living with him, because she didn't want to expose her child to disease, but she'd rented rooms for him and paid for a nurse to care for him with money she'd solicited from her new protector.'

'My father,' Roman guessed.

'Your father,' Catherine confirmed. 'I knew Elizabeth had left her husband. Even on the steppe I'd heard the scandal, that she'd left Komansky to live with Sergei. The unkind enjoyed repeating the gossip to me, using it as yet another example of Sergei's debauchery. His planned and calculated seduction of a happily married woman, enticing her away from her loving husband. God only knows that was nowhere near the truth, but I don't have to explain to you what the Komanskys are capable of.'

'You heard about Adele's beating.'

Catherine nodded. 'What I didn't know when I arrived in Moscow to answer Elizabeth's summons was that she'd had a child. Hardly expected at her age. I pleaded with her to return here with me so we could bring her daughter up together.'

'She wouldn't come?'

'I tried everything I knew to make her change her mind, but she realised that her reputation had gone and with it all hope of respectability, not only for her but her child. She reminded me that society was unforgiving to those who break its strict moral rules.

'But she trusted your father to care for her, which he did until the day he died – and afterwards. She opened her salon with money he left her. To return to that trip to Moscow, I tried to reimburse your father for the money he'd given Elizabeth to clear Sergei's debts and pay for his living expenses. Your father wouldn't hear of it.'

'He cleared Sonya's father's debts but wouldn't allow her mother to keep her child?' Roman shook his head in disgust.

'No. Your father offered, but Elizabeth was insistent that I should take her daughter, although it was obvious she dreaded being parted from her. She was so adamant, that your father and I felt we had no choice but to obey her. She told me in confidence that your father loathed children and that in time he would allow his dislike to show and drive a wedge either between her and her child or her and your father.'

Roman gave a sardonic laugh. 'She was right. My father had no time for children. So you took Sonya.'

'I took Sonya and brought her back here, much to Nicholas's disgust. He tried to stop his children from playing with her. He wanted me to raise Sonya as a servant rather than a member of the family.'

'But you wouldn't listen to him.'

'Not just me, his children. You've seen how close Sonya and Alexei are. Sonya's presence just gave me and Nicholas one more thing to quarrel over. But to return to the point of this discussion: Koshka is a successful courtesan. There are people in St Petersburg who know her real identity.'

'If they really know Koshka they will respect her too much to want to hurt her.'

'Komansky knows, as does Nicholas Beletsky, and neither of them respect Koshka. They might have told Levsky and others who Koshka is. Then there are servants, past and present; not all keep secrets.'

'You want Sonya to know that her mother is still alive?'

'Before someone else tells her, yes,' Catherine confirmed.

'And you want her to know her mother's true identity?'

'For the same reason.'

'The secret isn't ours to tell.' Roman took his cigar case from his pocket.

'It's Koshka's, and she needs to realise the devastating effect it could have on Sonya if she hears it from the wrong people. Tell me truthfully, have you never thought of telling Sonya exactly who her mother is?'

'I've thought about it,' Roman admitted. 'I've been bracing myself to call on Koshka before the wedding with the intention of trying to persuade her to meet Sonya and attend our wedding.'

'Good luck.' Catherine left her chair.

'You're handing me the task?' Despite the circumstances Roman couldn't conceal his amusement at Catherine's total abdication of responsibility.

'I've failed to make Koshka see sense in the matter. It's your turn to try.'

'I'll call in and see Koshka tomorrow and warn her of the consequences should Sonya find out her mother's identity from someone less sympathetic.'

'Thank you, Roman.' Catherine kissed his cheek. 'You will take care of Sonya for me.'

'In every way possible while I still breathe, and financially afterwards. I promise you, Catherine. In that respect I am my father's son.'

Catherine hesitated. She wanted to ask him if he loved Sonya but sensed that he would resent the question, especially in view of what Koshka had told her about Sonya loving Nathan Kharber.

He looked at her expectantly.

'You'll be the first to know the outcome of my discussion with Koshka.'

'I don't doubt it. I have something for you.'

She slipped her hand into the pocket of her dress and pulled out a key. She took his hand, pressed it into his palm and folded his fingers over it.

He opened his hand. 'A key?'

'A master key that will open any door of this house, including the communicating doors between the wing where you sleep and this wing. The pillars that lead up to the balcony are covered in ice. I'd hate for you to slip and break your neck on the way up to the balcony and French doors of Sonya's room.'

'You know?'

'I know everything that goes on in this house, Roman.'

'I'm sorry.'

'Sorry you took advantage of my hospitality, and my niece's innocence, to seduce her, or sorry you were found out?'

'All three.'

'Sleep well in my niece's bed, Roman.'

'I will, Catherine.' He dared to rise and kiss her cheek.

After Catherine left, Roman made his way to the only door that connected the wing of the house John Hughes was renting to Catherine's wing. He climbed the stairs, walked to the end of the first floor corridor, and slipped the key into the lock. It turned easily. He opened the door and found himself in the corridor that housed Catherine and Sonya's bedrooms.

He walked down the corridor, and knowing that Sonya was expecting him to walk through the French doors that opened on to the balcony, slipped the key into the lock of her bedroom and turned it.

'Roman!' She sat up in bed as he walked in.

He held his finger to his lips, locked the door, and set the key on her dressing table, before bolting the French doors and pulling the drapes.

'You walked up the stairs? How did you have a key?'

'I came in through the connecting door to the east wing. Your aunt gave me a master key. She knows where I've been spending my nights.' He shrugged off his jacket and tossed it on to a chair.

'Did she say anything?'

'She asked me to take care of you.'

'Was she angry?'

'Hardly, she gave me the master key. After all,' he smiled, 'a few more days and we'll be married, and until then,' he stooped down and kissed her lips, 'your aunt recognises that we need to practise.'

Madam Koshka's salon April 1872

Roman waited for Fritz to open the door to Koshka's boudoir before entering and presenting her with a bouquet of flowers.

'For me, how lovely.' She set down her pen and took them from him. 'The scent is divine. It's rare to find hothouse blooms that hold their perfume.'

'It is, and I can take no credit. The scent is the result of Catherine's gardener's experiments with rose bushes and trees. They are a gift from her. I'm only the delivery boy.'

'Please thank her for me.'

'I will.'

'And excuse my manners. Please sit down, pour yourself a drink, or would you prefer coffee?'

'A small brandy would go down well. I've a feeling I'll soon be needing the courage.' He waited while she opened the door and passed the bouquet to Fritz, together with instructions to give the flowers to one of the maids, to be put in water.

She closed the door and returned to her seat by the desk. 'A few more days and you'll be a married man.'

'I'm here to invite you to the wedding.'

'I will be there, as I was at Alexei and Ruth's, sitting at the back of the church with the veiled widows.'

'That is what I was afraid you'd say. You do realise that after we're married I will be taking Sonya to St Petersburg.'

'You're honeymooning there?'

'St Petersburg will be our first stop, I've made plans for us to travel around Europe. We're visiting St Petersburg first because I have business to conduct with Grand Duke Konstantin on Mr Hughes's behalf. The New Russia Company have placed bids on several government contracts, and I have undertaken to do all I can to secure them.'

'A worthy cause. Even I can see that Russia needs to modernise and industrialise.'

'I need your help, Koshka.'

'Really?' She filled two glasses and handed him one.

'Catherine and I agree that in taking Sonya from here to St Petersburg I will be exposing her to people who know more about her parents' past than she does.'

Koshka drained her glass.

'She needs to know the truth, Koshka.'

'She knows her father is in a sanatorium.'

'Her father is not the problem, as you well know.'

'Her mother is dead.'

Roman took a deep breath. 'Too many people know that is not the case. Komansky...'

'Didn't see me when Fritz threw him out. If he had, he'd have created a scene.'

'And the next time he walks in?'

'Fritz has taken care that Komansky won't get past the door.'

'Komansky isn't the only one who knows your real identity. Nicholas Beletsky...'

'He hasn't said anything, has he?'

'He told Sonya that her mother is – is, not was – a whore before Catherine and I could stop him. If Sonya and I meet him in public in St Petersburg, I might not be able to prevent him from saying more.'

'What do you want me to do, Roman?'

'Meet Sonya. Tell her the truth before someone else relates a distorted version of the facts. Introduce yourself.'

'And if she can't forgive me for abandoning her, or being a whore?'

'You didn't abandon her, you gave her to Catherine to bring up so that should tell you something about the kind of woman she has become. And when all is said and done, you're her mother. I need look no further to see where Sonya has inherited her beauty, generosity, and kindness. Please, Koshka, for all our sakes, meet Sonya and tell her the truth.' He looked at her. It seemed a long time before she nodded agreement. 'Soon?' he pressed.

'But not in public.'

'Of course.'

'And on one condition.' Koshka opened her drawer, and extracted the album she'd secreted at the back. 'That you give her this, not as a gift but as a loan, and that you and Catherine tell Sonya the truth before I see her.'

'Where and when will you meet Sonya?'

'Catherine's house on your wedding day – but only after you and Catherine have spoken to her.'

Chapter Thirty-one

Madam Koshka's salon April 1872

'Are you sure you're, all right?' Praskovia whispered to Sarah for the tenth time in as many minutes as they entered the church on Catherine's estate.

'Quite sure, and not so loud.' Sarah glanced up at Richard. Fortunately, he'd gone ahead to talk to John Hughes, who was sitting in the front pew with Catherine and Ruth, so he hadn't heard Praskovia.

Praskovia beckoned to the nursemaid she'd engaged to help her with Pavlo. 'Please sit on the end of the pew behind me, Galina, and if Pavlo makes a sound during the service take him from me and carry him into the vestry.'

'Yes, madam.' The girl curtsied and perched on the edge of the pew ready to stand if anyone should want to go into the pew ahead of her.

'I can see you grimacing,' Praskovia warned Sarah as they sat behind Catherine and John.

'False labour,' Sarah dismissed. 'These are the slow contractions that come the week before the birth. You know how much you suffered with backache before Pavlo was born. I'll be fine,' Sarah smiled at Glyn who was standing next to Roman in front of the altar.

Richard returned, reached for Sarah's hand and squeezed it.

'You, sure you're all right? You look...'

'What?' Sarah interrupted.

'Odd?' Richard suggested warily.

'I'm fine.'

The choir broke into song, and everyone turned towards the door. Alexei led Sonya inside, Anna straightening the train of Sonya's dress as she followed them.

A gasp rippled through the congregation, and Catherine brushed a tear from her eye at the sight of the dress she had worn to marry Alexei Ignatov, a man twenty years older than her with the reputation of a rake and a womaniser. She looked from Sonya to Roman. The dress was the same. The bride, beautiful – far more beautiful than her – or so she believed. The groom? Would Sonya be able to turn a blind eye to Roman's faults as she'd managed to do with her Alexei?

'I thought Roman said he wanted a small wedding,' John whispered below the level of the choir. 'The church is as packed as it was for Alexei and Ruth's.'

'It's not every day that a prince is married in the Donbas,' Catherine whispered in reply.

The bridal party reached the altar. Alexei placed Sonya's hand in Roman's and stepped back beside Ruth. Father Grigor held out his hand to Glyn who handed him the betrothal rings. The priest recited a blessing and bible passage before blessing the couple. Then proceeded to repeat the ritual three times. Sarah knew every ceremony was repeated three times in the Russian Orthodox church to represent the Holy Trinity, but it made for very long services and for all the excuses she had given Praskovia, she knew she was in labour.

Glyn, in his capacity as koumbaros or best man – a solemn position that Father Grigor had warned him before he'd accepted the position at Alexei's wedding, and repeated when he'd agreed to act as Roman's koumbaros, made him an important person in the couple's lives – moved next to Roman.

Father Grigor and Anna stood either side of Sonya. After the rings had been blessed for the last time, Father Grigor made the sign of the cross, pressed the rings against the bride and bridegroom's forehead three times, then exchanged the rings between the couple's fingers three times, to signify that the weakness of one would be compensated by the strength of the other, before finally setting the rings on the third finger of the right hand.

Father Grigor solemnly lit two candles and placed them in Roman and Sonya's left hands, where Sarah knew from witnessing Alexei's wedding to Ruth, they would remain for the remainder of the service. The priest joined Roman and Sonya's right hands while praying for their marriage.

A ripple akin to a sigh rippled through the audience as Father Grigor opened a box on a side table and extracted two magnificent crowns, wrought in gleaming silver and gold studded with emeralds. The crosses on the top of each crown were joined by white ribbon to symbolize the unity of marriage. Alexei changed the crowns between Sonya and Roman's heads three times.

Sarah had no experience of kings and queens or royal courts, but she imagined the crowns Roman had provided would not look out of place in the reception room of the Winter Palace, after having heard Richard and Glyn's description of the place. Alexei and Ruth had been crowned during their marriage, but their crowns had been garlanded white roses on simple wooden frameworks that Alexei had asked Pyotr to carve for them. She knew, from something Alexei had said, that the crowns would be treasured by the married couple for life. Alexei's grandfather and his mother Olga had both been buried with theirs.

Sarah's pains intensified as Father Grigor read yet more Bible passages. At the end of the reading he offered Roman and Sonya a gold chalice, referring to it as a "common cup", something Sarah took to be an irony considering the ornate design etched on the sides and the gems studded below the rim.

The bride and groom took three sips of wine from a shared cup, while Father Grigor reminded them that the Common Cup ritual was based on the wedding at Cana, where Jesus turned water into wine. He told the congregation that the cup represented life and symbolized the mutual sharing of joys and sorrows, an indication that from that moment on the bride and groom would share everything, doubling their joys and dividing their sorrows.

Sarah gripped the back of the pew in front of her. Her knuckles whitened as she fought the pain of yet another contraction. Richard looked at her in concern as Father Grigor and Alexei led Roman and Sonya three times around the altar. The choir began to sing the first of three hymns.

'I'm taking you outside,' Richard murmured.

'I can't move for a moment.'

Without hesitation Richard swept Sarah up into his arms.

Praskovia moved and Richard carried Sarah out of the pew. Father Grigor stared at them for an instant before running to open the vestry door. He tripped over his cassock and slammed into the door, hitting his forehead. When he finally wrenched it open, he ushered Richard and Sarah inside. Anna left the side of the altar. Father Grigor dived into the vestry and handed her one of his spare clean robes. She slipped it over her bridesmaid's dress and closed the door behind her.

Father Grigor returned to the front of the altar in time for the last hymn. He waited until the last note had been sung, before reciting the parting blessings upon the newly-weds.

He repeated the words but it was obvious to everyone in the congregation that he wasn't listening to his own speech. He looked from Roman to the vestry door as he recited, 'Be thou magnified, O Bridegroom, as Abraham, and blessed as Isaac and multiply as Jacob. Walk in peace and work in righteousness, as the commandments of God.'

As he turned to Sonya a baby wailed behind the door of the vestry. Smiling broadly, the priest recited, 'And thou O Bride, be though magnified as Sarah, glad as Rebecca, and multiply like unto Rachel, rejoicing in thine own husband, fulfilling the conditions of the law, for so it is well pleasing unto God.

The congregation joined him in the final ancient phrase.

'Na zisete – may you live!'

'As well we might,' Father Grigor added, 'with another new soul in the world.'

Glyn and Praskovia's house April 1872

'You will apologise to Roman and Sonya for us for interrupting their wedding,' Sarah asked Ruth, as she, Alexei, Glyn, and Praskovia visited her bedroom shortly after they'd returned home.

'Apologise,' Alexei laughed, 'they think it's funny! Roman says he only hopes his children will be born as quickly, and Sonya said your son will be a blessed and holy child after being born in a church.'

'Not too holy, I hope. I wouldn't like a monk in the family!' Richard qualified. He was sitting next to Sarah on the bed, his left arm wrapped around her, while he gently stroked his son's cheek with his right index finger.

'It's entirely my fault for ignoring Praskovia. As a nurse I should have known better,' Sarah looked down at her son. 'But at first I really thought they were false labour pains and by the time I realised they weren't it was too late to walk out of the church unobtrusively, or even with any dignity.'

'At least you saw most of the wedding. I'm only sorry you'll miss the wedding breakfast,' Praskovia commiserated.

'Tell Roman and Sonya we'll be with them in spirit,' Richard added

'There's nothing like a quiet night in with the family.' Glyn moved the shawl from Pavlo's head so he could see his face. 'I recommend it.'

'I'm looking forward to it.' Richard couldn't tear his gaze away from his son. 'You will watch Morgan and Owen for me and make sure that they don't disgrace themselves.'

'They won't,' Anna bustled in with a tray, which she set on the bedside table.

'I'll speak to the boys before they go to Mrs Ignatova's. You can watch them while I stay and look after Sarah...'

'I don't need looking after and the bridesmaid needs to be at the wedding breakfast with the bride and groom so it's time my midwife was on her way,' Sarah interrupted.

'As I'm staying here to take care of my wife and son, you go to the party with the others,' Richard added.

'A man look after a new mother and child?' Anna questioned in astonishment.

'I'll supervise him,' Sarah said. 'Go, have fun. You need it the way you work.'

'That's an order from your big brother and sister-in-law,' Richard added firmly.

'Along with a huge thank you from both of us for our son.' Sarah gripped Anna's hand.

'I was determined to deliver your baby after missing Praskovia's.'

'Have you a name picked out so we can toast the unexpected guest at the wedding after drinking the bride and groom's health?' Glyn asked.

'We couldn't make up our minds which Mr Edwards to name him after if he turned out to be a boy, so we decided to call him Edward, and as I have my father's name and saw no point in repeating it, we thought we'd name him Edward David Victor after the brothers we lost to the cholera.' Richard looked to Anna for approval. Too overcome by emotion to speak, she smiled through her tears and nodded.

'Hear that, Pavlo.' Praskovia lifted her baby in her arms and kissed his cheek. 'You have a playmate. Edward.'

'Everyone out,' Anna shouted in her best authoritative nurses' voice. 'Someone go and make sure the sleighs are harnessed and waiting.' She straightened the bedcover and lifted the tray in front of Sarah. 'I'll be back early.'

'No, you won't,' Richard countered. 'Go and enjoy yourself, sis, see you in the morning.'

Sarah smiled at her. 'Thank you again for our son. Next time I promise I'll have a girl so we can name her Maryanna after you and your mother.'

Catherine Ignatova's house April 1872

'Abandoned your bride already, Roman?' Catherine joined him at one of the tables the waiters had used to lay out the champagne glasses.

'Mr Hughes invited her to dance. It would have been churlish of her to refuse.'

'It would. He dances so well for a man of his size.'

'Better than me?' Roman raised an eyebrow.

'Stop fishing for compliments, it doesn't become you. You don't mind moving into my half of the house until you and Sonya leave on your honeymoon?'

'Not at all, Catherine. As Sonya is used to living in this half, it made more sense and it makes very little difference to me as I have been eating most of my meals here. The only thing I will have to sacrifice is my own bedroom in favour of Sonya's. And while we're talking of rooms, thank you for the loan of this.' He pressed the master key she had given him into her hand.

'Thank you for returning it.' She dropped it into her reticule.

He looked at her over the rim of his glass. 'Thank you for being so understanding.'

'It's hard to believe from the way I look now but I was young once, and I know young people are human. Just one thing, Roman: she is my niece. Please don't hurt her – in any way.'

'I promise you I never will – intentionally.' He glanced over his shoulder to the doorway as a figure walked in, swathed in black lace veils. 'If you'll excuse me, one of my father's closest friends has just entered.'

'I saw her at the service but she left before I could speak to her.'

'I know she would like to wish the bride well. Will you meet her with me and introduce her to Sonya.'

'It would be my pleasure, Roman.' She took his arm when he offered it to her. 'I'm glad we understand one another.'

'I know you're only concerned for Sonya, Catherine. As am I.'

They walked over to Koshka who was standing in the doorway.

'I'm so glad you came,' Catherine embraced her.

'The bride looked so happy in the church. You're a lucky man, Roman, she's very beautiful, as is the bridesmaid.'

'You recall the dresses?' Catherine asked.

'Unchanged in a world I no longer recognise.'

'The music will stop in a moment,' Roman prophesised. 'I'll reclaim my bride and introduce you.'

'I have a sleigh waiting, Roman...'

'It can wait five minutes. We'll go into the library and wait for you and Sonya there, Roman. How would you like us to introduce you?' Catherine asked.

'You've told her?'

'Everything,' Roman assured Koshka, 'which is why Elizabeth Tsetovna would be appropriate. It was the name you used when you lived with her father?'

'It was. Does she know the name I have used for so many years?'

'She does.'

'It would not be appropriate in this house.'

The music ended. Catherine and Koshka left for the library.

John Hughes walked Sonya to Roman.

'My mother?' Sonya asked.

'Is in the library with your aunt.'

Sonya led the way. She walked to the veiled woman sitting beside Catherine, took a package from the table next to them and handed it to Koshka.

'Thank you for allowing me to look at this album.'

326

Koshka took it. 'My most treasured possession. Roman and Catherine have told you...'

'That you are my mother, yes. Thank you for allowing them to.' Sonya knelt before Koshka and took her hands.

'There is no need for that,' Koshka said in embarrassment.

'There is. I've thought about nothing except meeting you since the moment Aunt Catherine and Roman told me that you gave birth to me. You are my mother. You cared enough for me to hand me over to a woman who would love me and give me a life you couldn't. I don't think I could ever be so brave and unselfish as to give up a child of mine. Not knowing how much I would suffer after such a parting.'

Koshka lifted her veil and took Sonya's hand. 'Not only beautiful but understanding.'

Oblivious to the tears coursing down her cheeks, she forced a smile.

Sonya kneeled upright and kissed Koshka's cheek.

Koshka gripped Sonya's hands more tightly for an instant then relinquished them. 'My very best wishes for your future, my dear, you make a beautiful bride.' She rose to her feet and grasped Roman's arm. 'Roman, look after her.'

'I have just made a solemn promise in church to do just that.'

'I cannot stay as I have a sleigh waiting. I just wanted to look upon your face once more, my dear. I can see that you have made Roman very happy. Roman, always try to make your bride as happy as she makes you. God bless you. Both of you.'

'When we return to Hughesovka may I call on you?' Sonya asked.

'That wouldn't be proper, my dear.'

'But we will see one another again.'

'God willing.' Koshka embraced Catherine, then Roman, and finally Sonya, before walking quickly away.

Alexei and Ruth's cottage April 1872

'I've decided, I like being married to you,' Alexei declared as Ruth rubbed soap into his hair and down his back.

'I could turn into a screaming shrew next week.' They were in the washing room of the Banya attached to their cottage.

'Then I'd have to chastise you with a venik.' Alexei referred to the bundles of birch twigs found in every Banya.

'I've been meaning to ask about those. Do you ever beat yourself with a venik?' Ruth questioned curiously.

'Misha and I tried it once when we were young. We took it in turns to beat one another. Misha always did enjoy hurting people. For me it was the first and the last time ... but perhaps I should try it again with you.' He wiped away the soap that had trickled down his face, opened his eyes and looked at her.

'Miriam insisted a good beating improves circulations and the colour of the skin.'

'You girls whipped one another?'

She laughed. 'That expression on your face is half reproof, half excitement.'

'I was anticipating whipping you.'

'I would whip you back, and not with a venik. The kitchen broom would stimulate your circulation more.'

'In that case I'll settle for a gentle embrace.' He fondled Ruth's breasts as she continued to rub soap in his hair.

'Close your eyes.'

Thinking more soap was trickling down his forehead he complied without question. She picked up a bucket of cold water and tipped it over his head.

'You could have put some warm water in,' he gasped when he could speak again.

'My brother says cold water is better for you than a beating with a venik, and as he's a doctor he should know.'

'For that I demand you warm me up.'

'It's almost time for you to go to work.'

'Mr Hughes gave all of us the morning off. Just as well, after the excitement of the wedding and Sarah and Richard's baby.'

'Sarah and Praskovia's babies are beautiful. Do you think ours will be as wonderful?'

'More so, because it will be ours.' He pushed the door to the steam room open, then stopped and looked back at her. 'Are you...'

'Sarah thinks our baby will be born in about six to seven months.'

'Why didn't you say something sooner?'

'Because I wanted to be sure.'

'I love you, Mrs Beletskaya. Come to bed.'

'After the steam room,' she whispered.

Catherine Ignatova's house May 1872

'You ready for your goodbye breakfast?' Roman watched Sonya open her eyes.

'No,' She closed her eyes again and inched across the bed until the full length of her body nestled against his.

'We have to leave within the hour if we are to get to the Monstov house before sunset tonight,' he warned.

'Do you never use inns?' She'd watched him map a route for them to follow from Hughesovka to St Petersburg, stopping over every night at the private country houses of aristocrats and wealthy socialites he was acquainted with, but whom she knew only by reputation.

'Not if I can help it. There are areas of Russia and even Western Europe where there are no houses worth speaking of, only shepherds' huts, small farms, and hovels. The few inns in those wild places aren't even worthy of the name. When I venture into such primitive territory I camp.'

'Camp – in a tent?' she asked in amusement.

'It's what generals do, and provided you have the right equipment and enough servants to do the hard work it can be comfortable. But whenever possible it makes sense to take advantage of the generosity and hospitality of friends and acquaintances, provided you're in a position to reciprocate. It's wasteful to keep a full complement of staff with nothing better to do than sample your wine cellar and eat food stocks in a house that's empty for most of the year. The best way I know of monitoring the industry or otherwise of housekeepers, butlers, and footmen is to give your friends permission to call unexpectedly on your property whenever they are in the area. It also,' he kissed her gently on the lips, 'means you have more privacy than you would staying in a hotel. Which is extremely important when planning a belated honeymoon. Time to rise.' He gave her another kiss before swinging his legs out of the bed and on to the floor.

'I'm missing you already.'

'You won't be once we start travelling for days on end cooped up in the same coach. But if everything goes according to plan we'll be in St Petersburg five or six days from now and then we'll see more people than any sane man wants to in one lifetime.' He went into the bathroom but left the door open. 'I'm looking forward to introducing you to the city.'

'I've been there,' she reminded him.

'Not with me. I can't wait to show you my St Petersburg.' He lifted his robe from a hook inside the bathroom and slipped it on.

'Which is different to everyone else's St Petersburg?'

'We have rather a nice palace there that I inherited from my father. After my mother's death, he would never allow anyone to touch her possessions other than to dust them, but you don't have to go into her suite if you don't want to.'

'I'd like to see it.'

He smiled. 'Thank you. It might not be quite so painful for me to see it with you. I hated going into her rooms with my father because it upset him. In fact it was the only time I ever saw him show any emotion when I was growing up. That will be our morning coffee and hot water.' He opened the door and took the tray from the waiting maid. 'Good morning and thank you.'

'Good morning, your Excellency.' She dropped a curtsey, turned, and ran. The footman echoed her 'Good morning' before carrying two large jugs into the bathroom. He left them, bowed, and scurried after the maid.

'Your aunt's servants appear to be terrified of me.' Roman set the tray on Sonya's bedside table. He went into the bathroom, filled his shaving bowl with hot water, and proceeded to lather his shaving brush.

'I think they are more embarrassed than afraid because they regard us as honeymooners.'

'They obviously have no inkling that we practised first.'

'I would be concerned if they did.' Sonya poured two cups of coffee, slipped out of the bed, and carried one into the bathroom for him.

'Much as I enjoy admiring you in your natural state, my sweet, when we're travelling it might be as well to wear a robe in the bedroom in case someone walks in on us. Several of my friends run bachelor establishments with solely male staff.'

She reached for her dressing gown.

'Really?'

'You find that hard to believe?'

'Not if there's a brothel or accommodating females nearby.'

'It's good to know my wife is acquainted with the world.'

'How could I fail to be when I've been married to you for a month?'

'True.'

She fetched her coffee, sat on a stool, and watched him run the cut-throat razor over his lathered cheek. He winked at her in the mirror when he saw her watching him.

'You said we'll stay in St Petersburg about three or four weeks,' she said thoughtfully.

'I may be able to complete my business in less time. As soon as I do, and you've tired of the city, we'll travel on to Moscow by train which, as I have my own railway car, will be more comfortable than a carriage. Once I've done what I have to there we'll proceed overland by train to Britain, via Dover and the English Channel, visiting Konigsberg, Berlin, and Paris en route.'

'You have business in every city?'

'No, Konigsberg, Berlin, and Paris will be purely for our pleasure. I will however have meetings to arrange in London, which shouldn't prove too onerous for you, as there are wonderful shops there.' He rinsed the blade in the bowl of water. 'The Crawshay works in Merthyr won't prove quite so interesting or scenic but I'll try to conclude my business there as quickly as I can.'

'I'd like to see the town where Sarah, Glyn, Anna, and Richard came from, after hearing them talk about it. The Crawshay works are ironworks aren't they?'

'Yes.'

'Aren't they in competition with Mr Hughes's works here?'

'Yes.'

'Then why would Mr Hughes want to do business with them?' she asked curiously.

'Will you promise not to repeat what I'm about to tell you?'

'Of course.'

'It's insurance.'

'Insurance,' she repeated in bewilderment.

'The Tsar wants rails to build a Russian railway that will stretch across the country from east to west, north to south, and every other direction, connecting every major town and city in "all the Russias". Mr Hughes has promised to deliver them but the works here has only just gone into production. It would be optimistic to believe that everything the New Russia Company will produce in Hughesovka will turn out to be absolutely perfect at the first attempt, so we're making plans to secure a "just in case" backup source.'

'You'll import them from Wales?'

'Only if we have to and only as a last resort, and even then, we may have to lie as to where they come from to escape import duty.'

'How will you import them – if you need them?'

'As scrap iron to be melted down.' He finished shaving and soaked a towel in hot water before wiping his face. 'I'll check my old room in Mr Hughes's wing of the house. I'll dress there and make sure nothing I'm likely to need has been left behind. He went into the bedroom. 'This room already looks rather empty and forlorn.'

'It does, doesn't it?' she agreed.

'After we leave Wales we'll resume our honeymoon. We'll take the ferry back to France and return to my railway car. Travel south, pick up my yacht in Marseille, sail to Rome, Naples, Capri – you must see Capri – Sicily, and on to Greece, and Constantinople of course...'

'Of course.'

'Are you making fun of me?' His voice was serious but his eyes shone.

'Just a little, perhaps.' She watched him over the rim of her coffee cup.

'I was going to say, then on to Yalta so you can visit our summer house.'

'From there into the Sea of Azov and back here by Christmas,' she said hopefully.

'Christmas may be a little ambitious.' '

I wouldn't like to be away from Kira and baby Pavlo and Edward too long. And Alexei and Ruth...'

'Ruth is pregnant?' he guessed.

'The baby won't be born until Christmas, I would like to be back for the birth.'

'I can make no promises.'

'I know.' She rang for her maid to help her dress and pack the last of the things she wanted to take with her.

'Except one,' he qualified. 'I promise to do all I can to combat your homesickness.'

'Thank you.'

'I know you're going to miss your family and friends, especially Catherine. She's been mother, father, aunt, and grandparents all wrapped in one to you. But I promise you we'll be back, princess. I just can't promise you when that will be. But whenever it is, our house should be finished given the money that I've, or rather Hans on my behalf has, been throwing at the builders.'

'You promised you would never call me princess again,' she admonished him.

'No I didn't. The first time I took you on to my boat you asked me to make that the first and last time that I would call you princess. I didn't answer and silently reserved the right to call you princess any time I chose to.'

'If you must call me anything other than Sonya, I prefer "my sweet".'

'I'll try to remember.' He went to the door. Sonya waylaid and hugged him.

'I'm only going to another wing of the house.'

'I know, but I won't see you until breakfast.'

He laughed and left.

After he'd gone Sonya sat on the bed and looked around the room. The house Roman was building in the town would be beautiful when it was finished, but if they moved into it on their return, she realised, she had spent the very last night not only in her room, but in the house that had been home to her ever since she could remember.

The momentous change in her life had happened almost without her even noticing it.

Hughesovka May 1872

Sonya stood in the hall alongside Sarah, Ruth, and Praskovia, part of yet separate from the bustle around her. Already she felt like an outsider, watching a scene she no longer had a role in. Then she looked past the men gathered around Roman and Mr Hughes and saw her Aunt Catherine watching her. She crossed the hall and embraced her.

'No tears.' Catherine warned ironically considering her own eyes were damp. 'Time passes so quickly you'll be back here before you know it.'

'Before you've even had time to miss me.' As Sonya hugged Catherine, she noticed for the first time how old and frail her aunt had suddenly become.

'Don't forget to send me postcards from every city you visit so I can see how much has changed in the world since I travelled with your uncle.'

'I'll look for the very best scenes that I can find, and I'll write at least once a week to let you know all my news.'

Catherine looked over Sonya's shoulder for Roman. He saw and read the signal in her eyes. He joined them and gently extricated Sonya from her aunt's arms.

'Time we were off, pr –'

'Say "princess" and I'll start calling you "frog",' she warned. The ensuing laughter lightened the atmosphere.

Richard, John Hughes, and Glyn shook hands with Roman and hugged Sonya. Glyn was the last to say goodbye to Sonya and claimed a kiss.

'As your koumbaros I believe I can do that.'

'You can indeed,' Father Grigor asserted, before following suit and kissing Sonya's other cheek.

'Cousin,' Alexei gave her a bear hug.

Sonya stared into his eyes. 'Look after your wife – and daughter.'

'It's a boy,' Alexei said firmly.

'Girl,' Ruth countered.

'Ruth and I are right, Alexei, I see you surrounded by women for the rest of your life. At least nine girls?' Sonya winked at Ruth.

'At least,' Ruth agreed seriously.

'Then pity help me!'

'You need women to keep you in order,' Sonya teased before saying her goodbyes to Praskovia, Sarah, and their babies.

'Anna begged me to ask you to stop off at the hospital,' Sarah said. 'Poor girl was quite tearful this morning at the thought of you leaving. If you do stop off and she does cry, don't worry, we'll soon dry her tears.'

'I'll write to all of you...'

'Not in the same week or you won't have time for anything else.' Impatient with the prolonged leave-taking, Roman took Sonya's arm and hooked it into his own. Too choked to speak, Catherine kissed his cheek and held Sonya briefly in her arms for a final embrace.

As Roman led Sonya to the door she looked back at Praskovia and Sarah's babies. 'The next time I see those two they'll be running around.'

'With our daughter calling out to Aunt Sonya to come and play,' Ruth smiled.

'I'll be her cousin twice removed,' Sonya reminded.

'I prefer aunt– and godmother. We won't have her christened until you're back,' Alexei said.

'Just make sure you return within forty days of the birth so you can stand godparent,' Father Grigor cautioned.

'We'll try.' Roman eased Sonya out of the door. 'We've kept Manfred, Hans, and the coachmen waiting quite long enough.' He helped Sonya into the back of the carriage he'd chosen for the first leg of their journey. Another three of his carriages carrying his staff and a wagon filled with their luggage were ranged behind.

'I feel like royalty,' Sonya pulled down the carriage window and waved to the assembled estate staff as they drove through the gates of Catherine's grounds and headed for the town.

'You are, but very minor. When we reach St Petersburg you'll discover princes and princesses are absolutely the lowest grade in the aristocratic pecking order.'

'I don't even want to be in the pecking order.' She sat back in her seat. 'I'm exactly who and where I want to be.'

'Which is?'

'Mrs Nadolnaya in a coach with Mr Nadolny, heading north.' She leaned on his shoulder and watched as the buildings on the outskirts of the embryonic town came into view.

'Do you want to stop off at the hospital?' Roman asked when they reached the main street.

'Please,' she reached for his hand, 'but only to see Anna.'

'And the other nurses?'

'Whoever's on duty.'

'I'm not jealous of Nathan Kharber. Not now I've enticed you into my bed and my life and you're wearing my ring. Slow down please,' Roman ordered their driver as they drew closer to Koshka's house.

The driver reined in the horses. Sonya looked up and saw a black veiled figure sitting at one of the first floor windows.

'I suggested we stopped to say goodbye but she refused, on the grounds that it wouldn't be socially acceptable for a young, newly married, respectable woman to call on a lady of her profession.'

'Perhaps a small family dinner when we return?'

'I will try to persuade her.' He lifted her hand to his lips and kissed it.

'It seems like the whole town is out to wave us off.' Roman saluted Vlad and Alf who were standing in the doorway of the New Russia Company headquarters. He turned and saw Anna leaning on the gate of the hospital. 'Stop, please,' he called out to the driver.

Sonya opened the door, climbed down, and hugged Anna.

'You're a good friend, Sonya. I love you and I'll miss you.'

'I'll miss you too, Anna, and I'll write. Don't work yourself to death while I'm gone and keep an eye on Ruth for me.'

'I'm hoping to deliver her baby.' Anna stepped back so Yulia, Miriam, and the other nurses who'd come outside could say their goodbyes.

Sonya glanced over her shoulder at Roman who hadn't left the carriage. 'I have to go.' She looked towards the door as Nathan walked out flanked by the porters.

'We all wanted to wish you and Prince Roman well.'

'Thank you, Kolya, Bogdan, Maxim.'

'Miss ... my apologies, Princess.'

'Please call me Mrs Nadolnaya, Dr Kharber, it's who I am now,' Sonya said as she shook Nathan's hand.

'We'll miss you,' the nurses chorused.

'We'll be back, if not at the end of this year then early next.'

Roman left the carriage, shook Nathan's hand without looking at him, kissed the girls' cheeks, and gave Anna an extra hug. He helped Sonya back into the carriage.

Sonya leaned out of the window as they drove off. The girls and Nathan had returned inside but Anna and Maxim had remained at the gate and were still waving.

Roman wrapped his arm around Sonya's shoulders. 'We'll be back.'

'I know we will.'

'But not until you've seen a great deal more of what this world has to offer.'

Sonya leaned out and returned Anna's wave. Maxim had retreated to the hospital but Anna still stood, alone and forlorn, at the gate.

The carriage turned a corner and she was lost to view.

Epilogue

Owen Parry's cottage, Broadway, Treforest, Pontypridd 1956

After eighty-four years I can still see that train of carriages, bearing Roman Nadolny's blue, red, and white coat of arms, bumping towards the steppe over the rutted street strewn with building rubble. The snow had gone, the last vestiges melting as the sun had risen that morning. A few householders, Praskovia, Madam Koshka, and the hotel manager among them, had planted fruit trees in their gardens. Some had taken well and the air was redolent with the scent of cherry and apple blossom.

Although dawn hadn't long broken, traders were setting up their stalls in preparation for the weekly market. A Cossack woman was unpacking loaves of bread as long and thick as a cavalry officer's thighs from her cart, and arranging them on a barrow covered with a white embroidered cloth, edged with crochet. A Russian peasant was building pyramids of vegetables on the stall next to her. Further down the street Levi and Ruben Goldberg were hooking sides of beef, mutton, and goat around the shuttered stall the shtetl carpenter had designed and crafted. Ruth said it was the first time a Jewish trader had dared venture outside of the shtetl to offer wares to Christians. A German trader had brought cooking pots; lacking a stall he was laying them on a length of tarpaulin on the ground. A Pole was displaying bags and baskets to advantage on a trellis of scaffolding, a Lithuanian dried fish, and a Turk was unwrapping his spices next to a dairyman's wife who was selling milk, sour cream, and cheeses.

Hughesovka was growing and all I wanted to do was hold up my hand, halt progress, and freeze it in that exact moment. I hated change and I recall feeling both angry and bereft as I watched Roman and Sonya drive out of town on that beautiful May morning in 1872. I knew Sonya hoped to return before Christmas; Roman, more cautiously, had suggested they would be away for a year. None of us suspected that four long years would pass before they returned.

Perhaps I was averse to change because I had lost so many people I'd loved. My father, mother, three of my brothers, and my two sisters, Dr Peter Edwards who had been so kind to me – all had died long before the Biblically allotted span, and all before my fifteenth birthday. There were also other losses, not as devastating, but still losses that affected me and made me yearn for a security I hadn't felt since my father had been killed "by the iron".

Richard was a loving and kind brother, but much as I adored Sarah I felt I'd lost something of his loyalty towards me when he married her. Glyn and Praskovia, Alexei and Ruth: they were thoughtful and caring, but they had one another, while I had no one to love who was solely special to me.

So I threw myself into the one institution that, although constantly growing and changing, needed me – the hospital. I started my shifts early and remained on the wards long past the time they were due to end. When I wasn't actually caring for patients I studied every textbook and copy of The Lancet I could lay my hands on. I volunteered to help Dr Kharber in surgery every time he called for a nurse to assist, and overloaded myself with work because it was preferable to dealing with the loneliness that gnawed at me even when I was in a room full of people. I think I found that solitude bit even harder and more painfully when I was in company.

Sarah made a point of visiting the hospital every day, but gradually over those four years, without either of us actually noticing how or when it happened, I assumed responsibility for more and more of her duties, including the nurses' training, the ordering of medicines and supplies, and the drawing up of staff rotas, for the porters as well as the nurses.

I was honoured when Sarah and Richard asked me to stand godmother to my nephew Edward, who soon became "Ted" simply because that was his first word. I also stood godmother to Glyn and Praskovia's son Pavlo, and Alexei and Ruth's twin daughters, Olga and Catherine, named for Alexei's mother and grandmother. The first – but not the last – pair of twins I delivered.

Before Roman and Sonya returned, there were more babies. Another boy for Glyn and Praskovia, whom they named Tom, and Sarah and Richard's daughter, Maryanna.

The one person who seemed to understand that it was possible to feel acutely lonely even when surrounded by people was Catherine Ignatova. I grew to know, admire, respect, and gradually love her during those years. At the outset of our relationship I felt she solicited my companionship as a substitute for Sonya's – and Olga's, the daughter she had lost – but I soon realised how wrong I was.

Catherine saw beyond the façade of competence I cultivated and strove to show the world. She saw my insecurities and understood just how terrified I was of making mistakes, not only as a nurse but socially. She taught me that all men – and women – even those with titles, are equal, and the only thing that matters is how we live our lives between birth and death and the kindness we show to one another.

She sent me notes, inviting me to share meals with her and always phrasing them so it sounded as though I was the one bestowing the favour by visiting her. She invited me to spend my days off at her home, and sought me out at the parties and social events that became more frequent as the works grew in capacity and output and Mr Hughes and his managers finally found the time for leisure.

Catherine organised balls, card parties, dinners, and recitals. Mr Hughes invited musicians, dancers, and actors to perform in Catherine's home, and on the makeshift stage he had constructed in the hall at company headquarters as an interim measure until he could build a theatre. He chose the companies, and paid all their expenses to travel to Hughesovka as well as their fees.

Occasionally I saw Alice Perkins, now Razina, and Glyn's wife Betty at the market or in the street. Like Glyn, Richard, and Sarah I always acknowledged them, although they invariably looked straight through me, just as they did the others, including my younger brothers Morgan and Owen. I presumed that Betty and Alice spent most of their time running their boarding house and surmised that they probably invested as much effort in avoiding us as we did them.

Misha occasionally visited his mother Yelena and brother Pyotr, but tried to avoid Praskovia. On the rare occasions he didn't succeed we heard raised voices in the kitchen quarters. There was a great deal of speculation among both the Russians and the Welsh as to why Misha persisted in living in barracks even on his days off, when his wife helped run a boarding house in town. But then no one really knows what goes on in a marriage except those directly involved. Like Praskovia, I felt it was no one's business but Misha's and Alice's as to why they had chosen not to live together, or whether or not they would eventually decide to have children.

Looking through the photographs, letters, and diaries of those years between 1872 and 1876, I realise now that it was a relatively content and quiet, if not always happy, time for me. Work, interspersed with summer carriage rides and picnics on the steppe, boating on the rivers, winter hunting expeditions in horse-drawn troika sleighs, and parties in Catherine Ignatova's ballroom in the company of the same relatively small circle of friends, made for repetitive, comfortable, and comforting memories.

Sonya kept her promise and wrote frequently to all of us. A son, Andrei, was born to her and Roman in London in January 1873 and his arrival explained the delay in their return journey. From London they travelled to Merthyr in the spring of 1873 and Sonya sent us more letters from the Welsh iron town than any other place they visited on their travels, principally because, I suspected, Roman wouldn't allow her to venture out into the Merthyr streets alone. They stayed with the Crawshays at Cyfarthfa Castle, and for the first time since I'd reached Hughesovka I wished I'd been there so I could tell all my old neighbours, like Maggie Two Suits and Jenny Swine, that I knew someone who was acquainted well enough with the Crawshays to receive an invitation to actually stay in the castle.

The Nadolnys remained in Britain for a year so Roman could oversee business interests he'd inherited from his father. They left Britain in 1874 for France, Italy, and Greece, and eventually arrived in Yalta in late 1875, where Sonya gave birth to a second son whom they named Spartak. Then in the spring of 1876 Sonya sent the letters we'd all been waiting for. She and Roman were returning to Hughesovka, but not alone. They were returning as part of a Romanov Grand Ducal party to inspect the works and – everyone in the town hoped – to give Hughesovka a very public royal seal of approval...

But they didn't come alone. Others came, including the Paskeys with the intention of disrupting the royal visit and destroying John Hughes's hope of legitimising his iron town on the steppe. They brought death, destruction, and tragedies that affected us all.

The repercussions of that visit echoed down the years and changed many lives. But the one thing it could not change was the progress of John Hughes's dream that grew more tangible and substantial with every passing day – Hughesovka.

A DRAGON'S LEGACY

Book Three in the Tsar's Dragons series

The Tsar's Dragons
Princes and Peasants

CATRIN COLLIER

When one has nothing left . . . but memories, one guards
and dusts them with especial care.

Saki (H. H. Munro)
The Wolves of Cernogratz

DEDICATION

For the men in my life, John and Ralph

I couldn't function without you

Press article
Nikita and Mrs Khrushchev's ten-day state visit to Britain

April 1956
Premier and Mrs Khrushchev were guests of honour at a state banquet in Buckingham Palace yesterday. During the course of the evening Mr Khrushchev questioned The Duke of Edinburgh and the Prime Minister, Sir Anthony Eden as to the history of Welshman, John Hughes, who founded the town of Hughesovka in the Ukraine where Mr Khrushchev was born, which has since been renamed Donetsk.
Neither the Duke nor the Prime Minister had heard of John Hughes. Therefore, they could give Mr Khrushchev no information regarding the man, or even confirm his existence.

CHAPTER ONE

The hospital Hughesovka January 1889

'I can't stand the pain . . . '

'The pain of childbirth is a burden every woman must bear as punishment for Eve's sin in the Garden of Eden, Mrs Grisha.' The young Dutch trainee nurse's lecture inflamed Alice Grisha's temper. Her authoritative "I know better than you" sanctimonious delivery even more.

'I'm in agony and you couldn't give a kopek!'

'Of course I care . . . '

'No, you don't!' Alice gave a blood curdling scream, waved her arms and knocked over the water jug and glass on the trolley next to her bed.

Hearing voices raised in anger followed by a crash, Nurse Yulia and Matron Anna Parry ran into the delivery room. Yulia grabbed the trainee and hauled her out into the corridor. Anna called for a ward maid to clear the mess of spilled water and shards of ceramic and glass before unhooking Mrs Grisha's chart from the foot of the bed and checking it.

'It won't be much longer now, Mrs Grisha?' Anna replaced the chart, wrung a flannel in iced water and wiped Alice's forehead before reaching for her hand and holding it.

'I'm in agony . . . that stupid girl . . . ' Alice glared at the door as she gasped in pain, although Yulia had closed it behind her, '. . . she told me that women have to suffer-' she clenched her teeth as another pain spasm took hold.

Anna wrung out the cloth in iced water again and placed it on Alice Grisha's head. 'I'm sorry, Mrs Grisha, but to some degree the trainee is right. We cannot give women opiates to mitigate the pain of childbirth except in extreme cases as the drug could affect the baby.'

'The baby isn't the one who's suffering! I am!' Alice thrashed around in the bed and threw her arms in the air again.

'Please, Mrs Grisha, this hysteria isn't good for you or your child.' Anna kept her voice, soft, low but Alice wasn't in a mood to be placated.

Alice stared at Anna as she breathed out slowly through narrowed eyes. 'I know you.'

'I expect you do. I live in Hughesovka.'

'I've seen you with Glyn Edwards's mistress. The Cossack ...'

Anna closed out the tirade of invective that flowed from Alice Grisha's mouth. She was used to the curses and anger of women in labour and understood the relief they gained from venting their feelings. But she knew and respected Glyn Edwards and his mistress Praskovia who had lived happily as man and wife for twenty years. She was also aware that Glyn's legal wife Betty Edwards was Alice Grisha's closest friend.

She couldn't understand why Glyn's wife Betty hadn't given him a divorce when he'd made it clear that he would never return to her. Or why Betty kept their daughter, Harriet, from him and least of all why Betty had persisted in living Hughesovka after Glyn had begged her to return to her home town of Merthyr.

All women in labour shouted and a few (who had the vocabulary) cursed, which was understandable given the pain they suffered but there was a streak of coarseness in Alice's language she' seldom heard from a woman and she wondered if Alice's vulgarity was a result of Betty Edward's influence, or Alice's husband.

Gavril Grisha was a legend in Hughesovka. Feared by the workers because he'd set up a union that had established a stranglehold on every job in the town. Tolerated by the managers in the works and collieries because he simplified the process of hiring and firing, Gavril Grisha was a force to be reckoned with.

No man was appointed to any position in a colliery or ironworks below management level without Grisha's "blessing" and paying his "union dues". The first lesson every newly appointed manager learned was that if men Grisha disapproved of were appointed to lucrative positions, Grisha had no compunction about using his power to organise "accidents" or strikes that would disrupt production and in severe cases halt it and cause closure of the offending colliery or plant.

Anna saw Alice grimace, folded back the sheet and checked the baby's progress. 'Your baby is almost here, Mrs Grisha. Push when I tell you please.'

'You're only saying that so you won't have to give me something for the pain. I can pay for it . . . '

'Push please, Mrs Grisha,' Anna reiterated. 'That's it, just once more . . .'

Alice grunted and pushed. Anna caught the baby as it slid from the birth canal. She smiled as she looked down at the child. No matter what the circumstances or how angry the mother, she never failed to be moved by the miracle of new life entering the world.

'You have a fine son, Mrs Grisha.'

'Send a message to my husband. He'll want to see him.'

Yulia knocked and entered the cubicle. She smiled at the bundle in Anna's hands. 'Congratulations on a fine son, Mrs Grisha.'

'Thank you. I hope you told that girl . . . '

'I've spoken to her, Mrs Grisha,' Yulia broke in.

'I have you have. Send word to my husband . . . '

'We'll tidy you up first and settle you down in a room with your baby.' Anna tied off and cut the umbilical cord, wrapped the baby in a sheet and carried him over to a basin of water.

'Shall I help you bathe, find you a clean nightgown, brush your hair and add a dab of scent first, Mrs Grisha?' Yulia asked, emulating Anna's calm. 'You'll want to look your best for him.'

Alice glared for a moment, considered, then acquiesced. While Yulia saw to the mother, Anna bathed the child, dressed him in a napkin and gown, and wrapped him a cotton blanket before handing him to Alice.

'Have you chosen a name for him, Mrs Grisha?' she asked

'Gavril.' Alice looked down at the child. 'For his father. Gavril Grisha. Gavril means "Worships God" and Grisha means "Watchful".'

'A very apt name as all children are God given,' Anna bundled the soiled linen together. 'I'll send a porter to fetch your husband. Congratulations Mrs Grisha.'

'I don't want anyone here to tell a soul that Gavril Grisha has a son before he sees the child for himself.'

'The staff in this hospital never discuss the patients outside of these walls, Mrs Grisha. We're far too busy to gossip.'

'Your shift ended hours ago, Matron,' Yulia reminded as the ward maid brought in a clean nightgown for Alice.

'So, it did.' Anna smiled at Yulia and the ward maid. 'I'll see you in the morning. Good night, Mrs Grisha, and son, and congratulations again. The best days in this hospital are the ones when babies are born.'

Richard and Sarah Parry's house, Hughesovka January 1889

Anna Parry took the key her brother had insisted she keep when she'd moved out of his house from her handbag, slipped it in the lock and turned it. The door opened and she stepped inside the hall. She muffled the sound by closing her hand over the lock, but Richard had heard her and was standing in the open doorway of his study.

'I wouldn't have called in this late if I hadn't seen the lamp burning in your study,' she apologised.

'Don't tell me.' He held up his hand as though to ward off her excuses. 'You had to work late – again – and on Sarah's birthday?' he reproached.

'I'm sorry to have missed Sarah's birthday dinner.' Anna shrugged off her nurses' cloak and hung it in the alcove that held all the family's coats and scarves. She set a package wrapped in blue crepe paper on the hall table. 'We had a glut of babies. Six today. Four boys and two girls.'

'As Sarah is well acquainted with the rigours of your vocation, I've no doubt she'll forgive you.'

'One of the babies is Alf Mahony's. His wife Tonia went into labour this afternoon and an hour later he had a fifth son. They're naming him Dafydd.'

Richard smiled. 'He'll be pleased to finally have a son with a Welsh name.'

'Boris is Welsh and Russian.'

'That's debatable but Bogdan, Anatoly and Artyom, aren't, and I've seen Alf's face when the Welsh boys call Bogdan "Boggy".'

'What's worse is the child answers to it with a smile on his face.' Anna balanced her hat on the hook that held her cloak.

'Are you hungry?'

'No, thank you, I ate in the hospital.'

'I opened a bottle of German wine. Sarah only managed half a glass before she fell asleep sitting in her chair.'

'A glass would go down nicely. I'm surprised to see you still up.' She followed him into his study. 'Last minute arrangements for the Grand Duke's visit tomorrow?'

'As if Mr Hughes would trust me with those?' Richard took a glass from the cupboard behind his desk and filled it for her. 'I've been ordering more wooden pit props from Poland. Alexei and I are extending the shaft in the "Six Bears" pit. You will take tomorrow afternoon off, so you can attend the lunch Mr Hughes has arranged for the Grand Dukes and their royal party in the hotel?'

'Barring an epidemic or catastrophe, I'll be there.'

'Right, I'll warn everyone I meet on my way to the office tomorrow, no epidemics, catastrophes, babies or broken bones allowed until further notice.' He picked up the order forms he'd been working on and closed them into a file. 'Enough for today.'

His eyes narrowed as he gave his sister an appraising look. Like him she had the black curly hair and blue eyes of their Irish mother. But there were dark shadows beneath her eyes, and she was thin, hardly surprising given the hours she worked and the meals she missed. 'You promised me when the new nurses and doctors Mr Hughes engaged for the hospital arrived, you'd cut your shifts down to one a day and five a week. That was three years ago and you're still working around the clock.'

'We're still waiting on two doctors, one Dutch, one German and four Austrian nurses. But you should be having this conversation with your wife as well as me. Do you know the staff call her Matron number two because she calls in almost every day?'

'Only for an hour or two, or so she tells me. Do you mind?'

'What if I told you that I was at loggerheads with Sarah? You'd divorce her?' she teased.

He frowned. 'You know perfectly well I could no more divorce Sarah than I could stop breathing.'

'Just as well, I love her almost as dearly as you, not least because she keeps you, Owen and Morgan in order. But Morgan and Owen are both less troublesome brothers than you were.'

'I'm loathe to admit it but they probably are. Has Morgan or Kira said anything to you about setting the date for their wedding?'

'Other than a vague "this summer" no.'

'They are happy together, aren't they?' he frowned at her.

'You do realise that you are asking a confirmed spinster who has no experience of romance that question?'

'Anyone can see that Morgan is very fond of Kira . . . '
Richard faltered when she burst out laughing.

'What is so funny?'

'You,' she smiled. 'For Kira's sake, I hope that Morgan is more than "very fond" of her.'

'You know what I mean,' he snapped,

'I'm not sure that I do, but if you are asking for my opinion, Morgan and Kira appear to be as besotted with one another as you and Sarah.'

'I see.'

'If you do, you see more than me. Whatever's between them, Kira doesn't talk about it. Nor do I expect her to. And to change the subject from our brother's love life, Alice Grisha gave birth today as well as Tonia Mahoney. In between cursing everyone in sight, and me and Praskovia in particular, she asked me not to tell anyone Grisha was a father until he saw the child. Which he should have done by now, so I'm not betraying her request.'

'Why Praskovia?'

'Because she knows I'm Praskovia's friend, and Betty is hers. Betty hates Praskovia and by extension presumably me.'

'I'll never understand why Betty didn't return to Merthyr when she arrived here twenty years ago and found Glyn living with Praskovia.'

'I'll never understand why Betty kept Harriet from Glyn. A father and daughter have the right to know one another.'

'They do,' he agreed.

'In case you need more details to congratulate Grisha when you next see him, Alice told me his son will be named Gavril Grisha after him. His hair is fair like Alice's at the moment, but that might change to Grisha's red.' She took the glass of wine he'd poured for her. 'Thank you.'

'You can be infuriating. Do you know that?'

'So, people tell me, but why in particular at this moment?'

'Are you telling me about Grisha's son because you expect me to broadcast the news.'

'That, brother, is entirely up to you.' She sipped the wine. 'Mm this is good.'

'That's my sister. Ask her a question and she'll change the subject.'

'I resent that comment.'

'Truth hurts.' He refilled his own glass.

'What about Owen?'

'What about him?' Anna curled up in the visitor's chair set in front of his desk.

'Do you think if he was sweet on a girl he'd tell me?'

'I think he's twenty-eight years old and that's his business.'

'Like you he lives for work. The metallurgical laboratory sees more of him than we do.'

'According to Kira it sees more of Morgan as well.'

'So, Kira does talk about Morgan?'

'She mentions him now and again when he's promised to take her somewhere and doesn't turn up because he's decided to work late. But to return to Owen, there's a very attractive female chemist working there by the name of Francine.'

'Really . . . '

'Before you ask me any more questions I can't answer, that's all I know. Owen brought her into the hospital with minor chemical burns.'

'But he brought her in?'

'From what I gathered he was with her when a bottle of acid she was holding exploded.'

'It would be nice to see Morgan and Owen settled.'

'So, says the happily married man who wants to pair up the entire world population.'

'Is it so bad for me to want to see everyone in my family happy?'

'Only when you interfere in their personal lives.'

Richard recognised the edge in her voice and changed the subject. 'To quote Varvara,' he referred to their Russian housekeeper, "My eyes are clapping". It's been a long day and tomorrow promises to be even longer. Time for bed.'

'And time I left,' she agreed savouring a last mouthful of wine. 'That really is good. You must give me the name and vintage.'

'Alexei choose it. I've no doubt he presented some to Catherine for her cellar.' He rose to his feet when she left her chair. 'You do have a new, and I hope fashionable expensive dress for tomorrow?'

'You wouldn't know expensive from cheap or fashionable from sackcloth. I thought I'd wear my matron's uniform.'

'Anna . . . '

'Don't worry, Sarah and Catherine picked it out for me because they don't trust me to do my own shopping. Your women won't let you down.' On impulse, she kissed his cheek before fetching her cloak from the hall. 'Sweet dreams until I see you tomorrow.'

'You too, Anna.' He walked her to the carriage Catherine had put at her sole disposal and handed her inside. As usual there were two grooms sitting side by side on the box. Both wore pistols in their belts. He hadn't needed to check if they were armed. Catherine was as cautious with his sister's safety as she was her granddaughters.

Richard spent ten minutes putting his desk and study in order before closing the door and climbing the stairs to his bedroom. Life was good, twenty years after he'd arrived penniless in Hughesovka he and his business partner, Alexei Beletsky had made enough money to consider themselves wealthy, even after they'd reinvested the largest slice of their profits financing the leases of new collieries and extending the shafts of their existing enterprises.

His house in Hughesovka had been designed by the same German architect John Hughes had commissioned to build his own mansion. He'd finished repaying the low interest loan he'd taken out with the company to pay for it five years ago and, despite Sarah's protests, with money he'd earned, not her first husband's life insurance. He and Alexei had also bought palatial adjoining houses for their families in St Petersburg as well as an office in the business quarter from which they ran the export department of their collieries. John Hughes's New Russia Company bought all the high-grade anthracite coal their pits produced but their collieries also yielded a fair amount of low grade coal that they sold abroad for use in steam engines.

He looked around the wood panelled walls of the study and hall, and sank his slippered feet into the deep pile of the French stair carpet. For all the comfort and luxury his home afforded, acquired with money he'd earned, he felt as though he didn't belong within its walls. The insecurities of the barefoot gutter snipe who'd begun his working life operating the "traps" – air vents - in a Merthyr colliery before his fifth birthday was ingrained in him, along with a sense of inferiority he found difficult to shake, especially in the company of those he regarded his "superiors". Although . . .

He went into his bedroom, closed the door and leaned back against it. All uncertainties, dissipated whenever he looked at his wife.

Blissfully happy, there were still times when he found it difficult to believe that she was actually his. He'd never anticipated anyone like her or their children, Ted and daughter Maryanna in his life, and was simply grateful that they were.

'I didn't expect you to be still awake after falling asleep in your chair earlier.' He shrugged off his jacket and waistcoat and hung them on his valet stand.

'As if I could sleep for long without you lying next to me.' Sarah set aside the book she'd been reading and raised her head to receive his kiss. 'I heard Anna come in but I was already in bed. She was late.'

'She asked me to give you her apologies for missing your birthday dinner and left a gift for you. It's on the hall table. There were six births in the hospital today and you know Anna, she thinks the hospital will fall down if she's not there to supervise it, just like the last matron,' he joked.

'She takes her duties seriously . . . '

'As did you, before you put our children's needs before those of the hospital,' he interrupted.

'Until I realised that Anna was even more capable of running the place and keeping the nurses in order than me.'

'My mother used to say Anna was born old. She was the one who kept our family together when our brothers and sisters were taken by cholera in Merthyr in '66. Their deaths broke our mother. She lost the will to live. Anna was only nine but she was the one who made the decision to take in washing to pay the rent and somehow found time to do it in between working shifts in a pub.' He pulled his shirt over his head.

'Why do men do that?' Sarah eyed him quizzically.

'Do what?'

'Lift their arms over their shoulders to grab the back of their shirt between their shoulder blades so they can heave it over their heads without undoing more than the top couple of buttons. Wouldn't it be easier to unbutton your shirt all the way down and slip it off like a jacket?'

'If it was, I'd remove it that way.'

'I can't see that it's more convenient to behave like a contortionist. Think of the poor laundress. Have you any idea what it's like unfasten buttons when a shirt is wet?'

'I've never thought about it,' he replied.

'Which says a lot about how long-suffering Anna was when she did your washing.'

'I had no idea you noticed the way I undressed.'

'It's not only men who like to see the opposite sex undressing.'

'And what would you know about men ogling naked women?' he enquired suspiciously.

She winked suggestively. 'I've seen the photographs they collect.'

'I haven't any.'

'None that I've found – as yet.' She raised her eyebrows.

'There are none.'

'And before we married?'

'I'd be lying if I said I never looked at those that fell into my lap.'

'Fell?'

'I never went searching for them. So where did you see them? Your patients. The porters at the hospital . . . '

'Both are too terrified of the nurses to smuggle in salacious postcards. I don't have to go further than your brother Owen's pockets when he forgets to empty them for the laundry. Varvara was shocked when she found them. But then she's never married or had much to do with men – young or old. I told her it was normal for men to be interested in naked ladies and in fact I'd be worried if Morgan and Owen weren't.'

'I'll take a look in their pockets tomorrow to spare Varvara – and your blushes.' He unfastened his belt and unbuttoned his flies.

'Don't, your brothers would be mortified.'

'You didn't tell Owen that you and Varvara had seen them?'

'No. Owen might suspect that we had if he remembered he'd left them in his pocket. I put the ones Varvara found in one of the drawers in his bedroom but he didn't mention them to me and I certainly didn't say anything about them to him.'

'When did you see them?'

'Last week.'

'And you waited until now to tell me?'

'I wouldn't have told you now if it hadn't come up in conversation. Your brothers are grown men. We were discussing the way you undress. Please take off your socks before you remove your underclothes.'

'Do you have any particular reason for making that request?' he asked.

'A nude man with socks on looks as odd as a dog in Wellington boots.' She turned down the lamp and settled back on the pillows.

'And how many dogs in Wellington boots have you seen.' He frowned, 'Forget I asked, I'm more interested in the number of nude men with socks on that you've studied.'

'Glanced at in a professional capacity not studied. Probably hundreds if not thousands,' she replied. 'A nurse has no time for modesty – false or otherwise.'

'Sometimes I'd rather not be reminded of the humiliations nurses enjoy inflicting on their male patients.'

'Nurses never set out to humiliate unless their patients are being difficult. Finish undressing and come to bed.'

'Is there any special way you'd like me to finish?'

'Quickly.'

'You're cold?'

'Yes but that's not the only reason.' She crooked her finger. 'I want you.'

'For what?'

'Come here and you'll find out.'

'That sounds as though it could be painful or dangerous.'

'That depends on your definition of danger.'

'Yesterday you found my first grey hair. You want to give me even more?'

'A grey hair isn't life threatening,' she smiled.

'It's a portend of old age that doesn't enhance my good looks.'

'You're handsome enough to overcome it.'

He dropped his socks on a chair and folded his underclothes on top. She turned back the bedclothes. He climbed in, stretched out beside her, and melded the full length of his naked body alongside hers before returning the kiss she gave him with interest.

'You could have come to bed an hour ago,' she moved on top him.

'I could have but anticipation is ninety percent of the pleasure.'

'Really?' She gasped as he rolled over and pinned her beneath him.

'Not really. This is,' he whispered as he entered her.

Catherine Ignatova's house Hughesovka January 1889

Anna said goodnight to the night porter who manned Catherine's front door and crept up the stairs to her bedroom. The room was beautiful, originally furnished for Catherine's daughter Olga before her marriage, it had later been used by Catherine's orphaned niece, Sonya before she'd married Roman Nadolny. It had been redecorated for her after she'd accepted Catherine's invitation to live with her and Kira.

Smaller than the state rooms and guest bedrooms in the mansion, it was still large enough to contain everything a young girl or in her case, woman, could possibly want. The furniture was French Empire, enamelled white and ornamented by gilding. A four-poster bed hung with blue and white silk curtains, that matched the bedcover and pillows, dominated the centre of the wall opposite the windows that overlooked the gardens. French doors opened on to a balcony that encircled the first floor of the house. A desk and chair stood to the left of the French doors, a matching dressing table and chair to the right. A cheval mirror, two bookshelves, bedside cabinets and a Dutch tiled stove completed the furniture. Doors led to a small bathroom fitted with a marble washstand and slipper bath and another door led into a walk-in clothes and linen cupboard.

She turned up the oil lamp on the bedside cabinet and turned down the wicks on the ones on the desk and dressing table before checking her reflection in the mirror. A white ghost stared back at her in the subdued glow. She took the pins from her hair, picked up her hairbrush and tugged it through her waist-length hair before plaiting it, as she did every night. She looked at the amber coloured silk gown and matching silk shoes Catherine's maid had laid out in readiness for the lunch tomorrow. As she'd promised Richard, he wouldn't have cause to reproach her for her dress.

Too tired to do more than wash her hands and face, she undressed quickly, pulled on her nightdress and fell into bed but, exhausted as she was, sleep eluded her.

Every time she saw Richard she took delight in his happy marriage. But occasionally it made her feel – not envious - she could never envy Richard anything that brought him joy, but conscious that something was missing from her life.

She lived in luxury, enjoyed Catherine and Kira's love and the love of her brothers, niece, nephew, Sarah and her godchildren and had found her vocation in nursing. She'd made many real friends in the town, yet whenever she was alone, especially at bedtime and in the early morning, she felt oddly empty.

Richard had Sarah and their children. Morgan and Owen one another and their girlfriends. Praskovia had Glyn Edwards and their children, her closest friend Ruth was happily married to Alexei Beletsky with twin daughters and another child on the way.

She was grateful, but she knew there could be more to her life – if she ever found the courage to overcome the degradation and shame of her past. Could she ever trust a man – any man other than her brothers? John Hughes, Glyn Edwards and his older brother Edward Edwards had never been anything other than kind to her but she still flinched whenever they drew near her. Could she ever bear a man to touch her the way the way the Paskey brothers had when they'd beaten and raped her in Merthyr.

She been twelve years old. Yet twenty years later the woman she'd become still woke in the early hours with the rotting food and ale stench of their breath in her nostrils and the clammy feel of their sweating calloused hands on her bare skin as they'd stripped her clothes from her body.

She shuddered at the memory that was never far from the surface of her mind.

There was little point in thinking of any kind of life beyond the one she had. She'd been defiled. No man would ever want her, so there was no point in wondering if she could bear one to touch her. Better to concentrate on her career, her brother's family and her friends. As long as there were people, there would be a need for nurses. And it was something to be needed if only by strangers.

THE TSAR'S DRAGONS
series by
Catrin Collier

In 1869, Tsar Alexander II decided to drag Russia into the industrial age. He began by inviting Welsh businessman John Hughes to build an ironworks. A charismatic visionary, John persuaded influential people to invest in his venture, while concealing his greatest secret – he couldn't even write his own name.

Hughes recruited adventurers prepared to sacrifice everything to ensure the success of Hughesovka (Donetsk, Ukraine). Young Welsh men and women fleeing violence in their home country; Jews who have accepted Russian anti-Semitism as their fate and Russian aristocrats, all see a future in the Welshman's plans.

In a place where murderers, whores, and illicit love affairs flourish, The Tsar's Dragons is their story of a new beginning in Hughesovka, a town of opportunity.

The
LONG ROAD TO BAGHDAD
series by
Catrin Collier
An epic story of an incendiary love that threatened to set the desert alight as war raged between the British and Ottoman Empires.

Catrin Collier was born and brought up in Pontypridd. She lives in Swansea with her husband, three cats and whichever of her children choose to visit.
Visit her website at www.catrincollier.co.uk.

Princes and Peasants
A Dragon's Legacy

CRIME (as Katherine John)
Trevor Joseph series
Without Trace
Midnight Murders
Murder of a Dead Man
Black Daffodil
A Well Deserved Murder
Destruction of Evidence
The Vanished

By Any Other Name
The Amber Knight
The Defeated Aristocrat

MODERN FICTION (as Caro French)
The Farcreek Trilogy
Lady Luck
Lady Lay
Lady Chance

Quick Reads
Black eyed Devils - Catrin Collier
The Corpse's Tale - Katherine John

Short Stories as Catrin Collier
Poppies at the Well
Christmas Eve at the Workhouse
Not Quite Leningrad

Short Stories as Katherine John
The Ghost before Christmas

Printed in Great Britain
by Amazon